To Ian & Phia

love from

Amanda

CW01621596

Taurus

First published in Great Britain in 2019

ISBN 978-1-9997160-1-1

Author's notes and acknowledgements

This historical novel is set against some of the traumatic events which occurred during the first stage in the transformation of the Roman Republic to the Roman Empire, and its effects on the people involved. It should be noted that Gaius Octavius and his contemporaries never used the name Octavian. He was not given the title Augustus until 27 BC, some seventeen years after the assassination of Julius Caesar.

I have no evidence that Titus Statilius Taurus was ever called Marcellus by his family, or wrote poetry. We do know that Caesar wrote poetry, although none survives, and that Quintus Cicero managed to write four Greek tragedies while campaigning with Caesar in Gaul.

I am indebted to Cheryl Walker's dissertation, 'Hostages in Republican Rome' for information describing the Celtic tribes' method of transforming prisoners-of-war into 'dedicated' slaves, swearing loyalty to their new owners at the altar.

Different Ancient Roman historians give differing accounts of the same events, making it impossible on occasion to know exactly where everyone was. I have chosen what would appear to be the most likely locations.

I have used italics to indicate that the Gauls were speaking in their own language.

I am so grateful for the assistance I have received in writing this book. I wish to thank Callum Mathie, who gave me information about camp-sites and tents; my brilliant readers, Stephen Allison, Andrew Long, Lauren Mulherron, and Tony Strachan, for their many suggestions and encouragement. Also my thanks go to Michael Evans, who meticulously proof-read the book, and offered much helpful advice.

Especial thanks to my son Jody MacKenzie, who once again designed the beautiful cover, and without whose technical expertise the book would have remained in the iPad.

And lastly to my wonderful husband John, who has so patiently put up with an author wife, who is frequently lost in her own thoughts of the past.

Cover : The Farnese Bull. *Museum of Naples.*

Introduction

By the time Gaius Octavius was born on September 23rd, 63 BC, the Roman Republic had already existed for centuries. The stability of the Roman political system and its gradually evolving and ruthlessly efficient army had enabled the Republic to expand with remarkable success. Rome held sway over many conquered countries, huge 'provinces' extending from Spain in the west to Syria in the east. And in the next few years Gaius's great uncle, Julius Caesar, was about to add Gaul to Rome's many conquests. The enslavement of war captives acquired during these conquests was regarded as essential, and the resultant forced labour increased the general prosperity of Roman citizens. More than half the population of the Republic were slaves with no legal status whatsoever.

Ethnic and racial integration and assimilation occurred due to the extraordinary social mobility. Enslaved prisoners of war, if they were submissive and cooperative with their owners, could eventually be freed. They would be allowed to vote as freedmen, and their children would automatically become Roman citizens. The Romans were anything but racist. A Roman citizen, whether a Gaul or an Egyptian, was an integral part of the system with the same legal protection as everyone else.

The Roman Republic modelled itself on the Greek Athenian democratic system. Senators, equites (knights), commoners, freedmen, and slaves made up a clearly defined class structure. The patriarchs of the wealthiest and oldest families became Senators and took their place in the Senate, the legislative assembly. The Senate chose two Consuls to rule for a given year, able to initiate legislation, and thus become the most powerful men in Rome. After their year of service they would be rewarded by full governorship of one of the many Roman provinces, a route to riches. In order to be considered for election as Consul, a candidate had to follow the 'cursus honorum,' the path to honour, during which time he would fulfil certain prescribed military and civilian roles. The young men filling these increasingly powerful positions were expected to have reached a specific age first. The two Consuls could make laws only if both agreed, (either could veto the other) and if the law was debated and passed by the Senate before sundown. There were also two tribunes of the people representing the common citizens, the plebeians, who also had the vital power of veto.

Gaius Octavius was born into a world where the invasion and conquest of other countries was considered a perfectly acceptable method of gaining power and wealth. As he grew up the legal foundations of the Republic were already beginning to crumble. The rules governing the cursus honorum were being ignored. Legions of soldiers were showing loyalty to their general, rather than to the Senate, as the general was responsible for their pay, and the grants of land given when the soldiers were discharged from service. Meanwhile, the disparity between rich and poor grew wider. The common people, the plebeians, supported the Populares political party in the Senate, hoping for improved legal protection, and a more equitable way of distributing wealth. Julius Caesar became their chosen leader. The old aristocratic families, which wanted the existing conditions to continue, supported the Optimates party, whose spokesman was the renowned Marcus Cicero. These contrary desires had already resulted in a recent civil war.

Pompey the Great, just ten years older than Julius Caesar, flouted many of the laws previously considered inviolate. He achieved astonishing political success by his military exploits. He became Consul, without following the cursus honorum. Military might had begun to supersede the rule of law. Filibustering techniques and other legal irregularities arose in the Senate. The days of the Republic were numbered. The convulsive upheaval resulting in the birth of the Empire was marked by bloody civil wars, lasting many years. Many famous citizens lost their lives, to be replaced by the up-and-coming but inexperienced young men, such as Marcus Agrippa, Titus Statilius Taurus, and Gaius Octavius. These 'new men' held the highest positions at an astonishingly young age, contrary to all the laws of the Republic, because their power derived from the legionaries who supported them. The name 'Caesar' proved to be an overwhelming and enduring rallying cry for the troops. Eventually 'Caesar' became a part of the title of the Emperor, but that is for another book.

WESTERN ROMAN REPUBLIC 44BC

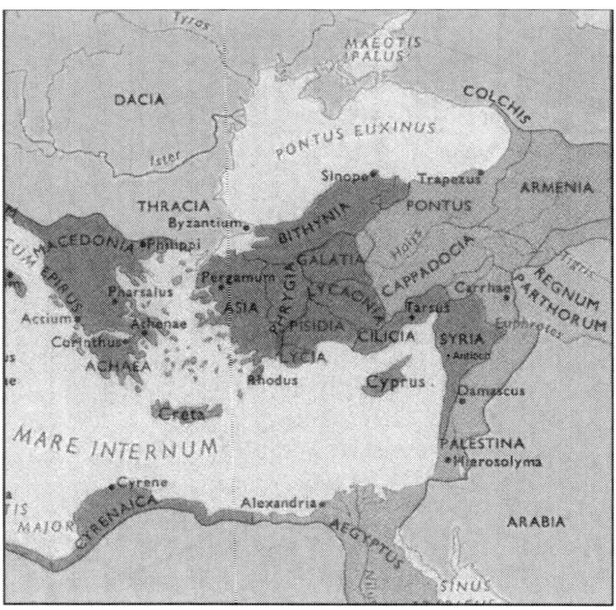

EASTERN ROMAN REPUBLIC 44BC

Table of Contents

Dramatis Personae

Italics denote fictional characters.

Ariovistus, the German King
Gaius Julius Caesar, Governor of Cisalpine and Transalpine Gaul
58 BC

Household of Marcus Statilius Taurus :–
Marcus Statilius Taurus
Caecilia, wife of Marcus
Lucanus Statilius Taurus, 'Luke,' elder son of Marcus
Portia, wife of Lucanus
Titus Statilius Taurus, known as Marcellus, elder son of Lucanus and Portia
Decimus Statilius Taurus, 'Dessy', younger son of Marcus
Ennius, tutor to Marcellus
Ambrosius, tutor to Marcellus

Household of Decimus Statilius Taurus :–
Cierán, a Helvetian slave
Laeforis, a Helvetian slave
Ethela, a German slave
Óengus, a Belgian slave
Darreth, brother of Óengus
Antonius Musa, physician and surgeon

Household of Cassius Domitius :–
Cassius Domitius, Centurion. A friend of Decimus

Agatha, wife of Cassius Domitius
Adrianus Domitius, son of Cassius Domitius

Household of Egnatius Juvenalis :–
Egnatius Juvenalis, wealthy citizen
Veronica, his daughter
Dora, a maid

Household of Gaius Octavius :–
Gaius Octavius, Governor of Macedonia
Atia, wife of Gaius Octavius
Octavia, their daughter
Gaius Octavius, their son

Household of Gnaeus Pompeius :–
Gnaeus Pompey, Roman Senator and general
Julia Caesar, his fifth wife
Gnaeus Pompeius, his elder son
Sextus Pompeius, his younger son

Lucius Marcius Philippus, Roman Senator
Claudius Marcellus, Roman Senator
Mark Antony, Roman Senator and general
Cleopatra, Queen Of Egypt
Marcus Cicero, Roman Senator
Quintus Cicero, younger brother of Marcus, Roman Senator and general

BOOK 1

Si brevis es gloriosior
Ed illustre nomen
Quod milite et politicum
Magna erit fama

Fragment attributed to 'Marcellus'

"Though small, you will be honoured,
"And with your illustrious name,
"As a soldier and a statesman,
"Great will be your fame."

Prologue

Bibracte (Autun), Gaul, September, 58 BC

All the hot summer long the morning mists rolled up from the rivers, cleared from the nearby hills and vanished into the sky. The wild flowers bloomed fiercely in the sun. Fruit grew succulent, ripening on long stems, glistening with syrup oozing from their burst skins, bending branches to the ground with their weight.

On the east side of the Rhine, the German women and children wandered out among the fields and forests accompanied by armed lookouts, always aware of the fragility of peace. They picked the mushrooms, blackberries, blueberries and juniper, apples, pears, quinces and plums. Their menfolk hunted the deer and wild boar, or crossed the Rhine in their ships, and raided the stores and barns of the local Gallic tribes to get prisoners and the precious corn. The Germans were famed for fighting, not farming. It was the proud boast of Ariovistus, the German king, that he had spent the last fourteen years campaigning, never sleeping in a bed in a house. Though he had managed to acquire two wives and several children.

At summer's end the tranquillity was broken. A cavalry party of returning German scouts galloped furiously across the meadows, trampling the flowers under their hooves. They rushed back to cross the Rhine from the rich pastures of central Gaul, not bothering with prisoners or booty in their haste. They were eager to inform their king of the impending danger. The Roman legions were on the march again!

Ariovistus received increasingly unsettling reports about the Roman Republic and its expansionist intentions. The Roman Senate had appointed Gaius Julius Caesar to be Governor of Transalpine Gaul, after his year as Consul in Rome. During that period he had sensibly declared Ariovistus to be a 'Friend and Brother of the Roman people.' But now this adventurer was forgetting his place in the world. Apparently Caesar had taken upon himself the chastising of the Helvetians for some error they had committed against the Romans forty-odd years ago. And his justification for this reckless warmongering? He had been ordered to do this by the Gods!

The Roman legions had invaded Celtic Gaul, fought a major battle, and slaughtered two thirds of the Helvetians, men, women, and children alike, without mercy. Now their army was camped in the southern part of Gaul, amongst the wealthy Aeduan and Sequani tribes. Ariovistus regarded the Aedui and Sequani as vassals for him to plunder and enslave. He was not going to allow any mercenary opportunist from the south to meddle with his indisputable sphere of influence. So he summoned his vast forces, his cavalry with their highly specialised foot-soldiers, his many archers, together with a huge mass of light infantry. The Germans embarked once more in their ships, and sailed westwards across the Rhine. They brought their women and children with them, so they would be able to witness their king's glorious victory over these upstart Romans. Then they marched swiftly to secure a stronghold, and sufficient provisions for war.

Gaius Julius Caesar had other ideas. The defeat of the Helvetians had proved to be highly lucrative. He was convinced that there was much more wealth to be had in the rest of Gaul. And he needed money, lots of money, to realise his ambition of becoming the most important and feared man in Rome. He had managed to contain his political rivals, Gnaeus Pompeius and Licinius Crassus by forming an alliance with both, an unofficial 'triumvirate.' Pompey was now married to his daughter Julia. But Pompey had looted vast quantities of treasure from his conquests in the East, and was now almost as wealthy as Crassus, the richest man in Rome. Both were in a position to buy votes and heavily influence the Senate. He needed to be able to do the same.

Caesar knew that the German king had crossed the Rhine many times before, always with a considerable force, and had successfully obtained tribute and hostages from the most important Gallic tribes in the south of the country. Ariovistus appeared to be thinking of settling all of Gaul for his own people. Outrageous! Caesar decided the tribute and hostages would be better under the aegis of the Roman Republic, and more particularly, himself. If he defeated the Germans, he would placate his supposed Gallic allies, the Aeduans. And also establish the right to keep his own army firmly fixed in the middle of this immense and rich country over the winter months, so he could annex the rest of it next year. Not a problem. He had the best fighting force in the world.

Caesar had six legions, each legion comprising six thousand soldiers, divided into ten cohorts of six centuries. Each centuria had its own standard, and was made up of ten units of ten men who shared a tent, a millstone, a mule, and a cooking pot. Thirty-six thousand men in total. He thought it would be sufficient.

BOOK 1 : CHAPTER 1

Vesontio (Besançon), Gaul, September, 58 BC

Decimus Statilius Taurus, 'Dessy' to his friends, was the decanus in charge of the tent. He was young, only twenty-three years of age, but he'd had seven years' experience, having joined the army when only sixteen. His men found the conjunction of his name and title hilarious. They chanted 'Decimus the decanus' as they were marched along, vying with each other to concoct some juicy ribald songs about his sexual prowess or deficiency thereof. There were ten of them altogether in the tent, Dessy the decanus, seven legionaries, who were his tent-mates, and two non-combatants, the slaves of the legion, whose job was to look after the soldiers and the mule. One of the non-coms used to be bone-idle until Decimus thrashed him. Then he made a rapid improvement. Dessy had a heavy hand, and a way of wielding a stick that was not conducive to laziness.

The non-com had stupidly allowed the fire-pot to go out. A twenty-mile march on a drenching wet day made the legionaries cold and hungry. They wanted warmth and hot food. But after using their remaining strength to construct their temporary camp, they were horrified to find the non-com unsuccessfully attempting to make a fire with wet wood-shavings. He was in great danger of being kicked to death. Dessy intervened, coaxing a pailful of glowing embers from the adjacent tent, and promising dire retribution for the culprit, duly carried out.

Strangely, the non-com didn't bear any grudge. No one complained when Dessy punished them: it happened only if well-deserved. On the contrary, he somehow made them all feel special to him. The men called it 'Dessy magic.' His tent was always the first to be erected, with everything properly in place, and the first to be dismantled, with everything correctly stowed away. If any of them got into trouble he would plead with the centurion in charge, and get them out of it again. Dessy was so persuasive.

"We're the best," said Dessy.

"We're the best," the tent agreed, and they were.

At present Decimus knew that the men were restless and resentful. They'd stopped singing and sulked instead. They didn't want to fight the Germans. The legionaries were tired. They had fought a long campaign all summer against the tough Helvetians, and won the final major battle with some hard fighting. The Helvetian forces were comprehensively defeated, with many killed, a few enslaved, and the rest sent back with the old men, women and children, to Switzerland. There was booty enough for all. It was September already. Surely it was time to stop fighting, have a good night's sleep, and then go home.

Despite their constant grumblings, the legions were force-marched eastwards by day, and also by part of the night, with no chance of a decent meal, and hardly any time to stop and rest. Even the water fetched by the non-coms had to be swigged down whilst still moving.

They captured some German scouts, prowling around in the woods outside their temporary camp. Centurion Pullo, an older man with grizzled grey hair and a misleadingly fatherly air, brought one of them over to Decimus.

"Here, Dessy, see if you can get any information out of this one. The others we caught were too badly injured to survive. You managed fine with those Helvetians a month ago."

"But they were little more than children, Sir," Decimus replied, looking askance at the heavily-chained, half-naked man being dragged towards him. He didn't want a reputation for extracting information from prisoners. It was a horrible task. Those Helvetian spies had been desperate to pour out all the information they knew, just as soon as they were promised a nice quick death at the end. Not that they got it. Centurion Pullo had taken them away to be used as target practise.

"And I don't speak their language," Dessy added hastily. He was feeling quite anxious. The centurion gestured to the man beside him and explained that he was an interpreter. Decimus looked at the German and his heart sank. The captive was huge and muscular, with tawny hair and beard, drooping moustache, and sandy eyebrows and lashes. His freckled face was pale though. Clearly he had lost a lot of blood. His arms and legs were covered with lacerations that someone had roughly bandaged. Even so, blood was still oozing out of the dressings. Perhaps he wouldn't last long. Oddly, he was smiling a little. Decimus could visualise him putting up a brilliant show in the arena, and an equally brilliant show for anyone trying to get him to talk.

Reluctantly Decimus summoned his men. Even the older ones were perturbed. He sent for some wine, and had the prisoner laid out on a trestle table. He started to question him politely, via the interpreter.

"You serve under the German King, Ariovistus?"

Smilingly, his prisoner agreed.

"Were you sent to spy on us?"

"Of course," said the German cheerfully.

"I need some information from you," Decimus explained. "I'll tell you what I want to know, and if you help me I can promise...." His voice trailed off. What could he promise this man? "What do you wish for, right now? A quick death?"

The prisoner looked amused when he heard the words. "A quick death? No, not that," he rasped out. "I want to fuck with you, little man." He paused for a moment, clenching his fists to overcome the pain of his wounds. Then he continued, his voice getting weaker. "You are so pretty, with your curly brown hair, and that little skirt you wear over your britches."

The prisoner watched closely while this was being translated. When everyone laughed, the prisoner joined in, trying to lift himself up, gasping and panting with the effort. Dessy was thinking quickly, even as his respect for his victim increased. He looked closely at the German. The freckles were scattered over the man's skin like so many pale oat-flakes. His eyes were a little unfocused. It was pure bravado, Dessy realised quite suddenly. Of course, even this man would be scared underneath the bluster, however much he tried to hide his fear. Decimus pulled the man up into a sitting position, so he could breathe more easily, and ordered one of his men to support him.

"So what would you report back to your king, about us?" Dessy asked. "That we are little and pretty?"

"So few of you, too."

"Thirty-six thousand men," Dessy replied. "Quite enough."

"But you are all so small. No way can you fight us and win. And you are all so soft, with your baths and your perfume." The German coughed and clutched his chest. He picked up Decimus's sleeve and fingered it. "You wear fine linen as well. My king has not slept in a house for the last fourteen years. We are hard men. We fight our campaigns winter and summer. You should run away quickly, little man. You haven't a chance against us. We will eat you for breakfast." The German laughed and coughed again. "And that would be sad."

"We can hold our liquor, though. Unlike the Germans," said Decimus.

"Who says we can't hold our liquor?"

"The Gauls."

"They lie," said the prisoner indignantly.

"I will drink you under this table. Isn't that right?" Dessy appealed to his men. They roared their agreement.

By the time the German was thoroughly befuddled with wine and blood loss, Dessy had found out a considerable amount of useful information, by dint of disparaging the tactics of Ariovistus. The Romans were heavily outnumbered. Ariovistus was making for the strategically important town of Vesontio, with its plentiful supplies and secure position. Decimus discovered that Vesontio was a town on a high hill, which was almost enclosed by the river Doubs, making a virtually impregnable citadel, a town of the Sequani tribe. He reported all this to his superior, with the suggestion that the German be released, to convey to his king the intelligence that the Roman army was small both in numbers and in height. This idea was received favourably. Dessy was told to prepare his prisoner for immediate release, and get him a horse.

"But I don't have the money for a horse, Sir," Decimus protested.

"Then get a loan," snapped the legate.

The German couldn't understand what was happening at first. Dessy told him he would stay the night, as he was sure the man wouldn't survive otherwise, being empty of blood but full of wine. Then in the morning he would be sent off to report back to his king. The German became effusive in his thanks, and swore to be Dessy's brother hereafter, promising that if Dessy were to be captured when the two armies finally locked together, he would seek him out and treat him as kindly. In the morning, despite his injuries, he insisted on giving Dessy a bear hug, nearly cracking his ribs, before riding off on a horse ludicrously too small for his huge bulk. But Dessy couldn't afford any better beast.

After receiving this precious information, Caesar ordered the disgusted legionaries to march at full speed to Vesontio. They arrived in good time, ahead of the German forces, seized the town with no trouble, and set up camp on the flat plain next to the river, but outwith the town ramparts.

It was hot and smelly in the tent, but the mosquitoes outside were worse, driving the men mad. The repellant concoctions produced by the locals were effective only for a short while, so they sat in a circle round the oil lamps, scratching at their skin, cursing, and contemplating an uncertain future. The men had already heard the rumours while hobnobbing with the slaves and camp servants. Their officers were terrified! Some were openly weeping in their tents, others were making their wills, and still others begging Caesar for permission to leave camp and hurry back to Rome. And all because of the Germans. The men pondered the information they'd had from their Gallic allies.

Germans.... The Germans were ten feet tall.... A German never knows when he's beaten.... Germans never are beaten.... Their gaze alone is enough to scare the wits out of you.... German women have cunts as hard as concrete. You would have to prise their slits apart with a crowbar! This information caused a bout of hilarity, coming as it did from the youngest tent occupant, a fifteen-year-old novice.

"What do you know about cunts, young'n?" asked one soldier.

"Loads," said another. "He's only just come out of his mother's."

There was a brief respite as the boy attempted to strangle the last speaker, and Decimus had to pull him off, while the others convulsed with laughter. But they soon continued to frighten themselves again. Germans chop their prisoners' balls off..... The Germans spread their prisoners' brains on bread..... The Germans roast their prisoners over slow fires.... The Germans……..'

"I don't believe it. It's all rubbish," declared Decimus.

"No, it's true. Honest. I heard it from one of they Gauls. They're terrified of the Germans. And with good reason, seemingly. What about that one you was questioning? The size of him, remember?"

Dessy remembered only too well. His chest was still a bit painful when he took a deep breath. But he wasn't going to change his stance.

"Look, the Helvetians defeated the Germans, and we've defeated the Helvetians."

The tent remained unconvinced.

All the same, many hard marching days later, when Decimus stood in line finally facing the German foe, he discovered his body wasn't so sanguine as his mind. His heart was racing, and his mouth was dry with anticipation of the battle ahead. Nevertheless, as soon as the trumpets sounded the signal to advance, Decimus was in there, pulling his squad with him. He was determined to shield the young novice, though. The boy was expected to hurl his spear, and then retreat back through the ranks. The armies fell on each other with such force that there was no room for javelins to be thrown, so he thrust the boy back through the lines to safety. Then he turned and hurled himself into the thick of the fighting, pulling off the enemy's shields, and stabbing, stabbing, stabbing with his short sword. Slippery bodies piled up under his feet, covered with blood and spilled guts. It was getting harder and harder to keep his balance. Still he pressed forwards, over the muddled heaps of slain and injured, enemy and friend alike.

Dusk was falling. It was becoming difficult to see. The long day's battle was over, the German line broken finally by the third wave of veteran Roman troops, and the relentless barrage of bolts from Roman catapults and scorpios. Caesar was victorious again. The ragged residue of the German enemy turned tail and ran, leaving behind their wagons, baggage, and the defenceless women and children. Some of the German men managed to reach their small boats and escape across the Rhine, Ariovistus among them. But many more were slaughtered.

The Romans returned from their pursuit, exhausted and elated, walking slowly up the slope of the battlefield, where the enemy had been foolhardy enough to attempt to engage a far superior force, not in numbers admittedly, but in military expertise. The legionaries were busy slitting the throats of those Germans too injured to be saleable, and rounding up any less injured, tying them up, and dragging them back to camp to claim as war prizes. They were happily rounding up the women and children as well. It would be a good night. One daughter of the German king was taken alive.

Decimus was feeling dizzy and faint from lack of blood after the battle. He had fought hard all day, encouraging those around him, charging forwards every time he saw the slightest opening in the enemy line, wielding his sword gripped tight in his right hand with terrible effect. He felt darts, arrows, and even javelins thud into his shield, jarring his left arm increasingly painfully. But still he held on grimly. He knew some of his opponents' sword thrusts had penetrated his skin, but he suppressed the desire to stop and inspect the damage. He was still on his feet, just, when the German lines broke and started their headlong retreat.

He watched without curiosity as blood dripped from his arm and thigh into the soil, running down his limbs in sticky red rivulets. Now he had difficulty in standing up, and fell back onto the cold earth. Cassius Domitius, his centurion and greatest friend, loomed over him, his face blurred, issuing orders. Dessy felt himself lifted up and placed on a couple of shields, acting as an improvised stretcher. The men heaved him back to their camp, and then carried him tenderly over to the hospital tent, where he was lowered on a wooden operating table.

Decimus gasped with shock as his wounds were disinfected, then gripped the table-sides with white-knuckled hands as the orderly started to stitch him back together. The orderly started with the deepest cuts first. Dessy managed to lift himself up and tried to concentrate on what was happening to him.

"What are you doing to me?"

"Putting you back together again, Sir," replied the orderly.

"How?"

"Just like your wife sews material. Not quite like your wife, though, as I use a curved needle, and some special thread made out of cattle intestines. Your body will absorb it."

"But why?"

The orderly laughed. "Wounds heal up so much better if the edges of the skin are pulled together. Even the Ancient Egyptians knew that."

"I don't have a wife."

"Maybe you should get one, Sir."

Cassius Domitius made an appearance.

"Are you mad?" Cassius demanded in fury. "Don't you know when to stop?"

"I wasn't really thinking. Just fighting mad."

"You need a cool head, sometimes, Dessy. Anyway, thank the Gods you're safe. Your men are terrified they'll get someone else instead of you, so you'd better hurry up and recover."

"The Decanus is likely to be feverish for a week or two," explained the orderly hesitantly. Sometimes he was blamed if things went wrong. Better to issue a warning.

"A week or two?" Dessy exclaimed. "But I feel okay, just a bit battered."

The orderly became serious. "Sir, your wounds will become infected, despite the vinegar. And you will be feverish and weak, as I've said. Don't rush things. You need to rest up."

"No problem," said Cassius. "He's not going to be allowed to move until your master agrees."

Dessy thought he would be in for a boring couple of weeks, but the orderly was right. He developed a raging fever, and didn't know much of what was happening for a fortnight. His men and the non-coms looked after him, especially the youngest legionary, who had lost his heart to Dessy. There was also a strange face which floated in and out of his consciousness, a pale face with a dark shadow across it. When it appeared he felt reassured, and his body ached less. He felt unseen hands wash him gently, and strong arms hold him up to drink from a cup.

Cassius kept a close eye on him, ensuring that everything was done for his comfort.

When the fever subsided, Decimus was astonished to find just how weak he felt. This was the first time he had been seriously wounded. Inwardly he was scared, terrified that this might be permanent and ruin all his careful plans for his future. For Dessy had specific plans, which involved promotion and war spoils in abundance. He was a younger son, and knew he would need to make his own way in the world. He came from a good but not particularly rich family. His father and grandfather had both been centurions, and both had to some extent increased the family fortunes. But Dessy didn't get on with his father, who was a stubborn man with deeply conservative views. Dessy had flung away to join the army after a bitter row, and seriously thought that if he'd stayed at home any longer, he might have killed the old bastard. Dessy had a temper.

"Do you want a go with our woman?" asked one of his men, breaking into his musings.

"What woman?"

"This woman. The German woman."

A tall woman was pulled forwards out of the shadows. Dessy looked at her in surprise. He hadn't noticed her before. She had bruises on her cheek and neck, and a deep festering cut on her left breast, showing through the torn remnants of her dress. She stared at him with blank eyes. He recognised her as his unknown nurse. He had no desire for her whatsoever. Perhaps this was also the result of his fever.

"She looks a bit battered."

"We made the young'n have a go first, but she was squirming and screaming. So we had to duff her up a bit."

"Did he manage?" Dessy inquired with interest.

"Not really. He had a go, though. So we let him off. He managed alright after the rest of us."

Once Decimus was able to stand steadily on his own two feet, he took the woman by the hand and led her over to the hospital tent. He couldn't find his orderly, and none of the surgeons wanted to help her, so he decided to do the stitching himself. He ordered one of the slaves to fetch vinegar, needle and suture material. He managed to swab the wound, the woman keeping quite still. Fortunately his orderly arrived, just as he was about to start.

"Would you like me to take over, Sir?" asked the orderly.

"No, just watch me, and see if I do it right."

"You're doing fine. She'll have a bad scar, though."

Decimus had been thinking a lot over the last few days, having nothing much else to do.

"These women don't usually last long. Why is that?" he asked.

"They pick up infections from the men. And they have dreadful tears inside after they've been raped a few times. No, they don't last long."

"Tell me something. Is there any way someone could be deliberately badly hurt, but could recover completely?"

"Why do you ask?"

"I was tasked with questioning one of the German prisoners. He was a magnificent specimen. Friendly and funny as well. I really didn't want to hurt him."

The orderly thought for a bit while he was bandaging the woman. "Joints, probably."

"What do you mean, joints?"

The orderly took hold of Dessy's hand and bent back his middle finger painfully. "Joints, like this, that enable you to move, to hold, to fight, to make love. If you dislocate a joint, it is sometimes possible to put it back, to 'reduce' it, without too much damage. And dislocation of joints is painful. Would you like me to demonstrate?"

Decimus snatched his hand back. "Listen, if anyone comes in with a dislocated joint, can you get hold of me? So I can see how to put it right?"

"If you wish, Sir."

"What's your name?"

"Musa. Antonius Musa. I'm available for hire, Sir," the orderly finished, with a bitter edge to his voice. "I'm the property of the surgeon Ruteus."

"I'll remember that," promised Dessy.

The woman lasted one more day. When Decimus returned to the tent the following evening, he found a scene of devastation. The woman was lying dead on the floor, her face as pale as a ghost. A deep gash over her wrist showed where she had bled, quite deliberately, all over the men's bedding, apart from his own, he realised. She'd finished by cutting her throat, the youngster's dagger still clutched in her hand.

"Didn't anyone keep an eye on her?" Decimus asked.

"The young'n was supposed to."

The boy was upset. "How could I look after her? I had to go to drill and weapons training. I couldn't stay with her all the time." He'd liked the woman.

BOOK 1 : CHAPTER 2

Vesontio (Besançon), Gaul, September, 58 BC

Cassius came with a surprise one afternoon, when the legions were in the throes of packing up in readiness for their winter quarters.

"You are invited to dine with our Commander," he informed an astonished Decimus. "Don't look so worried. I'll be there as well."

Cassius wasn't at all concerned about how his junior would perform. Dessy was good-looking, intelligent, and spoke well, and had apprised himself of much military literature. He knew how to win battles, and even better, how to describe how to win battles.

The food was superb, but the rest of the guests were a little overwhelming, as they included all the generals of each legion, most of whom drank a lot and spoke loudly. Dessy found that he was grateful for the presence of Cassius. They were seated at a small table apart from the generals, as rank had to be observed at all times. Dessy sat quietly, ate the meal, which wasn't quite as elaborate as that served to his senior officers, and said nothing unless spoken to. He made sure his answers were short and to the point. He drank abstemiously, following his centurion's example. It was as well to keep one's wits when dining with the most powerful men in Gaul.

At the end of the meal, Caesar told Cassius and Decimus to wait while the other guests left. His secretary had spent the afternoon finding out all there was to know about the Statilius family. All satisfactory, according to Dessy's tent-mates. High ranking, but somewhat impoverished, originating from the Lucania region.

. "Now, Dessy," his commander started.

Decimus rose instantly to his feet, and stood at attention.

"I thought you would like to know that at the parade tomorrow I will single you out for some praise."

"Thank you, Sir. I'll look forward to that," smiled Dessy, intrigued that Caesar should use his nickname.

"I am promoting you to centurion rank."

Decimus was speechless.

"And as this will cause you some financial difficulties, I am awarding you a grant of five hundred gold pieces. You will need to buy a horse, and at least a couple of slaves."

Caesar laughed at Dessy's consternation.

"As you know, I don't do these things lightly. You fought brilliantly. And acted with consideration for your men at all times. To me that is of the utmost importance. Now I wish you to take the place of young Aetius of the tenth legion, whom we so sadly lost from illness the other day. You may leave your men, or take them with you, if you prefer."

Decimus stammered his thanks as his commander gestured for him to sit down again. He sat with thoughts whirling round his head. Taking the place of Aetius Florianus would mean jumping over several centurions in rank, who were older and had served for longer than him. It might lead to problems. Well, he would just have to deal with it when the time came.

"What do you think, Cassius?" Caesar enquired.

"It is well deserved, Sir. He will be superb."

"Well, Centurion," Caesar continued, attempting to put the young man at ease, "have you any thoughts as to how to spend the rest of your prize?"

"Oh," Decimus sat thinking for a few moments, then with a smile on his face he fumbled in the pouch he wore at his belt. "I've been carrying this around all season, Sir," he said.

Caesar smoothed out the parchment and read aloud, "To Decimus Statilius Taurus, greetings from your nephew Marcellus." He looked up, feigning surprise. "I thought your brother's child was called Titus. Titus Statilius Taurus, is it not?"

Decimus was by now astonished. How on earth did Caesar know about his nephew?

"Yes, Sir," he answered. "But there are so many relations named 'Titus' in our family. After the naming ceremony the baby was very cross with us all. He looked just like a tiny version of my father Marcus, so I suggested we should have called him Marcellus, and that name stuck."

"I see," his commander laughed. His attention returned to the scrap of parchment. "This is obviously written by a scribe, but the next part is in his own hand?"

"Yes, Sir. I think he means a horse."

"'I wont a hose for my burthday I luv you.' Apart from the letter 's' being the wrong way round, he has a good hand. When is his birthday?"

"The twenty-third of September. He will be just five years old."

"Well, that is a coincidence. My sister's grandson, Gaius Octavius, will also be five years old on the twenty-third of September."

Everyone knows that, thought Decimus to himself. The Games celebrating the birth of little Gaius Octavius had lasted for many days.

"Is your nephew in Rome?"

"Yes, Sir."

"And do you intend to buy him a horse?"

"Now I can," Dessy laughed. "I've seen some of those sturdy little ponies from the North. One of them would be perfect for him."

"Then perhaps you could buy one on my behalf, for my great-nephew."

"It will be a pleasure, Sir."

"Good. Perhaps you will also engage to transport them to Rome. I understand you are to go and help with the recruitment of two new legions for me, in the Province."

This was all news to Decimus. Horses, slaves, and he would need to buy a centurion's armour and the helmet with its transverse crest. He could see his award disappearing rapidly on a horse for an unknown little boy.

The next day was a momentous one for Decimus. He was the last to be brought forward for commendation by his general, and the only one to be promoted. He received the vine-staff, his badge of office as a centurion, from the hands of his commander. He was overcome; tears were beginning to form. Hastily he wiped them away with his hand. The parade broke out into loud cheers.

Caesar made a mental note. He hadn't realised how popular this promotion would be.

"Salute the parade, Dessy," he said, smiling encouragement.

As if in a dream, Decimus turned and raised his hand in salute. The legionaries went wild. Dessy hadn't realised how well-liked he was, either.

The tent were mightily relieved to find that they were to be transferred to the tenth legion, along with their newly promoted centurion. They celebrated in style that night, able for once to shove thoughts of the German woman firmly to the backs of their minds. Thank the Gods.

On the following day Decimus was pleased to find that he was to share a tent and servants with Cassius initially, who was also to go to Rome, in part to aid the military tribunes with recruitment.

"You'll miss them," said Cassius.

"Miss who?"

"The tent. It's never quite the same." Although Cassius could remember so clearly the young Dessy he had shared a tent with, when he too was a mere decanus. He remembered how Dessy had stood transfixed with shock the first time his javelin had caused one of the enemy to fall down dead. He'd had to grab him, and haul him away from danger. Afterwards Dessy had confided his jumbled thoughts to him, about killing a fellow man, and did it always have to be like this? Man against man? And Cassius had gently put him right.

Cassius gave him some good financial advice and told him where the best horse dealers and slave merchants were to be found. Decimus soon found a horse for himself that he liked the look of; a young, recently broken but still spirited colt, at a fair price. The horse dealer threw in a fine leather saddle and bridle. However the small ponies proved to be more expensive than Dessy had expected. But the slaves were cheaper.

The slave dealer thought he could spot a potential good customer, as Decimus spoke nicely and grammatically, and would probably climb up the centurion ranks quickly, needing ever more attendants, as long as he stayed alive, that is. He advised Dessy to buy a couple of untrained youngsters, two of the Helvetians whom Centurion Pullo had estimated were too young to bear arms. Unknown to the higher authorities, the slave dealer and Centurion Pullo had an arrangement concerning captives, to the mutual benefit of both. The Helvetian boys were still traumatised from seeing thousands of their older comrades slaughtered en masse. The dealer thought Dessy would have no trouble with either of them, but they didn't speak any Latin, hence the reduced price.

The slaves were nervous. Not surprising as they both had some nasty bruises, presumably from previous rough handling when they were captured. Their hands were tied in front of them, but even so it was difficult for Dessy to assess them physically, as they kept cowering away from him. He should have brought his friendly orderly along, he realised. He was pretty sure the boys were bruised and not broken, but it would have been good to have an expert opinion. Dessy became slightly exasperated. The dealer, returning from serving another customer, explained that these young ones, being barbarians, were unhappy at being stripped naked. But the rules of hygiene precluded any wearing apparel. Unschooled slaves such as these had to be kept tied up or chained, and any clothes would inevitably become heavily soiled. Although Dessy noticed that the two boys were decidedly mucky around their nether regions. The poor kids were evidently just human cattle as far as the dealer was concerned.

The dealer slapped the boys round the face, and yelled at them in their own barbarous tongue. Then each one stood still and submissive. One of them, the fairer one, was decidedly tearful. His name was Cierán. At least it sounded like Cierán. The dealer thought he was about seventeen years of age, but the fair ones were slow to produce beards, apparently. The other was called Laeforis. They both looked to be severely undernourished.

Decimus was delighted with the price. Once he had handed over the money, the dealer slid his hand round the genitals of the fair boy, gripping him firmly, as the terrified youngster tried to move backwards.

"Do you want them castrated? No extra charge."

The boy seemed to understand the words. His face drained of colour. He stared at his putative new master in shock.

Dessy shook his head. "No. I can’t get on with eunuchs somehow. They give me the creeps."

The boy brought his hands up to his face, and shuddered. Was there to be no respite from this nightmare?

Dessy ordered his men to take the rest of his new acquisitions back to camp, while he rode the horse, which proved to be just as good as promised. As he rode back he thought about buying his own woman, something to keep him warm on the journey south, he smiled to himself. It was such a nuisance having to search out the brothels in each town as they passed through. And the women brought by their pimp owners to service the needs of the legions, either looked like the back of a horse or were priced extortionately. He would hire the orderly Musa, and ensure the woman wasn't ripped inside.

He was feeling pleased with himself, but Cassius was right, he realised. The tent were treating him differently. There was a distance now between them, no longer the usual joshing and joking. They spoke with the caution of men in the presence of one far more powerful. Dessy wasn't yet used to it.

His new slaves were brought to his tent. Dessy made them sit on the ground, and then broke apart a small loaf of bread and handed a portion to each boy.

"There you are," said Dessy. "Now eat."

Laeforis turned to his companion in confusion. "*He hasn't blessed the bread,*" he whispered. "*What do you think it means, Sir?*"

"He thinks we're animals," answered Cierán sadly.

"No! Be quiet. Only speak when you're spoken to," said Dessy sharply.

They looked up in bewilderment at this strange master. Never in their lives had they eaten unblessed bread. It was a terrible blasphemy.

Dessy was getting impatient. "Come on. Hurry up. What's the matter with you? It's perfectly good bread. You eat bread, don't you?"

Cierán took the pieces of broken bread, spread out his hands and whispered the usual Gallic blessing, thinking he would be punished for speaking at any moment. He handed a piece back to Laeforis.

"Oh," said Dessy, as realisation dawned. "Sorry about that. I forgot. I didn't think you kids...."

But here his voice trailed off. After all it was well known that the Gauls were a superstitious bunch, so terrified of their Gods, that they spent half their lives trying to propitiate them with elaborate ceremonies, and even human sacrifice, Dessy had heard. Still, he should have blessed the food. He must stop being so careless. Decimus patted Cierán on the head and told him he was a good boy.

Cierán recoiled in horror, and snarled, "*I'm not a dog*!"

Dessy wasn't going to let this piece of insolence pass. He grabbed hold of Cierán's hair, pulled his head back, and slapped him hard across the face. The boy should have been beaten for that, but after all, it was only their first night with him.

"Don't you ever speak to me like that again, boy!" said Dessy angrily. Cierán's words were meaningless to Dessy, but the tone was pure aggression.

Cierán was looking at him with open resentment, but he couldn't keep it up, he was too scared. Dessy waited until he was sure the boy was properly submissive, with eyes downcast, and sniffing a bit to keep back the tears. Quite deliberately Dessy reached out, grasping Cierán's shoulder with one hand, as he stroked the boy's golden hair with the other.

"You are my property. I will do whatever I like with you. Understand?"

Cierán nodded, and moved his hands in a gesture of capitulation.

"Good," said Decimus. "But you must say, 'Yes, Master.' So say it."

Cierán mumbled the words.

"Louder," snapped Dessy.

Cierán managed to say the words louder this time.

"Now eat," Dessy ordered.

The boys sighed with relief as the tense atmosphere dissipated. They hastily muttered their thanks, almost the only Latin they knew, and started to eat. Then Dessy told the servants to make sure the boys were given a decent meal.

The two Helvetian boys stared in amazement at the meal proffered by Cassius's servants. They could see chunks of meat, with carrots, onions, and beans in a thick rich stew. They had eaten nothing as good for weeks. In fact Laeforis had never eaten anything as good. That night they slept outside the tent on the ground, and were given a threadbare blanket to keep out the chill night air. The boys huddled together. Cierán found his thoughts whirling round and getting nowhere. He felt so miserable. Even the good food hadn't helped his bleak mood. He had tried to kill himself after the battle was lost, before surrendering his weapons, but when he turned the sharp point of his sword to his chest, he found he lacked the courage to proceed. A bitter blow. So now his life was forfeited to this master, one of the enemy, a Roman centurion. He was nothing, just a cowardly slave, a piece of property without a soul to call his own.

The following morning Decimus had the boys taken to the bath house and scrubbed clean, and their hair washed, but not cut. He liked their long flowing locks. It made them look a little exotic, he thought. And neither of them appeared to have head lice, fortunately. Then he took the pair of them to the camp altar. He wished to beg the Goddess Victoria to keep them fit and healthy so they could serve him for many years to come. To his surprise, when he turned round to bring them to kneel for the blessing at the feet of the goddess, the boys were white and sweating with fear.

"What's the matter with you both?" Dessy asked in astonishment.

Cierán's lips were moving as he prayed desperately for it to be quick, over soon, not the horrible prolonged affair that he'd heard about, with his liver torn out and eaten in front of him, and.......

The senior officer acting as priest explained. "They think you are going to sacrifice them. Look at them. Poor ignorant little devils."

Decimus took Cierán by the wrist, and spoke slowly and soothingly. "Nothing bad is going to happen to you. Just kneel down and receive the blessing." He might as well have saved his breath. When he tried to pull the boy forward to kneel, at first Cierán struggled and cried out, but then the blood drained from his face, his eyelids fluttered and he crumpled fainting into his master's arms.

"Here, you might as well lay him on the altar until he comes round," said the tribune.

Dessy lifted the boy up easily. He was surprisingly light, despite his long limbs. When Laeforis saw what was happening he jumped to the wrong conclusion. He started yelling hysterically, and tried to interpose his body between Decimus and Cierán.

"No, no, please. No eat! No kill! Please no kill," he wept.

"He's not going to be killed, you idiot. He's going to receive a blessing. That's all," Dessy shouted. "Not kill, no!" He turned to the tribune. "What's he talking about? No eat?"

"Better get an interpreter," suggested the tribune.

More expense, thought Decimus, but he agreed. By the time the interpreter arrived Cierán had come round, but Laeforis was still sobbing. The interpreter tried to explain the Romans to the Gauls and the Gauls to the Romans, without much success. But once Cierán had fully recovered consciousness, and was soothed and settled, the boys knelt obediently to receive the blessings of the goddess. They thought it made up for the lack of reverence for the bread at least. But they didn't entirely believe the interpreter.

A camp servant appeared with the branding iron Decimus had ordered, and asked if the branding was to be done now. Dessy thought it as well to get everything over and finished with. He expected the boys would make a fuss, so sent for his men to come and help hold them still. He asked the interpreter to explain to his slaves that as they were unable to speak Latin, he had to ensure they were at least easily identifiable. Dessy thought the boys would find branding was better than wearing an iron collar. After all, it was soon over, and they would forget all about it in a week or two, when their skin had healed. More to the point, it was much less expensive. There were over forty thousand men and boys milling around in camp, almost as many servants as soldiers. The boys might get lost or stolen. And now they were cleaned up, Dessy could see that they looked rather nice, especially Cierán, with his long fair hair.

Despite the explanation, the boys were still upset, struggling and protesting vociferously. Laeforis was dealt with first, but to Dessy's consternation Cierán promptly passed out again. He came round with a moan and then lapsed into a hopeless sobbing from the searing pain of his burnt buttock. Dessy waited impatiently until he had recovered sufficiently, and then marched the boy over to the hospital tent, to find his friendly orderly.

"Is anything wrong with him?" Dessy demanded. He would be entitled to return the boy to the dealer, if so.

"Does he have a name?" Musa asked.

Dessy thought for a moment. "Yes. Sounds like Ceres. Cierán, something like that."

Fortunately the orderly could find nothing seriously wrong. He surmised that the fainting was merely because Cierán was traumatised and terrified. He attempted to explain this to Dessy, but Dessy couldn't understand, as he thought he had been exceptionally kind. Few other masters would have bothered to try and explain their decisions to their new slaves.

That night, when Decimus ordered the boys outside to sleep, Cierán stood hesitating for a moment. Then with a tiny shrug of his shoulders, he dropped to his knees at his master's feet and kissed his hand. This was the way he had always bid goodnight to his father, and the way his own servants had always behaved. He waited expectantly for his master's words of blessing and dismissal, but as none came he stood up again in bewilderment, and bowed the polite Gallic half-bow. Laeforis followed suit.

Dessy had a feeling he was expected to say something, but didn't know what. He decided he would find out in the morning, as he thought the boys' actions were very sweet, and should be encouraged.

The Helvetians boys lay on the ground face down, trying to come to terms with the day's events. They knew from their own experience that prisoners taken in war by their own countrymen, were given special status, not treated like the usual domestic servants. They were allowed to swear loyalty at the altar to their new masters, and become faithful dedicated slaves, never chained, and certainly never branded. They were expected to adopt the allegiances of their owners, fight on their behalf, and never, ever try to escape.

"*We were taken to the altar this morning,*" whispered Laeforis. "*Do you think we are dedicated slaves, Sir?*"

"*But we weren't asked to swear anything, were we? And we've been branded. I don't feel dedicated. I feel humiliated. And sore,*" Cierán whispered back. "*Listen, you tried to protect me today, thank you for that.*"

"*Of course. You are the son of the chief.*"

Cierán began to feel a little more hopeful. He was still someone of importance to this boy, then. "*I'm the son of a dead man. So let us see this through together, Laeforis. Whatever comes, bad or good."*

"*Yes, Sir. That will be good.*"

Laeforis had only ever seen Cierán in the distance before, on horseback, with his father the chief, commanding his men. Now circumstance had thrown them together he felt proud to have made such a friend, rather than humiliated, and when Cierán's hand came over to grip his own, he felt an odd surge of happiness.

Their master yelled at them to shut up. They gave up whispering, and found sleep came easily, despite the branding. They were mentally and emotionally exhausted, and physically still weak from lack of food.

BOOK 1 : CHAPTER 3

Vesontio (Besançon), Gaul, to Rome, Italy, Autumn, 58 BC

The next day Dessy and the orderly sought out a suitable girl slave. The dealer had a large group of women and children of all ages. After Dessy had made his choice, Musa confirmed that she was relatively undamaged internally, the girl being one of the captive German women. She had been punched in the face, and had a black eye, several bruises, and a cut lip, not a particularly pretty sight. And someone had taken a stick to her. Back and buttocks showed areas of purplish contusions. But something about her appealed to Decimus.

After the sale was completed Dessy discovered from the orderly that the girl wasn't just undamaged inside, somehow she was still a virgin. This information made him look at the girl with new eyes. Apparently her name was Ethela. She was dressed in a ragged shapeless garment of undyed wool reaching only to her knees. She had small breasts, and a narrow waist, with a tangle of straight light-brown hair. Yet again it was obvious that she was terrified of him, even though he had done his best to be gentle. Before they returned to the camp he had bought her a wooden comb, a small hand-mirror of bronze work, and a length of blue-dyed material.

Dessy brought the girl into his tent. He ordered his men to look after his slave boys for half an hour, then he laid out his cloak on a blanket on the ground. He stripped off, already half-aroused, and approached the girl. She gazed at him, wide-eyed with terror. As he pulled her dress up, she burst into frightened sobs and tried to back away. This wasn't at all how he expected her to behave. He had to man-handle her down onto the ground.

The girl didn't seem to appreciate her luck. She was going to be just for his own use after all, not stuck in some ghastly brothel, or suffering multiple assaults from the troops. Dessy tried to explain to her in a gentle manner, and soothe her fear, but it didn't seem to work, so he gave up. But forcing himself on her wasn't all that successful. The initial contact was painful for both of them, until her blood acted as a lubricant. Dessy thought he must do something about it in future. Use some oil or something.

When he withdrew he found his penis covered in blood and spunk, so he got to his feet, pulled his cloak from under the girl, wrapped it round his shoulders, and walked off to the bath house to get cleaned up. Halfway through being dried he remembered the other German woman. For the Gods' sakes! He had left the girl surrounded by sharp implements! He pushed the attendant out of the way, grabbed his cloak, and hurried back to his tent.

The girl was lying motionless on the floor. Dessy was seized with panic. He knelt down and turned her onto her back. She was trembling, clutching her dress to her body. The blanket was soaked with blood, semen and urine, he realised. What a fool he was. The girl didn't know to use the wooden bucket. In fact he should probably get her a chamber-pot, he though ruefully. More money. On the other hand, he was going to save a fortune on professional women.

Dessy woke up the next morning with his usual erection, but something felt wrong. His first pee was agony! He pulled back his foreskin and examined himself. He had tiny abrasions all over his prepuce. No wonder he was sore. Fucking virgins was clearly overrated, or there should be some warnings of problems beforehand. He couldn't remember anyone ever telling him.

It came to him that Ethela might also have problems. She was such a frightened shy thing. Last night he couldn't persuade her to use the bucket at first. She had just stood and sobbed. Cassius's servants rigged up a blanket across one end of the tent, to give her a little privacy, and that seemed to work.

He pulled the blanket aside to find the petrified girl perched on the bucket, in the very act of urination. She gave a startled cry, and then started to sob yet again. Dessy let the 'curtain' fall back. One of his old tent-mates popped his head round the tent flap, and asked if his centurion had any orders for him this morning. He was an older man, never likely to climb up the ranks, but Dessy knew him to be reliable. Dessy brought his cloak and the blanket out, and asked if they could be cleaned up.

"You had a good night, then, last night, Sir," smiled the legionary.

"No," said Dessy ruefully. "The young'n was right about German women."

"Castoreum, that's what you need. I'll get you some from the apothecary, Sir."

" Would it help the girl as well? I think she's sore too."

"I'll ask, Sir."

Decimus knew the man was already turning rude rhymes over in his mind. Raw and sore, he thought would be appropriate. Oh well, he would just have to put up with it.

Ethela appeared to spend all her time in a damp heap behind the blanket curtain. One evening he got fed up with her and shouted, "Ethela, stop snivelling." There was silence. Dessy was trying to learn the names of the men in his centuria. Cassius had told him to learn five or six to start with, and to use them. All the other legionaries would presume he knew each one of them. But he did want to know each one, and Ethela was not helping his concentration.

Unbidden, again the awful image of the other German woman flicked into his mind. The rust-red blood, coalescing in dark pools from her neck to her waist, and onto the ground at her side. He remembered the sickly sweet smell of death, and the flies. Especially the flies, clustered round the throat wound like a black scarf, that rose and disintegrated at his approach.

He sighed heavily, walked over to the girl, picked her up off the ground, and pulled her to sit on the bed with him, one arm round her waist, the other holding the list of names. Her bruising was subsiding. She was beginning to look quite pretty. He gently kissed her cheek. Unfortunately she still stared blankly at the tent wall. He hadn't tried anything for a bit, but now he felt normal again, so he decided it was time for another go. This time more successful. And the oil had worked. He didn't feel sore at all the next morning.

Dessy presented his commander with one of the little ponies, the better one, he thought. Cassius reasoned that the subsequent journey to Rome would enable his protégé to establish the exact relationship he wanted with the legionaries. It would be a good time for Dessy to find his feet. He couldn't think of any disadvantages. Dessy's only problem was his occasional inexplicable acts of kindness, seemingly as surprising to himself as to his comrades.

Decimus enjoyed the journey back to Rome. He assumed he would be able to train the slave boys on the way. He was delighted with the girl. Alright, she was still terrified of him, and jumped with nervousness whenever he touched or spoke to her. But at least she was beginning to be a bit more cooperative.

Somehow he had overlooked the problem of menstruation. He had never given the subject much thought, not having any sisters. When Ethela obstinately rejected his advances one evening, attempting to push him away, he lost his temper with her. The Helvetian boys weren't helping, trying to get his attention, and going on about girls doing something, but he couldn't make out what they were saying. Dessy shouted at them all, slapped Ethela hard, yanked up her dress, and then felt guilty when confronted by the hysterically sobbing girl with the blood running down her legs. She held her sore face in one hand, and clutched her soiled dress with the other, quite distraught. Dessy had to waste a lot of time petting her and stroking her until she had calmed down a bit. And he realised that the Helvetian boys were horrified at his brutality, staring at him in shock.

Again his tent rallied round, finding Ethela suitable underclothes and linen cloths from the nearest brothel. Dessy was discovering how indispensable they were to him. He felt so much better having them around while he was feeling his way with his new command. Apart from Ethela, the problems were mainly his two new slave boys. They couldn't understand him even when he shouted at them. Slapping them didn't seem to help much, either. He'd assumed they would be quick to pick up Latin, but they were surprisingly slow. Only a few words penetrated, 'Master,' 'whip,' 'bread,' 'water,' 'horse,' and not much else. Unfortunately the more he shouted the more nervous and clumsy they became, especially Cierán, who dissolved into tears as soon as he raised his voice. He decided that when he returned to campaigning he would have to try a different approach.

Decimus was accommodated in the military forts along the Via Aemilia and the Via Aurelia on the coastal route, and was given great hospitality. Two particular scenes concerning his new slaves were engraved on his mind. He was on his way to the commandant's office when he caught sight of the three of them returning from stabling his horse. Cierán and Laeforis were throwing an apple to each other, while Ethela was attempting to intercept it. They were all laughing; happy children at play. He watched as Ethela stamped her foot in mock anger, and shouted at the boys. Cierán promptly gave the courteous Gallic half-bow, and handed her the apple. Ethela was about to take a bite when they saw their master. All three slaves froze in fear, Ethela swiftly hiding the apple behind her back. Dessy walked over to the little group, and held out his hand. Ethela gave him the apple, looking at him with apprehension. Dessy rubbed the apple on his tunic, and handed it to her.

"For you, Ethela," he said with a smile. But she didn't smile back.

On another occasion he found his three slaves bent over the cooking fire, as Ethela poured some gloopy liquid onto a flat metal tray. They straightened up as soon as they saw him. Ethela took hold of the tray with a cloth, and tried to flip over the contents.

"*It's stuck. I need something to turn it over,*" said Ethela, in a panic.

Cierán ran over to him, and touched the hilt of his sword. "Please?" he said, "For Ethela?" He pointed to the girl. Dessy swore at him. Cierán turned away, shrugging his shoulders. Dessy looked at the gloopy mixture, smelt the tantalising aroma, and suddenly realised what his slave girl was doing.

"Ethela," he shouted. He walked swiftly to her side and handed her the sword. The slave boys were watchful, uncertain how their actions would be interpreted by this unfathomable master.

Ethela stood silently for a moment, watching her pancake cook. Then she took Dessy's sword and flipped it over. The smell was so appetising. She called out orders in German. The boys rushed to obey her, fetching a plate. Cierán offered his master the pancake and the honey jar.

"*Pancakes*," Cierán explained. "Good, Master?"

More than good. It was delicious.

Dessy approached Ethela to thank her, but she backed away hastily, turning to find Cierán.

"He's not angry," Cierán told her.

"*Maybe not this time*," whispered Ethela. "*What if he finds out?"*

"He won't."

Letters were waiting for Dessy from his father. Apparently as soon as news of his promotion had reached Rome, his father had arranged a marriage for him, into a wealthy family. His bride was named Veronica, fifteen years old, and with a considerable dowry. Decimus was a little surprised by this news. He had thought to choose his own bride. But being totally dependent on his father for everything so far, apart from this award from Caesar, he knew he could not refuse. His father still had the total power of the paterfamilias, and did not take well to disagreements from his offspring. One of the many reasons why Dessy chose the army as his profession. But now he was home, with his father Marcus and elder brother Lucanus clad in their togas to honour him, and his wildly excited little nephew standing at the door to greet him.

BOOK 1 : CHAPTER 4

Villa of Marcus Statilius Taurus, Rome, Winter, 58/57 BC.

Titus Statilius Taurus, known in the family as 'Marcellus,' knew that Uncle Dessy had done something astonishing, something that had mightily impressed Grandfather. A difficult feat. Marcellus knew he had never done such a thing himself. And his new pony was the result. He loved the pony. It was a sturdy beast, with a long black mane and tail, a great desire for carrots and apples, and a fondness for getting its own way.

Marcellus was to be present at his uncle's wedding to a girl called Veronica. His so-called tutor, an unpleasant over-fastidious but ignorant man named Ennius, brushed off his questions as to the significance of the married state.

Marcellus had an ally. More than one, actually. A few months ago he found the groom's son, Rufus, a slave boy about the same age as himself, playing in the stable yard with a tiny beautifully-carved wooden horse. Marcellus promptly snatched the toy off him. Rufus started to howl, not that he thought it would do any good. Ennius came into the yard to tell his charge off for playing with the slaves again, misread the situation and slapped Rufus hard. Rufus's nose started to bleed, which made him cry more. Marcellus felt guilty, and gave the boy back his wooden horse, but Ennius wrenched it away again, saying, "You wicked ungrateful boy. How dare you take this off the young master. I will have you well whipped."

"No, it isn't mine. It's his," Marcellus shouted.

"Nonsense. Since when did a slave have a toy like this? You must have forgotten who gave it to you, Master Marcellus. You are so careless with your possessions. You really must pay more attention. How many times do I have to tell you the same thing?"

With that comment ensuring that Marcellus was in the wrong, as usual, Ennius retired to have his afternoon nap, which seemed to Marcellus to get longer and longer every day.

"Stupid man," said Marcellus, and handed back the horse again. "Where from did you get it? It's beautiful. Just like real. What do you call it?"

The slave boy rubbed his nose on his sleeve and sniffed his tears back. "I call him 'Lightning.' My Dad make him for me. Do you think I'll have to be whipped, Master Mark?"

"No. I'll go and see Grandfer about it right now."

Marcellus thought he knew just where the seat of power was in this household. With a strong feeling of righteous anger on the innocent boy's behalf, Marcellus became bold enough to confront his grandfather in his study, something he wasn't usually allowed to do. He knocked firmly on the door and entered.

"I have to right a justice, Grandfer," he said with a comical air of importance.

His grandfather was feeling tolerant, having just finished a large luncheon, washed down with excellent wine. He laughed and paid attention for once. This would be a good story to tell his cronies about his grandson. 'Right a justice,' indeed. Well, good for the boy.

It certainly sounded as if Ennius had jumped to a hasty conclusion. Grandfather promised to sort everything out. Which meant that Marcellus was allowed to play with the slave boy. Rufus was the youngest of the family, and had big brothers, who were properly deferential to Marcellus. His mother and father were pleased at their son's increased status as playmate to young Master Marcellus. The groom carved an equally lovely horse for Marcellus, who called it 'Thunderer.'

Ennius was not pleased to be overruled. Henceforth he blamed every piece of bad behaviour from Marcellus as due to the malign influence of the slave boy and his family. Marcellus was learning to ignore Ennius. He would have liked to have big brothers as well. But he only had little sisters, who were useless to play with, and cried at every opportunity. Unfortunately Ennius didn't like being ignored. He informed his small charge that as soon as he reached the age of five his punishments would be physical, not verbal as they had been in the past.

"As you know, Master Marcellus, your grandfather always quotes Cicero as saying, 'Show me a boy who has not been beaten, and I will show you an ignoramus.'"

Once he was home his mother was the first person Dessy wanted to talk to about this marriage. Lady Caecilia had been stricken with arthritis for several years, and rarely left her bedroom. She found little relief from pain, and was now no longer able to travel to the baths, even in a litter. Massage no longer helped. Her limbs were bent up awkwardly with strictures, and moved only a little. Walking was almost impossible. Her husband Marcus adored her. To see the care Marcus lavished on his wife when she ventured into company was quite affecting. He became tender and considerate. But she couldn't help Decimus in this case. She hadn't met his bride, and only knew of the family through hearsay. She told him he must decide for himself.

Dessy confronted his father almost immediately afterwards.

"Why on earth have you arranged for me to marry this Veronica Juvenalis? I've never heard of the family before. And according to the gossip in the barracks, her elder sisters are a pair of vulgar sluts."

"Not at all, my boy. Not at all. Certainly the older sisters are a lively bunch, but they are respectably married. The point is that the family might be low-born, but they are rich. Veronica comes with a large dowry."

"That's not what I want," said Dessy in exasperation. "You found a delightful wife for my brother, reserved, intelligent, and beautiful into the bargain."

"Your brother needed a wife to match his social position. Lucanus intends to climb high. As you are aware, he is bidding to be appointed as one of the Quaestors. We must help him in any way we can."

"Not at the cost of my future happiness. Lucanus would never agree to that."

"But he may have need of your wife’s money, in times to come. Look, Decimus, you will be perfectly happy. After you've fucked the girl a few times, and got her pregnant, she’ll settle down. And what about your slave girl?" Marcus asked. "I understand from my steward that she is to be yours exclusively. So if you're in love with the girl, it hardly matters what your feelings are about your future wife."

"I'm not in love with her, of course not. You are insulting, Father. How could I be in love with a slave? But she's a timid, shy little thing, easily upset. The other woman in our tent cut her throat. I don't want Ethela to do the same. I think she can just about manage me."

His father often boasted that he'd had every servant girl in his house, but Dessy had overheard one such coupling, and it wasn't pretty.

"The needs of the family come before your desires, Decimus. Let's face it. How long will it be before you are off again?"

"We're here for four months."

"If you were to fall in love with your wife, what a wrench it would be to leave her. If you cannot stand her, after a reasonable amount of time I will allow you to divorce."

"Allow me?" spluttered Dessy, now really angry. "You will allow nothing any more to me. I will marry the girl so as not to disgrace the family by seeming unreliable, as you have already signed the marriage contracts. But don't you dare take any more decisions about me on my behalf."

"I still have the authority of a father," Marcus insisted, "I could cut you off without a denarius, and turn you out of the house."

"That would suit me fine. I'll take myself off to the barracks."

They both had raised their voices so much, Lucanus came to intervene between them and keep the peace as usual.

"Please don't do any such thing, Dessy. Marcellus would be heartbroken, and so would I, and so would Father," he added with a smile, "although he would never acknowledge it."

Marcus was convinced that once his son appreciated the large estate and wealth that his bride would bring to the marriage, he would rapidly become reconciled. He didn't know his son very well.

BOOK 1 : CHAPTER 5

House of Lucius Marcius Philippus, Rome, Winter, 58 BC

An invitation arrived which partly alleviated the bad feeling between Marcus and his younger son, who was always the awkward one of the two, he reflected, whereas Lucanus did as he was told, and did it with a pleasant deference to his sire. So far Marcus remained unaware that Lucanus agreed with everything his father said, and then quietly ordered affairs to his own liking. As he was much better at running the house and estates than his father, no one bothered to inform Marcus.

The invitation was to visit the house of little Gaius Octavius, so the child could thank Centurion Decimus for choosing such a lovely pony for him. The invitation came from Gaius Julius Caesar himself. Caesar had heard that the up-and-coming Lucanus Statilius Taurus, elder brother of one of his own centurions, was endeavouring to be appointed to the post of Quaestor. And was likely to succeed, according to the local gossip. Admittedly only the first early stage of Civil Service positions, the beginning of the long arduous path to governing, and if successful, he mustn't be allowed to think himself of any importance yet. Caesar wanted to look the man over. Lucanus Taurus might be useful in the future. He would be a member of the Senate, if elected. A big jump for one from the Equites rank.

Marcellus accompanied his father and uncle to the house, but unfortunately Gaius Octavius was in bed with a feverish cough, so they did not get to meet him after all. Julius Caesar was clad in his official robes, having spent the morning dealing with petitioners for his favours, one of whom was seated beside him. A richly dressed, handsome young man, about the same age as Decimus, wearing a supercilious smile of disdain. Neither of them bothered to rise out of their chairs to greet these relatively unimportant guests, and Caesar pointedly didn't asked them to sit down either.

Lucanus turned to one of the servants, snapped his fingers impatiently, and ordered the startled man to bring chairs for them at once. He had no intention of being upstaged by Caesar. As the servant rushed off to obey this peremptory command, Lucanus turned to Caesar with a charming smile.

"Servants, these days. One wonders what gets into their heads. Half the time they seem to be dreaming, instead of concentrating," he said. He gathered the folds of his toga about him and sat down on one of the hastily proffered chairs. "Here, Dessy," he continued, waving his young brother to the other seat. "No doubt Lady Atia's household is in disarray, with the sickness of her little boy."

Caesar wondered if he had underestimated the Statilius family. He became gracious, introducing the young man as Mark Antony. Lucanus gave a small bow and said that he knew of Antony, and was pleased to make his acquaintance, as his reputation had preceded him. Antony scowled, knowing full well his reputation was dire, being that of a dissolute youth, now in considerable debt, which is why he had applied to Caesar, his mother's cousin.

Unfortunately Caesar indulged his gift for manipulation. He thought he would be entertained if he set the two young men against each other, so he spent some time extolling Decimus's courage on the battlefield, and suggested that Antony might give consideration to a military career, which would solve his financial problems, he added with a laugh. The two young men stared at each other with mutual antipathy.

Marcellus was invited to hand over the poem he had written in honour of Gaius Octavius. Caesar opened the tiny scroll, and read the poem out loud.

"Though small, you will be honoured,
"And with your illustrious name,
"As a soldier and a statesman,
"Great will be your fame."

Caesar smiled, and pulled Marcellus forward against his knees.

"Very good. Very good indeed. I approve the sentiments. But I see you have trouble writing the letter 's.' I had just such trouble when I was young."

This was news to Marcellus. Ennius had made him write out all the 's's again facing backwards, and had shouted a lot as well. Lucanus was privately amazed that Ennius hadn't corrected his son's handwriting. He thought he would need to ask his wife to check a little more on Marcellus and his progress.

Caesar was explaining, "Look, this is what I did. If you think of your 's' as a snake, you can make him face the letters you are still to write on the page. Then he will always be the correct way round."

"Yes, Sir. Thank you," said Marcellus. He had tried a similar trick, but Ennius hadn't agreed. Marcellus was now convinced that Ennius was teaching him wrongly, but was it on purpose? So he could hit Marcellus some more? He wasn't sure, but he knew Ennius was his enemy.

A harassed Lady Atia entered the room. What the hell was Uncle Julius thinking of, to be using her house to entertain when Gaius Octavius was so sick? So typical of him, she thought. He never cares about anyone but himself. Other people were merely there to be used to achieve his ends. She hated him, and especially hated the speculative way he looked at her.

Atia was accompanied by her daughter Octavia, a pretty girl of about eleven years. They both bowed to the guests, Atia apologising for not being present to greet them at the start of the visit. Octavia stared at Mark Antony. She remembered she had met him before, in Macedonia, when her father was governor. He had stayed with them for a few days while on his way to Athens. He had ignored her completely, so she made sure she only bowed to the Statilius family, and felt an inward satisfaction, though no one else noticed.

Decimus looked at Atia and marvelled. What a startlingly beautiful woman, with her lovely expressive face. She was tall and slender, and elegantly dressed, but her clothes were a little disarranged, and soft tendrils of brown hair were escaping from the cap she wore. She was clearly agitated, but trying to hide the fact. Poor woman. He thought she must wish her unwelcome visitors to go as soon as possible. Following his brother's example, Dessy refused to be intimidated by his commander's presence. He stood up, bowed to her, and with his delightful smile and real warmth, said that they were obviously taking up her valuable time, which would be much better spent with her little boy. Lucanus added his voice to his brother's. Lady Atia looked at Decimus at last, aware of a tall, good-looking young man, who was actively trying to help her. She felt a rush of gratitude. Her little son was so ill, feverish, coughing and wheezing, she could hardly think straight for anxiety about him.

Caesar wasn't having any of it. "My dear niece, I'm sure you can spare us half an hour of your time. Gaius Octavius will come to no harm. Indeed your apprehension on his behalf may worsen his condition."

"Whatever you say, Uncle Julius, of course."

Atia sat fuming inwardly for the allotted time, but made an effort to be interested in the charming young man, and managed as well to hope to congratulate Lucanus on his new appointment in the near future. Atia was politically astute, too much so sometimes for Uncle Julius. She could see through his little stratagems, and passed this ability on to her children.

Decimus had enough sense not to talk about the war. Instead he spoke about the new buildings he had seen, of how much Rome had changed for the better. Atia said that she thought too much decoration detracted from the lines of a building, and spoke about the architectural purity of the Greek temples she had seen in Macedonia. This was a none-too-subtle dig at Uncle Julius, who endeavoured to embellish every important public building with elaborate facades. This led to a heated discussion with Dessy, who loved the intricacy and craftsmanship he had seen at the Theatre of Pompey, now nearing completion. Atia managed to subdue her anxiety for a tiny period, which made her grateful to this sweet-natured young man.

Caesar tapped Atia's daughter lightly on the shoulder, making her jump.

"Octavia, my dear, take young Marcellus into the garden. He is a budding poet. I expect he would like to commune with the flowers."

Octavia laughed delightfully, Marcellus thought. He had never seen such a pretty girl with such a lovely laugh before.

Caesar enjoyed keeping his niece present against her will, but permitted her to retire after a short time, as he wanted to question Decimus about the progress of the recruitment process. He intended to keep a close eye in the future on Centurion Decimus, an extraordinarily brave man. If he had the subtlety of his brother he could prove useful. After all, Decimus had successfully obtained information from the German prisoner by trickery. And the man appeared quite taken with Atia. That too might prove useful. He would suggest to his niece that she should get to know the Statilius family better.

To his great relief, Octavia took an overawed Marcellus by the hand. Together they walked through the house to the enclosed garden. There were still masses of flowers blooming profusely, giving off a mixture of musky scents in the warm autumn sunshine, anemones, nepeta, acanthus, asters, and more. Octavia waited expectantly to see how Marcellus would commune with them, but he just held her hand tightly and said nothing, being rather unnerved by his meeting with the great Julius Caesar.

"What shall we play?" asked Octavia, to break the ice.

"Uncle Dessy is going to be married. Let's play weddings."

Octavia thought it was a funny game for a little boy. Her brother Gaius Octavius always wanted to fight with a wooden sword, or play with bow and arrows, which Octavia thought quite boring. She wasn't interested in his descriptions of the imaginary foes he had managed to kill. But she went along with him, being a good-natured girl. She thought weddings would be a lot more fun. Sure enough, they were. Marcellus sat on the ground and made a wreath of flowers for her hair, avoiding the prickly roses, while Octavia pretended to bake the sacrificial cakes. Then she crouched down so that Marcellus could place the wreath on her dark curls. Marcellus thought she looked even more lovely with flowers in her hair. He plucked up his courage and kissed her cheek.

"There," he said. "Now we are properly married, 'Tavia."

"Oh good," said Octavia. "Now we can have babies."

"Shall we go to the shop and buy some?" Marcellus asked doubtfully, not being quite sure about the baby idea. His mother had babies. They weren't much fun, as far as he could see. They got ill and died, and his mother cried a lot.

Octavia smiled. She already knew about babies, her nurse had told her with unremitting detail, but she liked the shop idea. So they pretended to go to a baby shop, which turned out to be Octavia's bedroom. She had a large collection of dolls. Marcellus said he only wanted boy babies, because he was fed up with little sisters. So Octavia obligingly pinned up the dolls' clothes so the dolls looked more like boys. They collected four boy baby dolls from the bedroom and took them back into the garden. Octavia wondered why she had never thought of boy dolls herself. She had only a little time to spend with her collection, but she had a vivid imagination, and gave each one a life story, and here was a little boy with an imagination to rival her own. Then Marcellus kissed Octavia again, because she smelt lovely, and had such warm soft skin. So then she kissed him back, and he felt transported to another place, a magic place, where he would live with Octavia and the babies, and Ennius wouldn't be allowed in the house. He asked Octavia what commune meant.

"I think it means that a garden with flowers is a quiet and beautiful place, with the noises of the world shut out, so you can have the space in your mind for poems to enter."

Marcellus liked that idea. He told Octavia about Ennius, and pulled out the bit of parchment on which he had written the first version of the poem for Gaius Octavius. Ennius had crossed out his writings.

"He said I made the 's's the wrong way round," Marcellus explained. "But your uncle said his were the wrong way round. Now I don't know which is the right way."

Octavia was perturbed, especially when Marcellus showed her the sore places on his back where Ennius had beaten him. "Your way is the right way. Come along inside. We must show this to your father."

The children didn't get any chance to explain because the visit was coming to an end. The adults were all on their feet, and farewells were being taken.

"Never mind," whispered Octavia. "I'll show it to my Great Uncle Julius."

As they walked home Lucanus turned to his brother in excitement.

"You have done me a great deal of good, Dessy. Won't Father be amazed?"

Caesar had so enjoyed verbally sparring with him all afternoon, he had eventually suggested he would support Lucanus in his bid to become Quaestor, even though he couldn't force Lucanus to declare for one or the other political party in the Senate. Luke was too wise to commit himself fully at this early stage of his career.

"An interesting family," Caesar observed to Mark Antony after they had left. "I think young Lucanus will go as far as Consul one day. I'll get Atia to befriend his wife, so we have some idea of his policies. And Atia can have the handsome centurion as a reward for her services, although I won't tell her that."

Antony wasn't interested in the slightest in the Statilius family. Nor was he interested in Atia.

"However before they arrived we were discussing your debts, were we not, Antony? I was glad to hear of your studies in Athens. Always strive for improvement. With me as your patron you will become a man of stature. So I suggest I buy your loyalty by paying all your creditors in full."

"Can you buy loyalty?" Antony asked in surprise.

"Certainly. I buy the loyalty of my troops by paying them double the usual army rate. But I also have to be successful, and they must continue to believe I will always succeed. Now I have written to the Proconsul in Syria on your behalf. He is happy to have you as one of his cavalry officers. So you have a chance to prove your worth to me in a military way. And you may well acquire a fortune yourself. These Eastern countries have temples stuffed with gold. The monetary rewards may be enormous. And I've heard the women are beautiful."

In bed that night, Marcellus pondered on Gaius Octavius, the unknown boy. Octavia had said she like being called 'Tavia,' and that it would be Marcellus's special name for her. No one else would be allowed to call her that.

BOOK 1 : CHAPTER 6

House of Lucius Marcius Philippus

Octavia collected up the dolls and put them back in their correct places in her bedroom. She liked order, and she liked the secure feeling it gave her, to make some order in her life. Ever since her father died a year ago, Octavia felt as if she were floating in a cold sea, pulled by currents against which she could make no headway. Often when she went to bed she lay frightened in the dark, unable to sleep.

During the day, after her lessons, Octavia spent an increasing amount of time at her mother's side as she learnt how to run a large house efficiently. She was aware that she would be married in only a few years, and then she would be totally in charge of the household. That was a pleasing idea, although she didn't like the thought of what she must endure to achieve that state. Sometimes she wished her nurse wasn't quite so informative.

Octavia was pleased to learn that Great Uncle Julius was to leave Rome tomorrow, and return to Cisalpine Gaul. Where, he told her mother, he would ensure Roman justice prevailed over his area of governance. Octavia did not like the smile on her great uncle's face when he said this. When Great Uncle Julius stared at her he seemed to be looking right through her to the other side. She didn't like this disquieting look in his eyes. And when he told her she was a pretty girl, she didn't take it as a compliment, but more of an unseen threat. He embraced her a little too tightly as he kissed her goodnight. Her nurse had told her to be careful.

"Don't let him get too near you, ducky. He's not a nice man."

Octavia agreed with this summation of Great Uncle Julius's character. But how could she keep him at arm's length? Despite his menacing presence hovering over her in the background, she had managed to enjoy playing with little Marcellus today.

Octavia curled up on her bed and thought about the other visitors. She decided she liked Centurion Decimus, but she did not like Mark Antony, the unpleasant young man she had first encountered in Macedonia. Octavia lay in bed thinking about the past, conjuring up the turmoil of those last years.

Gaius Octavius, her father, had been the Governor of Macedonia. Many Roman citizens came to stay and were warmly welcomed at the governor's palace, while on route to various Greek cities. Mark Antony was one of them, on his way to Athens, where, he informed the governor, he hoped to learn from the Greek philosophers and teachers there. Octavia didn't think he would learn much. He drank a lot of her father's best wine morning noon and night, tried to borrow money from him, and wandered unsteadily around the palace.

Octavia had been ordered to practise her skills as a hostess, and show him around the gardens. But he wasn't able to recognise any of the exotic flowers or plants her mother was so proud of, and appeared totally disinterested, his gaze wandering off repeatedly to look at the girls picking the fruit, and grinning and winking at her pretty young nursemaid. The next afternoon, during siesta time, Octavia heard shrieks for help coming from the dining room, and found her nursemaid screaming, being bent over a side table by Antony. He had one hand lifting up her skirt to reveal her bottom, the other in the dark patch between her legs.

When Octavia ran over shouting at him to leave Sufi alone, he desisted at once, with a shamefaced look. Straight away Octavia told her mother about the strange behaviour of their guest. That night she heard her mother and father discuss Antony, her father describing him as a dissolute, impecunious libertine, words Octavia didn't know, but remembered, writing them down on a scrap of papyrus, awaiting future explanation. They were bad words, she was sure, and Antony was therefore a bad man. After that Sufi disappeared. Octavia never found out what happened to her. A much older plain-featured nursemaid looked after her instead, whom she liked well enough. But she missed Sufi, who could run and dance and knew lots of games to play.

Now to take out and examine those extra painful memories. Octavia didn't do this often. She remembered how pleased her father was at being recalled to Rome when his period of office ended. He had seemed like a young boy, full of high spirits. To start with she had felt a little sad to be leaving Macedonia, where, despite the occasional badly-behaving visitor, she had been so happy in her father's palace. She enjoyed her lessons with her tutor, and discovered what all those long words meant, amongst other things. And her mother was less disposed to make her practise working with her spindle, which Octavia found so dull. While spinning she allowed her mind to fill with the characters she had read about, Ulysses' adventures, and Jason with the Argonauts, Persephone trapped underground, and Theseus defeating the Minotaur. The stories of Gods and Goddesses fascinated her. How weird they were, always jealous or violent, causing mayhem more often than not.

Gaius Octavius liked to be known here among the Macedonians, as a patron of the arts. Poets and musicians were always welcome at the Governor's palace, and would be sure of adequate payment for their recitations and performances. Octavia found her soul yearning for the cadences and rhythms of the poems read aloud, as well as the complex meanings hidden in the words, puzzles that her brain loved to tease out. She learned some of them off by heart. And the music appealed to something in her that she couldn't even name, a deep longing for understanding.

Father often told her things he kept from others. She was his secret repository.

"I'm glad to return. I wish to stand for Consul," he told her.

"Consul, Father?"

"That's right, darling. One of the most important men in Rome. Shh…it's a secret," he laughed at her. "Tell no one, not even your dolls."

This was a standing joke between them.

Mother needed her as well. Her little brother, also Gaius Octavius, was nearly four years old and already quite demanding. Octavia smiled to herself. She still knew how to manage him better than his nurse.

Octavia remembered standing in the middle of the enormous house and surveying the scene with some relish. There was so much activity. The servants were rushing about removing the woven hangings from the walls, wrapping up the precious vases, loading beds and bedding onto the mules and wagons, which were carrying all the Governor's household goods down to the small harbour. There everything was transferred to the waiting fleet of ships, that would take them to mainland Italy and thence to Rome. The secretaries scurried around as documents were archived or destroyed according to the Governor's whim. The household was packed up, every lamp, every blanket, every slave and horse had to be found accommodation. They were sailing to the south of Italy first.

It was so exciting, thought Octavia. At last they were returning to Rome. What fun! Then perhaps she would see her cousin Julia, whom she admired so much. Her father was engaged in sorting out all the paperwork for the new Governor who would take his place. Octavia was so proud of her wonderful father. Marcus Cicero himself had declared that he had governed wisely and justly, and would no doubt help him to the coveted role of Consul.

She walked into the large hall where her father dispensed justice, wishing to see if she could be of any help to him. To her surprise he was standing by his desk, rubbing his chest with his hands. He looked pale and uncertain, so unlike the commanding figure she knew. There were no servants around. He must have dismissed them, she realised in alarm.

"Father, what's the matter?"

"Nothing, my dear, nothing. Just a bit of indigestion. Don't worry your mother, now. I will be well directly."

"I'll call your physician, Father."

"No, Octavia. You will do no such thing. I am fine." No way could he admit to any weakness. Not now. Not when he was so near the prize.

He was sweating, she remembered, a sheen of moisture on his face. And he tried to smile at her, which made him look worse. How she longed for help, but he was adamant.

At last he recovered a little, the colour returned to his face. "All the work is done, my dear. I will be able to rest on the ship. Stop looking so anxious."

So she had tried hard not to look worried, although from that day onwards the uneasy feeling never completely left her.

The time came to embark. The gulls screamed and wheeled overhead, hoping for scraps. The harbour smelt of rotting seaweed and rotting fish, an unforgettable stench. Octavia remembered the ship unfurling its sails as it was towed out of the harbour, clawing its way through innumerable other vessels. The sailors had to fend off the boats blocking their passage, and as they did so Octavia could feel the ship protesting a little, gently rocking. The ship would use rowers more than sail, her father explained, as the winds were blowing from the west. The ship would have to tack its way back to Italy.

Octavia held tightly onto the rail, the wind cooling her. She remembered leaning over the side of the ship, staring into the crystal clear waters. Then she saw it. A pod of dolphins was following the ship. They were playful, leaping out of the water with a smile, or standing on their tails. Octavia was entranced. Surely this must be a good omen? She tried to convince herself that all would be well.

They made landfall at Brundisium. Everything was reversed. The harbour had the same smell, the same gulls shrieked overhead. All the household goods were removed from the ships, and loaded again on wagons and pack mules. Octavia travelled in a litter with her nurse, while her mother was in another litter with her small son. After a couple of days they arrived at Nola, close to Naples. But that night at supper her father gave a strange sound, a cry almost.

"What is it, my dear?" asked Atia in alarm, rising to her feet. "You don't look well."

Gaius Octavius sat rubbing his chest, and came up with the same desperately wrong answer.

"A touch of indigestion, I fear. Nothing at all. Nothing to worry about."

But there was no hiding it now. Again his face was moist with sweat. He sat with his arms wrapped round his chest, gripping himself tightly. Gasps of pain broke from him. Then he gave a groan.

"Oh, this is......"

Atia shouted for help, calling on the servants and the Gods to do something, anything. The physician arrived almost immediately. After a brief examination they could see the answer in his face.

"His colour is bad, very bad. The pulse is erratic, almost undetectable. The pain is immense. I fear the worst, dear lady. I'm so sorry. There is nothing I can do to help."

"A prayer. A prayer, or a sacrifice to the Gods. Promise them anything, anything," cried Atia.

Her husband only spoke a few more words.

"Look out for the children," he whispered to Atia.

Octavia saw his face turn a greyish-blue colour. His lips were deep purple. He hardly appeared to be breathing, just a shallow useless tiny movement of his chest. He made a small sighing noise. It was for the last time.

The children were sitting perched on the edge of their father's couch, Octavia in shock, Gaius not understanding.

"Why doesn't Daddy wake up?" he demanded querulously. "Why is he such a funny colour?"

"Hush darling, hush," said his sister. "Daddy isn't well."

But she knew. She knew. Looking at his face where once there had been laughter and tears, she knew that her beloved father had gone somewhere she couldn't follow. And she had let it happen. She had known and done nothing. It was all her fault.

When the shattered group arrived at Rome, still clad in their black clothes of mourning following the funeral rites, they were met by Great Uncle Julius. Octavia never forgot that first sombre meeting.

"My dear niece," said Caesar. "What a shock for us all. But I am glad to see you are not pining away completely. You must take care of yourself. Appearances matter. We must make sure the plebeians know that we carry on regardless of misfortune. It will be my sad duty to find you another husband in due course."

Octavia remembered the look of disbelief on her mother's face at the words.

"My daughter Julia is to marry Gnaeus Pompeius shortly. Despite your grief I wish you all to be present to celebrate the addition to our family of a great statesman."

Octavia was told she would be one of the attendants at the wedding. She took her place at the nuptials with a heavy heart. She didn't think she would ever be happy again. And poor Julia was being married to an old man, she realised in horror when she first caught sight of Pompey. Beautiful Julia, so young and so fresh was going to have to endure……. Here Octavia's mind gave up. Would the same fate fall on her? Marriage to a disgusting fat old man, who'd had four wives already?

BOOK 1: CHAPTER 7

House of Marcus Statilius Taurus, Winter 58/57 BC

Marcellus was intrigued to find that Uncle Dessy had slave boys of his very own. They did not belong to Grandfather, unlike everyone else. Big boys, though. Not the sort to play with. Uncle Dessy shouted at them a lot, and called them rude names, according to Ennius when Marcellus asked him what the words meant. There was a girl, too, who cried.

The Helvetian slave boys liked Marcellus, and helped him to groom his little pony. They were not quite sure of his position in the house, and assumed he was one of the slave children. They came across him only when he went to the stables, as he still had his meals with his little sisters. He was not yet considered old enough to behave properly in the dining room. Also Marcellus had strict instructions from his mother and Uncle Dessy, that he should wear only old clothes that wouldn't matter too much when grooming and riding the pony. Sometimes Rufus was allowed to ride the pony as well. Not for long. Marcellus could be unselfish, but only for a short time, until his love of riding the pony got the better of him and he ordered Rufus to get off. Rufus meekly obeyed.

When Marcellus tried to help the Helvetians to groom the big horses, they were happy to show him how to use a curry comb, how to brush down coats till they gleamed, how to plait the horses' manes and tails, how to polish their hooves until they shone. Marcellus liked listening to the boys' speech. He thought it had a beautiful lilting sound, like a poem or a song. He realised that they were speaking another language, and began little by little to understand what they were talking about. Words like '*horse*' and '*harness*' and '*reins*' stopped being strange and became familiar. He liked the sound of their names, Cierán, and Laeforis.

One morning Ennius overdid the chastisement, making Marcellus extremely sore and unhappy. Marcellus made his way to the stables and curled up in a corner with his pony and sobbed. The Gallic boys spent time trying to comfort him when they should have been working. But then they heard their master shouting that his horse hadn't been bridled or saddled as ordered, before he went out hunting. Uncle Dessy yelled at Cierán, told him he was lazy and called him rude names again, whereupon Cierán shouted one back at him, which sealed his fate, as this made Uncle Dessy very angry indeed. Dessy knew the boys hated being stripped and beaten, so he reserved such punishment for misdemeanours he considered severe. He tied Cierán up and beat him with a stick until he cried, which Marcellus didn't like at all. But when Decimus went to untie Cierán, thinking he had been punished enough, he heard Marcellus's sobs, so he walked round to investigate. He had the stout stick still in his grasp. Laeforis misunderstood. He moved quickly to interpose his body between Marcellus and his master.

"No, no! Not hit! Little boy. Not hit little boy!" Laeforis protested. "Please, please, Master. Already hit bad!"

"Get out of my way," said Decimus angrily. He shoved Laeforis violently aside. Laeforis fell backwards and hit his head with a sickening thwack against the doorpost. He slid slowly down the door, and ended up on the ground. He sat looking dazed, then put a hand to the back of his head, and then looked at it again. His hand was covered in blood. Marcellus howled with shock.

Dessy looked at the two frightened boys, and knew it was mostly his fault.

"Mark, stop crying. Go and fetch the steward. Now. Right away."

Marcellus ran to the steward's cubby hole and pushed open the door. He was surprised to see the steward on a bed with his back towards him. The steward was naked, lying astride what appeared to be another naked person underneath him. Marcellus couldn't tell if this was a boy or a girl. He could see the white buttocks of the steward moving up and down rhythmically. How odd. Marcellus didn't bother to find out what was going on.

"Uncle Dessy wants you in the stables right away," he shouted, and pushed the door shut again.

Dessy went over to his slave, and crouched down, looking at him anxiously.

"Hey, are you alright, boy?" he asked him, a hand on his shoulder. Laeforis was looking bewildered, his eyes unfocused, as if he was drunk. "Can you stand up? I'll get you to that bench over there, alright?"

Laeforis understood the import of the words and nodded. Dessy heaved him to his feet, and half carried, half dragged him over to the bench. Marcellus arrived back, followed a little while later by the steward, hastily adjusting his clothes. Dessy then finished untying Cierán, realising as he did so that he now had one sore slave and one wounded slave. Not good. And his horse still hadn't been bridled or saddled. Clearly he wasn't going hunting this morning after all. He would have to see to Laeforis. He told the steward to organise the care of his horse, then ordered dressings and vinegar.

Laeforis had a deep split at the back of his scalp, gaping wide open. Fortunately the bleeding was slowing to a trickle. Decimus was sure the wound should be sutured, so he sent for a surgeon. To Laeforis's surprise his master carefully and sensitively bathed the wound, and then tried and failed to explain the next procedure. Decimus wasn't sure if Helvetians knew about suturing wounds, even if the Ancient Egyptians did. However once the surgeon arrived Laeforis submitted obediently enough. Cierán looked pale when he saw the gash in his friend's scalp, so he was sent away in case he fainted again.

Decimus performed the stitching under the surgeon's supervision, and proved to be quite adept with the needle. Dessy came to the conclusion that it would be a lot simpler if he could do some stitching himself when back with the legions, so after the surgeon had finished fixing the dressings, he made inquires about surgical needles and sewing materials, and went back with the surgeon to purchase what he thought he might need in the future.

As he walked back to his house Decimus started to think about Laeforis. Twice the boy had attempted to stop him by putting himself in the way. Once when he had thought Dessy was going to sacrifice Cierán, and now when he thought he was going to beat Marcellus. 'Already hit bad,' he had shouted. Quite brave of him, Dessy realised, as he had just witnessed his friend being punished, and must have known his master was angry with the pair of them.

Decimus sent for Marcellus and became aware that the little boy wasn't walking easily. Something was wrong. When he saw the appalling bruises on his nephew's body, Dessy lost his temper again. He picked up Marcellus, and stormed into the salon. He found his father, brother, and sister-in-law present, so he was able to yell at all of them.

"Marcellus says Ennius is allowed to beat him, is that right?"

Marcus trotted out his usual line about 'ignoramus's and beating boys.' One he had used repeatedly when Lucanus and Decimus were children, and had complained bitterly about their treatment.

Dessy wasn't going to let history repeat itself. "It was Cato, not Cicero, you stupid bastard. Look what that swine has done to my nephew. He's only five years old!"

He pulled off Marcellus's tunic. The little boy had swollen and tender multicoloured bruises all over his back and bottom. He started to cry, because he didn't like Uncle Dessy shouting, and he was even more sore now than he was this morning. Dessy picked him up in his arms to comfort him, which was difficult, as however he held him at least one part of his little body was made more painful. Marcellus put his arms round his uncle's neck, and pressed his cheek against his face.

Both Marcellus's parents and even his grandfather were horrified at the state of him. Marcus was so shocked, he was even prepared to overlook being called a 'stupid bastard' by his son. It took some time before Marcellus could be questioned. Haltingly, amidst sobs, he told them about the 's' problem. And he told how Cierán and Laeforis were trying to make him better this morning. The adults discovered that Ennius had fed Marcellus many stories about Spartan boys and their ability to put up with pain. So Marcellus thought he wasn't allowed to complain. Ever.

Dessy had to hand it to his father. He was decisive. Ennius was sent for. He was sentenced to twenty lashes, and was told he would be sold in the morning with the advice that he was never to be allowed near children. "Any children," Dessy added, "slave children as well."

Marcellus found Ennius's sobs and entreaties upsetting, so he was sent away for a soothing bath, and was to be allowed to eat in the dining room as a special treat, perched on the end of Uncle Dessy's couch.

Decimus summoned his slaves to his bedroom. He inspected Cierán's back, feeling a little guilty for having punished the boy. He decided to have his slaves in attendance at the meal, so he could keep an eye on them both. Cierán's back was in a worse state than that of his nephew's.

Halfway through the meal Marcellus slid off the couch and walked over to Cierán, holding an apple in his hand. He handed the apple to Cierán, then put his arms round the boy's neck, said something, and kissed his cheek. Dessy could see that Cierán was tearful yet again.

"What was that for? A thank you?"

"No," Marcellus answered. "It's a birthday present."

"Cierán's birthday? How do you know?"

"'Cos he telled me. He's big now. He's fifteen years old. That's big, isn't it?"

"Told me," Decimus corrected, automatically. "How did he tell you?"

"He tolded me yesterday. He said, '*Tomorrow is my birthday,*' and I said, '*How old shall you be,*' and he said, '*Fifteen,*' so I givved him a present."

"I *gave* him a present."

"Did you, Uncle Dessy? What did you gave him?"

Decimus laughed and abandoned further attempts to correct his nephew's grammar.

Marcellus had a nice time explaining all the foreign words he knew. But he didn't know how to say 'I'm sorry I punished you,' a phrase which Dessy would have found useful.

As the evening wore on Marcellus became silent. Decimus didn't notice at first, as he was talking animatedly to the other guests about the Gauls and the German fighters, and explaining Caesar's military tactics. Eventually he turned round to find his miserable little nephew had tears rolling down his cheeks.

"What's the matter, baby boy?" Dessy asked.

"I'm not a baby," said Marcellus tearfully.

"Well you're crying like one."

"I don't want Ennius to put me to bed."

"Of course he won't. Don't be silly. He's locked up in the cellar."

"I'm not silly," said Marcellus, crying harder. "And Laeforis is crying as well. He's not a baby, is he?"

Dessy looked across at his boys to see it was all too true. His slaves were curled up on the floor. Cierán had a protective arm round Laeforis, who had his head on Cierán's shoulder, and was softly sobbing. His head ached dreadfully, and the noise and music in the dining room was making it so much worse. He thought that even the stables would be preferable.

Dessy sighed. He was having such a good time with the adulation of his father's friends. He would have to do some sorting out. He thought he would start with his nephew.

"Shall I put you to bed, then?"

"No."

"Who, then?"

"I want Cierán to put me to bed."

"Alright. But I need to get Laeforis to bed as well. His head is hurting him, isn't it? Where do the boys sleep?"

"In the stables."

"Don't be absurd. How can they sleep in the stables?"

By now little Marcellus was getting very fed up, so he shouted to start with. Decimus found out a lot of things he hadn't known before. As he had given no orders about his slaves' sleeping arrangements, the steward hadn't bothered to make any either. Dessy discovered that his boys slept on the stable floor, which they hated, as it was hard and cold, and they had to take off their scanty clothes, so as not to get them dirty. That Laeforis wasn't used to horses, and was a little afraid of them. That the boys had to wake before day break, so as to wash themselves all over with the freezing cold water from the pump, so they could greet the sun at dawn in a state of purity, and the sun would 'breathe into their souls'. Marcellus was a little hazy on this point. And that the house-girls and the steward all peeked at the naked boys, but the boys didn't know. And Marcellus thought the boys would be happy to sleep in his room with him because he didn't snore, unlike Uncle Dessy.

"Did the boys say that I snore?" Dessy enquired, frowning.

Marcellus was well aware that the boys were woken frequently outside their master's tent in the camp, by his loud snores. Laeforis had done a hilarious imitation. But Marcellus had no intention of getting them into further trouble. So he explained that Uncle Dessy was in the bedroom furthest away from everyone else, so as not to wake the entire household, his mother had said.

After this torrent of information, Decimus walked over to the boys. Cierán looked up at him fearfully, trying and failing to get Laeforis to stand. Dessy stooped down, and put a reassuring hand on the boy's shoulder. Then he was able to summon and yell at the lazy steward, and order palliasses for his boys to be put in his nephew's bedroom. He wandered over to Portia, his sister-in-law, to explain matters.

"But are your slaves safe?" Portia asked anxiously.

Dessy exploded. "Good heavens, woman, of course they're safe. Do you think I would bring slaves to this house if they weren't safe?"

Lucanus was about to chide his brother for his rudeness to his wife, when they all turned to look at the boys. Cierán picked up Marcellus in his arms, and kissed him. Whereupon Marcellus put his arms around Cierán's neck and howled that nobody loved him. Cierán tried ineffectually to calm him down, but to start with he couldn't be placated.

"Uncle Dessy says I'm a silly baby. I'm not, I'm not, am I, Cierán?" sobbed Marcellus.

Cierán looked helplessly at his master. Disagreeing with Decimus had led to punishment in the all-too-recent past. Dessy took over, telling Marcellus that everyone loved him. He was actually a big brave boy. Dessy was just teasing him about being a silly baby. He suggested that Marcellus was almost grown up, and so should bid goodnight to his parents by kissing his father's hand and his mother's cheek, and then bow to all the guests. Then they would take him off to bed and tuck him in. As this wasn't quite how little Roman boys usually behaved, Lucanus and Portia were surprised but pleased by their son's good manners. The dinner guests were impressed.

Decimus had to support Laeforis to the bedroom, gratified to see his orders had been swiftly carried out. He decided to review his expenditure, to think more about his slaves' welfare. He had been remiss. The boys needed winter clothes, decent boots, and cloaks. He would enlist Portia's help in the morning.

After all, he was soon to be rich. Money worries would disappear with this marriage, so his father said.

When Portia came to kiss her son goodnight, she found Laeforis fast asleep with his head cradled in his arms, almost hidden under the coverlet. Cierán was softly singing a Helvetian lullaby to help Marcellus to sleep as well. Marcellus loved to hear the boys sing.

The next morning found Laeforis still unwell, so he was ordered to stay in bed, while a sore Cierán accompanied his master on various expeditions for his master's wedding preparations. He saw a great deal more of the city he had heard so much about. Decimus organised new clothes for himself as well as his slaves. Marriage was proving to be an expensive business so far.

BOOK 1 : CHAPTER 8

Villa of Egnatius Juvenalis

Grandfather and Marcellus had already visited the house of the lady Uncle Dessy was going to marry. Her name was Veronica, a plump spoilt fifteen-year-old, with little thought in her head but food, clothes, and jewellery. She had two married older sisters, who gave her a lot of inside knowledge about the transformation from virgin to matron, most of it highly coloured and spiced with many hoots and screams of laughter. Marcellus didn't like them much. The three of them looked at him and giggled and tittered and whispered comments about him he didn't understand, making him feel thoroughly uncomfortable. Then they giggled and tittered again. He thought they were quite unpleasant. He wondered if Uncle Dessy would think the same. Grandfather could have chosen better. He should have selected someone like Octavia, Marcellus reflected.

Veronica was poorly educated for a Roman girl, her father Egnatius Juvenalis believing that books were for men only, and then only in minute amounts. He didn't like to think of his girls soiling their minds with poetry or prose. Girls should be kept in blissful ignorance. He thoroughly approved of this marriage to one of equestrian rank, even though the Statilius family were not particularly well off. Veronica's father could have bought their estates ten times over. He considered Decimus to be the ideal mate for Veronica, a real man, an army man, who would be able to handle her, Veronica's father having given up the unequal struggle years ago. Although he was an astute businessman, his relentlessly cheerful wife and brash uncouth daughters ran rings round him. He would do anything to keep the peace in his house.

This time Marcellus was invited to go with Uncle Dessy and his father to meet Veronica again, to discuss the final arrangements for the wedding. He met a little girl at their house, much the same age as himself, but she was nothing like Octavia. When they were introduced she stuck her tongue out at him, which he thought very rude, but everyone else in the Juvenalis family appeared to find amusing. They were both to shout the ritual obscenities at the marriage ceremony, which would be a strictly middle class affair. Veronica and her sisters, with much nudging and giggling, took the children off to teach them the rude words. Marcellus found the whole process baffling. He was told to admire the wedding dress and translucent flame-coloured veil, which Veronica insisted she had spun and woven herself. This announcement caused a great deal of sniggering from her two elder sisters.

Marcellus was intrigued to find how different was the bride's house from his own, with plump cushions, vibrant wall paintings of banquets, and ladies wearing very little in the way of clothing. There were exquisite mosaics on the floors, a garden full of flowers, and beautiful furniture brilliantly inlaid with patterns and pictures of the gods and goddesses. On one table he found Hercules cleaning out the Augean stables with a horse most realistically watching his efforts. Marcellus was fascinated, and would like to have explored the entire house. He was taken outside to the household hearth and told that here he would light the nuptial torch of Ceres to start the marriage procession. Marcellus wondered what Veronica would think when she came to his own more Spartan house. He thought she might find it difficult to get comfortable on their hard wooden-slatted beds, with only a thin horsehair mattress on top. Bony little Marcellus found it pretty uncomfortable himself sometimes.

Unknown to Marcellus, his uncle was just as horrified as he was at the thought of marriage to this girl. He didn't like her short stature, or her plump appearance, or the multiplicity of necklaces, bracelets, and rings that she wore. The way she was stuffing herself with sweetmeats was disgusting. If she kept on at this rate she would soon be spherical, he thought miserably. Worse though was her impoverished conversation. Veronica and her mother and sisters could talk of nothing but inanities, or comment with much giggling on the physical attributes of gladiators they had seen. Dessy called the visit to a halt as soon as he could without causing offence. He walked back to his house in a state of indecision. Should he really allow this marriage to go ahead? He was sure he would never be in love with this insipid, shallow, overdressed girl. The more he thought about it the more he realised he was in a trap devised by his father. He couldn't back out now.

To Dessy's astonishment, Caesar sent a lavish wedding present, a magnificent silver dinner service. Luke knew it was partly a bribe for his favour, but expressed his admiration none the less. It showed that his brother was pretty highly favoured by his commander. Caesar thoroughly approved of his centurion's marriage into a wealthy family of plebeians. Another handle he could pull in the future if necessary.

Dessy was pleased to see Cassius and his wife at the wedding, with their small solemn son Adrianus, who was just two years older than Marcellus. The little boys took to one another at once. Also, his friendly tribune had been invited. The tribune appeared with an astonishing looking flame-haired concubine, one of the recently captured Helvetians, apparently, a high class one at that, who outshone every other woman present. She had such a regal air. She looked with disapproval at everything, and asked Decimus in a clear voice, and in perfect Greek, at what stage would he rape his bride, and did everybody get to watch the procedure? The tribune tried to shut her up and pretend it was a joke. Some of the guests laughed uncertainly. Fortunately the Juvenalis family were unfamiliar with the Greek language, but Veronica was aware of the woman's disdain and was furious.

"How dare he bring that slut to my wedding," she hissed at Decimus.

Decimus was as surprised as Veronica, but he could hardly say so. "He's my senior officer. I cannot afford to offend him," he explained.

The tribune hesitantly asked if Decimus's slave boys could be summoned, so that the concubine could talk to them.

"It might make her feel more at home," he told Decimus apologetically. "She's not very happy. That's why I brought her." Which seemed a really stupid reason to Dessy.

Dessy's slave boys were excited by the presence of the concubine. They tentatively edged forwards, and kissed her feet. After that the concubine lost all interest in the proceedings, and talked with great animation only to the slave boys. When Dessy moved to stop them, the tribune asked if they might be permitted to carry on. "They are from her country," he explained. "Perhaps it will help her to feel more settled here."

Decimus agreed immediately. His boys' faces were lit with a happiness he had never seen before. They appeared overwhelmed, looking at the flame-haired girl as if they could hardly believe she was real, and willing to talk to them alone. Perhaps they would feel more settled as well.

Veronica was happy too, now she thought she was again the centre of attention. Although she began to realise that almost every male in the room was occupied in covertly watching the Helvetian girl. Although many compliments came her way, the male gaze invariably ended up in the wrong direction. Veronica was understandably annoyed. However she realised that her new husband was concentrating his attention solely on her. That pleased her. And her new sister-in-law made much of her.

Decimus was appalled to discover that he did not take to Veronica in any way. It wasn't just her lack of height, or her rounded form, but especially he didn't like her breasts, which were big for a girl of her age, and seemed to occupy most of her thorax. And her speech and manner confirmed his worst fears every time she opened her mouth. She was common. He was marrying a girl for her money. He was beginning to despise himself.

Marcellus and Adrian were quickly bored by the speeches. And as despite his hopes, Octavia and her mother hadn't appeared, even though they were invited, Marcellus led his new friend out to the courtyard, and introduced him to his pony and his slave companions. They had a wonderful evening, with the big boys helping the little boys to career round the stable yard on the pony. Marcellus and Adrian made repeated forays into the wedding feast and commandeered plenty of food for everyone. Marcellus even managed to procure some wine, but the big boys thought it too dangerous, fearing an unpleasant retribution. So he took it back again, nearly getting caught by the steward. Adrian promised to try and come back soon.

When his relatives left, Dessy was confronted not by the shy bride of his romantic imaginings, but by a fifteen-year-old girl who appeared almost brazen in her approach. She was sitting up naked on the matrimonial bed with a look of joyous expectation. She was still wearing masses of jewellery. He found he didn't like it when her little red tongue came out to moisten her lips, reminding him of a snake. The mass of curly black pubic hair below the plump white belly he found repulsive. So he abandoned his thoughts of tender coaxings and caresses, and just got on with the job. The girl appeared to be perfectly satisfied, however, pulling his face down to hers, and kissing him passionately on the lips, which caused further arousal. After his second performance, and he felt a little like a performing animal, she lay back with a sigh of contentment and went fast asleep, leaving Dessy wide awake, pondering an uncertain future. He felt more drawn to her maid, who had kept her eyes modestly downwards during his efforts with Veronica. He left his new wife to go to his own room and his slave girl, though he didn't want any more sex. Ethela was fast asleep on her thin mattress on the floor. He could see her brown lashes resting delicately on her cheeks, as her breasts rose and fell with her quiet breathing. He felt a rush of affection for her. She was the antithesis of his vulgar low-class wife. How he regretted ever agreeing to his father's demands. He must have been mad!

Veronica was furious when she found him absent the next morning, feeling hideously insulted. She knew the news would be all over the household in no time. Her sisters had told her about Dessy's slave girl, but Veronica was conceited enough to think she would be preferred over any other girl, especially a slave. She thought she knew a great deal about men, marriage, and sex, but she knew nothing at all about love and loyalty. She was a girl who was too stupid to realise the extent of her own ignorance. She was apt to copy the habits of her elder sisters, thinking that they had all the answers to the world's problems, most of which circulated around men and how to manage them by giving or withholding sexual favours. She had reckoned without Dessy. He felt no fondness for her. Indeed when he discovered her beating her maid in the morning, with a savageness that sickened him, he wrested the stick from her grasp, snapped it in two, and declared that if he ever saw her hitting a servant again, he would do the same to her. He failed to realise how angry his bride was at his desertion of the marriage bed. Sex with her meant nothing to Dessy.

Veronica's female relations appeared as visitors later in the day, eagerly awaiting the stories of the bridal night. When a weeping Veronica told her mother that her new husband had disappeared overnight, her mother told her to dry her tears and stop worrying.

"He would be exhausted, my love. Don't make yourself anxious. I expect you led him such a dance last night that he needed to get his breath back. They're not all the same. Some can keep it up for hours, but some can't. But from what you say it sounds as if you've managed him fine." But even she was shocked when she discovered Decimus had abandoned her daughter for his slave girl.

As the days went by, even conceited little Veronica realised how much her new husband despised her. Her mother's explanations no longer held true. He hardly bothered to talk to her. His coldness towards her pushed her to ever more desperate measures, which were invariably unsuccessful. Increasingly Dessy took his pleasures at the brothel and the baths, or with his slave girl. He visited Veronica's bedroom rarely now. His wife was merely a duty he had to perform for the sake of the family, but in no time he stopped any pretence that it was enjoyable. He preferred her gentle maid with her fair hair and quiet demeanour.

Despite her sister-in-law's protestations Veronica grew ever more convinced that Decimus would never love her. She thought increasingly about obtaining some poison and doing away with the slave girl. But her mother was aghast at the idea.

"Don't even think it, my darling. It would cause so much trouble. You must just bide your time until Decimus comes back to his senses."

BOOK 1 : CHAPTER 9

Villa of Marcus Statilius Taurus, Rome, Winter 58 /57 BC

The first casualty was Decimus's own slave girl. It became clear that she was pregnant. Her periods stopped, she was slightly sick each morning, and she began to increase in girth. Dessy decided against having her aborted, as he knew that often the outcome was poor, resulting in death or chronic illness, or at least that's what his sister-in-law Portia told him when he mentioned the possibility. He thought that a pregnant girl might be less alluring, but found he still wanted to have sex with her. So he did. With her he had always tried to be as kind and gentle as circumstances allowed. Obviously he'd had to be a bit rough to start with, as she was so uncooperative at the beginning. When he realised that now she was finding it hard, he used the girls at the public baths instead. He still liked cuddling her, so instead of shoving her out of his bed as he was used to do when he had finished with her, he kept her with him throughout the night, even though she disturbed him by getting up frequently to pass urine, or muttering strange German words in her sleep. He supposed his snores disturbed her.

When Veronica heard about this she wept and pulled her hair. When this didn't work she decided to have hysterics, screaming loudly and throwing herself on the floor. This always used to bring her father round to her way of thinking. Dessy merely apologised for his wife's behaviour to his sister-in-law, and took himself off to the army garrison. So Veronica lay in wait for him when he eventually returned to the house, wearing a more revealing dress, or trying to hug him and kiss him. Sometimes Decimus felt he had no option but to perform his matrimonial duties, and could bring himself to get on with it. This made Veronica happy, he could see that. But sometimes he found her so repellant it was difficult to disengage himself without losing his temper. And it was difficult. The more he rejected her the more she tried to cling to him.

One morning he woke to find Ethela sitting up in bed staring silently at him. As he reached out to stroke her bare shoulder, she reacted as if she had been stung, pulling away abruptly. He found this tiny incident oddly upsetting. He didn't know anything about her, and hadn't ever bothered to find out. The Helvetian boys spoke to her in German, so he supposed he could ask them how old she was, for instance. But now he didn't want to know. He didn't want to find out that she was little more than a child, and that she hated him.

Two months after her wedding Veronica started to be violently sick, not just in the morning but all through the day, and sometimes at night as well. She lost all interest in sex, which was a relief for Dessy. Weight fell off her rapidly. Her mother was delighted.

"You're pregnant," she explained to her tearful daughter.

Decimus informed Veronica that he would take her maid Dora as his concubine, as his own was no longer able to function properly. Veronica was far too ill to protest. So the last two months of his leave were spent quite pleasantly. The shy maid couldn't refuse him, being a slave. And he found her much to his liking. But he still preferred Ethela. So he began to teach her some Latin words, simple ones to start with, and praised her when she got them right. He bought her little presents almost every day, ribbons for her hair, a pretty coral and silver necklace, soft leather slippers for her feet, which were small and shapely for a girl of her height. It appeared to be working. Ethela sometimes smiled. And once she kissed him, almost spontaneously, when he gave her a crystal jewel box. Occasionally he remembered to bring a gift to his wife as well, which made Veronica more hopeful. Finally he plucked up courage and enlisted the help of his slave boys and his nephew, but he didn't probe too deeply. Ethela was fourteen years old, he discovered, which was a great relief to him. So at least she wasn't quite a child.

The nearer it came to the time when he would journey north, gathering up the two newly recruited legions on the way, the more Decimus thought about his role in the army. He didn't think he would have too many problems being in charge of a centuria. Already the men at the army garrison respected him and obeyed him promptly, realising that he demanded instant obedience. And that they would be punished if he didn't get it. He hoped that his success at getting prisoners to talk would soon be forgotten by his seniors. But before he left for the north he was summoned for a heart-to-heart talk with Lucanus, his elder brother whom he loved and revered, a man so unlike himself.

There was a problem worrying Lucanus. He explained that Dessy must treat Veronica better. The household slaves were already picking up on his despising of her. She was pregnant, she was sick, and she needed his help.

"She's only a little girl, Dessy, when all is said and done. Be kind to her."

"Alright. But I'm not going to pretend I love her. I hate pretence."

"It is your duty to love her. You are ten years older. You are a man. She will be the mother of your children. Have some respect."

His brother's words about Veronica weren't in vain. Dessy started to make a real effort, and no sooner had he done so than he found Veronica was actually terrified of the thought of pregnancy and childbirth, having been fed alarming stories by her sisters. So he started petting her, taking her onto his knee as if she were a little girl again, telling her how lovely she looked, and that she mustn't worry about anything. Although he might be unable to get leave when the baby was due, he was convinced his sister-in-law and Veronica's own mother would make sure everything was fine.

Gradually he came to realise that he was fond of the girl, but only as a man might be fond of his dog. It was so much easier to treat her as a pet, now she was no longer a recipient of his physical self. Fortunately Veronica was too inexperienced to understand that she wasn't after all the great love of his life. She began to feel much happier, especially as she knew that Dessy's slave girl was no longer able to perform satisfactorily either.

Before her new husband left for the North, Veronica suggested that she should move back to her father's more luxurious house, a measure Decimus approved of. He would have quite liked her to stay there permanently, but that was too much to hope for. When he thought about the forthcoming baby he could only envisage a boy. Decimus couldn't bring himself to think of a daughter, fearing it would turn out just like Veronica. Meanwhile his slave girl was heavily pregnant, and now Dora, Veronica's maid, appeared to be pregnant as well. Marcus was delighted at this evidence of his son's virility, assuring Dessy that any of his offspring, as well as his legitimate heir, would be reared in his house, without any difficulty, even if the slave babies turned out to be girls. Marcus had a wonderful time boasting at the public baths of his son's prowess to his friends, who were suitably impressed.

Veronica's maid would move back with her mistress, although Veronica had threatened to sell her. Here her father intervened for once. She could not sell a slave while the woman was pregnant with the master's child. Her father was a little shocked at his daughter, and remonstrated, causing Veronica to produce floods of tears. For once in his life her father remained firm.

At the first stirrings of spring Decimus rode out with his father-in-law to inspect his bride's estates. Egnatius was so proud of Decimus, assuring him that he would be only too delighted to manage the estates on his behalf, if Dessy, could he call him Dessy? would allow. But perhaps he would prefer his brother, could he call him Luke? his brother's management? Dessy disclaimed all knowledge of farming, and assured Egnatius of his gratitude. The amount of money his father-in-law suggested he should receive annually from the profits took his breath away. And made him think furiously. Egnatius hoped Dessy wasn't offended by Veronica's removal to her father's house. Dessy reassured him fervently on this point.

Once they were home Decimus put his ideas into practise. He could no longer fool himself. He should never have agreed to this marriage. It was a disaster. He decided that the only way forward was to avoid any monetary reward to himself for such an egregious error. He went to the temple of Victoria, the Goddess whose favour he frequently sought. He vowed that all monies coming from the marriage should be put aside and used solely for Veronica and any children of the marriage. He would manage his household by himself, with nothing, not a denarius, from the

Juvenalis family to help him. He swore this to the Goddess, and promised her a decent sacrifice using his own funds, just as soon as he had any. Afterwards he felt a great deal better.

When he tentatively explained his decision to Egnatius, he discovered his father-in-law to be an enthusiast for this scheme.

"I'll keep it for you, certainly. You have a good businessman's head on your shoulders, Dessy, my boy. May I call you Dessy? Oh yes, you said. Money should work for you," Egnatius continued. "I'll see to it that your profits will be safely lent out at a good rate of interest."

This wasn't quite what Decimus had intended, but after all, it would all be for his family, not for himself. So he thanked Egnatius for his understanding and his help.

BOOK 1: CHAPTER 10

Villa of Marcus Statilius Taurus

Despite Uncle Julius's clear instructions that she should befriend Portia, and report everything that Lucanus said and did back to him, Atia waited a little while before she visited the Statilius family. She wanted to see the handsome young centurion again, but she was worried. Had she shown by even a flicker, that she found herself attracted to him? Had she avoided the scrutiny of Uncle Julius, who used everything and everyone to his own advantage? He had wasted no time in marrying her off after the death of her first husband.

She'd been married to Gaius Octavius at fifteen, when he was a good-looking thirty-year-old widower, with a daughter, Octavia. Her Octavia was born a year later. She was twenty-two when Gaius Octavius Junior was born, such a joy for them all. Then her darling husband died when she was only twenty-six. For the last three years she had been the wife of a man nearly old enough to be her grandfather, let alone her father, Lucius Marcius Philippus, another widower, with one son and one daughter. Even now Uncle Julius was endeavouring to get him elected Consul. At least Philippus had great affection for her children, though unlikely to have any more of his own. Lucky Portia to have a young husband like Lucanus.

Octavia had told her mother all about the fun she'd had with Marcellus. Atia was determined that no son of hers would be friends with a boy who played with dolls. She had a good idea of how little Marcellus would turn out in the future; not a child to be emulated. So although she was happy for Octavia to accompany her on a social visit, she left Gaius Octavius Junior behind.

Marcellus and Adrian were perfectly happy to welcome Octavia, or 'Tavia, into their circle of friends. Marcellus introduced her as his wife.

"We have four boy babies," he added proudly.

"All at once?" Adrian asked. He looked at Octavia with respect. "Jupiter, that must have been hard."

Octavia laughed aloud, the beautiful gurgling laugh that Marcellus loved so much. "It was easy. We bought them from the baby shop."

Adrian found this unconvincing. At seven years of age he knew a lot more than Marcellus, but not enough to challenge this self-possessed girl. Octavia soon discovered that after all Marcellus was much like other boys. She was happy to referee their mock sword fights, when the boys pretended to be gladiators. She was good at bandaging their imaginary wounds. Marcellus contrived to get wounded often, as he loved being fussed over by his 'wife.' He told Octavia that his uncle stitched wounds up with a needle and twine stuff. Laeforis was produced to prove this statement, as neither Adrian nor Octavia believed him.

The boys encouraged her to ride the pony, which she did with some trepidation, and without telling her mother, who she knew would forbid such pastimes as not for girls. Many things were not for girls, Octavia had discovered as she grew up. Girls don't run, they don't argue with their stepfathers, they don't drive chariots or fight wars, although Octavia had heard that some had been known to fight in the arena, to the shock of their male relatives. They didn't even have their own names, but had to share with all the other girls in the family. So as there was already an Octavia, Octavia Major, she was only Octavia Minor, which made her feel small and insignificant. Life for her was becoming ever more circumscribed.

Marcellus assured her that when they were properly married she could do whatever she wished. Octavia secretly longed for such an outcome, knowing it to be impossible. Juicy young girls from important families seemed destined to be married to powerful elderly statesmen. She was sure such a fate awaited her.

Meanwhile her mother was at pains to discover the times when Decimus was at home, rather than at the army barracks or out with his father-in-law. She thought she was being subtle, but Portia had a fair idea of what was in the wind, especially as both parties were in the habit of blushing furiously when they did eventually meet up.

Lucanus was an astute young man. "Lady Atia wants to know what I'm up to, but she also wants to see my good-looking young brother," he teased Dessy, who flushed crimson and protested that, for the Gods' sake, he had only just married Veronica.

"Cut it out, Luke. I thought you were worried about the servants. You're giving them something to talk about."

"Keep your hair on. No one's listening. I learnt to be cautious as soon as I started canvassing for Quaestor. Look, if you're really not interested I'll make sure you don't meet her, because the pair of you give yourselves away every time."

Dessy said nothing.

"I see. You want to go on seeing her."

"Why not? She talks intelligently, and has much knowledge of politics, so she should be a help to you. I don't get much intelligent conversation from my wife, do I?"

Lucanus laughed aloud. "Oh, so it's all for my benefit that she comes?"

"I think she has taken to Portia, for which I don't blame her. You are so lucky, Luke, to have married such a lovely girl."

"She told me last night that she thinks she is expecting another child. Let us hope that this time the child will survive."

The last two boy babies had come into the world, only to leave it again before the first week of life was over. Portia had been very depressed after each tragedy. Luke thought this should be the last try for another child. After all they had Marcellus and two little girls. Quite enough. Would an affair help or hinder Dessy? Lucanus could see how taken his brother was with the elegant, cultured Atia. He was aware also that Veronica was never going to be the love of his brother's life. On balance he decided it would do Decimus no great harm, and after all nothing would happen before Decimus returned to Gaul, there simply wasn't time. Such an affair would have to be kept well hidden from the world, Luke thought. No one outside the family must ever know.

BOOK 1 : CHAPTER 11

Rome, 57 BC

It was good that Ennius had been sold, Marcellus thought to himself, but he still regretted the punishment that had been inflicted on his former tutor beforehand. Anyone's distress found a resonance within him. When Rufus was thrashed by his father, Marcellus stood nearby and cried with him, until the groom noticed. Then thankfully he stopped.

But the new preceptor that Grandfather had bought for him came with disadvantages as well. Ambrosius was a small fussy man, who had heard about the previous tutor's fate, and had no intention of suffering anything similar. So Marcellus was spared any further physical punishment. Furthermore Ambrosius agreed with his pupil about the way the 's' letter faced. So that was two problems solved. But Ambrosius was of limited intellect and had little imagination. Marcellus found him deadly dull. He knew no stories, a little history, and a lot of Homer. He placed great emphasis on strange things, like tidy hair and clean hands and tunics, items which were of no importance to a lively boy, who loved riding his pony. Marcellus was a bright child, but was having trouble trying to learn to write Latin and Greek simultaneously.

His father Lucanus liked the look of Adrianus, the son of Cassius, and invited him to come and play with Marcellus whenever he liked. Which meant nearly every day after Marcellus had finished his lessons. Thankfully.

Marcellus was hoping to see Uncle Dessy soon, so he could tell him his problems, but he had to wait all summer. Uncle

Dessy was back in Gaul with Caesar and had taken Laeforis and Cierán with him. Marcellus was upset when the two straw mattresses in his room disappeared. He had felt so safe when the big boys were sleeping with him.

Every now and then Marcellus went with his mother and little sisters to visit Aunt Veronica, and take a present of flowers or fruit, or cakes from their own kitchens. Grandfather especially liked cake, and so did Marcellus. He enjoyed these expeditions, as invariably Aunt Veronica declined the cakes, so Marcellus and his sisters ate them for her. Aunt Veronica was getting very fat, Marcellus thought, although how she managed it was beyond him, as she ate nothing that he could see. In fact he usually crept out of the salon quite quickly, and went to find Veronica's father, if he was at home. An exciting man, who often had some new thing to be admired, a beautiful expensive vase, or a lovely mirror, or better still, a brand new chariot equipped with perfectly matched horses. A charioteer came as well, so that Veronica's father could be driven at a sedate pace through the countryside on his way to his vast fruitful estates. He promised that one day Marcellus could accompany him. But secretly Egnatius preferred his luxuriously-padded litter.

Marcellus was able to explore the house to his heart's content. When at home Egnatius came with him often on these expeditions, as he loved Marcellus's enthusiastic praise for everything he saw.

"Only the best quality," his host would explain. "It come all the way from Egypt, Marcellus. What do you think of that, eh?"

And Marcellus would stand amazed at the elaborately carved desk, or casket, or side table. Veronica's father tried to press presents on him, but Portia would always insist that they be returned. She wasn't sure that her husband wished to be indebted to the Juvenalis family. He hadn't the same regard for their money as his father. Unfortunately the mosaic floor which should have been installed was only half completed as Veronica couldn't cope with the noise. Marcellus admired the plan for it, an elaborate geometric pattern of sea nymphs and dolphins, with Europa and the bull most realistically portrayed in the centre. Veronica’s father and Marcellus became good friends. When Veronica or his wife had been more than usually trying, Egnatius would put his hands on his hips, shake his head in bewilderment, and say to Marcellus, "Women, eh? Who can understand what they're on about? Not you or I. Eh, Marcellus?"

And Marcellus would shake his head in turn, and agree.

Veronica might have increased in girth, but her face was pinched and ill-looking. She still had to cope each day, either with overt sickness or constant nausea. She began to dread waking up in the mornings. Her back ached and the baby kicked her constantly, even when she was trying to snatch some sleep. Her mother was at a loss. Neither of her elder daughters had suffered in this way. The best physicians in Rome had no answers either. Although every preparation was tried, and failed to make any difference. For Veronica the final straw came when she was ensconced in the family’s latrine, trying to evacuate her severely constipated bowels. She was seized with a violent pain around her anus. She screamed for her mother to come and look, to come and help her. A dark plum-coloured mass was protruding from her rectum. According to their physician, Veronica had developed something called ‘prolapsing haemorrhoids,’ for which he had no cure.

She liked visitors, because for a short spell they took her mind off the problems with her body. She lay on her couch on a cushion without its centre, and attempted to listen to Portia's news. Portia didn't gossip, though, which would have been much more to Veronica's taste. At the end of her pregnancy she was dragging herself around, hardly able to walk, she was so uncomfortable. Her head ached alarmingly.

Her maid-servant had no problems. Which was fortunate, as Veronica wasn't prepared to make any allowances for her pregnant state, and constantly reiterated that she would be sold as soon as the baby was born. But Dora's baby would belong to Decimus, her husband, and he alone would decide its fate. Veronica hoped it would be exposed, to die in a pot at the door of her father's villa.

Atia's visits to Portia didn't stop with Decimus's return to campaigning. She discovered she liked Portia. They were both aware of the politics of these visits, but that didn't impinge on their friendship. Adrian was brought by his mother Agatha each day to join the circle, which Portia liked very much, as they became good friends as well. After the boys had finished their lessons with Ambrosius, the women would take the children to the baths in the afternoon, as Cassius wanted his son to learn how to swim, and one of the public baths nearby had a large pool. Portia had a circle of interesting friends, who met up most days for a massage, baths, and an exchange of information, often political, which Portia duly relayed back to Lucanus. Sometimes there was entertainment as well in the paelestra, dancers, or acrobats, or a short play. Very occasionally Veronica and her mother would join them. Veronica's luxurious residence had its own set of baths, and Veronica's mother assured Portia that she would be welcome at any time. But Portia found the Juvenalis family as wearing as Decimus, and took up the invitation only occasionally.

Veronica floated on her back in the pool like a beached whale. Marcellus was intrigued to see that sometimes her stomach moved around like a wave as well. Portia decided it was a good time to explain some basic facts to her son, without going into too many details. Difficult, as Marcellus was consumed with curiosity, and asked innumerable questions afterwards, which Portia dealt with by telling him to apply to his father or Ambrosius.

BOOK 1 : CHAPTER 12

Gaul, 57 BC

The newly-recruited legionaries were having difficulty getting to grips with their young centurion. He was good-looking, with a tall, tanned, muscular frame, the scars of recent battles apparent for all to see when he stripped in the bath-house. One or two of the more impressionable youngsters had already begun to hero-worship him, striving to earn a friendly word of encouragement or a pat on the back, and blushing furiously when they had achieved their goal. But they soon discovered it took a great deal of effort to win his praise.

It was rumoured that he had been promoted in the field for showing exceptional bravery. A shield with one hundred and thirteen holes in it, apparently his, was displayed in front of the centurions' mess. He seemed always to be smiling and cheerful. And when a couple of his men developed a raging fever, he showed an almost womanly concern for their welfare, isolating them in a tent close to his own, and having them nursed by the camp servants.

But the more circumspect noticed his two slaves. They behaved impeccably, concentrating all their attention on their master, and responding instantly to the slightest look or gesture, as if failure to do so might result in severe penalty. And when one soldier, feeling like dodging sword-training, feigned illness, the centurion paraded his men, had the malingerer tied up to a whipping post and given twenty lashes, leaving his back raw and bleeding. "So," said their centurion, still smiling affably, "if you pretend illness, and fail to convince the camp doctors, you will be made to feel really ill for some time to come."

Decimus, in turn, was assessing the qualities of these all-too-raw recruits. They would need to be trained quickly, as he knew his commander was intending to engage shortly with the men of the Belgic Coalition in the north of Gaul, who were reputed to be fierce fighters. Dessy's men, being novices, would be placed in the front line, with the more experienced legionaries in the second line, while the third and last line was always composed of hardened veterans. That was the invariable battle order. It had worked miracles in the past, and wasn't about to be changed.

Decimus looked over the new recruits as they paraded. He would need to lick them into shape. They were the usual assortment, some stupid, some bright, some anxious and some already overconfident. First he assessed their fighting abilities. It was instantly apparent that some were skilled swordsmen, but some were not. Some could throw a javelin and hit a target, some could not. The hopeless ones he reassured swiftly, explaining that courage was far more important than skill, and in no time they would find themselves more proficient. Drill was relentless, twice a day for hours at a time, until they could perform the correct manoeuvres without conscious thought. He paired them up and taught them how to use the small scorpio catapult, and had bigger groups handling the huge ballista, the large-framed catapult capable of demolishing a town wall. Eventually Decimus divided them into squads of eight, and selected those he thought more capable of leadership to be in charge. He promoted the seemingly overconfident ones especially, telling them they were now a temporary decanus, but he would see how well they went on before making them permanent. As usual the eight men would share a tent, a mule, and a millstone for grinding their ration of corn, together with two non-combatants.

The legions marched north through Central Gaul, along roads paved with wooden planks, or tamped down gravel, not the solid surfaces of the Roman Republic. They came to the land of the Remi. The Remi tribal chiefs took one look at the disciplined Roman forces, now over sixty thousand strong, and decided to become allies. They handed over their terrified children as hostages, and swore to be loyal to Caesar, to fight for him, and keep him informed of the movements of the hostile Belgic tribes. They also agreed to provide corn and other necessities for a campaign.

Caesar sent for Decimus, and asked him about the state of readiness of his troops. Dessy had to admit that they were nowhere near competent enough to fight. He thought it would take another month of intensive work. So the two recently recruited legions were left behind in the base camp, while the rest of the army marched off to engage the vast enemy numbers of the Belgic Coalition. Caesar assumed that if Dessy’s men weren't ready, a group under a newly-appointed centurion desperate to show his worth, none of the others would be ready either.

Decimus was worried, thinking he had failed in some way. He applied for help to his friend Cassius. Cassius was reassuring.

"You're doing everything right, Dessy. It takes time. And you've had no time at all with them. Stop worrying. No one else is as far on as you. You're the best," he ended, and they both laughed, making Dessy feel so much better. What a good friend Cassius was to him.

They agreed that it was about time the new men found themselves acting on their own initiative. It would be good training for them. As they were in supposedly friendly territory,

Decimus's centuria was sent off in his chosen groups of eight legionaries, each group with a wagon, with instructions to forage in the surrounding countryside for food and fuel. They were to take the non-coms as well, to help with the cutting and loading, and were to return before sundown. They were given explicit instructions that they were not to engage with the natives in any way. If confronted, they were to back off and return to camp. The Remi were to be considered 'Friends and Brothers of the Roman People,' said Decimus. He couldn't foresee any problems. But that was the trouble with problems. It was always the unforeseen ones.

Late in the afternoon all but one of contuberniums had returned, loaded with wood. Food was almost unobtainable though, apart from some late apples, some winter cabbage, and a few carrots. The Remi had wisely decided to hide their supplies of corn and fodder from their 'friends and brothers,' knowing that they would otherwise starve.

Decimus decided to look for the missing men before the light failed. The sky looked ominous, full of dark clouds, heavy with rain. He summoned the men from his former tent, his contubernales. They had formed themselves into his unofficial bodyguard. Cassius was happy to assist, realising how anxious Dessy was. It wouldn't do to lose a whole squad of soldiers. The two centurions questioned the new recruits as to where they had last seen their misplaced comrades. An improvised map, drawn in the earth by one of the men, gave them a good idea of the direction. Dessy would remember him. He praised the men for their first efforts at self sufficiency, then dismissed them, ordering them to get fires going, collect their rations, and cook their supper.

Cassius and Decimus together with the bodyguard marched through the fertile countryside, encountering hostile glances from the half-starved peasants engaged in preparing the ground for the spring sowings. After travelling for five miles they found the woods where most of the returnees had split and chopped up fallen timber, and coppiced the willows. Dessy held up his hand. He thought he had heard something. They proceeded cautiously. There was always the chance that some farmer had objected to his fields being raided.

The first obvious sign of disaster was hanging from a tree. It was a dog, crucified, still just alive, with its tongue protruding grotesquely from its jaws. It was conscious of their presence, now emitting small whines of distress. Dessy thought he had never seen a more pitiful plea for mercy than the expression in the dog's eyes. He killed it with one clean stroke of his sword. He could hear the sighs of relief from his companions, or of breath hissing out through pursed lips.

Much worse was to come. The two centurions dismounted and walked towards the all-too-human sounds of terror. They found a scene of carnage. There were four pathetic victims, emaciated greyish-white corpses. A dead mutilated male, stripped of clothes, was lying half in and half out of a stream. Next to him was an equally dead naked female. The parents, Dessy supposed. Because here were the children. A young girl lying at an impossible angle, with her neck broken and her body defiled. Blood in crimson gobbets soaked all over her shift. Lying by her side was a dead toddler, no longer possible to say with any certainty whether a boy or a girl. And on the ground crouched a terrified little boy, still alive, and with no visible marks on his delicate skin. He was rocking rhythmically backwards and forwards, and the noises they had heard came from him, a high-pitched regular dreadful wailing.

Dessy swiftly assessed his legionaries. Seven of them were grouped together, but one was by himself on the earth by the wagon. Dessy walked over to this one first, one of his young hero-worshippers. The boy had his hands clasped together, and tears rolling down bruised cheeks. He had been beaten around the head and face. The non-coms were huddled cowering in the empty wagon. Decimus ordered them out. He turned towards the remaining soldiers, looking into their furtive faces under the helmets. A wave of anger at their stupidity surged inside him, but he remained calm. He made a sweeping gesture with his arm, encompassing the pathetic corpses, and spoke with a voice filled with quiet menace.

"These people are our allies, called ‘Friends and Brothers of the Roman People’ by our Commander. I believe I told you that no natives were to be harmed in any way."

"But Sir," protested the temporary decanus, "it were a joke, weren’t it? Thems is barbarians."

"No," said Dessy. "No joke." He pointed to the battered legionary. "Is he a joke as well?"

The men started to blame each other. But Dessy swiftly shut them up. He was white with inner fury, and the men were well aware of it. Decimus walked over to the wailing child and lifted him to his feet. The boy could hardly stand, he was so petrified. His bowels became liquid, faeces squirting down his thighs. Dessy ordered the beaten legionary to take the child over to the stream and wash him clean. He ordered the rest to make a pile of the wood they had managed to cut. The non-coms were told to light a pitch torch from the clay fire-pot they carried, and to thrust it through the woodpile to set the pyre ablaze.

"Now," said Decimus. "Dress them."

"Dress them? These.......?"

"These allies," cut in Decimus sharply.

The men found it difficult clothing dead uncooperative bodies, but they dared not refuse.

"Place them on the pyre."

They obeyed. Decimus stood at the foot of the burning logs. The wood was green, so there was a lot of smoke until the flames caught at the bodies. When the conflagration was well under way Decimus came to attention, raised his arm in salute, and intoned the prayer for the dead. Cassius and the battered legionary, staggering to his feet, came to join him. The non-coms felt brave enough to creep forwards and bow their heads. Decimus swivelled round at their approach. He gave a brief nod of approval.

Cassius collected the mens' cloaks and made a bed on the floor of the wagon. When the shivering boy was dried Dessy wrapped him up in the cloaks, laid him in the wagon, and told the injured legionary to get in beside him.

"Why have you been beaten up?" Decimus asked the man.

"I was trying to stop them, Sir. It was no good, just me and the non-coms against the rest. A couple of the others were dithering. That's why the bastard laid into me. They're all scared of him."

"Who? Your Decanus?"

"No, Sir. It was Vibius."

Silently and sullenly the men marched back to camp. To cap everything the sky became even darker before they had gone half a mile. A sudden sheet of lightning split the heavens, followed by a long rolling clap of thunder. The cloud burst over their heads. Drenching rain soon soaked everything. The horses splashed through the mire, their sides and underbellies becoming coated with mud, each individual hair ending in a small sticky spherical ball. Dessy draped his cloak over the man and boy in the wagon, but its shelter was soon ineffective. The men marched on, their minds whirling round, hardly noticing the downpour. Their centurions had said nothing as yet about punishment. They had an inkling that it was going to be bad.

When they arrived back at camp Decimus told the men that since they had failed to bring back any wood or food, they would have no rations for seven days, only barley bread. Then he dismissed them, after telling them to be ready for an early punishment parade at daybreak. He went to lift the child out of the wagon. He informed the battered legionary that he intended to make him the decanus in charge.

"As you seem to be the only one with any sense. Do you think you could manage it? If not, I'll split them up."

"I'll give it a go, Sir."

"Good. Remember I'll back you up. But don't take risks. After tomorrow they should be easy to handle. Let me know straightaway if you have any more problems with them."

"Yes, Sir. Thank you, Sir."

"I hope it compensates you for the flogging you will get tomorrow."

"Yes, Sir. It will."

Again good. The man knew better than to object, already aware that the contubernium would be punished as a unit, no exceptions.

"What are you going to do with the boy?" Cassius asked.

"I don't know. I wanted to salvage something from the wreckage, I suppose."

Dessy took the child back to his tent. He tried to explain what had happened to his boys, but he wasn't sure they understood. Cierán attempted to say something, but Dessy gave up trying to understand and brushed him away. He still had so much to do. The little boy said nothing at all. At least he had stopped wailing. Cassius's servants were enjoined to try and feed him.

Decimus asked to speak to his legate. He related the day's happenings, but the legate didn't seem to grasp the problem.

"They were from the Remi, do you say?"

"That's correct, Sir."

"I wouldn't bother too much about it, Dessy. They were only barbarians, and peasants, too, from what you say."

But Decimus was unhappy. "May I just check with one of the senior Remi, Sir? And I wish to punish the men severely."

"Certainly, certainly. They disobeyed a direct order. No problem at all, Dessy. Do whatever you like with them."

Dessy made his way to the part of the camp where the remainder of the Gallic auxiliary troops were stationed, cavalry for the most part. There were a few Aeduans from the South, but the majority were the local Remi. He asked to speak to a magistrate, if possible one that could speak Latin. He was ushered into a tent, invited to sit down, given a glass of excellent wine, and ordered to unburden himself. The magistrate listened patiently.

"What punishment do you have in mind?"

"I am going to have a punishment parade at dawn. All eight legionaries will be flogged, with a double punishment for the decanus. Will that be adequate?"

"I would like to be present."

"Sir, I would be most grateful. I thought I had sufficiently impressed upon them that we are allies. Either the words are meaningless to them, or they are too stupid to understand."

The magistrate laughed. "We are the barbarians, Centurion. They cannot get their heads round the fact that we behave just like them. They wish to feel superior."

At daybreak Decimus impressed on Cierán that his horse needed a thorough grooming, after riding through the storm last night. Again Cierán attempted to speak to him, but Dessy had no time for him.

The Remi magistrate brought a phalanx of stony-faced men with him. Decimus was feeling nervous, unsure as to what the Gauls would do. But they merely watched the proceedings. After the parade, which took some time, the magistrate invited Decimus to dine with him that evening. A relieved Dessy was pleased to accept. He went over to the stables to find Cierán leaning against the wooden stall, and doing very little. The horse was still in a dreadful state. Dessy got cross and shouted at the boy, who looked at him with bafflement. Later on he found the horse was still looking pretty bedraggled, so he yelled at Cierán again. It crossed his mind that the boy was behaving badly deliberately. However Dessy put the problem of Cierán to the back of his mind. He spent a convivial evening with several senior Remi, all of whom treated him with courtesy and friendliness. And the wine was superb.

The next morning Decimus was feeling irritable. His head thumped. The excellent wine, no doubt. He'd had far too much to drink. He took the recruits for yet another drill. They appeared to be a remarkably stupid bunch this morning, and kept getting everything wrong. He shouted himself hoarse, but there were still gross errors. He would have to keep them at it, but he found it so frustrating. Sword training came afterwards. At least here they were showing signs of improvement. Then javelin practise and the use of the ballistae. His headache just got worse the longer the day went on. Nevertheless he gathered them all together at the end of training, and sent for the ones he had punished the day before. These came walking stiffly and warily. Their backs were a mass of bruises, and all movement painful. The unfortunate decanus could hardly stand. Was something else going to happen to them? Decimus could see the fear in their faces, and smiled to himself.

"Gather round." Dessy waited while they shuffled closer, still keeping a respectful distance from him. "Listen to me. We're the best," he told them. "Now you say it."

"We're the best," they chorused, and most of them grinned with relief. After watching their fellow soldiers flogged yesterday they had tried hard to get everything right today, frightened of the consequences if they didn't meet their centurion's exacting standards. Probably the reason why they were worse than usual, some of them reflected. Trying too hard.

"Just you remember that. All of you. You as well." Dessy nodded to the little group of punished soldiers. "Right. Dismiss."

One of the men took his courage in his hands and tentatively asked if he could share his food with one of the miscreants. This pleased Decimus. At last they were beginning to think and act as a team.

"I hope you will always look after your comrades. One day you may have need of help yourself."

BOOK 1 : CHAPTER 13

North East Gaul

Dessy went over to the stables at the end of the day to see the state of the horses. He wanted to make sure Cierán had finally done a better job today, and he wasn't going to let the boy away with anything. To his horror he found Cierán sitting on the ground, leaning lazily back against the rail, and the horses' coats hardly touched. A spark of anger kindled in Dessy's brain. He shouted again at Cierán, but made no impression, so he lost his temper completely, tied the boy up and gave him ten lashes with the horse whip without the boy making a sound.

"And tonight you will serve me my supper," Decimus said when he cut the boy down. Cierán had tears running down his cheeks, but Dessy paid no attention. He took him by the shoulders and shook him hard, shouting, "Do you hear me? You will serve me tonight. And you will do so properly and correctly. Do you understand?"

"Yes, Master," said Cierán dully. It was their usual response to him whenever he shouted at them. Although Dessy knew in his heart that they often had no idea of what they were agreeing to.

Decimus ordered Cierán to finish grooming the horse, and stalked off to his tent. He discovered that the little boy still hadn't said a word. The servants had managed to spoon-feed him, though, which was progress of a sort. The child just sat staring into space. Every so often he would start rocking backwards and forwards, but made no sound, for which Dessy was thankful. He didn't feel like coping with the hideous wailing noise.

Cassius came to share supper with him, but found his friend silent for once. Cierán turned up eventually, and bowed in his master's direction. He took the plate of stew offered to him by Cassius's servant, and was about to serve it to his master when he gave a sudden gasping cry. He dropped the plate on the floor and ran out of the tent. Some hot food splashed onto Dessy's legs.

Decimus rose in fury, and followed him out. He was aghast to find Cierán kneeling on the ground a few yards from the tent entrance, his hands clutched to his stomach. Cierán started to retch. A stream of vomit hit the ground, but the boy continued to make horrible retching noises. Laeforis ran out of the tent to join them, anxious to prevent his friend from suffering any more punishment. He knelt down besides Cierán, placing a protective arm over his back, to deflect any further blows from their master.

"*What is it?*" he asked.

"*I can't hold it in, I've shat myself. Oh God*!"

Laeforis glanced down. A reddish brown stain was appearing at the back of Cierán's scanty underclothes. There was a strange unpleasant smell, but not the usual smell of shit.

Cierán gave another cry, and curled up, gripping his abdomen tightly. "*Oh God, Oh God*," he whispered. "*What am I going to do*?" He opened his eyes again to see his master's booted feet standing before him. Then he was sick again.

Dessy knelt by his side. "What is it?" he asked gently. "What's the matter, Cierán?"

Cassius thought it was pretty obvious. "The poor kid's ill, isn't he? Shall I send for a doctor, Dessy?"

Dessy thought quickly. How much would that cost? Oh well, he would just have to put up with it. The doctor couldn't understand anything Cierán said, so they needed an interpreter as well. When the interpreter eventually arrived, Dessy discovered his slave had been ill for two days, with an aching gut, nausea, and loose bowels. He exploded.

"Why didn't the silly chump tell me?"

Apparently the boy had tried to tell his master yesterday, but he didn’t have the right words and Decimus had brushed him off impatiently. Now Dessy remembered. It was just too difficult to communicate with him, Laeforis explained tearfully, and this evening in the stables Cierán had felt too ill and weak to make his case.

"Oh, hell! I should never have punished the poor kid. Tell him that, will you?" Dessy knelt down and grasped Cierán’s hand, which clutched his own convulsively as he was gripped with the dreadful spasms again. "I'm sorry, I'm sorry, my little one. I didn't realise you were so sick."

Cierán promptly vomited again, just to prove the point.

"He's not exactly little," murmured Cassius. It was true. The boys had shot up in the last few months. Cierán was now taller than his master. Cassius’s servants and a few of the legionaries helped to get the boy cleaned up and settled onto his straw mattress, with a bucket beside him. Laeforis was detailed to stay with him and attend only to him. Dessy would use Cassius’s servants.

By next evening it was obvious that Laeforis had become infected as well, and Cierán was getting worse. The discharge from his anus appeared to be more blood than anything else. He looked dreadful, with his skin taut over his face and a greyish complexion, despite the expensive medicine Dessy had purchased. It had no obvious effect. The boy was weaker, hardly able to sit up, let alone drink. And anything he did drink came back almost immediately. His eyes were sunken, his mouth dry, and his lips cracked. His breath was sour and sweet at the same time. Laeforis appeared to be heading the same way. Dessy was resigned. He wasn't sure that either boy would survive; the doctor put their chances at only fifty-fifty. Quite a few others were affected in the camp and there were already several deaths. Fortunately Cassius's servants so far remained free of it.

"I'll need to buy some slaves to look after my boys," Dessy explained to Cassius. "They are too weak to help themselves in any way, and the little boy needs spoon-feeding at present. I can't make use of your servants all the time. I'll get a couple of those new Belgian prisoners. They'll be cheap. If my boys get better, I'll sell the new ones on."

Cassius objected that it was no trouble, but Dessy was adamant. He was worried that his boys might infect Cassius's servants as well. They had been with Cassius for years, and he prized them highly.

There was by now a huge number of captured prisoners being auctioned off, fifty-three thousand from one town alone. Dessy inspected the ranks of men and boys. One of the captives was making a great fuss, unwilling to be parted from his companion, a friend or a brother perhaps. Dessy became interested. The boy was pulled away and punched repeatedly to make him keep still enough to be sold. Dessy got him for a knock-down price, as he looked to be so uncooperative. He was dragged over to stand by his new master, clad in only a pair of trousers, with no shoes or boots on his feet, and an expression of devastation on his bruised face. Dessy started bidding for the companion, and succeeded in no time. The dealer had so many to sell. He wanted to get rid of this mass of prisoners as soon as possible, and take his profit. The newly enslaved had an unpleasant habit of contracting fevers and dying.

The companion was brought over in turn. Dessy summoned the interpreter. The two slaves stared at each other.

"Now," said Decimus, via the interpreter, "You wish to stay together?"

They agreed, surprised.

"Then you," Dessy pointed to the one who had violently struggled, "you will kneel down and kiss my feet."

The prisoner recoiled at once, before this was even translated, and refused.

"Very well. Take them back to the dealer," Dessy ordered.

He turned away from them, and appeared to give his attention once more to the prisoners being sold.

He could hear an argument going on behind him, but ignored it.

"*Do it*!" said the elder prisoner.

"*How can I*?"

"*Just do it. We need to be together*."

The elder one managed to catch hold of Dessy's sleeve. "*Please, Sir,*" he said in Gallic. "*He will do as you ask*."

Dessy turned back to the two of them. The younger one looked at him in despair, then dropped to his knees. He leant forward and kissed Dessy's booted feet.

Decimus bent down, took hold of the boy's elbows, and pulled him upright again. The boy was crying now, hot tears of humiliation. Dessy fumbled in the pouch at his waist, and produced a handkerchief. He made to wipe the boy's tears away, but the boy reared back in alarm.

"No. Keep still," Dessy ordered.

The boy stood silently, with his head bowed.

"Gauls are brave," said Dessy. "Gauls don't cry. Isn't that right?"

The boy lifted his head as this was translated, but the tears continued to flow.

"Good," said Dessy. "What are you? Friends? Brothers?"

"*Brothers, Sir,*" the older one replied.

"And how old are you?"

Fifteen and seventeen, apparently. He had overestimated their ages. He found that the older one was named Óengus, the younger one was called Darreth.

"Now you will go with my men. You will be branded. That hurts. So you will be brave. And you won't cry."

"*No, Óengus, no*!"

The younger one was so upset. The elder one had his lips clamped tight together. He made an effort to speak.

"*We have no choice, have we*?" He sounded weary, defeated.

Dessy shrugged his shoulders. "If you wish you can try your luck with another master."

"*There's no point, is there? You are all the same. All cruel, all savages*."

"You are wrong. Like you, we are all different. But you will have to find that out for yourselves."

Decimus started to untie the thin rope binding the hands of the younger one.

"Don't ever cut rope," he said. "You just end up with pieces that are no use. Even rope costs money."

The boy started to massage his wrists, while Dessy untied his brother.

"Now listen to me. Afterwards you will be bathed. It doesn't hurt." Dessy looked at the pair of them. How was he going to get any semblance of cooperation? "It is hard for you, I know. Today is bad for you. It will get better, that I can promise you, as long as you are good children. So be good," he said. "Be good," he repeated. "You say it now. Be good."

The two boys dutifully repeated the mantra.

"*We are not to be tied up again, or chained, Sir? I mean after we've been bathed*?" asked the elder one. He had a comforting arm now around his brother's shoulders.

"I hope not. Chained men are a nuisance. Someone has to bring them food and water, or a shit-bucket. That wouldn't be much use to me. But it's up to you, isn't it? You must obey me. Again, that may be hard to start with."

Dessy called some of his legionaries over. "I want these two branded. The irons are in my tent. Then they are to be washed, fed, and clothes bought for them, boots as well. They are not to be ill treated in any way. Is that clear? Then bring them over to my tent."

Dessy handed over what he hoped would be enough money. There were little black dots dancing in front of his eyes. He brushed them away with his hands. Cassius walked over to join him, and inspect the new purchases.

"Fucking flies," said Dessy crossly. "They're there all the time. Drives me mad."

Cassius couldn't see any flies.

"Look, I'll need a few days to knock some sense into these new ones. Is that okay?"

"Sure, take as long as you like. I'll cover for you."

"Thanks."

Dessy went over to settle with the harassed dealer, and then came back to the centuria to finish teaching the day's manoeuvre, forming a circle. They weren't very good at it yet, but at least they were improving. His headache returned with a vengeance, so he went back to his tent for some water, and to see what had happened to his other boys. He took off his helmet, which made his headache lessen a little in intensity. The throbbing pain eased to a certain extent. He managed to hang up his sword, leant his shield against the tent pole, and unbuckled his breastplate.

Cierán was lying face down, looking practically moribund, he was upset to see. He managed to raise him up, but the boy was moaning in distress as soon as he touched him. Cierán's back was still a mass of bruises from the whipping. Dessy tried to persuade him to take a few sips of water.

"No, no," Cierán protested, crying weakly. "It hurt too much. Not drink. Hurt too much. Please, Master."

"I know, I know. But you must drink, the doctor says. Come on, Cierán, drink a little to please me."

He managed to coax the boy to swallow some water, and more of the medicine, then lowered him carefully back onto the palliasse. He knelt by the bedding, and stroked the boy's cheek. "Don't let him die, not till I've had a chance to put things right between us," he prayed to whichever God was listening. The little boy sat rocking himself in a corner of the tent. He still hadn't said a word.

Decimus sighed. Everything was going wrong. He sat on his bed, feeling depressed. The legionaries brought over his new acquisitions. They stood silently, with their long wet hair and bewildered expressions. Dessy looked up at them. He felt so tired. What an effort it was going to be to communicate.

The flies were back again. He leant forward to brush them away. As he did so, he was seized with a sudden violent spasm of pain in his abdomen. A powerful wave of nausea flowed up from under his rib cage. He started to retch. Saliva gushed into his mouth. He was going to be sick any instant, he knew. Quickly, one of the boys stepped forward.

"*Get a basin*," the boy snapped to his companion. He couldn't see anything to use, so passed Dessy his helmet, which Dessy rapidly filled with vomit. Luckily the other boy tipped the water out of the washing bowl, and brought it over. Now Decimus knew how his Helvetians were feeling. The pain in his stomach was fierce and unrelenting. Vomiting hadn't helped. Every so often the pain increased, causing him to retch and vomit again. It was exhausting.

After a while the new slave lifted the water jug to his lips. "Drink!" the boy commanded. Dessy looked up at him in surprise. "Be good," said the boy. "Drink." Dessy drank.

Cassius appeared to find out how Decimus was, as one of the legionaries had told him his fellow centurion looked awful, and was complaining of a bad headache. Cassius took charge with his usual efficiency. Dessy felt a profound relief at not having to think any more. Thinking was too much effort.

The illness swiftly became overwhelming. Decimus was delirious, tossing and turning in his bed, and talking nonsense. He slid into a strange period, where time became meaningless. Day and night merged into a feverish blur of sweat and heat, while his bowels twisted and writhed in perpetual agony.

His dreams or memories, he wasn't sure which, were all of "be good," and someone coaxing him repeatedly to drink. But he didn't want to drink. Some part of his brain knew that drinking caused the pain to intensify. But the voice was insistent.

Twelve days later Dessy came round again to full consciousness. He lay on his back, gazing at the tent roof, wondering why it seemed so difficult to move. He felt blessedly cool. The pain had vanished, thanks be to the Gods. After a while he managed to lift himself up, his gaze falling on two youngsters, who he thought were strangers at first. He couldn't work out why they were sitting on the ground in his tent. Then realisation dawned. He remembered their purchase. He looked round for the little boy, and felt a rush of relief when he saw him curled up on a blanket in the shadows.

Dessy tried to get up, but fell backwards onto the bed, he was so weak. One of the youngsters came over to help him. "Be good," said the boy sternly, and helped him to his feet. Dessy shook off the restraining arm and staggered to the back of the tent with panic in his breast. Cierán was lying under the raised tent flap, on a heap of straw covered by a sheet. Which was unstained, Dessy noticed, thankful that the Gods had answered his prayer. He must make some sacrifice in expiation. Cierán tried to rise, but Dessy shook his head.

"No, no. Lie down, lie down, Cierán. Where's Laeforis?" he queried.

Cierán pointed behind him. Just then Laeforis appeared at the tent entrance with Cassius. Decimus felt relief surge through him. The youngster came over to him again, and this time Dessy allowed himself to be helped into bed.

"Welcome back," said Cassius. "Will you please stop terrifying us? You've been making no sense for days."

"Days? Why, what day is it?"

Cassius told him.

"It's weird. I don't remember much of what was going on. Just that I felt so hot all the time, and the pain never let up."

"You owe your new kids a lot. They took over pretty comprehensively," Cassius said, smiling. "I'm afraid you've lost a couple of your men. But your contubernales were so concerned at your illness, they've been promising the Gods everything and more to ensure your safe recovery. And they helped a lot with looking after you. Your non-coms sorted out the bedding, which was quite a job to start with. And they helped to nurse your boys."

Decimus arranged for Cierán to lie next to him, as he wanted to monitor his progress. He noticed the look of dread in the boy's eyes at this unexpected development. He told the boy that he liked to hear him sing, which came as a surprise to Cierán. Dessy knew he had been too hard on his slaves, and now they were far too scared of him. He had been too preoccupied with training his centuria. Well, now he would have time to make amends. He must be more patient with them. Make sure they understood his orders properly. And he would need to pay more attention to them, when they were trying to tell him something.

He attempted to explain that they must learn to communicate better. Cassius thought it would be a good way to counteract the boredom of convalescence.

"Óengus can speak a little bit of Latin," he said. "And his brother has a lot more words than your Helvetians."

What a relief. Óengus could help with the language for all of them, and Dessy wouldn't have to keep forking out for an interpreter. Though he wouldn't be able to sell them on, as he had planned. Dessy knew it would have been too unjust, after they had acted like loyal servants, according to Cassius, as if they had been raised in his own household. How astonishing that they had taken his injunction to be good so much to heart. But now he was responsible for feeding and clothing four slaves, when he felt he earned barely enough money to support two. He would have to think of some way of getting extra money, as he was determined to stick to his vow.

The commander occasionally rewarded exceptional displays of courage with hard cash. The first soldier to climb the wall of a besieged city, or the first to land from a ship onto hostile shores would be awarded a 'mural crown' made of gold, but also a substantial amount of money. A risky business for the soldier concerned, though. Anyway, at present he was hardly strong enough to stand on two feet, let alone fight anyone. He would need to get fit again, and so would Cierán and Laeforis.

When they had all recovered some bodily strength, Decimus decided to teach his slaves a little sword play, as one day he might need them to fight for him. It would help with their recovery and help him as well. Cassius was happily undertaking the drilling of Dessy's centuria, as supervising a full day's training was still far too much for him. Decimus started with short sessions at first. He didn't want to exhaust himself or his slaves. He soon discovered that he could teach the boys nothing. On the contrary, they could teach him. Despite his weakness Cierán managed to win these practise bouts every time, and Dessy only succeeded in beating Laeforis a couple of times. To suggest, as Centurion Pullo did two years ago, that the boys were too young to fight, was clearly nonsense. Like Roman boys, they had been reared to use swords and javelins from an early age, and the two of them also had considerable natural ability. Cierán could throw a javelin further than anyone else, even though he had been so ill, and looked extraordinarily graceful while he was doing it. His technique was perfect.

The boys were hesitant at first, not sure how far to go, wondering all the time if they would be punished for winning. During one of these sessions Cierán managed to catch his master with a deadly thrust to his chest wall. Dessy fell back with a sharp yelp of pain. Cierán stood aghast. Dessy got to his feet, looked at his frightened slave, and laughed.

"You're so good. I'm simply going to have to get quicker." He tousled Cierán's short blond hair. "Did you fight? At Bibracte?"

The boy nodded, still looking terrified. Did this mean he would now be executed like his father? Dessy hastened to reassure him, becoming aware of his fear. He put an affectionate arm round the boy's shoulders, and hugged him, saying, "Well done, Cierán. You are so good, so agile. You had better start teaching me. I can't teach you anything."

The next day Decimus found he had a bruise on his chest wall the size of a dinner plate, when he stripped in the bath house. The other centurions crowded round him, seeking an explanation. Proudly Dessy pointed to Cierán. "I was well and truly beaten," he explained with a smile, "by a fifteen-year-old kid."

Decimus's appetite gradually returned. When Óengus offered him the bread one evening, the still dumb little boy snatched it out of his hand, and gave the loaf back to Óengus.

"What the hell?" said Dessy, half amused and half annoyed.

"You not do it right," said Óengus. "No thank the Gods for bread. Must thank. Ganainm not happy."

"Ganainm?"

"Small boy. Ganainm."

"Is that his name?" Dessy asked in surprise. He had never heard the child speak.

"Ganainm. No name. Mean 'no name,'" Óengus tried to explain, then he held his hands out over the loaf on the side table, and spoke the words of the blessing, albeit in Gallic, something Decimus rarely bothered to do. He felt guilty. And he still hadn't sacrificed. He'd better sort something out soon. He held up the piece of bread Óengus had just served him.

"Bread," he said. "Now you say it." He pointed at each boy in turn. Then, "Now say it in Gallic."

"Bread," they chorused, but the words they used were different. The northern language, Dessy realised, was not the same as that of the Helvetians and Aeduans.

"Bread," Dessy repeated. "You don't say it the same, do you? We can't keep talking so many different languages. I wish you all to learn to speak my language properly. We will set aside some time every day for this. And I will remember to bless the bread in future." And maybe try and learn some of the southern Gallic language himself, as the Belgian boys could understand the Helvetians. It might help him with the Gallic prisoners in the future. He was pleased to see his Helvetian slaves were beginning to grow in confidence, no longer expecting to be constantly shouted at or chastised.

He would need to take Óengus in hand, though, and make sure the boy knew that he was the master and Óengus was the slave. At present he wasn't sure Óengus understood. In this he was wrong. After the branding there was never any doubt in his slave's mind as to which was which. And the oppressive atmosphere of this enemy army, with its drills and parades and weapons far superior to anything the Belgians possessed, made Óengus and his brother Darreth feel thoroughly miserable.

Decimus sensed something of this when he summoned Óengus to kneel before him, prepared to give a lecture on the duties of slaves. Óengus came to him and knelt promptly and obediently, looking at him in fear. His confident manner had vanished. Óengus could cope with a sick centurion who lay on his bed, too weak to stand, and talking rubbish, but this centurion was different altogether, looking stern and grave. Óengus knew all about his master from the Helvetian boys. A man quick to use physical punishment if his inexplicable orders were not instantly obeyed. The Helvetians found him impossible to understand.

Decimus was aware of the boy's fear. He was about to launch into his speech when Óengus put a hand on his knee and asked why he and his brother had to be branded. Dessy saw the tears in the boy's eyes. He explained patiently.

"Hey, don't get upset. I'm sorry, Óengus, I'm sorry. It is an army requirement. All slaves must be readily identifiable. Either you are branded or you have to be fitted with an iron collar with my name and rank. You've seen them?"

The boy nodded. But he still looked miserable.

"There's no time for arguments over property in the army. I thought you would prefer to be branded. The collars are never removed. A constant reminder." Although perhaps sometimes that's a good thing. And branding was a much cheaper method of identifying slaves, but he wouldn't tell Óengus that. "I thought that if you were branded you would be able to put it to the back of your mind in a few weeks. Here," Decimus held out his hand. Óengus grasped it in his own. "I won't think any the less of you, I assure you."

"But you sell us, Master."

Decimus frowned. "Who told you that?"

"Centurion Cassius say when slaves better, we to be sold."

"Do you want to be sold?"

Óengus shook his head vigorously. "No, Master." There was always the possibility that the next master might be a lot worse than this one. And would no doubt repeat the branding, the thought of which terrified Óengus and Darreth.

Dessy smiled. "That's good. Because I want you to stay with me. You have been a great help to me, nursing me and my boys. I thank you for this. I swear I will never sell either of you, any of you if it comes to that. You are my responsibility."

"Sometime we not say good things. Not have the word? Not be bad. Not……." Óengus ran out of words.

"Yes. I know. I understand. I will be more careful, I promise."

It came to Dessy that the boy was reaching desperately for reassurance.

"Not good," said Óengus. "Brand not good."

"But I've just explained," Dessy started, when he realised what the boy was saying. "Here, Óengus, get up. Get up, boy."

He lifted the boy to his feet, turned him round, and pulled down his trousers, exposing his buttocks. The brand was a suppurating mess.

"Oh my God," whispered Decimus. "We must do something about this. Put it right."

"Have to do brand again?"

At this moment Dessy realised how frightened the boy was at the possibility. "No, no, of course not." Although he wasn't sure if his initials would still be clearly etched on the boy's skin. Well it was just too bad. "What about Darreth?"

"Darreth no good," said Óengus.

Decimus summoned Darreth in turn. His burn didn't look to be quite so badly infected. Decimus discovered that his slaves had been anointing themselves with some foul-smelling lotion that Cassius's servants had provided. Dessy marched the pair of them and the lotion over to the hospital tent, and managed to find his orderly. Musa pursed his lips when he smelt the lotion, and when he saw the state of Óengus.

"Poor lads," he said. "I'm afraid the treatment will be painful."

Only a few days later one of the senior tribunes appeared at Dessy's tent. He came with his dog at his heels, a beautiful golden hound. The dog wandered into the tent, looked round, saw Ganainm on the ground, sniffed him thoroughly, and then gave him a perfunctory lick. The boy slipped his hands round the dog's neck, and buried his face in its fur. Dessy was smiling at the spectacle, but the tribune's words wiped the smile from his face.

"Seeing as you are convalescing, Dessy, the legate has a job for you."

"Yes, Sir. What is it?"

It was bound to be something awful, he thought, if it took a tribune to order it.

"We've captured some prisoners. Some of the Bellovaci. So get to work on them. We need to know the enemy's geographical location, their communication routes, and the size of their forces. It would help if you could also find out where they are getting their supplies."

"Yes, Sir. Then what?"

"What do you mean?"

"What do you want me to do with them afterwards?"

The tribune found that highly amusing.

"Do whatever you like with them, Dessy. They're all yours."

The tribune was about to leave the tent, still chuckling. The dog shifted uneasily, gave Ganainm another lick, and let out a yelp. The tribune looked with amusement at the little boy and the dog.

"Do you want a dog, Dessy?"

"Maybe I'll have to get one, Sir. The boy doesn't talk. In fact he seems to have hardly any awareness of the world around him."

Seeing that the tribune was interested, Dessy gave him a brief summary of the little boy's history. Óengus listened intently. This shed new light on his master. The tribune offered to let Ganainm play with the dog, if it would help, and ordered the dog to stay with him, for the time being.

Decimus went out to inspect the prisoners. No wonder the tribune had found it funny. The four of them were in a dreadful state, one even worse than the other three, with a deep sword slash on his thigh, still bleeding a little. The arrows and darts fired at them as they were ambushed, were still sticking out of their bodies. They were chained with hands and feet brought tightly together, their faces grimaces of pain. Decimus touched one of the arrows, causing his victim to cry out sharply. The man broke into a sweat, beads of perspiration gathering on his forehead and upper lip.

Decimus decided to enlist the help of his contubernales and the hospital orderly, Musa, who was fortunately available for hire at the moment. When Decimus explained what he wanted, the orderly was worried.

"Sir, I have taken an oath to Asclepius. 'First, do no harm.'"

"I know. I know. It will be me doing the harm. But I think they are so badly wounded that I may only need to help them. The Gauls are not used to our sort of medicine. They will think they are being tortured. At least I hope that's what they'll think."

The worst affected prisoner was unchained and laid out on a bench, but strapped tightly to prevent any movement. Decimus made one of his men press on the wound to stop the blood flow.

The orderly attended to that wound first, the prisoner emitting moans of distress all the while.

"What now, Sir?" asked the orderly, when he'd finished.

"Look, if I so much as touch these arrows, it's agony for him. So what do I do?" Decimus demanded.

"The best way to deal with arrows is to break off the fletching, and push the arrow through to the other side," Musa explained.

Gingerly Decimus grasped the arrow and broke off the protruding end. The prisoner screamed.

"Jupiter! Are you sure this is right?" Decimus asked as he attempted to push the arrowhead through the skin of the man's arm, despite his weak cries of protest. "It's so tough."

"Believe me, it's the best way."

Decimus grasped the arrow shaft and forced it through. He dealt with another arrow in the same fashion, this time the man saying nothing.

"Oh, good. This is easier," said Decimus.

"Yes, Sir. Probably because he's dead," said the orderly.

"Oh!"

Decimus gazed in dismay at the corpse of the man. He hadn't managed to ask him a single question, he had been so concentrating on performing this novel surgical procedure. The pale bloodless face looked heavenwards, free of all expression, the grimaces of pain smoothed out. Decimus stepped back a pace and saluted his dead enemy. The contubernales heaved the body off the table, where it fell face downwards to the ground. The three remaining captives looked on in horror. The youngest one started to cry.

Decimus was going to order his men to dispose of the corpse when the orderly stopped him in his tracks.

"He'll be useful to practise on," Musa remarked.

Decimus was a little shocked. "What do you mean?"

"It will give you a feel for the force required to dislocate joints," the orderly explained. "If you are still interested. And then I can show you how to restore them. You won't want to practise on your own dead compatriots?"

"No, certainly not." Decimus was surprised at the orderly's apparent callousness. "But we had better do something about these others. So far I've no information to give to my superiors."

Fortunately the next victim proved more amenable to questioning. He had one arrow sticking out of his groin, so the orderly handled this one, having to cut it out, with Decimus all the while asking the prisoner about the information he needed. Then Dessy dealt with a couple more arrows, and cleaned and sutured the resulting wounds. As Dessy had hoped, the man thought he was suffering some refined torture after hearing the screams and cries of his comrade, all too aware of his painful death. Military details poured out of him, subsequently confirmed by interrogating the other wounded prisoners under similar circumstances. At the end of the day Decimus thought he had sufficient intelligence to alert his superiors, and also had managed to salvage the remaining three prisoners. He explained to the orderly that he needed to keep them alive, and he needed them to recover sufficiently, so he could sell them, as he had no money. He was determined to stick to his vow.

Between them, the orderly and Decimus organised the nursing of the prisoners by the camp servants, until they were well enough to be sold. Decimus made Óengus and Darreth spend some time teaching the prisoners enough Latin to impress the slave dealer. Afterwards Decimus and his centuria were reunited with their legion, and took part in the rest of the summer's campaign against the Bellovaci, acting as a rearguard protecting the baggage wagons. Dessy didn't receive any reward for exceptional bravery, but the income generated by the sale of the prisoners was quite enough for them all to live on comfortably for the time being. He was able to provide his new servants with warm winter cloaks, before the final military campaign of the season, and before cold weather set in.

It was some time before Dessy realised that although he was training his slaves, in a way they were also training him. He now made sure to bless the food every night. When his boys knelt to kiss his hand before their dismissal, he had learnt to say, 'Goodnight,' or 'May the Gods watch over you and keep you safe,' in both of their languages. He started to use their superb javelin technique and swordsmanship to train his own men. And he made a proper sacrifice to the Goddess Victoria, to thank her for her intervention, keeping him and his slaves alive to fight another day.

When Cierán tentatively asked why he'd had his hair cut short, Decimus tried to explain to him that it was because he had been so hot and feverish.

"The doctor said you must be cooled down, so your beautiful hair had to be cut. I've kept it for you. It's in the chest over there. I thought it might be important. You may grow it again, if you so wish."

Cierán looked at him in amazement, eyes shining with tears. "Yes, Master. Important for us. Thank you," he said, as he leant forward and kissed his master's hand.

Cierán grudgingly agreed to have his uneven hair neatly trimmed by the camp barber. He told his master that he did not wish to look like a Roman, which made Dessy laugh. "I don't know any Romans with your hair colour, Cierán."

Decimus gradually became aware that although Cierán was the youngest, he was also the most influential of his four slaves. The others all looked to him for guidance, and addressed him as '*Sir.*' It was Cierán who arranged the tasks to be done by each boy. He settled arguments, particularly those arising between Laeforis and Darreth, who did not always see eye to eye. He had the last word, usually quoting some words of wisdom from his deceased father. Sometimes Dessy became exasperated when one of the other slaves appeared to check with Cierán before carrying out an order. Cierán noticed, apologised, and scolded the culprit.

BOOK 1 : CHAPTER 14

North East Gaul, Autumn, 57 BC

The senior tribune and his dog came with letters for Dessy from his father and brother, and the unwelcome information that there was another captured spy to be interrogated. Decimus was troubled as he unsealed his father's letter. News from home was a rare occurrence.

Dessy smiled to himself as he read the first few lines. So he had sired a son and heir, a strong healthy child, according to his father Marcus. Egnatius had brought the child over to be accepted formally into the Statilius family. Fortunately Decimus's slave girl Ethela was able to act as a wet nurse, having been delivered of a boy a month previously. Why a wet nurse? Dessy frowned. Had he missed something? No. Here it was. His father had sad news to convey. Though Veronica appeared to have made a good recovery after the birth, she had died suddenly, only five days later. The doctors couldn't say why, but thought that her swollen right leg may have allowed some evil humour to form and stagnate.

At first Decimus experienced a feeling of profound relief that Veronica had died but not the baby, almost immediately followed by a wave of guilt flooding over him. His wife! A girl of fifteen, as his brother had so often pointed out. And her death pleased him? He felt sickened by his own thoughts. He opened his brother's letter quickly, knowing there would be a lot more information. As he read he found he didn't want to know the terrible details, that Veronica had suffered badly as the pregnancy went on, and of how much she was looking forward to the birth, so her troubles would be over. Then on the fifth day after delivery she had started coughing up blood. Dessy could imagine how terrified she would be. And here he was, the cause of her misery and death, a thousand miles away in North Gaul. He had been no help to her at all.

Lucanus amplified the information about Ethela. She'd had few problems carrying her own child, who was also a healthy boy, Dessy would be pleased to know, and she had copious supplies of milk. Veronica's devastated parents were happy for their new grandson to be reared in the Statilius family house. Veronica's mother asked that Veronica's maid be accommodated as well, as she couldn't bear to see the girl, especially as she was also having a trouble-free pregnancy, and carrying yet another of Dessy's offspring.

For a time Decimus sat staring at the tent wall with unfocused gaze, trying to take in the news. He would have to purchase some mourning clothes for himself and for his slaves. He would need to write letters, to his sister-in-law, thanking her for her help, to his father-in-law, lamenting the loss of his youngest child. And to his own father, for looking after his wife, child, and slaves. He couldn't think at present of any other obligations, though at the back of his mind he knew there were other things he should be doing.

The boys knew something was badly wrong. Laeforis attempted to serve his master breakfast, but Dessy pushed the plate away impatiently. He wasn't hungry in the slightest. But he had a job to do. He supposed he'd better get on with it.

Óengus intervened, pointing to the letter. "Bad news, Master?"

"My wife has died." Saying it made it real.

Cierán was shocked. "Lady Veronica? She dead, Master?"

"She dead," Decimus said wearily.

"And little baby?"

"Apparently the baby is fine. So is Ethela and her baby boy."

"Oh." Cierán poured out a beaker of wine, and handed it to his master. "My sister die too, but baby die as well. My sister very young, like Lady Veronica. Little girl only. Why they die, Master, the girls?"

"Why indeed, Cierán? I don't know. I just don't know. I suppose having babies is a dangerous thing to do." Dessy took a sip of the wine, and then put the beaker down on the side table. "No. I need a clear head. I have to torture another poor bugger this morning."

Unfortunately the captured spy wasn't wounded in any way, a nice-looking bearded young man, trying his best to appear brave. Someone had already stripped him of his clothes. Decimus walked slowly over to the hospital tent, seeking out his orderly again. His disjointed thoughts were whirling round in his head. This was different. He had to face it. If he questioned this man he would cause him much pain and suffering. There was no disguising it. This was cold-blooded torture. But visions of Veronica kept intruding. What she must have suffered. The pain of labour, and then the terror of impending doom as she coughed out her life blood.

'I can't do it, I can't do it, I can't do it,' his brain reiterated. 'Why me? In the Gods' name, why me? Especially today. Why do I have to be the vicious bastard that breaks the man's spirit by breaking his body?'

Some men would enjoy it, he knew. Vibius, for instance. But Vibius was a fool, a cruel fool admittedly. He would fail to obtain any information. Did the end ever justify the means? He didn't think so. What if he refused to interrogate the prisoner? No, that wouldn't work, he thought in despair. He would be charged with disobeying an order, and would be reduced to the ranks and punished as well, or executed, possibly. He wasn't sure if even his friendly tribune would be supportive. But he knew what had happened to spies in the past. The men just chopped bits off their victims, or shoved their limbs in the fire, the result often being that the poor creatures died of blood loss or shock before any information became available. That was the problem. 'I'm the best,' Dessy thought wryly to himself. It brought him no comfort.

He found that Musa would be available for hire later on. Good. He would have liked to stop and watch an amputation, thinking it might take his mind off Veronica for a bit, but there was no time. Presumably the surgeon Ruteus had no qualms about inflicting horrendous pain on his patient. Though he appeared to be half drunk. The patient looked much the same as the prisoner, brave on the outside and terrified underneath. He had been given a lot of wine himself, judging by the empty wine-skin lying on the floor.

Decimus sought out his friendly tribune. But it was just as he feared. There was no sympathy for him. And he wasn't prepared to tell the tribune about his wife's death. It just wasn't the done thing, making excuses.

"No, you cannot pick and choose which orders to obey," said the tribune. "You have taken the oath of loyalty to your Commander, and to your legion. You're a centurion, Dessy. You are a wonderful example to your men. And you are proving to be quite exceptional at obtaining information from the prisoners. So just get on with it."

The tribune's servant was intrigued. Afterwards he made haste to inform the rest of the camp that Centurion Decimus Taurus, the supposed Master Torturer, wasn't that keen on torturing anyone, and looked as miserable as sin at the prospect.

Decimus found he was beginning to think like a slave dealer himself. If he could get this prisoner to talk without too much damage, he would be able to sell him for a tidy sum. And then he felt ashamed of his own thoughts. Another uncomfortable feeling. He put the idea to the back of his mind, and resolved to concentrate on extracting information. That was what he was supposed to be doing, after all. And he thought he knew how. He was surprised to discover that the man could speak Latin, quite well too. Strange for a man so far from Rome. Decimus sent for an interpreter, though, just to be on the safe side.

"Would you like to use the latrine?" Decimus started. The man assented eagerly. Which confirmed to Decimus that he was in all probability terrified underneath his tough exterior. Dessy called on his contubernales to escort the prisoner. When he was brought back, Decimus pushed his naked victim down onto a bench. The young man couldn't help but shiver in fear.

"You're cold," said Decimus. He untied his own cloak and draped it round the prisoner's shoulders. "There. That's better."

He poured out a large beaker of wine for the prisoner, one for himself, and one for the interpreter, to his surprise. Decimus sat down on the bench next to the young man, put his arm round the man's shoulders, and gave him the beaker into his bound hands.

"Cheers," said Decimus, feeling anything but cheerful.

"Cheers," agreed the young man in astonishment. He drank the wine eagerly, desperate to block out the future.

"What is your name?" asked Dessy.

"My name is Mathghamhain."

"Mathghamhain?"

"That's correct." The prisoner smiled a little. "It means 'Son of the Bear' in your language."

Decimus talked to the prisoner for a considerable time, with great courtesy, waiting for the wine to take effect. He asked about the man's parents, his wife, and had he any little ones? Yes, the prisoner had two small children. He was from the Nervii, one of the reputedly fiercest tribes in Gaul. The wine loosened the man's tongue.

"I have a son," said Decimus. "But my wife died having him. I only got the news today."

The prisoner found himself saying he was sorry to hear it.

"She was fifteen years old," Decimus went on.

"Too young to die," suggested the prisoner.

"Yes. Far too young." Dessy gulped down the rest of his wine, and then was silent.

"Why are you telling me this?" asked the prisoner eventually.

"I don't have anyone else I can tell. Anyone who would understand. The legionaries aren't supposed to marry." Decimus fell quiet again. "I feel it was my fault," he whispered. "I didn't love her enough."

The prisoner frowned. "How could it be your fault? You couldn't predict what would happen. We must put our trust in the Gods, and hope they have a reason to take our loved ones from us."

"You're right, of course."

"We have lost a child," the prisoner continued. "A beautiful child, a little girl with blonde hair and the sweetest nature. The Gods want only the best for themselves."

Decimus realised that this was going to be even worse than his imaginings. He already liked the prisoner far too much. He hadn't the faintest idea why he had told him about Veronica. It was so strange. It was also so true. There was no one else he could tell. He'd tried telling Cassius this morning, but Cassius hadn't understood. Oh well, Decimus shook himself mentally. Time to start the serious stuff. Better get on with it, and stop procrastinating.

"I'm afraid I need answers to some questions," Dessy started apologetically.

"You won't get them," said the prisoner.

"According to our allies, the Aeduans, the Nervii are weak," lied Decimus. "Unwilling to fight."

"We are strong," claimed the young man. "We will not tamely surrender to Caesar. We are not the Aedui."

"But our scouts have reported that the Nervii have fled the district. There's no sign of them. They've run back to their homes."

"We have done no such thing."

"There is no sign of a single Nervii this side of the river Sambre. We can find no army to attack."

"I assure you there is an army camped on the north side of the river," said the young man indignantly.

"So what?" said Decimus, trying to put as much contempt into his voice as possible. "Even if there is an army, there's no way your pathetic forces can beat us. You have no heavy weapons, no large catapults, no battering rams."

"We know how to defeat you."

"How?"

The young man recollected himself. "Why don't you attack us and find out?"

"Listen. I have no wish to hurt you. I like you. But I need to know your battle plan."

"I don't like you, and I have no intention of giving you any information," said the young man.

"Of course you will give me the information. You are not a God. You won't be able to resist me for long. So I would prefer you to tell me now, then I can send you back to your wife and children ...." Dessy paused. There was no way he was going to sell this prisoner, he knew. "Unharmed," he finished.

"Send me back?" whispered the young man.

"Yes. I promise you. Whatever happens in the next hour, whether you talk sooner or later, I swear I will send you back."

The prisoner looked bewildered. "Surely you will send me back as a corpse?"

"No. I swear before all the Gods. I will send you home alive, and in one piece, I hope."

"I can tell you nothing," said the young man sadly. He'd known he was doomed from the moment of his capture, whether from these Romans, or from his fellow Gauls.

"Oh, fuck!" said Dessy in despair. He picked up the young man's hands. He hoped the orderly was right, and joints could be restored without too much damage occurring. The corpse hadn't been that forthcoming.

The young man's face was grey with pain and shock. He was trembling. The orderly Musa fastened a sling round the man's left wrist and tied it round his neck. Then he strapped the bent arm firmly to the prisoner's chest.

"He should keep that on for a few days. And it would be as well to give him some painkiller. I'll send some over if you like. Try and get him to move those fingers, then the swelling will reduce."

Dessy thanked him. He felt quite shaken. It had been so much more difficult than he'd expected. Thank the Gods for his contubernales, because without them he was sure he would have given up. They just obeyed his orders without questioning. He would have to pay for the orderly's services, and for the painkiller he supposed, and this time there would be no profit. He had the prisoner helped back to his tent. There was no point in having him chained up; he was too weak to do any damage.

Decimus went off to tell his commander that the Nervii were camped on the northern side of the river, and that they intended to attack the baggage trains which marched behind each separate legion. And that many of their supplies and arms came from Britannia, the country on the other side of the Channel. Caesar altered the disposition of his troops and baggage accordingly.

"How on earth do you do it?" asked Cassius, when he heard the result of the interrogation.

"Easy. I make love to them. Then I torture them. Then they talk," Dessy said bitterly.

He woke in the night. The prisoner was attempting to sit up, with little gasps of pain on each movement.

"What?" Dessy asked. "What's the matter?" Which was a really stupid question, he realised. He went over to try and help. The dim oil lamp showed the terrified prisoner frozen with fear. How long had he been awake and in agony?

"Do you need a piss?" asked Dessy softly, so as not to frighten him further. "It's not a problem."

With a sigh of relief the man nodded. Decimus woke Óengus. Between them they helped the prisoner outside to the urine bucket, then Óengus was told to get the man a piss-pot. Decimus administered some more painkiller, thinking it would do no harm. Gradually the prisoner closed his eyes and slept. Decimus couldn't sleep. He lay awake for the rest of the night.

The next morning Decimus felt so depressed he wanted to just turn over and stay in bed all day. Cierán knelt on the ground at his feet, lacing up his master's boots. He looked up suddenly to see Decimus staring blankly at the tent wall, the expression on his face one of despair, and a tear at the corner of his eye. Cierán snapped his fingers in front of his master's face.

"Stop it!" he said sternly. "Stop think so much bad thoughts. You not bad man, Dessy."

Decimus looked at him in astonishment.

"My father say, 'You tell a man by his slaves.' So. Look at us. You not bad," Cierán said with great emphasis. "You good," he finished.

Decimus wasn't sure whether to slap him for insolence or kiss him for understanding. In the end he did nothing, as Cierán continued to buckle him into his armour. When Cierán had finished he stood to attention, gave the polite half-bow of the Gauls, and opened his arms. "Now you hit me, if you want," he said. "But I have to tell you. Is important you know."

Decimus hugged him and told him he was an idiot. Cierán shrugged his shoulders. "Maybe," he said, "maybe not."

When the Roman army finally marched to engage the Nervii, the whole baggage train was now amalgamated into one enormous crowd of wagons, mules and servants. Decimus and his men, together with the two new legions, acted as a rearguard to protect it. His prisoner was made as comfortable as possible in one of the baggage wagons, along with Cierán and Laeforis, as Decimus thought they were all still too unfit to be on their feet and marching for any distance, and at speed.

The Nervii attacked across the river, before the Roman camp was fortified, and before the baggage had even arrived. When Decimus and his men came to the top of the hill overlooking the battlefield, it was clear that the Romans were being hard pressed. The camp orderlies and cavalry were scattered and the camp partially overrun by the enemy. Decimus yelled at his troops to keep in formation, but to charge down to their camp to give support. The battle was horrendous, with huge numbers of Romans dead and wounded, but the Nervii were defeated in the end.

Envoys from the remnants of the Nervii successfully sought peace terms from Caesar. They had lost the vast majority of their fighting strength and most of their leading citizens. Women, children and old men were the main survivors, unable to protect themselves from the rampaging Roman forces. Caesar was magnanimous in victory, and thought news of his clemency would play well in Rome, especially as his dispatches to the Senate kept emphasising how courageous was this defeated enemy, how hard they had fought, and with what skill, making his victory appear ever more glorious.

Decimus was worried that his prisoner was thinking of suicide, which was not in Dessy's plans for him at all. So he set guards to watch over the man. Then he searched out the camp silversmith and ordered him to fashion a necklace of two silver laurel leaves on a heavy silver chain, explaining that he needed it urgently to present to a brave man. The silversmith, no fool, began to speculate on the man in question, and soon hit upon the obvious answer. He spread the word.

After a week, while the envoys were still present and finalising the arrangements of their surrender, and when the prisoner had almost recovered his self-respect, Decimus ordered his men to parade the following morning and asked for the envoys to be there as well. In the morning Decimus was a little surprised to find the Remi magistrates present in addition to the stony-faced envoys, together with a squadron of cavalry. He wondered why, not aware that somehow word had got around, that the Nervii prisoner was to be honoured by a Roman centurion.

There was an unpleasant edge to the proceedings, Decimus felt. He hadn't wanted to make a huge song and dance about this ceremony of his, but he was doing nothing wrong, he told himself. He had been repeatedly assured that any prisoners he questioned were subsequently his, to do with them whatsoever he wished. When his men were drawn up stiffly at attention Decimus had the prisoner brought to the parade ground.

"We are here this morning to honour one of the bravest men I have ever met," said Decimus. His words were loudly repeated by the interpreter to a mostly silent crowd. One or two of his own men tried a subdued cheer, which rapidly tailed off. The Gauls weren't cheering. A disconcerted Dessy walked over to the prisoner, and started speaking again. "I wish you to accept this token. To us laurel leaves signify the highest praise we can bestow." He held out the chain. The prisoner took it. For a moment Decimus thought he was going to hurl it to the ground.

"I am to carry the burden of your conscience, am I?" whispered the prisoner, smiling mirthlessly. "Thank you for this." He finished speaking, overcome with emotion, knowing that with this action Dessy had signed and sealed his death warrant. An unpleasant death, too, probably. He prayed that his family would be spared.

Decimus didn't know what he meant. He took the chain from his prisoner's nerveless fingers, and slipped it over the man's head. Then he stepped two paces back, unsheathed his sword, and held it out in salute. This time his men banged their shields loudly with their swords, and cheered more heartily. But the Gauls still made not a sound.

"I told you I would give you back. I keep my promises." So saying Decimus took his prisoner by the arm and escorted him over to where the envoys were standing scowling at him. "You must return to your lands, to your wife and family," Dessy went on. "Your tribe have lost so many young men, the remainder will need everyone available to restore order in their ranks. Especially a man such as yourself."

"I betrayed them," said the prisoner. "So they will kill me."

"No, no," said Dessy anxiously. "You did no such thing. I am the betrayer, not you. I betrayed my own honour, by torturing an unarmed man. Will you forgive me?"

Decimus held out his hand.

"If I shake your hand they will kill my wife and children as well. But if you give me your sword, I will kill myself now, and save everyone a lot of trouble." The prisoner turned towards the envoys. "No? You can't put everything right, Dessy, however much you may want to. We have to accept the fate the Gods mete out to us."

The corpses were found just outside the camp gate the next morning. The 'son of the bear' had been defanged, and had his paws cut off and hung round his neck. His wife had been strangled with the silver chain, still in situ. At least the children had been swiftly dealt with. There was no attempt to hide them from Decimus. Someone was bound to tell him. The only consolation came from the orderly. Musa assured Decimus that the man had been mutilated after death, not before. He could explain, but Dessy no longer wanted to know, as the orderly couldn't tell him whether or not the wife and children had been dealt with first.

At least there were no complaints from his seniors afterwards, thankfully.

BOOK 1 : CHAPTER 15

North Gaul to Rome, Autumn 57 BC

The end of summer was spent subduing the remaining tribes of North East Gaul. Cierán thought his master might sink into despair. He had to search his memory for his father's words of wisdom, sometimes resorting to making them up. To his relief Decimus shook himself mentally, becoming resigned rather than depressed. And a little fatalistic, which he hadn't been before.

At the end of a successful campaign Caesar arranged for the legions to winter in Gaul, but he also sent for Decimus. Once again Dessy was invited to dine with his commander. This time his friendly tribune was the only other person present.

The conversation was limited at first to the straightforward affairs of the camp, the problems that might occur with the men in winter quarters, and possible solutions. Decimus had given a lot of thought to these problems. He was able to make sensible suggestions for the men's training, and also how to relieve the boredom that would inevitably occur with limited light and limited access to hunting and women. He thought it would be essential to organise a programme of team games between the centuriae, with small prizes for the winners.

"Like an Olympic Games, but with sword fighting and use of the ballistae as well," Decimus suggested. "Regular weapon and armour inspections could be instituted too, with penalties for poor maintenance. Otherwise the men will spend their time gambling, drinking and generally getting up to mischief, mostly picking fights with each other, or bullying the camp servants."

"I'm sure you're right," his commander agreed. "I will pass your suggestions on to my legates."

Decimus also thought the camp servants could be given some incentives for good behaviour. They still had a great deal of work to do, foraging in the surrounding countryside, chopping wood, preparing meals, maintaining latrines and bath houses.

Then the talk turned to prisoners-of-war, and their disposal. The commander told them the fabulous sum of money raised from their sale, for the Senate and people of Rome.

'And for you,' thought Dessy. He spent the meal wondering why he had been chosen for this honour, and presumed that some really disgusting order was about to be given him.

At the end of the meal the commander's conversation became much more personal.

"When you honoured your prisoner with a parade, your speech was reported to me," said Caesar. He paused, watching the colour rise in his centurion's face. Dessy sat staring straight ahead, his heart thumping in his chest, wondering just how much trouble he was in.

"You accused yourself of betrayal," his commander continued. "But if you hadn't given me the information you obtained, we may have lost the battle. It may well have been the deciding factor. The result was so finely balanced either way, because the Nervii fought so hard and so determinedly. I have brought you here tonight to reassure you. You betrayed no one, Dessy, when you interrogated the man."

"It was dreadful," said Decimus. "I hated doing it." There. That was the truth. And the end result didn't bear thinking about.

"I understand," said Caesar. But he didn't. Why waste sympathy on barbarians? They were uncivilised scum. Semisavages. The Aeduans and the Arverni were tolerable. At least some of them could speak Latin. But these Northerners were only fit for slavery, for the arena or the mines and quarries for the most part. So they could be of some use to the Republic. Still, Decimus was so good at his job. His skill was needed. Strange that such a courageous young man should be so squeamish about a little torture.

"Occasionally we are called on to perform tasks which are anathema to us, but which we know must be executed," Caesar continued. "For my own part I'm glad that our prisoners are questioned by a man of honour, a man who will endeavour to do his best for them. I can't relieve you of that obligation. Sometimes we have to compromise, Dessy, in order not to betray our own men. I have a further task for you, which I hope you will find more pleasant."

'Oh, God,' thought Dessy. 'What now?'

"I'm ordering you to take the sons of King Galba, hostages of mine, to Rome over winter. I want them installed in the house of my niece Atia. I wish young Gaius Octavius to have a smattering of the Gallic language. It is a vast country. It will be useful for him to know something of it in the future. And I would like the hostages to be brought up in the Roman fashion. So they learn our civilised ways."

Decimus was appalled. Was he to be some glorified nursemaid? And how could he afford to transport two princes? His commander smiled, well aware of his centurion's horror.

"Take your centuria with you. You can continue their training on the way. Although you have performed miracles with them so far. Naturally you will need a considerable amount of money for expenses. I propose to give you a grant of two thousand gold pieces. Will that be sufficient?"

Alright, a trip to Rome. Instead of kicking his heels in winter quarters in a hostile land. Decimus was relieved. But in a way he was aware that he was being bribed. Bribed to continue as 'Master Torturer,' as his contubernales mockingly now called him. Not to his face. They knew better. It looked as if he was destined to become Caesar's 'gofer.' Not a brilliant career. Still, the money was more than welcome. And he would get to see his family, and his sons, legitimate and illegitimate. Even better, he would see Ethela again. In some ways he had missed her most of all.

"I am sending a cohort with you, Dessy. You will be in charge. I presume that won't be a problem for you."

Ye Gods! To be in charge of a cohort! Six hundred men. With five centurions under him. Which could be a problem. Never mind. Problems were there to be solved.

Decimus left the praesidium wafted to Elysium in his imagination. He wasn't quite so elevated when he discovered that his commander was to journey with him. But Decimus was good, very good. He anticipated problems and solved them before they arose.

"You give me nothing to complain about," his commander teased him one morning.

"Would you prefer your eggs to be overcooked, or would you rather have cold bath water, Sir? I can arrange for both," said Dessy with a perfectly straight face.

Some of the other centurions sniggered.

"I would hate to put you to any extra trouble, Dessy."

Caesar decided entangling with the Statilius family led to him looking foolish. He desisted from any further attempts at frivolity, and pushed on ahead as soon as he reached Transalpine

Gaul, with a cavalry escort to ensure his personal safety. He no longer needed Decimus and his cohort.

King Galba's sons proved to be very young, very frightened children. They were imprisoned at Bibracte, in Aeduan territory, with hundreds of other terrified children. Decimus thought they looked ill-clothed and ill-fed. It turned out the little hostages had been robbed of their clothes, their jewellery, and the nurse that had been sent to care for them. Óengus and Darreth spoke the same language, and their tribe was an ally of King Galba's, so Decimus used them as nursemaids. Dessy had the children to eat with him every night, so they got used to him. He tried to explain everything that they saw on the way south that alarmed them.

His best move was to acquire a puppy, an exuberant bundle of energy with silky floppy ears, that cried out to be fondled. The puppy had an engaging affectionate nature, and rarely used his sharp milk teeth, only when the little boys overdid the petting, and he needed a nap, or a drink, or something to eat. And then only as a warning. He didn't bite, just made a little snapping gesture, immediately followed by an apologetic lick. Although Decimus had never owned a dog himself, his slaves were delighted with the purchase, like most boys. Óengus undertook the training of the animal. Decimus told Ganainm that the dog was his property. It was becoming clear that Ganainm understood some of what was said to him, especially when the Helvetian boys spoke to him. He even appeared to understand some Latin. But he still spoke not a word.

The hostages were transported by the wagon containing Dessy's tent and equipment, along with Ganainm and the puppy. Ganainm couldn't understand what they said. But they played a game with stones, and he joined in. All the little boys loved the puppy.

Cierán organised a rota, so each slave had a day driving the wagon instead of marching. Although Cierán enjoyed marching with Óengus, who thought deeply about things, and came up with many new and fascinating ideas. The two of them talked about anything and everything, and as their master was riding ahead with his centuria, no one ever told them off or stopped them. Cierán had to placate Laeforis, who was jealous of this new relationship, and felt that his position as Cierán's friend was being usurped by the Belgian boy.

Darreth made a great fuss whenever Cierán ordered him to do anything, coming up with all sorts of fatuous objections. He had to be constantly checked by his elder brother. Cierán found him wearing on occasion, although he usually managed to keep his temper with him, only lashing out occasionally when Darreth had proved to be even more obdurate than usual. Fortunately for his slaves, Decimus remained oblivious to any underlying friction between them. Cierán knew that his master would attempt to solve any such problems with a whip.

The further south they travelled, the lighter Dessy's mood became. They journeyed by the coast roads, skirting the Maritime Alps. How lovely it was to return to his own familiar landscapes, the neatly walled farms of the Province, the camaraderie of the military forts on the way, where Decimus was received according to his vastly increased status. He found the other centurions to be excellent company, although he was sorry Cassius wasn't with them. It was good to make new friends. They were surprisingly deferential, presumably because of his status as one of Caesar's favourite officers.

His only mistake was to question his boys about their past history on the journey, where he discovered, to his dismay, the consequences of the appalling behaviour of the Roman forces. Rape and death for his boys' mothers and sisters, death for little children, death for brave fathers and brothers. Cierán came from an affluent family, with extensive land holdings. Óengus and Darreth's father had been a magistrate. Even Laeforis had owned his own slaves. Decimus found that the Helvetians had a dream whereby they would return to their homes. Óengus was more realistic, aware that his lands would be occupied by the invading army. He knew there was no longer a home to go to, and that the relatives he remembered were most likely dead or sold. He said as much one evening.

"Óengus, you will stay with me. One day you will be freed, I promise," Dessy assured him. "All of you will be freedmen one day."

"As long as we be good," said Óengus.

"But if you killed, Master, what for us?" asked Laeforis. It was a question they had all wanted to ask, but had never dared.

"I don't intend to be killed, thank you," said Dessy. The boys laughed. But it was a serious question, and deserved a serious answer. "I have written my will. That is about what happens to my property when I am dead. You will belong to my son, but you will be under the care of my brother. After a period of time, I have suggested that you be freed, as long as you have remained faithful, and trustworthy. If I am killed, I want you to serve my son as well as you serve me."

"We serve you well, Master?" Cierán asked.

"Very well. You don't cry so much now, do you, Cierán," teased Dessy, "which is good."

"You no hit me so much," replied Cierán, smiling.

"I can remedy that," said Dessy, and leant over and cuffed him.

Everyone laughed again, a nice warm sound. It was the first time Cierán had ever ventured to attempt a joke, Dessy realised. He was becoming increasingly fond of them all.

They reached the Mediterranean coast, the sea sparkling in the autumn sun, looking so inviting and benevolent, thoughts of wrecking ships and drowning sailors clearly far from Neptune's mind at present. The Gauls asked if they would be permitted to swim. It was hot and dusty on the roads, although the surface was so much better now they were in Roman provincial territory. At first Decimus said nothing. The boys thought their request was going to be rejected. But Decimus was thinking hard, and thinking particularly about future campaigns. He decided that not only his boys should swim, but so could the entire cohort, non-coms as well, some of whom had never seen the sea before, let alone learnt to swim. He wasn't to take all the cohort to Rome, only his own trained centuria, so he stationed them at one of the maritime forts, with instructions that every man and boy was to learn to swim if they didn't already know how, and their achievement would be tested on his return, when he would fling them into water, watch the result, and punish any who were failures, as long as they didn't drown, he said, smiling.

BOOK 1 : CHAPTER 16

Villa of Marcus Statilius Taurus

Veronica's father called round to collect Marcellus. He wanted Marcellus to see the statue of Veronica in a niche above her elaborately carved sarcophagus in the family mausoleum, an ostentatious structure in keeping with the rest of the Juvenalis family's possessions. They walked hand in hand, both wearing the dark clothes of mourning, Egnatius in a toga, Marcellus in a charcoal-coloured tunic, accompanied by a posse of equally sombrely-clad slaves. When they arrived, Marcellus stood next to his companion, not knowing quite what to do, as Veronica's father was crying. Marcellus wasn't used to very grown-ups crying. He put his hand into Veronica's father's hand, and squeezed tight.

"I'm so sorry, Sir," he whispered miserably. To his surprise Egnatius carefully collected his tears into a tiny amphora, stoppered it, and gave it to one of the slaves, who placed it in a little gilded box. Egnatius sniffed, pulled a silk handkerchief out of the folds of his toga, and blew his nose vigorously.

"Sorry, young Marcellus. I shouldn't give way like that. But she was my little girl."

"Yes, Sir," agreed Marcellus, feeling more and more upset himself.

"A wonderful girl, Marcellus, wasn't she? Loved by all."

"Yes, Sir," said Marcellus, tears running down his own cheeks now.

Egnatius turned to look at him. He lifted his hands in a helpless gesture. "Now I didn't mean for you to be upset. My blame, Marcellus, my blame entirely."

He stood absentmindedly patting Marcellus's shoulder, lost in contemplation. Then he made an effort to pull himself together.

"What do you think of her statue? Just like her, don't you think? Beautiful."

"Yes, Sir," Marcellus agreed again. He felt this was one of those rare occasions when the truth wouldn't be adequate. The white marble statue of a slim elegant sylph-like girl bore no resemblance whatsoever to the Aunt Veronica he knew. Although he had difficulty remembering her before she turned into a large waterlogged shapeless lump, topped by a thin anxious face.

"You don't think your uncle might be cross with me, for taking this on myself, without consulting him?"

"No, Sir. He'll be really pleased." Marcellus felt he was on sure ground here.

Egnatius took the marble box, and reverently placed it at the feet of the statue.

"There, my love," he said. "Your father's tears will always be with you. The Gods bless you, my dear girl."

Now Egnatius took a gold necklace from a leather pouch, and carefully placed it round the neck of the sylph. "There you are, my darling. Daddy knows how you love pretty things." He blew his nose again. "I will try and bring my girl something she loves whenever I visit her. Don't you think she'll be pleased, Marcellus?"

Marcellus thought she would be delighted, and said so. They walked back together through the baking streets, each wrapped in his own thoughts. Just where was Veronica? Was she inside the sarcophagus? Would she like the necklace? Did dead people have to stay for ever encased in marble? Marcellus thought he would try to keep alive for as long as possible. He had accompanied his mother to their own mausoleum to visit the tiny marble boxes that presumably contained all that remained of his dead baby brothers. They must have been very tiny babies to fit in those little boxes. He didn't like going there, since his mother, like Veronica's father, always ended up crying.

This time Uncle Dessy had brought some little boys home with him. Foreign princes, who were to be turned into Romans. They were to be taken to Lady Atia's house, to teach the mysterious Gaius Octavius how to speak Gallic. Marcellus flattered himself that he could already speak Gallic. He had said '*Hello*' to Cierán and Laeforis. But now Uncle Dessy had new big boys, whose language Marcellus couldn't understand. Luckily they could speak enough Latin for him to cope with, and understood his attempts to speak the Helvetians' language. He liked these new boys. They wore trousers, so looked strange and foreign. But Uncle Dessy said they could dress as they pleased, and keep their hair long, seeing as their flowing locks were always neatly tied back or braided.

Marcellus was sad to see Cierán's hair had been cut short, because he was so hot when he was so ill, apparently, but knew it must have upset Cierán, as he had never ever cut his hair. Marcellus found his new acquaintances were as fastidious as Cierán and Laeforis, stripping as soon as they got up, and pouring buckets of water over themselves, and washing their hair, and repeating the process at night before their supper. Uncle Dessy had inspected their supper the first night they all arrived, and told the steward it wasn't good enough for his slaves. And when

Grandfather complained about the expense, Uncle Dessy merely asked him how much gold he should give him to ensure his slaves were properly fed. Uncle Dessy said his slaves were growing boys. Marcellus was surprised to learn that the boys would grow any more. They were already the tallest servants in the house, taller even than the groom.

After greeting his father Marcus, brother Lucanus, and little Marcellus, Dessy asked if his mother was well enough to see him, and was told she was desperate to greet her younger son. He had been absent so long. Portia came waddling towards him with some difficulty, as she was in the last stages of pregnancy herself, just like Veronica's maid, Dora. Lucanus had declared that this was to be the last child. He was so worried about his lovely wife. She had been in despair after the deaths of her last two babies. How he hoped this forthcoming child would be spared to them.

Lady Caecilia was looking greyer and smaller, thought Decimus. She could hardly move unaided, and the cruel arthritis crippling her joints caused her to have great difficulty sleeping. Tired lines were etched onto her face. But her face lit up when she saw her son, and she held her arms as wide as she could in greeting. Dessy hugged her, but felt her flinch a little. He realised instantly that he must have hurt her, the last thing on earth he wanted to do. Dessy adored his gentle mother. So he apologised, kissed his mother on the forehead, and then settled down by her side for a long chat. He was able to tell his mother problems that his father would dismiss out of hand. He didn't want to give her any worries about himself, though. She had dreaded his early entry into the army.

Afterwards Decimus asked to see his sons. Ethela was summoned. She appeared holding one baby, with a girl carrying another slightly older one. Marcus plucked the baby out of the girl's arms, but Portia stopped him immediately.

"Not that one, Father," she said firmly. "That is Ethela's child."

"Ooh, yes. Skinny little creature, aren't you?" Marcus said.

The baby gave a thin wail. Dessy walked over and held out his arms to receive the child. He'd seen starving children before. This little one was severely malnourished. Dessy wondered how it had happened.

"Does Ethela not have enough milk for the two children, Portia?" Dessy asked his sister-in-law.

"Father insists that your son and heir is always fed first," Portia explained. Thank goodness Dessy was home, and would countermand this dangerous instruction.

"I see," said Dessy. "But I want both my sons fed." He managed to keep his temper for once. He walked over to where Ethela was standing, holding a chubby infant in her arms, looking horribly like its mother, in Dessy's opinion. But the baby smiled a fat smile at him, looking very sweet. "Here, Ethela," Decimus said, holding out their child in his arms, "give milk, please. Come and sit down."

To everyone's horror Dessy pulled out a chair for her to sit on. Ethela flushed, and whispered that she could feed the baby outside. Dessy, now holding his plump son, held the door open so she could pass through with the baby. Portia followed them to Dessy's room.

Ethela was in floods of tears. Portia explained and apologised. She had been confined to bed with a kidney infection, and hadn't realised what was going on. Marcus made Ethela feed Veronica's baby in front of him, so he could ensure Decimus's legitimate heir was well fed. Poor Ethela was only able to properly feed her own child at night. Portia hoped that when Veronica's maid had her baby, any day now, they thought, there would be two mothers and three babies, and more milk available, but she had found a wet-nurse. Still Marcus insisted Ethela fed Veronica's baby, and so the wet-nurse was feeding Ethela's baby. Dessy said the babies were to be fed equally as much as possible, and attempted to convey this to Ethela. He said he wanted Ethela to stay in his room, at which Portia burst out laughing.

"And when the babies cry in the night, Dessy? It won't bother you?"

Dessy grinned. "Well perhaps not. What's the solution then, my darling sister?"

Portia told him that Ethela and the children would be in his room in the daytime if he so wished, and transfer to the nursery at night. The nursery had thick walls, she said with a mischievous smile. Dessy looked over to where Ethela was happily suckling her own baby, making little crooning noises to him.

"She's very young, but she's a good mother. To both babies," whispered Portia. She wondered how much Decimus was grieving for his wife. So far he had made no mention of her.

The next morning Decimus announced his intention of calling on the Juvenalis family. Luke suggested he take Marcellus with him, as Veronica's father was so fond of him. Decimus found it awkward to be hugged by his father-in-law. Egnatius was overcome.

"Dessy, my dear dear boy," he said, clutching him in a tight embrace. "We must be brave. We must bear this grief together. We'll get over it eventually. Given time." He paused to wipe streaming eyes, and then stood awkwardly patting Decimus on the shoulder.

Marcellus burst into tears, relieving the tension in the room, as Uncle Dessy and Veronica's father moved to comfort him simultaneously, and collided. They stood apologising to each other, as Uncle Dessy lifted Marcellus up into his arms. He hadn't thought Marcellus would be so upset, but of course the boy knew Veronica quite well, and this was the first adult death to impinge on his little life. Perhaps he shouldn't have brought him. He'd done so for his own selfish reasons.

Veronica's father now apologised for the sarcophagus. Here Marcellus dried his tears and intervened.

"It's really beautiful, Uncle Dessy. And the statue of Aunt Veronica is perfect." Even though it was nothing like his aunt, he thought, he had succeeded in telling the truth.

Egnatius explained that he would be unable to accompany Dessy to see it in the immediate future, as he had postponed an important business meeting now for too long, and he must set off in the morning. Perhaps Dessy wouldn't mind going with him again, once he had returned? Then he touchingly pleaded with Dessy to have a small part in the rearing of his grandchild. He was feeling overwhelmed by this tall, authoritative young man, who appeared to have grown in stature over the last year. He explained that as a wealthy man he could provide anything that the child needed, and would be honoured to do so, just as long as he caused no offence to the Statilius family.

Decimus looked at his father-in-law properly for the first time, and saw a man ennobled by his great love for his family. Alright, as a father he had failed his daughter in some ways, failed to educate her, failed to inculcate some of the Roman virtues. But his love for her transcended so much, and made him sincere and wholehearted in his grief.

"Sir," said Dessy. "I honour you as much as my own father. Although we have lost Veronica..." He could see a tear rolling down Egnatius's cheeks. "Temporarily lost Veronica," he amended hastily, "I hope, Sir, you will always be a father to me and a grandfather to our child." By now Dessy was affected himself. The two men clung to each other, choked emotionally. On recovering, Dessy was at pains to assure Egnatius that his help would be sought at every opportunity. He asked if his own father had put any difficulties in the way of Veronica's father seeing his grandchild.

"Not at all, Dessy. Not at all, my boy. Your family are always most welcoming. But I wanted your approval particularly."

With that Decimus felt able to take his leave, resolved in his heart to become less judgemental about Egnatius, and to learn to appreciate his many good points, generosity being one of the most obvious.

Life went on. Grief must be put aside. The usual rituals of the year must take their place as if nothing had occurred to upset the balance of Dessy's world. December was a time for feasting and fun, before the harsh reality of winter intervened. Decimus had never felt less like celebrating. He sensed an internal emptiness, after his meeting with Egnatius, as if his soul had evaporated away, leaving a husk of a man behind.

It was difficult to make Cierán understand. "It is Saturnalia. The slaves' festival. My father has designated you to be the host of the feast. The King of Saturnalia."

"Because I am son of the chief?" Cierán asked in surprise.

"No. Because you are the youngest male slave." And will make lots of mistakes, which everyone will find hilarious. Dessy hadn't known Cierán was the son of a chief. Interesting. Maybe that explained why the others all looked to him for guidance, even though he was his youngest slave. And why Laeforis had always performed the most menial tasks, like emptying the slop bucket.

"I will act as your slave," Dessy explained.

Cierán was shocked. "No, Sir. Not possible you to be my slave."

"It's a joke. The masters dress as slaves and serve the meal." And get drunk. "Father loves pretending to be a slave. It's a way of letting your hair down."

This was bad. "Do the others have their hair cut off as well? They not like this, Sir. Not a joke for them."

"No, no. I don't mean that. It's a way of bending the rules. For fun. Father will be the life and soul of the party. Your party. You will be in charge of the 'guests,' the household slaves."

"And girls?"

Dessy laughed. "Yes, and girls."

"We can fuck the girls?"

"No you bloody well cannot fuck the girls." He paused to think for a moment. "Look, afterwards I'll take you all out."

"For girls to fuck?"

Dessy wasn't sure why he was finding this conversation so disturbing. Somehow he had always thought of Cierán as sweetly innocent. Obviously not. Oh well. The boy was sixteen after all. "Yes. But we must be careful. The streets get rowdy."

"I make a speech?" Cierán asked doubtfully. His father always made a speech before an important feast. "My Latin not so good."

"It's a lot better than it was. You'll do fine. It doesn't matter if you make mistakes. It's all part of the fun."

"Then I wish for Ethela and Penelope."

That was a surprise. "Who's Penelope?"

"She help Lady Portia and Lady Caecilia. She teached to read and write letters."

Dessy hadn't noticed her. "She's *learnt* to read and write."

"Yes. She clever little girl. Can read books and write letters. Maybe when she big girl, she help me read and write."

"We'll see," was the only comment Dessy made, not sure if educating the boys would be helpful to him. Not that encouraging, Cierán thought sadly to himself.

In the afternoon the male slaves were all dressed in togas. Not proper togas. Quite short ones, with not a lot of material in them, and no purple stripe down the border. Dessy, Luke and Marcus were dressed as slaves but in clean fresh tunics, Cierán noted.

First the masters sacrificed a pig to the household Gods. The blood was mixed with flour and salt, made into tiny flat altar cakes, and baked over a griddle. Every member of the household was given one of the cakes. Marcellus kept his in his mouth and spat it out into a vase at the first opportunity, where its rancorous remains were found a week later by a slave doing the dusting. The carcass was taken away to be roasted on a spit set up in the courtyard. It would be eaten later that night.

Decimus placed a laurel wreath crown on Cierán's head. He stood back to admire his handiwork and felt the first misgivings. Cierán looked remarkably handsome, young, tall and elegant, like a youthful God. To Dessy's surprise he turned on his heel and walked off towards the kitchens.

"Hey, where are you going?"

Cierán turned to him. "When you be my slave, Master?"

"Well," said Dessy. "Now, I suppose."

"Then you not ask me where I go." Cierán smiled and touched his master's arm. "You not good slave, Dessy." He thought he'd better find out the limits of this slave idea quickly. And his master was frowning.

Dessy was worried that Cierán was taking the whole thing too seriously. "I think I'd better come with you."

"Sure," Cierán agreed. *"Óengus, come with me."*

There was a large amphora on the floor of the wine cellar. The sommelier was explaining that this would be the wine served at dinner tonight. Cierán picked up a ladle, dipped it in the wine and sipped. Then he offered the ladle to Óengus. Óengus choked and spat the wine out on the floor.

"*It's vinegar,*" he said.

"*Not even good vinegar*," said Cierán. "You will not serve this tonight. Better you should serve water than this."

Gingerly Decimus took a sip. "It's disgusting," he affirmed. "You! You'd better sort this out. Now."

The sommelier found Cierán and Óengus towering over him intimidating. And he had annoyed Centurion Decimus. A serious mistake. He was full of apologies, he must have got the vessels mixed up, he maintained. Hastily he produced an amphora of good wine, that was due to be served only to the masters. This met with approval from both Gauls and Dessy. They trooped into the main kitchens, and inspected the food. That at least passed muster. Everything was beautifully prepared, and in lavish quantities, under the aegis of a much slimmer Portia, now she had been safely delivered of her healthy baby boy a month ago. She was pleased to see Cierán in the kitchen, and told him he could taste anything he liked. The boys duly sampled some of the dishes, with great enthusiasm. There were a lot of unfamiliar flavours. Cierán had an earnest conversation with Portia about the ingredients, so she showed him some of the meats, fish, vegetables and spices the chefs had used. This led to Cierán summoning the chefs, shaking their hands, and making them a short speech of thanks. Portia thought he was enchanting. She wished her husband showed a little more interest in the way she ran her house.

When the time came a short while later for the festivities to start, Cierán found himself seated at the head of a long low banqueting table, with Ethela on his left and a pretty young Greek girl, aged about twelve, on his right. This was Penelope, Dessy discovered. He hoped this wasn't one of the girls Cierán wanted to fuck. She was just a child still. No, thank the Gods. Cierán was anxious to learn how to write his name, and Penelope would show him how. Was that alright? Dessy couldn't see any problem with that, and gave his consent.

Marcus carried his wife in his arms, settling her on a comfortable couch, propped up with cushions.

"My wife likes to see you all enjoying yourselves," Marcus explained to Cierán, "but she won't stay long."

Cierán rose to his feet and managed beautifully to welcome her as a star fallen from the heavens, come to grace their banquet. He bowed to her. He reminded his fellow slaves that this upside-down world would soon be righted, so it was best not to get too drunk or be too offensive. Then he called on all to rise, spread out his arms, and thanked the Gods for their bounty of food and wine, all this said in quite passable Latin. He repeated the blessing in his own language.

When the feast was well under way, with Marcus and his sons rushing around, plying the men with wine, and the noise reaching a crescendo, Cierán stood up again. He held up his hand for silence. With a smile he told the room that he had a slave available for hire. "His name is Dessy. He sings."

Lady Caecilia laughed aloud. "May I hire him, Cierán?"

Cierán graciously agreed, with Dessy protesting all the while, as he led him over to his mother. "Me? I can't sing. You know I can't sing!"

"Yes you can. I hear you. Not sing rude songs tonight. Sing a good song for your wonderful mother. The one about your home."

When the loud applause died down at the end of his rather good performance, Dessy told his mother how beautifully the Gauls sang. "Sometimes they sing together, Mother. Different notes in harmony. They may sing for you, if you ask them."

After the Gauls had indeed sung so beautifully, it brought tears to several eyes, without many knowing what the song was all about, Cierán ordered that everyone was to sing at the banquet. Marcus volunteered to start. He sang discordantly, but with great enthusiasm. After that the party became a little more riotous, each performer greeted with louder and louder applause. Cierán was too busy to keep order, as he was finding out from Penelope how to write his name. It was fascinating, this code of the Romans. He wanted to unlock its secrets.

A summons came from Lady Caecilia, delivered by an excited Marcellus, who was pretending to be her page boy. This was the first time ever he had been allowed to be present at the banquet. It could occasionally degenerate into a rough-house, when too much unaccustomed wine was consumed. However this was a rare event, and unlikely to happen with Decimus and Luke around to keep order. Cierán was asked to sit next to her and tell how come he was so good at running an event of which he had no prior knowledge. He explained about his father.

"My father important man, called Cierán like me, Cierán, the Wise and Just. We have many feasts. Must always taste the wine and food be good first. Then thank the Gods and the cooks."

"And where is your father now? I should like to meet him."

"Caesar ordered him be killed and his body be burnted on the fire. So my father no longer exist. His soul is burnted on the fire with his body. He is nothing now. But I remember how he say wise things. I tell some to Dessy."

"I'm glad you weren't killed, Cierán. You are much too young to die."

"I try to kill myself, but I not have the brave."

"No, dear. You didn't have the courage."

"I not have the courage," Cierán amended. "So now my soul belong to my master."

Caecilia reached out her small deformed hand and touched Cierán's own. "The Gods stayed your hand, dear." She decided further information might be even more upsetting, so she thanked Cierán and retired for the night.

When Marcus had drunk his fill and was collapsed in a chair, softly snoring away, his servants carried him to bed. Marcellus had climbed onto Óengus's lap and was fast asleep as well. The party was coming to a close. Decimus found his slaves looked anything but sleepy, regarding him with barely suppressed excitement. As the nearest and safest brothel was expensive, Dessy knew he was in for a costly night. At least he was feeling much more like his usual cheerful self, mostly thanks to Cierán.

BOOK 1 : CHAPTER 17

House of Marcus Statilius Taurus

After Saturnalia, Dessy's slaves were surprised and gratified to discover that their status amongst the other household slaves had increased markedly. No other male slave had ever been invited to sit next to Lady Caecilia, let alone chat away to her, as if he were a guest in actual fact. The menials started addressing them all as 'Sir.' Buckets of water were lined up for their use morning and evening; they no longer had to pump up the water themselves. Their clothes were whisked away and washed for them, their sandals and boots cleaned, their cloaks brushed and hung up to dry. 'I'll do that for you, Sir,' became the constant refrain. The boys enjoyed their moment in the sun, knowing their lives would return to normal once they were back in Gaul with their master. In the meantime it was pleasant to be treated so well. The steward invited them to dine with him and the other freedmen. He liked the look of Cierán, but was soon made to realise his mistake. Cierán reacted in fury when he casually dropped a hand on the boy's thigh. The steward was full of apologies.

Lady Atia came on a visit of condolence, partly to have a look at two barbarians that she had been told to her horror she was to welcome into her household. Her husband Philippus had said he approved of the project. Civilising the barbarians was high on his agenda. She found Dessy had not diminished in attraction since his absence. She felt so drawn towards him. But she must control her feelings and follow convention.

"I was so sorry to hear of your wife's death, Sir," she said. "What a dreadful blow for you to suffer."

"At least the child lives," Dessy replied soberly. "He seems a healthy little lad."

Atia said she had heard that Centurion Decimus had so far felt unable to visit his wife's tomb. "Would it help if I accompanied you?" she dared to ask.

Dessy thought it might help.

"Perhaps you will let me see the child?" asked Atia.

"Of course. Will you come this way? He's a bonny specimen. I've called him Lucas."

Dessy had met a lot of women in his life. He was increasingly fond of Ethela. Although while he was away in Gaul his imaginings thought of her as a sweetly affectionate girl, which didn't quite match up with the reality now he was home. He supposed she was too much taken up with the babies. He loved his sister-in-law as a sister. But he had never fallen in love, and almost never expected to, as if the grand passions of his fellow men were not for him.

But a single glance at the face of this woman had the strangest effect on him. He could hardly look away. He wanted to drink in every detail. Her soft cheeks with their bright complexion, her mouth, full and sweet, made for kissing, her hair rich and glossy with shades of chestnut amongst the dark curling tresses. He was desperate to take this wonderful smiling delicious creature into his arms and kiss her. He wondered if any thoughts like these were in any tiny way reciprocated.

Together they arrived at his bedroom. He placed his hand on Atia's back to guide her through the doorway, only the second time he had managed to touch her. They bent over the crib together. The baby caught sight of them smiling at him. He smiled a gummy grin back at them, a bright little boy with wide awake eyes, and a happy chuckling nature. He laughed aloud when his father picked up one of the toys in his crib, shaking it to make it rattle.

"Oh, what a lovely smile. Let me try," said Atia. Their hands touched as Dessy passed her the toy.

Ethela was busily occupied nursing her own child. Dessy couldn't keep his thoughts in any longer. He felt compelled to speak.

"I want to kiss you," he whispered, leaning in towards her.

Atia turned to face him, a look of surprise on her face turning to a smile. "That's good," she said softly, glancing at Ethela. "I want to kiss you."

At that Dessy carried out his dreams. She was in his arms in a tangle of clothes, and he was kissing her cheeks, her lips, her neck. He felt the warmth of her perfumed body against him. He felt they fitted together perfectly. He was murmuring endearments into her ear, stroking the glossy hair with his fingers, and a feeling of wonder, of ecstasy coursed through his body. He tried to lead her over to his bed, but she detached herself hastily, and pulled back in alarm. Ethela was looking at them curiously.

"No, no. Not today, not today. It's too dangerous," said Atia.

Dessy didn't know what she meant. "No, it's perfectly safe. Don't worry about Ethela. She's mine. She's my slave."

What fools men were, Atia thought to herself.

"Centurion Decimus, my husband is too old to make love to me. You have a habit of making babies. How am I to explain such an event to him?"

It wasn't strictly true. The beginning of each month appeared to remind Philippus that he was a married man. He would make his way to his wife's bedroom with a couple of servants in tow, in case he should need something. Atia would have preferred to go without an audience, even an audience of slaves. It took Philippus so long to get going.

"I want you. I want to make love to you. I've never felt like this before, never. You are the most wonderful woman I've ever seen. The most wonderful woman I've ever kissed."

"You know nothing about me. I might be the world's worst harridan."

"I know a lot about you. I know how much you care for your children. I know how much you loved your first husband."

"How do you know that?" Atia asked, a little alarmed.

"Marcellus never stops talking about your daughter. Children tell each other secrets. Then Marcellus tells his Uncle Dessy. Can we never be completely together then? Could you love me, do you think?"

"Let us take a little time to get to know each other better," Atia pleaded. She was in a state of shock. She hadn't thought through the consequences of this. A full-blown affair was a dangerous move. She wasn't sure she had the courage. If her husband ever found the two of them in bed together, he would be legally entitled to kill either or both of them. Should she be risking her life like this? Her children desperately needed her love and support. On the other hand no one had loved her properly for three years. She was deprived of physical affection. She had a great hunger to be touched, stroked, and caressed. And especially to be touched by this lovely man. She nuzzled into his neck, and kissed his cheek. She touched the line of his smiling lips with her finger.

"Unfortunately I don't have unlimited time," Dessy tried to explain his impatience. "I have to return to Gaul in the Spring.

Your uncle is thinking of conquering the entire country. And I will have to be there."

"First then, let us visit Veronica's tomb together, and ask for her blessing on us."

Decimus was unsure about this idea, but he would get Atia all to himself, so he agreed to the proposal. Marcellus was surprised to find that for once he wasn't wanted.

In the tomb there was a marble couch, ridiculous for their first coupling to take place in front of his dead wife, thought Decimus, but oh God, what a marvellous experience it would be. However he could see from Atia's face that such a proposal would meet with instant dismissal. She was praying. He composed himself and at last thought about Veronica, a vibrant life snuffed out in horrific circumstance. He prayed with sincerity for once, that she might now be happy in her afterlife. He was determined to kiss Atia goodbye, though, so he did.

"No," she said when he released her. "We must be careful. We can't just throw ourselves at each other. There are other people involved who might be hurt. My husband has a good nature, but it wouldn't extend to being cuckolded in his own house. Wait till I send for you."

"Make it soon, then, my sweetest love."

"As soon as can be, darling."

Decimus left the tomb enraptured. And went home ecstatic. Tomorrow would be an exciting day.

Atia wasn't used to planning underhand affairs. She had two inquisitive children, so would need to be very careful, she thought, especially after Decimus's comments about Marcellus. Another inquisitive child. Her husband was busily occupied in preparing for his role as Consul the following year. He was hardly ever at home, and dined out frequently, plotting the legislation he hoped to enact in the Senate, and making sure his fellow Consul would be onside. He hardly noticed whether she was there or not, Atia thought. She was pleased to find that the hostages were very young, and came with lovely manners already instilled in them. They bowed to her and kissed her hand, when Dessy brought them forward. Also one of Decimus's servants was designated to stay with the boys. A little boy who couldn't speak, but who could understand what was said to him. A useful child to have around. She wasn't so pleased about the dog, but everyone combined to persuade her that he was a great asset.

Atia decided to accommodate the young hostages in an annexe sometimes used for guests, a little apart from the main house, with its own tiny courtyard opening onto a grotto made of seashells, with a central fountain. There were three rooms available. She had all the rooms cleaned, side-tables, chests, beds and bedding installed, told her children that the hostages' accommodation was to be off limits to them, as they would want a little privacy, especially at first. They would have lessons with her children, and be taught everything a Roman youth was expected to learn. Then she wrote to Decimus, and suggested he come and inspect the hostages' accommodation, 'to see if it was suitable.'

Decimus felt like a young boy, delirious at the thought of seeing his love again, and the consequences. Atia led him over to the annexe. She was shy at first, so Dessy enjoyed taking everything slowly and patiently. For the first time ever he put someone else's pleasure before his own. He was gentle, tender, and sensitive, careful to take her body with him on this new adventure. He quickly realised that his love, although a few years older than he was, had little knowledge of sexual enjoyment. He thought correctly that her only experience had been with her two husbands.

He decided that as the hostage children didn't like parting from him, initially he would leave Óengus, Darreth, and Ganainm with them. Familiar faces for them. When he wanted time with Atia his slaves were ordered to take the children outside to play, while Atia slipped into the annexe unnoticed by all but her maid.

Caesar was amused to hear that Centurion Decimus's devotion to duty caused him to check on the hostages on a daily basis. How easy it was to manipulate people. But he kept his thoughts to himself, being anxious to keep Philippus on his side when Consul next year. He would be away, attempting to consolidate his Gallic conquests. He needed allies in Rome to protect his interests. Young Gaius Octavius's birthday celebrations had been postponed until his Great Uncle Julius was back in Rome. A special games had been organised. He would have an opportunity to watch the effect of his machinations.

It didn't take long for Lucanus to discover the real reason for his young brother's frequent visits to the house of Lucius Philippus, Consul-elect. Decimus was guileless.

"You are playing with fire, Dessy."

"This is the most glorious thing that's ever happened to me. I'll take care not to get burnt. Not a soul is witness. Not even the little dumb boy. Not even the dog."

After a time Dessy started to think, as he walked back to supposedly check on the hostages yet again. Having a fuck and having a shit were both pleasurable in their own way. But could a fuck with Ethela ever be like a fuck with Atia? He thought he might try and find out one night.

BOOK 1: CHAPTER 18

House of Lucius Philippus

Marcellus was surprised when he realised his father was nervous. This was new. His father and Uncle Dessy were hurrying with urgent strides towards Lady Atia's house, where at last he was to meet the mysterious Gaius Octavius. But his six-year-old legs were having difficulty in keeping up and he desperately wanted a pee. His willy was sticking straight out in front, as it did sometimes, whether he wanted to pee or not. It made his new best tunic bulge in front of him, and he thought everyone was looking at him and laughing. Ambrosius kept turning round to shout at him to keep up, so he couldn't stop and use one of the big leather urine buckets on the street.

At last they arrived at the house, and were ushered in by the porter. Marcellus hung back in the atrium. He thought if he pee'd into the pluvium, the central pool that collected rain-water from the roof, no one would ever know. He lifted up his tunic, but then caught sight of a tiny marble Cupid standing on a low plinth, a bow and arrow in his hands.

The Cupid was looking straight at him. The Cupid blinked, and then let out a wail of distress. Marcellus temporarily forgot his difficulties at this strange phenomenon. He walked over to examine the Cupid more closely. He discovered the child was coated all over with a shiny grey dust. Marcellus walked slowly round the plinth. He felt a frisson of fear shoot through him when he realised that the Cupid's wings were fastened through the skin of his back by wire pins. The pins were surrounded by swollen reddened flesh. There were dribbles of dried blood staining the base of the feathers glued onto some sort of wing-shaped frame.

The Cupid wailed again. Marcellus lifted him off the plinth and carried him into the house, with the Cupid's hot little hands clutched round his neck. To his relief he saw an open doorway at the end of a corridor, leading into what looked like a garden. He could hear a fountain splashing. Marcellus walked through the doorway into the blessedly familiar garden, carrying the crying Cupid with great difficulty, the plump little body slipping slowly out of his arms. The Cupid made a hiccupping sound, and then vomited over Marcellus's shoulder, and all down his new best tunic, which was already streaked with grey dust. Marcellus could feel the warmth and wetness seeping through the material, with the loathsome smell of sick. His mother was not going to be best pleased. He almost dropped the child, just managing to lower him onto the ground. He looked round, spying a healthy green laurel bush. With huge relief he lifted his soiled tunic, and allowed his urine to flush into the bush.

As his bladder emptied, a beautiful fair-haired apparition rose from the centre of the bush, wearing a wreath of laurel leaves in his hair. Marcellus was beginning to think this was a very strange house.

"You've pee'd all over me," said the apparition.

Marcellus was in no mood to be told off by a complete stranger. His best tunic was ruined. "Your Cupid has sicked all over me," he snapped back.

"It's not my Cupid."

"Well, whose is it?"

"No idea."

"You shouldn't have been inside the bush."

"I'm hiding from Octavia."

"Why?"

"They're going to make me shake hands with a lot of boring old men and listen to their boring speeches. It's for my birthday."

The Cupid wailed again, and was sick again.

"We have to do something with him," said Marcellus angrily. "He's so hot. I need to get his wings off and get this grey stuff off him as well. Look, there's wires right through his skin."

"But he's a slave child. He's not one of ours. He's hired. We don't have to do anything."

"Yes we do," shouted Marcellus. "He's a responsity. We have to be responsital for slaves. My Uncle Dessy says so."

"Alright. You hold him still."

Gaius Octavius touched one of the pairs of wings. The Cupid screamed.

"Now is not the time to show weakness," said Gaius Octavius, and pulled hard. The Cupid screamed again, but the first wire came out. Once all four wires were unfastened Gaius Octavius and Marcellus reviewed their handiwork. The Cupid now had red streaks of blood coursing from the wounds on his back through the grey marble dust coating his body.

The two little boys decided the best thing would be to shed their own soiled tunics. Then they washed themselves and the crying Cupid in the garden fountain. The Cupid stopped crying and shivered instead, so Marcellus pulled him out again.

"I'm going to be a Great Man," started Gaius Octavius conversationally, sitting on the edge of the fountain with his feet dangling in the water spray.

"Sez who?"

"Sez you." Gaius Octavius was surprised. "In your poem." He recited the poem Marcellus had forgotten about.

"Though small, you will be honoured,
"And with your illustrious name,
"As a soldier and a statesman,
"Great will be your fame."

"There you are. You wrote that. You're my best friend," Gaius Octavius concluded.

"I'm not. I'm Adrian's best friend. I don't like you. You are horrid to Cupids."

"It was your idea to get the wings off him," Gaius Octavius protested indignantly. "Anyway you do like me. You're to be my guest of honour at the Games tomorrow. We will start them together, after the sacrifice."

Marcellus digested this news in silence.

"Bring Adrian, if you want," Gaius said airily.

"Say some more sayings, then," Marcellus demanded.

"If you wish to eat the whole pie, it is best to take one slice at a time. That's another one. I've thought of lots of them for when I'm a Great Man. You will be a Great Man, too."

"No I won't." Marcellus felt it was time to assert himself.

"Yes you will, because you are my friend."

Marcellus wasn't going to take this. Clearly it was time for a scrap. The boys hurled themselves at each other, and fought long and hard till they found themselves at a standstill.

The hostages were hot and bothered in their annexe. Their fountain was a thin trickle of water into a shallow stone basin in the shape of a scallop shell. There was little shade. They decided to explore, following the sound of childish yelling voices. Marcellus broke off the fight, and welcomed them in Gallic, and succeeded at last in impressing Gaius. The hostages stripped off and sat themselves under the fountain as well, with much giggling. Ganainm joined in. Trousers were too hot to wear.

They heard a girl's voice, high pitched and sweet, calling, "Gaius Octavius, where are you?"

"That's my sister Octavia," explained Gaius.

"That's my wife 'Tavia."

"You are my brother, then. So you have to be my friend." Gaius was pleased. He loved getting his own way.

"Oh, alright," Marcellus agreed. He was too hot to fight any more.

To her horror Octavia found five naked little boys in the garden fountain, together with what looked like a severely ill child on the ground. She didn't have time to sort it all out before shocked adults appeared and demanded to know what was going on.

"When in Rome, do as Romans do," explained Marcellus.

"Meaning what exactly?" demanded his father.

"They don't have baths in Gaul."

"So we were showing them how," Gaius contributed, following Marcellus's lead. "Because they are our responsity. Centurion Decimus said so."

"Responsibility, not responsity," said Dessy, smiling.

The owner of the Cupid appeared, hiding his anger under a pretence of smiles and apologies. The Cupid took one look at him and started whimpering. The owner picked up the wings, handed the Cupid to his servant, and swiftly departed without his fee.

Not by the flicker of an eyelid had Dessy or Atia betrayed themselves. No one present could guess that only yesterday he had to cover her mouth in that same annexe, as their coupling resulted in them climaxing at the same time, a new experience for both.

Once the boys were dressed properly again, Marcellus in a fine borrowed tunic, the two boys wisely spent the rest of the afternoon on their best behaviour.

The Games were to celebrate a small but important boy's birthday, so no one was killed, and no blood was shed. The gladiators gave a rousing exhibition with their practise swords. There was a demonstration of tactics with real soldiers and real prisoners from one of the battles in Gaul. There were dancers, jugglers, musicians, and acrobats. The hostages were invited to attend as well as Adrian. Gaius Octavius stood on a plinth with Marcellus. They dropped their handkerchieves at the same time, to set the games going. All the little boys found it an exciting but tiring afternoon.

Atia decided Marcellus would be a good friend for her son after all, so Marcellus found himself often walking round to see Gaius Octavius, or Atia bringing her children to his own house. Marcellus insisted he be accompanied always by Adrian. The boys exhausted themselves playing with the hostage children and the puppy, but didn't learn much Gallic, as no one bothered to teach them formally. They were given lessons in sword play and wrestling by Óengus and Darreth. Real lessons were given by Gaius's tutor, whom he hated. He told the others that one day he would have him executed, which impressed Marcellus and Adrian, but the hostages were indifferent. They had seen too many such executions in their little lives.

One afternoon the Roman boys spent time making up important sayings for when they were the 'Great Men' Gaius insisted they would all become. They thought of quite a lot that pleased them, and some that were useless but hilarious.

"A wise man knows when to desist," claimed Adrian.

"Only the weak deserve pity," said Gaius.

"Clemency is the laurel crown of a great general." This was Marcellus.

"A Great Man is noted for his civilised conduct."

"No, for shitting on all equally," said Adrian. They collapsed into hysterical laughter.

"A fart is the greatest insult that can be bestowed." Gaius had just farted and thought this was unfair.

"A vomiting child hinders discussion, but leads to new experiences," claimed Marcellus.

Gaius thought that was enough to be going on with. He wasn't quite sure what clemency was. Marcellus's explanation that it meant being kind to Cupids he didn't really believe. They didn't always get on well. Gaius sometimes turned up with Agrippa, a slightly older and bigger boy, who tended to win all their many fights, which he carried out with ruthless determination. Often it was Adrian and Marcellus against Gaius and Agrippa. Marcellus continued to disagree that as Gaius's friend he too would be a Great Man. He wanted to be a poet and go in the army, a combined career Gaius thought was unlikely, and Agrippa openly jeered at.

Portia and Veronica's maid had both managed to produce boy babies, so at last Marcellus had four real boy babies for 'Tavia and him to play with. One day when Octavia appeared with her mother and brother, Marcellus ordered Ethela and the wet-nurse, to their horror, to bring the babies into the peristyle. 'Tavia admired the babies. Marcellus agreed with her that they should be taken back inside the house, when one of them started crying and set all the others off.

The more Marcellus saw of Octavia, the more he came to believe that his dream might actually come true. With Gaius and Adrian happy to go along with his imaginary marriage, and Octavia too kind-hearted to disabuse him, only Agrippa attempted to make him face reality.

"Do you know what you have to do to Octavia when you *are* married?" Agrippa demanded.

"Of course. I will kiss her and cuddle her, and read her my poems. And we will buy some babies, as she likes them to play with."

Agrippa laughed and said, "You have to put your smelly dick in her hole, you idiot."

Agrippa's use of the word 'dick' shocked and impressed the other boys. They knew it was exceptionally rude.

"What hole do you mean?" Marcellus demanded, feeling anxious.

"The one between her legs. All girls have a hole between their legs that their pee comes out of. You have to put your dick inside."

Marcellus was incensed at this piece of information. "You're a liar," he screamed. But he could remember that time when he had opened the door of the steward's room, to see him lying on top of another person, his naked bottom going up and down. Marcellus had often wondered just what was going on, but hadn't liked to ask.

After Agrippa and Gaius had gone home, Marcellus accosted one of his sisters, the spiky one, and asked to see the hole between her legs. She agreed, as long she could see his willy. Portia caught them in the act of this mutual bodily exploration, and stopped them immediately. She insisted later that Lucanus explain the facts of life to his son. But his explanation caused

Marcellus to become outraged. He simply refused to accept it, becoming angrier and angrier, so Lucanus decided to leave well alone for the time being, and wait for his son to grow up a little.

Marcellus wrote a poem every day for practice, as Uncle Dessy said practising was vital, thinking more of sword play and javelin throwing than poetry. His poems did get better, used better images, and conformed to the proper rhythms. They were picked to pieces pitilessly by his friends. But Marcellus took their criticisms on board, and each day tried a little harder.

He was sad when Uncle Dessy returned to the army, taking all the big boys with him, and Ethela, his son Lucas, and her own baby. He overheard the huge row Uncle Dessy had with Grandfather, who was appalled at the thought of his grandson being taken to stay in Gaul, when he should have been safe at home in Rome.

"You can’t trust barbarians, you fool," shouted his grandfather. "How dare you take such risks with the family."

"Rubbish," Dessy replied. "The Aeduans have been our faithful friends for many years. They are totally reliable. There will be no problem. You are living in the past, Father. Times have changed."

Decimus was worried about another matter, though. How was he going to cope now that his role in the army was also becoming more defined by his skill at eliciting information from prisoners, both the terrified and the brave? He thought that when he rejoined the legions he would have to lay down some ground rules. And explain that without them he wouldn't be able to continue. He had to have a free hand to promise freedom, or slavery, or death, quick or slow.

Before he left for the North he had a heart-to-heart talk with Lucanus, his adored and admired elder brother, a man so unlike himself. Dessy knew his brother was one of the few men who would climb up the social pole by being pleasant to all, kindhearted, and above all, a humanitarian. He would have been quite unable to torture anyone, Dessy reflected. In the past he would have said the same about himself. He was wrong, though, he was astonished to discover. Lucanus thought that if torture was necessary for the good of the Republic he would have to go along with it. "Surely, Dessy, the needs of your country come first, before any individual, especially before one of these barbarians?"

"But I'm the one that has to do it, or rather I'm the one that orders it to be done. These are men I admire. Worthy opponents. And I reduce them to human wrecks. One day I am dreading being ordered to elicit information from women or children. What am I to do then?"

Luke frowned. "But women and children won't be brave?"

"I suppose not."

"I had to perform some unpleasant tasks while I was doing my military service in the East. The moral responsibility lies with the one giving out the orders. When you order your men into battle, you are responsible for them, as their centurion. But if your legate tells you to hunt down the enemy women and children, as mine did, it is he who will answer to the Gods, not you."

Lucanus's words about torture came as something of a shock. No one else appeared to understand how he felt. Dessy wasn't naive. He knew some men with a lust for power thoroughly enjoyed inflicting terrible pain on other men, even on women and kids. The Quaestionarii rapidly became inured to the suffering, even of the innocents. And although the household slaves were rarely physically punished, partly because they were too well trained, and partly because the steward was a lazy piece of shit, the unspoken threat was always there. Obey or else! But a thrashing was not the same thing at all as being deliberately burnt or mutilated. Maybe he was worrying unduly. He was a recently appointed cohort commander. Training his new men should be enough to concern him.

Decimus installed Ethela and the children in the house of a Roman trader at Bibracte, in Central Gaul, one of the safest and richest towns of the Aeduan tribe, those faithful Gallic allies of Rome. He left Óengus and Darreth with her to help with the children, and any necessary household tasks. Many of the other officers were bringing their wives to Gaul. It appeared to be perfectly safe, almost a province of Rome already. The Arvernian and Aeduan magistrates meekly arranged for corn to be supplied to the invading Roman army, which was pushing ever further north and east.

Dessy had agreed with Atia that it would be far too dangerous to attempt to communicate by letter. Their final parting had been hard for both.

"Stay safe, darling. Don't take unnecessary risks."

"I won't, my dearest love. I will come back to you, I promise." Though how the hell he was supposed to avoid unnecessary risks as a centurion......No point in explaining the army to Atia. She wouldn't understand.

They didn't meet again for two years. It wasn't hard for Dessy. He was too busy fighting to give much thought to romance. And every so often he found himself back near Bibracte, and Ethela. But for Atia the years were long and empty. She kept close to Portia, hoping for scraps of information to come her way from the sparse letters Decimus wrote home to his brother.

Every time Dessy returned to Bibracte he experienced the shock of seeing how his little sons had changed, no longer babies, but now little boys. Mochán was slim, with fair hair, fair skin, and the brown eyes of his father. Lucas was much darker, with already a noticeable streak of determination. They chattered to each other and to Ethela in German, quite unconsciously changing to Gallic when talking to Óengus and Darreth. But Dessy was pleased to find that Óengus had managed to teach them some Latin. Ethela wanted him to get a tutor for Lucas, but Dessy said, "No, Ethela. For both boys."

"Mochán is a slave. He must know this," said his mother. Mochán must realise that for him life will be bad, she thought. He was such a beautiful boy. Her heart ached when she saw him. She was terrified of his future, and the thought that she might not be in it. That he might be sold. "Master Lucas is the master. He must know this as well."

"No, Ethela. Mochán is my son. He is entitled to as much love and protection from me as Lucas. I have ensured that you will both be freed if anything happens to me, with enough money for you to live on comfortably. But I want Lucas to be aware that Mochán is his brother. I want them to love and respect each other, as I love and respect my own brother. And the same holds true for little Manius, my other son in Rome. So even though Lucas is my heir, I want him to be able to count on his brothers for support. And I hope he will always help them in turn."

Ethela was in tears at the end of this speech. Dessy took her in his arms and kissed her.

"Do you understand, my lovely girl? You must stop worrying. There is nothing to worry about. Ever."

Ethela nodded. For the first time she put her arms around her master's neck, and hugged him back.

BOOK 1: CHAPTER 19

House of Lucius Philippus, Rome, 55 BC

Octavia received the news she had been dreading. Her stepfather arranged for her to marry Gaius Claudius Marcellus Minor, a man thirty-three years of age, only nineteen years older than she was. He had a daughter already married. The wedding wouldn't wait until the return of Great Uncle Julius from Gaul. Philippus did not approve of Great Uncle Julius, and had done all he could to obstruct him last year. In consequence Caesar had mobilised enough allies in the Senate to prevent Philippus from receiving a governorship, the usual reward for a Consul.

Miserably Octavia started work on spinning and weaving her wedding dress and veil, but the work made her more and more depressed. She didn't have time to play anymore, to Marcellus's disgust, pushing him away crossly for once, and telling him she had to work on her dress. But Marcellus carried a secret in his breast that he hugged to himself. One afternoon he had heard his mother and Lady Atia chatting about Octavia.

"Yes, she is to marry Marcellus," said Lady Atia in reply to Portia's question. "Without Uncle Julius's presence. He can stay in Gaul as far as we are concerned, the further away the better."

Marcellus was still worried about the physical consequences of marriage. He didn't want to ask his father. He hoped that maybe Uncle Dessy would be home before winter. He felt he would trust his information more than anyone else's. But Uncle Dessy could only pay the briefest of visits. He was busy recruiting replacements for the legionaries dead or injured in the last summer's campaign.

Atia could have screamed with frustration. She knew Dessy was coming to Rome. She couldn't get anywhere near him. Philippus was spending all his time at home on wedding preparations. Dessy was to be at the ceremony, but she wouldn't be able to touch him. Let alone speak to him. Every time Octavia opened her mouth to ask something about the arrangements, her mother snapped at her in irritation.

With little time to go to the wedding, Marcellus wasn't allowed anywhere near the bride, but he knew that was usual. His marriage poem was already written and beautifully copied out on vellum. Ambrosius said it was really good. When Gaius Octavius and Agrippa came to his house, and he talked about his forthcoming marriage they grinned at him but said nothing, secretly wondering what Marcellus would do when he discovered it wasn't to be, and hoping it would be something shocking. Adrian being two years older tried hard to persuade his friend that he must be mistaken, with no success.

Another Marcellus was equally worried about the marriage. Claudius Marcellus Minor could hardly turn down the offer from Consul Philippus to marry his step-daughter Octavia. But his first wife died soon after his daughter was born. Subsequently he had found his pleasures amongst the catamites at the baths. He couldn't even remember the last time he'd had intercourse with a woman. When he made an attempt with one of the girls at a high-class brothel, he hadn't been able to get an erection at all. Panicking, he returned to the baths to find he had no trouble with his favourite boy. But Octavia was a pretty young girl. Surely all would be well?

On the eve of her wedding Octavia sadly gathered together her dolls, games, and toys and one of her dresses. She walked with her mother to the temple of Juno to offer them all to the Goddess, but she kept back her favourite doll, one of the boy babies, now properly dressed like a boy. He was called Marcellus, and she whispered all her secrets and longings to him at night while she lay in bed. The Goddess Juno would not be pleased if she knew how much Octavia hated the idea of marriage with this Claudius Marcellus Minor, she thought to herself. Safer to keep hold of the doll. Octavia had another worry. Her periods, always a little erratic, had disappeared for the last two months. But now she could feel the familiar premenstrual ache in her abdomen.

Marcellus was allowed to light the torch of Ceres in the bride's house to start the wedding procession, which gave rise to the first misgivings in his mind. He had performed the same role for Aunt Veronica, but it hadn't led to his own marriage, but to Uncle Dessy's. He began to be anxious.

The ceremony was interminable, the deputy Pontifex Maximus droning on and on about the amalgamation of these two great families. The temple interior was hot and stuffy. The ten witnesses looked as if they were about to go to sleep. Little Marcellus thought the High Priest was making too much fuss about the Statilius family. Not yet notable for greatness. He didn't recognise any of the heroic acts mentioned as coming from his own family. It was a puzzle. It gradually dawned on him that the man the priest was referring to as the husband of Octavia, was a weedy perfumed youngish man called Claudius. Anger began to kindle inside Marcellus. Could Adrian be right after all? Were Gaius and Agrippa taking part in one huge joke at his expense? Now he discovered Octavia was sharing the spelt bread with this

Claudius. Rage boiled over in Marcellus's breast. When the priest asked Philippus for his stepdaughter's hand, and placed it in the weedy young man's, the result was as unexpected as it was shocking.

Marcellus erupted from the crowd of onlookers, hurled across the temple floor screaming at the top of his voice, "No, no, You shan't have her. You're not putting anything inside Octavia. I won't let you. I won't let you."

Marcellus butted the young man in the stomach, causing him to howl in anguish. The witnesses woke up, as the bride called out in alarm and the High Priest dropped the sacrificial knife.

"She's my Octavia, not yours. You go away. Go away!" Marcellus continued to scream at the top of his voice and pummel the young man. Decimus rushed over, lifted Marcellus up in the air, pinioning his arms, and took him outside, where he proceeded to administer a severe thrashing on the boy's backside. Once he was released, Marcellus shouted that he hated all of them.

"All of them," he reiterated. "And I hate you too," he yelled at Dessy. He was a ball of eight-year-old fury, standing with clenched fists and face white with anger. Decimus slapped him sharply across the face, causing Marcellus to trip and fall on the steep temple steps, grazing his knees and elbow. Blood trickled down his limbs, smudging and staining his tunic. Cierán gathered the livid struggling boy up into his arms, and carried him over to the nearby public fountain.

Inside the temple Lucanus, red-faced with embarrassment, apologised profusely to both families, and said his son had obviously gone mad due to the heat. Octavia was in tears, pleading for Marcellus not to be punished.

"He's only a little boy," she said again and again, to no avail. Who listened to the bride after all? Her mother told her abruptly to shut up.

Cierán was engaged in washing the grazes when Lucanus approached. He snapped an order to Dessy's other Gallic slaves. They immediately formed a protective guard around Marcellus.

"I wish to speak with my son," said Lucanus, baffled at this odd behaviour of slaves, almost as strange as his son's dreadful unprovoked attack on the bridegroom.

"My father say words cause more wounds than swords," said Cierán. He bowed, then turned to face his little charge.

"*Now, Master Marcellus, be brave and go with the Gods,*" he said. He clasped the boy's hand in his own and then propelled him towards his father.

It was just enough pause to make Lucanus consider his speech more carefully. He calmed down a little, and didn't shout, but explained simply that all the consequences might not be apparent immediately, but at the very least Marcellus had insulted two major families, and the High Priest of Rome. He wisely decided not to mention Octavia.

Marcellus was sent home in disgrace, surrounded by his bodyguard of Gauls, while Lucanus and Decimus returned to see just how much offence the child had caused.

Octavia was so upset, she forgot some vital parts of the ceremony. When processing to her husband's house she omitted to give any money to the locals, and arrived at his door tongue-tied and quite unable to remember how to respond to his greeting, until prompted by her mother. Atia was becoming increasingly cross with her daughter, but mentally blamed Marcellus.

Worse was to come. At the traditional sacrifice of a pig, the sacrificer pulled the knife swiftly across the sow's throat, and the red blood spurted out into the sacred chalice. At the same moment, Octavia felt the usual clot that heralded the onset of menses, slide down her vagina and onto her thighs. The smell of the pig's blood, the heat of the day, the tightly-knotted girdle round her waist, and her anxiety, caused her to feel light-headed. She slid to the ground in a tumble of creamy-white wool. The departing wedding guests correctly opined that the future for this marriage appeared somewhat shaky.

The marriage was supposed to be consummated in the dark, but the knot of the bride's girdle had been too enthusiastically tied by her stepfather Philippus, and Claudius couldn't get it undone. So he called for lights to be set in the bedroom. The lamps revealed a frightened fourteen-year-old girl with a red-stained dress and a bloodied matrimonial bed. Claudius was delighted. There would be no damage to his reputation after all.

"My sweet child, there is no need to be frightened of me, none whatsoever," said Claudius, to Octavia's huge relief. "In view of the circumstances I think we had better postpone our love-making a while. Do you mind?"

"No, Sir, Of course not," said Octavia.

"In that case, my dear, I will leave you in peace tonight."

Claudius kissed her cheek, gathered up the stained bedclothes and delivered them to his expectant servants. He went off to his own room with a feeling of reprieve. He thought his new wife a beautiful young girl, but unfortunately Octavia failed to rouse any sexual desire in him whatsoever.

Claudius waited for ten days before seeking out his new wife's bedroom. He found himself feeling anxious. He had managed to get himself aroused, but as he approached Octavia, to his alarm he could feel the tumescence dissipating.

Octavia was equally anxious, although so far her husband had been kindness itself to her. She lay rigid in the marriage bed as he approached, and then suddenly remembered her boy doll was lying next to her. Claudius picked up her hand and kissed it, but then wanted to know about the doll. He laughed when he heard that it was named Marcellus, and told his wife that of course she could keep the doll. Claudius stripped off his clothes and cuddled up next to her, but after a while he realised there was simply no way.

"My dear, I am so sorry. I am unable to perform satisfactorily at present. I will engage to do so in the future. I wonder if you would be kind enough not to mention this to anyone else. For a man to fail to make love to his beautiful wife, does not do his standing any good in our society."

Octavia hastened to reassure him. She would tell no one. Claudius didn't believe her, thinking all women were endless gossips. At first Octavia kept her promise. She never mentioned it to her mother.

Three days after the wedding, Gaius Octavius and Marcus Agrippa turned up to see Marcellus.

"My sister Octavia wants to hear your poem. You are to visit as soon as you can," said Gaius.

"You were brilliant," said Agrippa admiringly. "Didn't you wake everybody up! I thought I was going to wet myself laughing."

"Yes, it was superb," grinned Gaius. "That High Priest was so boring. I thought he'd never shut up."

"Has she forgiven me?" Marcellus asked, feeling so sorry to have ruined his true love's wedding.

"What for?" Agrippa was genuinely surprised. "She must have thought the old fart of a High Priest was awful. It was a great way to cut him short. Can I have you at my wedding, Marcellus? I'm intending to marry one of the Vestal Virgins tomorrow."

Marcellus and Gaius combined to shut the blasphemer up. But Agrippa shouted that Marcellus was a much worse blasphemer, after what he did in the temple, so the tables were turned. Without Adrian, Marcellus came off considerably worse. Agrippa used his muscles to good effect, pummelling Marcellus on all areas of his body. Nothing was out of bounds, according to Agrippa.

Thankfully Decimus arrived on the scene and took the three boys off to the Field of Mars to spend the afternoon practising javelin throwing. They were to watch and follow Cierán, who threw with astonishing accuracy over great length. Decimus wondered if his height helped. His technique couldn't be faulted.

Later Marcellus went with his father to the house of Claudius Marcellus Minor, to deliver his own hand-written tear-stained apology. They were surprisingly warmly welcomed. Marcellus was encouraged to read out his poem, which he had hastily amended that morning, so it wasn't quite so graphic. It was a poem about two love birds, acclaimed as exceptional by his small audience. Claudius told him he would always be welcome in his house, and suggested that Marcellus be hired out to other weddings to enliven proceedings, all this said with a pleasant smile.

"We will always be rivals for Octavia's affections, won't we, my little namesake?" Claudius said laughing. An idea flitted across his mind. Ridiculous. Well, put it aside, see how things go, but it was always useful to have something to fall back on if things didn’t work out.

BOOK 1: CHAPTER 20

North Gaul, 54 BC

Decimus had been promoted again during the previous year's campaign against the Germans, but he hadn't enjoyed it. The Gauls and Germans were finding out what happened if they dared to cross Caesar, slaughter being the optimum outcome. Caesar broke all the rules of warfare, seizing and holding the German envoys. Women and children weren't spared either, but were hunted down mercilessly. The Romans succeeded in building a bridge across the Rhine, no mean feat. Once across, their army rampaged savagely amongst the German lands, massacring all the inhabitants, burning buildings and destroying crops. Caesar's message to the German tribes was clear. Keep out of Gaul. Dessy was relieved when Caesar retreated back across the Rhine, in order to invade Britain, perhaps a bit more successfully this second time.

Decimus was now ranked higher in the legion than Cassius, which didn't worry Cass in the slightest. He knew just how good a fighter and organiser his friend was. He was proud of his part in Dessy's training and experience. Cassius went to Britain with Caesar, while Decimus was left behind in North Gaul with three legions under the command of Titus Labienus. Their present job was to guard the harbours, ensure an adequate supply of corn for the entire army, and find out what was happening in the rest of Gaul. As usual Dessy was roped in. He could now speak to some extent in both North and South Gallic, thanks to his slave boys.

Decimus found the Gauls to be in a state of high excitement. They were outraged at their princes being slaughtered by the Romans. They had been forced to watch the executions being carried out in a flagrantly disgusting manner, an unjustified prolonged public torture, as far as the Gauls were concerned. And the harvest was abysmal all over the country because of the terrible drought this year. People were hungry, and could see their situation becoming perilous during the winter months, as they now had a greedy foreign army to feed, as well as themselves.

Labienus found Dessy to be an invaluable aid in motivating his bored troops. Decimus made sure the legionaries and camp servants were always busily occupied. The soldiers were furious at being deprived of the opportunity to loot in Britain, thinking themselves hard done by. So Decimus encouraged boxing competitions, mock gladiatorial combats, and horse races, where many bets were laid and lost, as well as the usual competitive team games.

News came that Mark Antony was appointed quaestor to Caesar, his mother's cousin. Antony marched more new recruits up from Italy to join Labienus. He arrived at camp with a large quantity of baggage and some great wines, it was reputed, as well as the replacement legionaries. Decimus was interested to hear that Antony had become a rich and influential man, and had learnt a lot whilst on military matters in Syria, where he'd ended up in charge of the entire cavalry division. Apparently with great success. Decimus thought he would reserve judgement until he had seen the man in action.

Labienus arranged a dinner to welcome their new officer, a man already openly declaring his support for the Populares Party in the Senate, and thus to Julius Caesar, one of their main supporters. Labienus proceeded to introduce Mark Antony to the senior centurions and the military tribunes.

"And this is Decimus Taurus," explained Labienus. "Second Centurion of the Tenth Legion. An appropriate name," he added.

Dessy held out his hand. "We've met before," he said.

"I think not," said Antony.

"It was in Rome, at the house of Lady Atia. I was there with my brother Lucanus."

Antony decided this social upstart needed to be put in his place. How dare he claim acquaintance with his superior? Antony was deliberately insulting. "I m afraid I don't attempt to recall all the lower orders I meet."

"You had just applied to Caesar for help with your enormous debts, before you fled to Greece," said Decimus.

Antony looked him up and down. A smile of contempt crossed his features. "Oh yes, of course. I remember now. You are Lady Atia's reward."

Dessy fired up straight away. "Meaning what, exactly?"

Labienus intervened hastily. "Hey, we're here to fight the Gauls and the Brits. Not to fight each other."

"Well not for the moment," said Antony. "Maybe later."

His long-suffering secretary approached, and whispered something to him. Antony's expression changed immediately.

"Ah yes," said Antony. "There is a matter I wish to discuss with you, Centurion Taurus. I understand that pretty girl in Bibracte belongs to you. Ethela, is that right? I wish to purchase her."

"She's not for sale," snapped Decimus.

"Oh come on. Every slave has a price. How much do you want for her? A hundred sesterces? A thousand? Ten thousand?" Antony offered, laughing.

"She's not for sale," Decimus insisted. "She is the mother of my son. No sale."

Labienus put Antony right after the dinner. "Never get on the wrong side of the centurions, Antony. They will hang you out to dry."

Now he was in Gaul, Antony wished to reinforce his reputation as a hard fighting man, so the following morning he gathered the new recruits together on the parade ground.

"Now men, we are here to fight the Gauls and the Britons. I want to demonstrate to you that there is nothing to be afraid of. We will need a Gaul or a Briton first to demonstrate just how useless they are at fighting."

Antony turned to survey the scene. He caught sight of a tall blond youth carrying a bundle of throwing spears, walking next to a darker boy leading a horse. He thought he'd seen the blond boy around, but couldn't remember precisely where. The boy looked a likely specimen, so Antony sent some of the men to fetch him.

"Now, lad, are you a Gaul?" Antony asked Cierán.

"A Helvetian Gaul, Sir," Cierán replied, bowing politely.

"Perfect," smiled Antony. He addressed the recruits again. "Now men, you all know we beat the Helvetians. This strapping young lad is one of them, taken prisoner, no doubt. So who will volunteer to be the target for this lad?"

Not surprisingly there was no response.

Antony laughed. "Ten gold pieces to the one who volunteers."

One of the soldiers put his arm up, to the jeers and prophecies of doom from the others.

"Good lad," said Antony. "Go over there towards that catapult, and stop when I tell you."

The soldier walked away obediently, being ordered to halt after fifty yards. Antony picked up a javelin and tried to hand it to Cierán. Cierán backed away hastily.

"No, boy. I want you to throw the javelin. Look, there is your target."

The target capered around, waving his hands in the air. Cierán shook his head vigorously. Antony was furious to be openly disobeyed by a slave in front of the recruits. He struck Cierán across the face.

"I order you to throw this javelin at that target. Do you hear me, boy?" Antony shouted.

Again Cierán shook his head. "Not kill Roman. My master be angry if I kill Roman."

"Kill him? You'll get nowhere near him, you ape. Now do as you're told."

Decimus was inspecting the barns built to store the corn supplies, when Laeforis galloped up to him, yelling that Cierán needed help.

When Cierán again refused, Antony knocked him to the ground. He then proceeded to lash at him repeatedly with a horse whip, with Cierán trying to protect his head with his hands.

"Just what the hell do you think you're doing with my slave, Sir?" demanded Dessy, when he arrived out of breath and out of temper.

Just my luck, thought Antony. It would have to be Centurion Taurus's slave. Fuck! "He refused my order," he snarled. "I won't have it."

"What order?"

"It doesn't fucking matter what order. The point is he refused to carry it out."

Decimus pulled the shaken Cierán to his feet, put his arms round him to steady the boy, and wiped the tears from his face with his hand. They had a whispered consultation in Gallic. Cierán pointed out the target, who was now doing a little jig.

"My servant will obey your order, Sir. But to be on the safe side, I think we had better alter the target."

Decimus gave Laeforis his shield. Laeforis cantered his horse over to the ballista, which was at least twenty yards further on than the target, and hung up the shield on the cross-beam.

"Now, Cierán, throw the javelin," ordered his master.

The javelin whistled past the target, and struck the shield dead centre with a thud. The target stood rigid with shock.

"Now you, Laeforis," said Dessy. "From the same place."

Laeforis got down from the horse, and picked up a javelin from the pile, balancing it in his hand. Then he ran up and hurled the javelin. It struck the first javelin and split it in two down the middle. Cierán put his arm round his friend's neck and kissed his cheek.

"*Not bad*," he said, laughing and crying at the same time. He was very sore.

The target raced back to the rest of the group.

"These are Gauls," said Dessy, gesturing to his two slaves. "They are brave, skilled fighters, which is why I use them to train my own men. Never underestimate the enemy."

The sad news came that Caesar's daughter Julia had died in childbirth. His only legitimate daughter. The baby had died as well. Some of the men, and especially the superstitious Gauls, thought it to be an ill omen for the army.

In the midst of his grief Caesar knew he would somehow have to find another way to reinforce the alliance with Pompey. This had proved to be most beneficial. Caesar's term as Governor in Gaul had been extended for a further five years, due to the good offices of Pompey and Crassus, while they were both Consuls. At present Crassus's elder son was serving with him here in Gaul, not with any distinction, admittedly. Still, it meant that Crassus senior remained a staunch friend and ally. At the moment he was off with his younger son to wage war in Parthia, and would presumably return even richer and with greater prestige. Caesar's thoughts dwelt a lot on what to do about Pompey. Eventually he hit on a possible solution, though this might make him future enemies.

Dessy found the rest of the auxiliary troops of Gauls in camp becoming almost mutinous as winter approached. What was the point of allying themselves to Rome if it resulted in their wives and children starving? When the Romans returned from Britain in September, with not a lot to show for all their efforts, the Gallic Council was held at Samarobriva, to debate the precarious situation, of famine stalking an already starving nation.

Caesar decided to separate his forces in their winter quarters. Each legion was stationed in a different part of the country, in a well-fortified camp, so the feeding of the army didn't depend on one tribe only. Such tempting targets caused several of the Gallic tribes to combine together and attack two of the camps. So the Gauls had a partial revenge that winter, wiping out the fourteenth legion, together with their legates and Dessy's friendly tribune, and causing severe damage to another legion under the command of Quintus Cicero.

BOOK 1: CHAPTER 21

Villa of Claudius Marcellus

Cousin Julia was dead, as was also the little baby. Octavia was devastated by this loss, her one good friend, someone she could talk to about all her problems. And she did have problems that weren't quite like other people's. For instance she was unlikely to die in childbirth, for despite being married for a year Octavia was still a virgin. At first she had thought her husband's failure to make love to her was somehow her fault, after the disastrous start to their marriage. Claudius continued to be kind to her, and never reproached her in any way. Once he had apologised and promised things would change, but they never did.

And now she knew why. One day she ventured into her husband's bedroom, as she knew he was only with his close friend Favonius and a boy slave. The group sprang apart at her entrance. She was shocked to see her naked husband lying on his back, his penis engorged and erect, the boy agilely leaping off the bed, while Favonius looked on, laughing. They were all drunk, she realised. The slave boy as well. She never discussed this episode with Claudius, but no longer made any attempt to be sexually pleasing to him. Julia said he might find her repulsive, which was more than her pride could bear. She never ventured near his bedroom again unless she knew he was going to be away for a good long time.

Julia explained. Julia understood, and now Julia was no more.

Octavia had grown apart from her mother, who was in a perpetual bad temper with her these days, continually demanding that she produce offspring. Atia wanted grandchildren. Octavia didn't dare tell her the reason why she had failed to conceive. Thank goodness for Marcellus. He was far too young to confide in, but she knew he was a true friend. And he came often to the house with her brother Gaius Octavius, reading her his poems, telling her their exploits, and making her laugh. His uncle wasn't coming back to Rome this winter, he told her, as Caesar was too scared to leave Gaul, for fear of another rebellion. When she passed this scrap of information on to her mother, Atia reacted with shock.

"He's not coming?" Atia demanded. "Dessy's not coming home?"

"Not according to Marcellus, Mother. Great Uncle Julius thinks there may be further insurrection if he leaves Gaul."

"Damn these bloody Gauls," her mother yelled at her. At last Octavia began to understand her mother's attitude.

Then came more frightening news from Gaul. Great Uncle Julius had the temerity to offer Octavia as a wife to Pompey, now that Julia was dead. He presumably thought that he had enough power to force Claudius to divorce her. Octavia shuddered at the thought of having to marry that creepy old man. Claudius was very much against the idea, fortunately, as was her stepfather Philippus.

Claudius was furious with Caesar for daring to interfere with his marriage. He didn't want any tales told. He was hoping to be appointed Consul in the future, so he could work with Philippus on the 'Stop Caesar' party. Most of the Senate could see the danger in giving Caesar any more power.

Marcus Crassus was dead, slaughtered in Parthia, together with his legions and his younger son. The triumvirate was broken. Fifty-two year old Gnaeus Pompey didn't think Octavia would be much use to him politically. He didn't fancy her anyway. Too young and too virtuous, by all accounts. He was becoming increasingly worried about Caesar's continuing military success. And his popularity with the plebs. It almost seemed as if Caesar was bent on becoming the most powerful man in Rome rather than Pompey the Great. This was a severe blow to Pompey's self esteem. He decided to ally himself with the conservatives in the Senate and form a power base. He made overtures to Marcus Brutus and Cassius Longinus, both staunch republicans, as was Marcus Cicero and his brother Quintus, now returned from the fighting in Gaul. Unfortunately Quintus had lost almost a third of his legion during the summer to the Germans, by a total misjudgement. He'd had a stormy interview with Caesar afterwards, with his character shredded. He no longer felt disposed to admire Julius Caesar, and discovered many in the Senate who felt much the same.

To Octavia's great relief Pompey turned her down. Octavia went to the temple of Juno to offer up a sacrifice of a young goat, and give thanks for her answered prayers.

BOOK 1: CHAPTER 22

Gergovia, Central Gaul, 52 BC

The Gauls found their charismatic leader, Vercingetorix, a man who inspired the whole nation to combine to throw the Romans out of their country once and for all. He was successfully engaged in pursuing a scorched earth policy, and was now holed up with his army in Gergovia, a well-fortified town, while he encouraged the Aeduans and their allies to join him.

At first Caesar ordered a vast camp to be built opposite the town, then another smaller camp, joined by a trench to protect troops passing from one camp to another, in an attempt to cut off supplies to the Gauls. But news arrived that the Aeduans were at last preparing to ditch him and join with Vercingetorix. Caesar marched south with six legions to prevent such an dreadful realignment of forces against him, leaving few behind to defend the camp.

It was so hot. Inside the camp the ground was parched, the grass brown and shrivelled, with little for the cattle and horses to feed on. Decimus was exhausted. They couldn't go on like this. Soon the camp would be overrun. The Gauls were persistent, becoming ever bolder and closer each day. As the Primipilus of one of the remaining legions Decimus was ordered to attend the evening's strategy meeting. His opinions were invariably acted upon, but he had run out of ideas. He walked over to the praesidium, with the dust puffing up at each step he took, coating his boots with greyish powder, and making him cough.

The mounting casualty rate decided the legate to risk all in sending out a few of the remaining cavalry at night from the back of the camp, to try and find Caesar. Without his troops they were doomed. Decimus suggested that even the non-coms would have to be armed, however useless they were. They might inflict some damage, however slight. And they could shout and bang their shields, if nothing else. This was agreed. At the end of the meeting Decimus was ordered to get a few hour's well-earned sleep.

When Decimus trailed wearily back to his tent, he informed Cierán and Laeforis that they would have to fight by his side in the morning. He knew it would be a problem convincing them, but they too would die if the camp was overrun.

"I need you with me, to fight with me. Otherwise we will all die. You as well. Do you understand, both of you?"

Cierán was shocked. He immediately protested. "No, Master. We not fight with you. My father say Roman fight Roman, but Helvetians never to fight Helvetians."

"I don't care what your fucking father said," Dessy shouted at him, "you will do as I say. I own you. You obey me. That's what's going to happen."

Cierán was shaking his head resolutely. "No, Master. Not to happen. Not possible to happen."

The silly idiot, Decimus thought wearily. He couldn't be bothered to explain to his slave exactly how easy it was going to be to obtain obedience to his command. He was just too tired. He put his hands on Cierán's shoulders, gently kissed him on the cheek, and said, "Get some sleep, you foolish boy, and wake up a wiser man."

Decimus spent half an hour writing a letter to his brother. But the Gods knew if it would ever reach him. He sealed it and then turned in, feeling so dispirited. He knew he would be allowed to sleep through the night. He had spent the previous three days and nights fighting, with no sleep at all, until his orders had stopped making any sense.

When he woke the next morning he experienced a feeling of relief that he was still alive. They had not been overrun. Not yet. He yelled for Cierán to arm him, as usual, and for Laeforis to get him something to eat while he was doing so. Laeforis walked off to get the day's bread ration. But there was no sign of Cierán. He had vanished. Off to sort out the horses, Dessy assumed, still feeling sleepy.

"Cierán gone," Laeforis announced, when he returned with the bread.

"What?" Dessy jumped out of bed in alarm.

"Cierán gone," repeated Laeforis firmly.

"What do you mean gone? Gone where?"

"Cierán say I have to stay and serve you, but not to fight, because you not sworn us. He gone away."

"What do you mean, not sworn us?"

"We not sworn at the altar. So we cannot fight with you."

Decimus didn't know what he was talking about. "I don't understand. You must explain."

"You take us to the altar, but we not say words. You have us branded. So, not sworn slaves."

"So did the idiot try to kill himself?" Decimus asked in anguish, "if he wasn't sworn?"

"No, Master. Just gone."

It was true. Cierán had gone, vanished in the night. There was no trace of him in camp. No one had seen him leave. Decimus felt something akin to despair. He hadn't realised how much he had come to depend on the boy, how much he loved him. His beautiful boy with his golden hair, perfect body, and perfect manners, so reliable, so steady, so pleasant to have around, with his songs and quaint sayings. Gone to join the enemy.

"Why have you stayed, Laeforis? Why didn't you leave with Cierán?" Decimus asked.

"He order me to stay and serve you. He say important I serve you. You need to be cared for. You not able to care for you."

"But why do you obey him and not me?"

Laeforis looked at him as if he was daft. "Cierán is son of the chief. Of course I obey him. He say you not make me fight."

As usual Cierán was correct.

It was dusk, thank the Gods. The Gauls retreated behind the fastness of their defences. There would be a break from the constant fighting. Decimus didn't think the enemy would try to attack on a moonless night. They could all get some sleep, now that Caesar was back with the rest of the legions. As was his friendly tribune, appearing after eighteen month's absence, without any explanation as to how he had managed to avoid being annihilated with the rest of the fourteenth legion. Rumour had it that he had been enslaved. If so, he didn't look any the worse for it. If anything he seemed to have become far more competent as an officer.

Dessy walked back from headquarters to the tent he shared again with Cassius, now he had only Laeforis and Ganainm. Cassius's slaves were busy preparing the evening meal, a couple of roasted partridges. At least the food had been good here, even if nothing else was. The slaves hastened to help him out of his armour. Decimus dropped his cloak on his bed, and stood in the centre of the tent.

"Don't I get a kiss, then?" he asked.

Ganainm ran to him at once, to be embraced gently.

"Alright, my little one?" enquired his master.

The boy nodded.

"Well, what has Caesar decided?" Cassius demanded.

"He's insane, if you ask me. He wants to make an all-out attack. But the place is so well fortified. He thinks he can trick them, but I feel Vercingetorix is unlikely to fall into any traps. And look how many troops he has under his command. I argued against it, but Caesar didn't listen to me."

"That's new."

They had a short discussion about the pros and cons of the plan. Cassius agreed it was full of holes. They ate the supper and became more cheerful. Cassius started reading a letter just delivered, the first communications they had received from Italy in months.

"Fuck!" he said.

The slaves became tense. A master swearing boded ill for the immediate future. They had better tread warily.

"Anything wrong?" asked Decimus.

"I'll say. My darling brother-in-law wishes to call in the loan he made me, so I could get my horses and servants. Where on earth am I going to get the wherewithal here? We haven't received any prize money yet from Avericum."

"It will come. At least our revered Commander knows how to keep his troops sweet. Money and women, in that order. Anyway, you always told me never to borrow money."

"Yes. Because of my experiences with my fucking brother-in-law. He keeps upping the interest. There's no way I can repay him. What the hell am I going to do?"

"I can lend you the money. Don't worry. No interest."

"I thought you didn't have much yourself," said Cassius.

"I'm a relatively rich man," explained Decimus. "My wife brought me a large dowry, but usually I keep the money for my son. You are an exception, though. So no problem."

Cassius thanked him, but was unusually silent for the rest of the evening.

As Decimus expected, Caesar's plan was disastrous. The Gauls were tricked initially into thinking they were being attacked by the cavalry at their weakest point, but soon realised their mistake. The Roman troops pushed forwards, overcoming the first line of defences, thinking they were winning easily. Decimus was worried to see how quickly the legions advanced, hardly bothering to keep in formation, despite his shouted orders. One centuria in particular was thrusting against the town walls, with many others rushing to fill in behind. In consternation Dessy observed Cassius clambering up the wall, just as Caesar realised the day was lost and ordered the trumpets to sound the retreat. Unknown to Cassius and his men, Decimus could see the Gauls piling up in huge numbers to defend the wall. Cassius reached the top of the wall and waved his sword, encouraging his troops to join him, oblivious to the signals.

"Cass, Cass, Cass! Get down! Get back for the Gods' sake!" Decimus screamed.

The figure in the distance waved again in acknowledgment. To his horror Dessy saw the dark silhouette suddenly jerk, bend over, then topple backwards off the wall. He knew then his best friend was dead. Dead because he wanted the money he would get from Caesar for being first on top of the enemy's walls. The mural crown. Why didn't the fool rely on me? thought Dessy in despair. Perhaps he didn't believe me, when I offered to lend him the money. Or he was too proud to take it.

With tears streaming from his eyes, Decimus turned to face his soldiers, yelling and screaming at them to retreat back to the camp.

The casualties were enormous, forty-six centurions dead, a third of the men wounded or killed. The hospital tent was overrun. Ruteus, the surgeon in charge, couldn't keep up, especially as he wasn't a very good surgeon. He was bawled out by his commander for sheer incompetence, and developed a black mood as a result. When the last casualty was dispatched for the night, the light being too bad for any more work, Ruteus sat in the officers' mess, nursing his sense of grievance with copious beakers of wine.

Decimus's orderly burst into his tent, in a state of distress.

"Sir, Sir! My master Ruteus is blind drunk. He is gambling with me as a stake. So far he has won, but Sir, I don't wish to be owned by General Labienus, or Quaestor Mark Antony. Is there anything you can do?"

Decimus looked at Musa, trying to rouse himself to feel any emotion other than grief. There was no way he ever gambled. He couldn't understand the fools that spent the summer campaigning, only to lose all their salary on the throw of the dice. But what use was money after all? It didn't win you real friends, or keep slaves loyal. Nevertheless he knew somewhere at the back of his mind that he was fond of the orderly. He explained sluggishly that he didn't think he could do much, but all the same he would come over to the officers' mess. He thought he might be able to persuade his friendly tribune to take part, or even the medical officer, who surely appreciated the skill of the orderly, while he was forced to work under Ruteus's supervision.

Ruteus was indeed drunk, Dessy found when he had dragged himself over. He had won a considerable amount of money, and had no need to stake his slave. Perhaps this was some sort of punishment, Decimus surmised. He was quite correct. Ruteus knew how much more skilled Musa was, and resented him professionally, whilst making a lot of money out of him. Dessy moved over to the gaming table.

Ruteus grinned to see him. "Want to try your luck against me?" he asked. "What will you stake? Four thousand gold pieces?"

Decimus had a moment's insanity. Most unusual for him. But he felt fatalistic, numb, but also a sense of mild outrage on the orderly's behalf. What a way to treat a competent loyal servant.

"He's worth more than that," said Dessy.

"How much will you stake, then?" Ruteus was too drunk to appreciate that a centurion, even a primus pilus, was hardly going to have the wherewithal to produce such a vast sum of money.

"Five thousand gold pieces," declared Decimus. He would take his whole life earning enough to pay this back, he realised. Who cared? He didn't.

The senior officers crowded round him. Dessy hadn't known how popular he was amongst his superiors.

Ruteus threw the dice first. He threw a four and a six. The mess groaned in unison. No one wanted Ruteus to win. An unpleasant man even when sober, which was seldom.

Dessy sent up a forlorn prayer to the Goddess Fortuna. He threw the dice with a careless abandon. Two sixes! The room erupted into cheers. Dessy sat in stunned silence, staring at the dice. Antony's heavy congratulatory blow on his shoulder served to rouse him from his stupor.

"Well done, Dessy. Serves the lazy bastard right," Antony declared, expressing the general view. The mess roared their approval.

"Best of three throws," said Ruteus, realising too late what a dreadful error he had made.

"No." Dessy was emphatic. "One throw is enough for me. My nerves couldn't cope with more."

Ruteus tried to think of a way out, but failed. The whole mess had witnessed the transaction.

Decimus turned to Musa, and managed to make one of the most meaningful speeches of his life.

"You are a doctor, highly skilled in both medicine and in surgical procedures, much more so than me. I am sorry that you have been debased in this fashion. I will never let such a thing happen to you again. But in the meantime, may I say how proud I am to know you are to become a part of my household."

The orderly was overcome. He just managed to whisper his thanks.

The Aeduans joined forces with Vercingetorix. News came of the slaughter of the Roman traders in Bibracte, their capital city. For Decimus it was all of a piece. His life had disintegrated. Now he had lost his sons and Ethela from his own misjudgment, as well as Óengus and Darreth. It made little difference to his mood, except that he started to hate the Gauls with an intensity that frightened Laeforis and Ganainm, who were often the recipients of his invective. The death of Cassius changed him in ways he wasn't aware of himself. He was now a vicious bunch of muscle and bone, living in order to kill or be killed. Violent death was everywhere around. He accepted it, his own as well as the enemy's. Rationality had gone, and with it some tangible force for good had disappeared. The smiling carefree officer vanished, replaced by a much harder and less principled man, Dessy knew something was missing in himself, but at first he couldn't find what was lacking. He needed Cierán, but Cierán had gone for good.

Vercingetorix was emboldened to attack the Roman Army as it was in full retreat, but miscalculated severely, and lost the major battle. Mark Antony succeeding in defeating the Gallic cavalry with his brilliant tactics. The Gauls hastily retreated and holed up at Alesia, a fortified hilltop town with little in the way of supplies, and a civilian population needing to be fed. But they weren't fed. Instead they were expelled from the town. Caesar refused to allow his men to feed them either. So they starved to death.

The Romans had completed extraordinarily elaborate siege works, stretching for miles. They also reinforced their outer defences against the Gauls, whose relieving army was again defeated by Mark Antony's cavalry. Decimus was forced to admit that in the field Antony was invincible, keeping men and horses in tight formation, knowing exactly where and when to attack. After months on starvation rations the Gauls surrendered. Vercingetorix was handed over to Caesar.

Decimus spent hours trailing around the lines of prisoners, searching for Cierán. Every so often he would catch a glimpse of a blond head, only for his hopes to be dashed. He made Laeforis search as well. Then he yelled at him for not doing his work properly, when Laeforis returned miserably to his tent, having failed to find any trace of his friend amongst the Helvetians. Several of the prisoners remembered Cierán. Decimus lost count of the number of times he was told about the wisdom and mercy of Cierán's father, and how proud he had been of his young son. But the Helvetian prisoners all insisted both Cierán and his father had perished six years ago, murdered by the Romans at the battle of Bibracte.

Laeforis was just as upset as Decimus, but got no understanding from his master. He became depressed. He had no idea where Cierán had gone, and presumed he must have been killed almost as soon as he joined the enemy forces. He wasn't much help to Decimus. He knew how Cierán would have changed his master's mood, telling stories, singing songs, and speaking the wise words of his father, but he couldn't bring himself to do anything helpful as he mourned his friend. Meanwhile Decimus threw himself into his work with a rigour that astonished his colleagues.

Decimus was given the pick of the captives to have or sell as slaves. He chose ten men, and took them to the altar, this time to swear an oath of loyalty to him. Much to his surprise they did just that. So he armed them, and ordered his tent to train them. Letters arrived from home, but he didn't want to read them any more. Letters from home were always bad news. He presumed they would be scolding him for risking and losing his sons' lives. He kept them in a little wooden box, but didn't unseal them.

There was no chance to go back to Rome that winter, as Caesar started campaigning again almost immediately. His headquarters were in Bibracte under Mark Antony, so Decimus was able to visit the house of the trader, where he had left his sons and his slaves. And see for himself that it was an empty shell, no people, no furniture or fittings. Just blood, blood everywhere, There were still streaks of rust-coloured bloodstains splashed all over the walls and on the floor. He stood in the middle of the room where he had last seen them all and started to weep.

Ganainm ran to him, put his arms round him and hugged him tightly. He tried to speak, speak for the first time in years. It came out as a series of squeaks.

"I'm here, Master." He tried again. "I'm here, Sir."

Decimus didn't even notice, shoving him roughly out of the way. Laeforis noticed though, putting his arms around the distraught boy and leading him out of the room.

Some of the Roman traders and slave dealers who had escaped the slaughter, started to trickle back into Bibracte. One night in the officers' mess, Antony leant back in his chair, put his feet on the table and asked Decimus if his slave girl Ethela was back in Bibracte.

"Yes, she's here," answered Dessy.

"Good," said Antony. "I think I'll have to requisition her, unless you've decided to sell after all?" He only made the suggestion to annoy Decimus, who was remarkably morose these days, drinking heavily all night and saying nothing.

To his surprise Decimus said, "Sure, I'll sell. Would you like to see her before we decide on the price? We'll go in the morning at first light."

They rode in silence down the hill to the now so familiar house. Antony was shocked to see the main door hanging loose on its hinges, but he followed Decimus inside the building. He was curious. Decimus led him to the empty room of slaughter. He pointed to the sheets of dried blood on the wall.

"There she is," he said. He pointed to the floor. "Those are my sons." He gestured towards the other side of the room. "And these are my slaves. You can have Ethela and welcome. You'll have to scrape her off the wall, though."

With that he walked over to the wall, placing his hands flat on the stained surface. "I'm so sorry," he whispered. "I'm so sorry."

The dreadful look on his face shocked Antony. Wordlessly he put his arm around Dessy and led him out of the house. He kept looking at his grim-faced companion on the way back to headquarters. At last he plucked up his courage.

"Dessy, maybe it's time to go home."

"No, no. I don't want to go home." Home to face the justifiable wrath of his father, and the appalling sorrow of Egnatius and Luke. The unspoken reproaches of his darling mother, who adored all of her grandsons, bond or free. "Are you suggesting that there's anything wrong with my work?"

"Nothing of the sort. Your work is exemplary, as always." High praise this from Antony.

"I'm staying in Gaul. I want to kill Gauls."

Decimus made a costly sacrifice to the Goddess Victoria, but his heart wasn't in it. He stopped cutting his hair and trimming his beard. He took a perverse pleasure in unleashing his ten Gauls on their fellow men during that year's bloody campaigning, and made a lot of money from rounding up and selling the natives.

The following year, though still comparatively young, he was made Camp Prefect. His logistical skills were superb, and his ability to enthuse his troops undiminished, despite his inward heartache. He was with Mark Antony and four legions in winter quarters. They spent the winter sniping at each other, to Caesar's great amusement.

BOOK 1: CHAPTER 23

Villa of Marcus Statilius Taurus, Rome, 51 BC

Agatha's brother wasted no time in arranging a marriage for his sister, almost as soon as the news came of Cassius Domitius's death. She was to be married to a rich man living in Capua, a wealthy merchant who openly declared his allegiance to Pompey, insisting that Pompey was the only man who stood between Rome and Caesar's dictatorship.

Portia organised a dinner to bid farewell to her, and to her son Adrian. Despite the well-known views of Agatha's future husband, Portia invited Atia and her son, Gaius Octavius, as well as Agrippa. The boys had been firm friends for years.

Adrian was devastated to be saying goodbye to his friends. Marcellus promised to write frequently, and send him his poems for his appraisal. Gaius gave him a beautiful jewelled dagger, while Agrippa gave him a set of toy soldiers, so he could practise military manoeuvres, a pastime that Agrippa loved almost more than playing with hoops or marbles.

A letter arrived from Decimus. At last he was coming home. But strangely it said nothing about his boys, or Cierán. Portia rushed round to tell Atia the good news.

There was no pleasure in this journey south. Dessy hardly spoke to his men or his slaves, only to give them necessary orders. His mood infected all his companions. When he arrived in Rome, Decimus dismissed his bodyguard, telling them to return to barracks, along with Cassius's slaves. Decimus had promised to keep them. With only Laeforis and Ganainm attending him, he rode through the familiar streets. The crowds of people hastened to clear a path for this obvious hero, with his battle honours adorning his breastplate. He reined in when he arrived at his own street, slowing his mount to a walk, putting off the evil moment. He thought with anguish about the coming confrontation with his father, where he would be told he was a naive fool to trust the barbarians. Much worse would be the meeting with Egnatius his father-in-law, to explain just how he had lost Veronica's only precious child.

Dessy arrived at the door of the house. He took some deep breaths to calm his nerves, knowing that inside these familiar walls, there would be constant reminders of everything he had loved and lost. He rapped on the outer door leading to the stables, to be admitted by the astonished porter, who couldn't understand this subdued approach. The porter knew that the family were planning a huge celebration for Master Decimus's safe return. Laeforis and Ganainm were brusquely ordered to stable the horses.

Dessy walked through the archway into the courtyard. He stood stunned, rigid with shock. He could see a pretty young woman on a stool, and a circle of small boys and bigger boys and girls sitting on the ground around a man with long blond hair, who had his back to him. The man was chained to the whipping post.

Cierán twisted round to see who this was, who had arrived unannounced by the porter. He took one look at his master, and jumped to his feet, his chains clinking in protest.

"Uncle Dessy," cried Marcellus. He leapt up, heedlessly dropping his tablet and stylus on the ground, and ran over for a hug. Dessy had his arms round the boy, but was looking straight at Cierán.

"Cierán," he croaked, hardly able to believe his eyes.

"Master, you're home safely," said Cierán, and bowed deeply. "Thanks be to the Gods." Then he turned to the children and said, "Master Lucas, greet your father."

A small boy detached himself from the group of excited whispering children and approached Decimus hesitantly. He hadn't seen his father for two years, so wasn't sure what to do, and didn't recognise this man with his long dark hair and untrimmed beard. Dessy solved his problem by lifting him up into his arms and kissing him. He did the same with his other small sons. Then he turned to face Cierán, took him in his arms and crushed him to his chest, despite being hindered by the chains. He was speechless to start with, and they both had tears running down their cheeks.

Cierán was worried, though he didn't show it. There had been no word at all from his master, despite Lucanus's repeated attempts to ask his brother whether any punishment was to be imposed on this disobedient but heroic slave. Marcus had been predicting dire consequences for him, ever since the news came that Dessy was coming home, whereas Lucanus was constantly reassuring.

"Why are you chained? Who ordered this?"

"It was your distinguished father, Master, because I do a bad thing. I disobey you. He say you will have me crucified. But when your father goes for his siesta, your brother has me unchained. He say I do good things as well."

Decimus looked round at the group, hardly daring to ask, his voice shaking. "Ethela?"

"She probably feeding the baby, now," Cierán answered. "Master Marcellus, please to tell Ethela that the master is here."

"What baby?"

"Your baby, Master. Little girl. We call her Ella," Cierán explained. "When she was born Ethela had to lie on the ground by the roadside, and tell us what to do. It hurts the girls bad to have babies. But Ethela made no noise in case we were found out. She is one brave girl."

Decimus shouted for the steward, insisting that the chains be instantly removed.

"You not mad with me?" Cierán asked, rubbing his wrists.

Dessy shook his head. "How could I possibly be mad with you? You have made me so happy. How did you manage to save them all?"

"I am very bad man," Cierán confessed. "I take letter you write to your brother. So I say to all, very important I must take letter to Rome, with your sons and your slave girl. It is your orders." He bowed again. "Master, can I greet my friends?"

"Of course."

Ganainm and Laeforis came forward to be hugged, and then found themselves being embraced by Óengus and Darreth in turn.

"*I'm sorry, I'm sorry,*" whispered Cierán to Laeforis, "*but I couldn't tell you my plan. The master would have made you tell him everything.*"

Hardly pausing to greet his father and brother, who had just emerged from the house, Decimus rushed to his bedroom, to find Ethela was indeed feeding the baby. She looked up at him with such an expression of joy, he felt his heart leap within him. He knelt on the ground and put his arms round both of them.

Portia came running into the room and hugged him with enthusiasm. "Darling Dessy. You found Cierán. Isn't he a marvel? So brave of him. So clever of him to rescue them all. Look at Ella. Isn't she lovely?"

She certainly was. A beautiful little girl with blonde hair, and with her mother's blue eyes.

"We've missed you so much for the last two years," Portia continued. "Atia is dying to see you."

Ethela made a little moue of disgust.

In the evening Decimus insisted that they dine in Gallic fashion, with his slaves at the table. He had Ethela next to him on his couch. He couldn't stop touching her, stroking her arm, playing with her hair, or picking up her hand and kissing her fingers. A problem bubbled to the surface of his mind. It needed solving.

"Ethela, are you jealous of Lady Atia?"

Ethela laughed. To her Atia was just a scrawny old lady. She had no idea why Dessy was so enamoured of her. "Why I be jealous of her, Master? Cierán tell me that Mark Antony offer ten thousand sesterces for me, and you say 'not for sale.' You must like me a little bit, I think. But when I am old and ugly, then you will sell me."

"Cierán said you were so brave, making no sound when you had baby Ella. I will free you, my lovely girl, as soon as it can be arranged."

"And Mochán?" Ethela was tense with hope.

"And Mochán and Ella. All of you."

Dessy looked at his slave girl. Her eyes were shining with unshed tears. She was so beautiful, he realised. He loved her so much. He leant forward and softly kissed her sweet mouth. "You like *me*, don't you? A little bit?"

"I not like your hair and beard."

"I'll have to do something about it, then."

"Before you come to bed," said Ethela firmly.

When Cierán tried to explain, Decimus began to understand how hard it had been for his slaves, to keep Ethela and all the children safe on their long journey through enemy lines. Especially when Darreth behaved like a complete idiot, and nearly got them all killed, Cierán thought, but he had promised Óengus to say nothing of this to their master.

"I hear from the Aeduans in camp that their countrymen intend to desert Caesar and join Vercingetorix. They mean to attack the Romans in Bibracte, so I know Ethela and your sons in great danger. But I cannot tell you. You are the enemy still, although you are my master." Cierán wasn't sure that his master would understand his thinking, but Decimus just nodded.

"You write letter to your brother, and seal it. So I take the letter and go out with the cavalry." He made it sound simple, but Decimus knew better.

"And just how did you manage that?"

Cierán smiled. "I take three horses and two slaves from the Remi, so I look like cavalryman."

"Two slaves?"

"Yes. Two Remi slaves. They think they will be killed if they stay in camp. They *want* to come with me. Here they are." Cierán waved an imperious arm and gestured to two servants standing nearby, with anxious expressions on their faces. They dropped instantly onto their knees. Cierán smiled. "They think maybe you punish them. I say no, you no punish them."

"No, of course not," said Dessy in astonishment.

"I take gold as well. Gold from the Remi. Traitors." Cierán shrugged his shoulders, expressing his contempt for all things Remi. "So I reach Bibracte and your letter work like a magic spell. I say my orders are to take your son to Rome, with all your servants."

"You are my bravest boy. Thank you, Cierán. I thank you from the bottom of my heart. I am so sorry you were chained up."

"It is good, Master. Lady Portia's secretary teach me to read and write in the mornings."

"The girl on a stool?"

"Yes. Penelope. She is a good teacher. She teach your boys, and Óengus and Darreth as well. Ethela too. Lady Caecilia say...." Cierán hesitated, then started again. "Lady Caecilia *says* it is good to learn. I wish to marry Penelope, but she won't marry a slave." Cierán smiled at his master.

"I am going to free all of you. Ethela as well. You are heroes. I wish you to stay with me, but I know how you long to go home."

Cierán shook his head. "Not any more. We travelled through my country, Helvetia. I find my uncle has take over all our land. He let us sleep in the cow-shed." Cierán pulled a face of disgust. "When we leave he say, 'Don't come back.' I am son of the chief, you see. My father was Cierán, the Wise and Just. My people wanted me to stay, but that would mean war between my uncle and me. Not good for my people."

"I searched for you amongst the prisoners after Alesia. I thought you must have gone to join Vercingetorix. Many of them knew of you and your father. They told me stories about his wisdom. How he spent one hundred years, untying the Gordian Knot."

Cierán laughed. "No, only ninety-nine years, my father say. It teached him patience."

Dessy stared at him.

"He was making a joke, Master. Did you hear the story about the baby that two women claimed? So he order the baby to be cut in two pieces? I've heard three different endings, but my father say he never did any such thing. Some other wise man, maybe."

"Did my father ever find out that you were released in the afternoons?"

Cierán's eyes sparkled with laughter. "Yes, Master. Sometimes I read to Lady Caecilia. She has difficulty holding a book now. So one afternoon your father walk in. He is shocked. He ask me what I am doing without the chains. So I kneel down and say to him that he is wise and just, like my own father, so he chain me only in the mornings. He is very pleased to be told he is wise and just."

Decimus freed all of his slaves, the children and Ethela as well. The men were given the name Statilius Taurus to add to their own, as was customary. When Dessy discovered that Óengus had fallen heavily for Veronica's maid, he freed her as well. He didn't think he would have any more use for her. In fact he wondered why he had so much as looked at her; she was such a shy mouse-like creature. She no longer appealed, now he had his darling Ethela. Although Portia maintained that Dora was a good mother to her son Manius. Clearly a lot of things had been going on in the house while he was away.

Poor Laeforis was upset to find that Dessy's other slaves had all been taught to read and write, while he was left behind in Gaul with his foul-tempered master. Darreth wasted no opportunity in making him feel ignorant. Decimus told him that now he was free, it would be put right. Laeforis had patiently coped with his master's fury and frustration, despite his own grief. Decimus knew he owed him a lot.

After the ceremony, to Dessy's astonishment, he found Ganainm in floods of tears in the corner of his bedroom.

"Hey, baby boy. What's the matter with you?" Dessy asked in consternation.

It took some time for Cierán to work it out. "He want to be freed, too, Master."

Dessy pulled the miserable boy down to sit beside him on his bed, one arm round his waist. "I can't free you, Ganainm. You are from the Remi tribe, our allies. You were never a slave. But I would like you to stay with me. Will you, please?" He held out his hand.

Ganainm stopped whimpering, sighed with relief, put his hand into Dessy's, and nodded.

"Thank you," said Dessy.

Decimus lay in bed that night feeling so happy, with his arms round his newly freed woman, sure he had done the right thing. And now he had another child, he thought to himself. Such a beautiful child too, with her golden hair just like Cierán's. His mind jumped immediately to the next thought. So could it possibly be that Cierán and Ethela.........?

He tightened his grip round Ethela.

"Mmm?" she said.

He kissed her mouth. "Go back to sleep."

No, no, no! Don't think it. He would be forced to kill them, Ella as well. So don't think it. Don't *ever* think it! Don't even let the possibility enter into his mind. That would be disastrous.

BOOK 2

Nos sibi reserat genitale secretum universum.
Simul tetigit nos ita gaudium haec mirantibus
Inmortales, tantum obtinere censuimus quasi
uni iacebat corpus nos novae spes
amor noster tenet clavis nos creatum est ipsa vita.

Fragment attributed to 'Marcellus'

"We have unlocked the secrets of the Universe
"Together we have touched such joy, such wonder
"As we thought only the immortals could obtain.
"When our bodies lay together we made a new hope,
"Our love holds the key. We have created life itself.

BOOK 2 : CHAPTER 1

House of Claudius Marcellus, 51/ 50 BC

Nothing much had changed for Octavia. She was as virginal as ever, her husband making no further attempts to do anything about the situation. He encouraged her to visit his sister, who had a little girl of two years. Little Cornelia was sweet, lovable and affectionate. Octavia loved to visit. Unfortunately the little girl had a wine-stain mark on part of her face and neck. Her father hoped she would become a Vestal Virgin, as her marriage prospects were so poor. He needed to get some use out of her in the future.

The Senate was gradually coming round to the opinion that Pompey was a safer bet, after his year as sole Consul favoured them rather than his former father-in-law, Julius Caesar, the so-called 'Man of the People.' Lucius Philippus spent most evenings at his stepdaughter Octavia's house, plotting with her husband Claudius and his fellow conspirators. He rarely brought his wife, and Atia didn't often come to visit herself. When she did, her comments were invariably acerbic. Octavia was always relieved when her mother went home again.

Octavia was given a list of dinner guests she was to invite each night, mostly the Senators jealous of Caesar's increasing power, Marcus Cicero, Marcus Brutus, Cassius Longinus, and many others. This time the dinner was special, given to celebrate Claudius's election to be Consul the following year. Philippus had managed to swing the vote at the popular assembly. Octavia sat on her husband's couch, saying nothing, but noting everything.

Philippus repeatedly harangued his fellow diners, attempting to rustle up and consolidate support. "Look, these Gallic wars have admittedly extended Roman rule as far as the Channel and the Rhine, but that's given Caesar a fortune. He's busy bribing the plebs with banquets and games. We must stop him. If we're not careful, we'll have another Sulla."

The support was quickly forthcoming. "Yes, and it's given him extraordinary military power as well. He has ten legions of veteran soldiers under his command. He's rather usurped Pompey as the strong man of Rome, I'm afraid," said Claudius Marcellus.

"I've heard that Pompey is coming round to our point of view. Sound him out, would you, Philippus?" Cato asked.

"Do you think Caesar will tamely disband his troops in order to stand for Consul as a private citizen? He has to be here personally, in Rome. He's not allowed to bring an army with him," Brutus argued.

"But that's what Pompey did ten years ago."

"Didn't do him a lot of good, though, did it? He had to choose between having a Triumph and becoming Consul, and he chose the Triumph."

"He didn't need to be Consul then. He had an alliance with Caesar and Crassus. But Crassus is dead, and so is Julia. And Pompey is coming to realise that only he and the Senate stand between Caesar and tyranny," said Brutus. "We must stand firm."

The conflict between Caesar and Pompey, predicted so often by Adrian's stepfather, finally broke out. To Octavia's horror it was her husband Claudius Marcellus's actions as Consul which finally precipitated the crisis. When they discovered what was going on in the Senate, Octavia, Atia, and Portia thought the men's actions were insane. Did they want another civil war? Apparently they did.

Lucanus came limping back from the Senate, supported by his slaves, with a bloodied swelling on his jaw and his toga torn.

"What happened to you, Luke? Did someone attack you in the street?" Decimus asked in shock.

Lucanus sat down wearily, while Portia rushed around with a bowl of water and a cloth.

"No, I was attacked in the Senate! It was a riot today. A big fight between those supporting Caesar and the others siding with Pompey. I got up to speak, to get them to calm down, because they were all shouting and swearing so loudly at each other no one could hear a word. But someone grabbed my toga and ripped it, and then someone else swung at me. Then Cassius trod on my foot, I'm not sure whether by design or not. So I thought it best to retire while I was still in one piece."

Decimus turned to find Ganainm standing next to him, proffering a glass of wine. Dessy handed it to his brother, horrified to see Luke's hand shaking a little as he gratefully gulped it down.

"Explain," said Dessy.

"I don't know how much you are aware of your commander's plans?"

"He hasn't confided in me, but we all know he wants a Triumph. He damn well deserves one, too. I'm pretty sure he wants to be Consul as well."

"You left Caesar at Ravenna, outside Italy?"

"Yes. He is camping quite legitimately with only the thirteenth legion. What's wrong with that?"

"Nothing, as yet. He's sent Mark Antony with a letter to the Senate, explaining that he wants to stand for Consul whilst remaining in Cisalpine Gaul. When Claudius Marcellus read it out, there was uproar. Everyone knows this is strictly against the laws of the Republic. To be elected he has to be present in Rome, and without an army."

"Couldn't they make an exception for him? He has achieved so much."

"It won't happen, Dessy. He has many enemies in the Senate. The new Consul, Claudius Marcellus, hates him. Caesar offered his wife to Pompey without consulting him, making him look weak and powerless. He is getting his revenge, now. Unfortunately Caesar is well aware that he will be prosecuted if he returns to Rome as a private citizen without Consular immunity."

"Why, Luke? On what grounds?"

"Mainly on the grounds that he has conducted illegal wars, without Senatorial approval. After all, he had no permission to go to Britain, let alone conquer Celtic Gaul. And he is thought to have committed war crimes against some of the Gallic princes. On his own admission he had two of them flogged to death, and had others murdered. Anyway, Claudius has turned him down on both counts. Even worse he's refused to allow any of Caesar's reports to be read or debated in the Senate House."

Marcus was astonished and flattered when Mark Antony asked if he could come round and discuss the present situation with him. He was thrilled to be in the midst of the political controversy. It was years since anyone had actively sought his opinion. Although he soon realised that it was his sons' opinions that were being sought.

Cierán met Antony and his escort at the door. Antony took one look at him, and jabbed him in the chest with his finger.

"I know you. Now why do I know you?" Antony demanded.

"When you were stationed in North Gaul, you ordered me to throw a javelin at a legionary, Sir. And I refused."

Antony laughed. "Yes, now I remember. Stubborn bastard, aren't you?"

Cierán smiled and agreed.

Marcus summoned his two sons to the conference.

"At present Pompey controls two legions, stationed just outside Rome," Lucanus explained. "They are supposedly to be used in a war against Parthia. He has six more legions in Spain, the province he governs."

"Well, how can we persuade the Senate to listen to Caesar? The last thing we want is a civil war," said Antony. "The plebeians are scared stiff."

Marcus agreed. "I've lived through and fought in previous civil wars. Dreadful. They should be avoided at all costs."

"I think, Sir, that we must attempt to persuade the Senate to give in to Caesar's not unreasonable demands," Antony declared.

"Not everyone agrees that his demands are reasonable," said Luke. "There are a great many unreasonable people in the Senate at the moment."

"At present he can send for and easily mobilise his troops in Gaul, eight legions of battle-hardened troops. What do you think, Dessy?"

Decimus spoke slowly. "I think Caesar and Pompey have been desperate to have a go at each other, ever since the deaths of Julia and Crassus. Each wants to be top dog. I don't think anyone can stop them fighting for the prize. I can't see either of them backing down and disbanding their troops."

Antony sighed and agreed. "I think you may be right, Dessy." He gestured in Cierán's direction. "You'll need your javelin thrower, then."

Lucanus couldn't name any additional supporters of Caesar in the Senate that weren't already known. Opinions had coalesced around either Caesar or Pompey. The Caesarian faction was outnumbered. After the conversation petered out, with no obvious solution, Antony rose and took his leave.

"I presume Caesar can count on your support?" Antony asked the brothers, as he was on his way out.

"Of course," said Lucanus.

"I'm Caesar's man," said Dessy. "I always will be. Almost everything I have comes from him, including my javelin thrower."

Decimus decided it was time for a show of force. He accompanied his brother to the Senate sessions, surrounded by his ten heavily-armed Gauls, but had to remain outside. Meanwhile the Senate argued backwards and forwards that Caesar and Pompey should both disband their armies. Mark Antony used his veto against the many proposals from Claudius and Lentulus, the other Consul, that would be injurious to Caesar. With Pompey breathing over his shoulder, Claudius Marcellus demanded that only Caesar disband his army and return to Rome. This proposal was carried, with shouts and cheers from Pompey's supporters drowning out the opposition. Mark Antony was man-handled out of the Senate. He staggered out of the door, almost falling into Dessy's arms.

"Stupid bastards," Antony snarled. "They won't listen to me. They don't know what they've let themselves in for."

Dessy and the Gauls accompanied Antony back to his house. Antony didn't hang around. Decimus was impressed with the speed at which preparations were made for his journey north. When it was time to set off Antony mounted his horse, then leaned down and grasped Dessy's hand.

"You'll be sent for. You've had a nice long leave."

"Of course, Sir," Dessy agreed soberly. "No problem."

Antony raced back to Caesar. Which all left Caesar with no option but to cross the Rubicon with the thirteenth legion, and enter Italy under arms, having prudently sent for his other legions in Gaul. He declared publicly that this stain on his reputation, his dignity, couldn't be borne, and could be resolved only by brute force.

Pompey with his two legions and most of the Senate fled to Capua. To everyone's surprise Titus Labienus, Caesar's successful second-in-command throughout those Gallic wars, sided with Pompey and the Senate.

Decimus had to use all his powers of persuasion on Cierán to get him to fight alongside him. He realised that the other Gauls would obey Cierán, as the son of the chief, rather than him, even though Cierán wasn't their own chief.

"You get to kill Romans, revenge for your defeat," Dessy started. "Revenge for your father's death."

Cierán thought he should be fighting on the other side, in that case. Caesar caused his father's death, not Pompey. Wisely he said nothing of this to Decimus.

"Maybe Helvetians fight for Pompey and Labienus."

"I've not heard of any, truly. Plenty of Gauls, but mostly the Aeduans, Belgae, Nervii. If we come across any Helvetians on the other side, you have my permission not to fight them."

"Your men will think I'm a coward."

"No they won't." Dessy thought for a moment. What else? "You will become rich. There is always booty to be shared out. Sometimes slaves and horses as well as money. You will need money when Penelope has her child." Cierán's wife was due to give birth in the next month. Now Cierán was looking thoughtful. "Look, I'll give you Cassius's slaves. Okay, they're not very bright, but they can cook. And they know how things are done in the army. You'll get your own tent."

That seemed to clinch it. Cierán burst out laughing. "How will I be able to sleep without your gentle snores as a lullaby, Master?"

To Dessy's surprise Cierán said he wished first to speak to Marcus before finally making up his mind. "Will you ask him for me, Sir?"

Dessy agreed, intrigued. He accompanied his freedman to the resulting interview. Cierán started by kneeling at the feet of Marcus and kissing his hand.

"Sir," he said when he got up again. "You are like my own father, wise and just. Dessy wishes me to fight alongside him. I am worried though, that there may be opponents from my own country. I would be grateful for your opinion on the matter."

"My dear boy, from my own selfish point of view I would be delighted if you fought alongside my son. As we know, Dessy sometimes, not often admittedly, but sometimes makes rash decisions."

"Since when have I ever made rash decisions?" Decimus protested angrily.

His father ignored him. He could have mentioned the appalling risk Dessy had taken with little Lucas and the others, and this dangerous affair with Lady Atia. But knowing Dessy, it would just lead to a shouting match. "You are so steady and reliable, Cierán," Marcus continued. "You would be an asset, an invaluable counterbalance of reasoned argument."

"But am I to fight my own countrymen?"

"My boy, your father must be so proud of you. I truly believe that he would see nothing wrong with you committing yourself to fight with Dessy, even though there is a remote chance that you may harm some of your fellow countrymen. Dessy is Caesar's man, which you may not agree with. But you are Dessy's man, are you not? So go with my blessing. I hope and pray I speak for your father."

"Thank you, Sir. I will abide by your decision." Cierán kissed Marcus's hand again before leaving the room.

Afterwards Cierán explained. "When your father had me chained I think he later regretted his decision, but he could never say so. Every morning he would come to ensure I was well, and in no danger from anyone. I think he was worried about your steward." Cierán smiled. "You are fortunate to have such a wise father."

Decimus made each of his Gauls into a decurion in charge of thirty auxiliary cavalrymen, but with Cierán in overall command. Their troops were a mixture of nationalities, but mostly Gauls and Spanish. He found Cierán to be a harsh disciplinarian, but his men were swiftly turned into a properly functioning unit. Although Cierán was always most concerned for their welfare, ensuring his men and his slaves were adequately clothed and fed.

The war had now been raging for three years. First Caesar defeated six legions in Spain, then, despite an enormous setback at Dyrrachium, he defeated Pompey's forces at Pharsalus. The fleeing Pompey was killed by the Egyptians, but like the Hydra, others arose to take his place. His allies Scipio, Cato, and King Juba carried on the war in Africa, together with Labienus and Pompey's two sons, Gnaeus and Sextus.

Caesar decided it was time for his great nephew to do a little fighting, and sent for him, but Atia and Philippus refused to allow him to go, to Gaius's disgust. Lucanus was co-opted by Caesar, to fight alongside Decimus in the African campaign, during which time Luke came to realise just how competent a soldier Dessy was. It was funny to be taking orders from his younger brother, but Decimus was so good at his job, it was a pleasure to see him in action. As well, Luke discovered that Cierán and his fellow Gauls had proved to be great fighters, armed with nerves of steel. Cierán had absorbed many of his master's precepts over the years. He had become a brilliant tactician. Each Gaul was now a senior officer in charge of a thousand cavalrymen, again with Cierán in overall command. He was forced to keep a close check on Darreth, whose exuberance sometimes led him to act precipitately, leading to problems in the field. But Óengus and Laeforis were always rock solid and reliable. Luke found that watching the horses and riders' manoeuvres in close formation almost took his breath away. They moved as an astonishing cohesive whole. Then the mass of men and horses split down the middle, circling round the enemy, hurling their javelins with terrible effect.

All the Gauls were now well off, with their own tents, slaves, and horses. The campaigns in Egypt and the Middle East had proved highly lucrative for all. Caesar was full of praise for them. After the rather disgusting end of the war at Thapsus, where the opposing forces were massacred, they all returned to Rome for the Triumphs.

Rome had never seen Triumphs like this before, four in all, outdoing even Pompey the Great in magnificence, games, and public banquets. Gaius Octavius was pleased to be awarded military honours for the African Triumph, even though he hadn't participated. He rode alongside Caesar's chariot. His friends were jealous, and made many disparaging remarks and snide comments. But Caesar wasn't able to rest on his laurel crowns for long. It turned out that the remnants of the Pompeian forces in Africa had fled to Further Spain, with Titus Labienus, and Pompey's two sons, Gnaeus Pompey and his younger brother Sextus. Apparently they were busy raising troops and coercing the population into giving large quantities of money to their cause. They would have to be dealt with.

Decimus was given the unenviable task of rounding up all the legionaries who had just been discharged, and forming them into their legions once more. He was successful, being his usual persuasive self. The troops were promised more land and more pay. Before setting out with his legions for Further Spain to settle the war once and for all, Caesar asked Decimus to dine with the other senior officers.

During the course of the evening Caesar made a point of praising Dessy's achievements, and said, "Dessy, I would like you to use your powers of persuasion on my niece, Atia."

This elicited a crack of laughter from Mark Antony. Decimus scowled at him.

"I want her son, young Gaius Octavius and any of his friends that would like to join us to come with us to Further Spain. I think we will soon be finishing off these rebellious individuals, once and for all. I would like Gaius Octavius to be there to witness my triumph. Take all the time you need."

This caused another snort of derision from Antony. One day that bastard is going to get his comeuppance, Dessy thought to himself. And the sooner the better. To his astonishment Caesar still intended to leave Antony in charge of Italy when the rest of them set off for Further Spain, despite the mounting evidence of his incompetence.

Lady Atia remained unconvinced of the necessity for her son's presence in a war at so tender an age, so Dessy gave up trying for the moment, and just delighted in their present encounters. They were now so attuned to each other that love-making was an exquisite joy for both. Atia found herself wondering how on earth she was going to cope when Dessy left her yet again for war. Should she be one of those dreadful women who kept a slave for sex, or should she be one of those who visited the gladiators the night before the Games? She knew she would never stoop so low, but it was hard and getting ever harder.

BOOK 2 : CHAPTER 2

Further Spain, 46 BC

Adrian arrived from Capua by night with devastating news. He was forced by his stepfather to take up a position as military tribune with the remnants of the Pompeian forces in Spain, despite his father having died fighting for Caesar. No arguments prevailed against his stepfather and uncle. Despite this, the hastily summoned Gaius Octavius and Marcus Agrippa were generous with their good wishes for his success. The parting with Marcellus was tearful on both sides.

Adrian took ship at Ostia, and sailed first to the Balearic Islands, to the military base there, still held by the Pompeian forces, and then to Cartagena. After that it was a long slow journey through Further Spain. Adrian made friends easily with Maximus, another new junior tribune with no military experience. Both were from equally unimportant families. They arrived at the well-fortified camp of Gnaeus Pompey, outside Córduba, and reported at once to the praesidium, where they were received by Titus Labienus, the second in command. The Camp Prefect arranged for their accommodation. They were to share a tent initially. A servant was deputed to show them and their slaves to their quarters, and then take them to the officers' mess for a banquet to welcome them both. Adrian and Maximus found themselves enthusiastically received by their fellow officers.

They survived the initiation ceremony, which Adrian hated, but which Max accepted with his usual stoicism. Three weeks later all the junior officers were summoned to a strategy meeting at headquarters. They were told of the plans to ambush

Caesar's forces on the march. The plans were rolled out and the details hammered home. Then Labienus, smiling like a crocodile, asked for volunteers for a dangerous assignment.

"I'm sure our new officers will be happy to seize this chance for glory, will they not?" he asked, smiling directly at Adrian.

Reluctantly Adrian stood up. Silently Max joined him.

They were each given a few legionaries, two smelly Spanish guides, and a rudimentary map, and sent off to ascertain the location of the enemy camp. Adrian wondered why they were obliged to wear full uniform and armour. He was told he might need to fight, if any small parties of enemy were found. But otherwise they were to keep under cover. Max said he thought they employed scouts to do this, rather than raw rookies. Both were sure they were putting their heads in a noose, but didn't want to upset the other by saying so outright.

Max said that they should separate, and explore the wide valley on both sides. So that's what they did. They filled their wine-skins with water from the clear stream running along the valley bottom. The guides were marching swiftly, but always moving from cover to cover, along the edges of woods, or in culverts. Adrian found it hard to keep up; his armour was heavy and bulky. The vegetation was lush, difficult to wade through, with trails of ivy and brambles trying to trip them up. It was so hot at midday, he told the men to stop and rest in the shade. There was no sign of any camp so far.

After marching for what seemed like many miles it became too dark to proceed further. Adrian suggested they bivouac for the night. The legionaries produced some bread and smoked ham for his supper, and helped him off with his armour. The guides curled up on the ground, but the legionaries formed their cloaks round their spears to make a shelter for their officer. Adrian sorted out the guard rota, though he had no idea how they would know when to change, but the men just accepted his orders. He lay wrapped in his cloak on the cold ground and wondered what the hell he was doing. And was Max doing the same? He hoped so.

He woke stiff and sore the next morning. The guides had vanished in the night, the guard baffled and angry. Adrian told them it wasn't their fault. It was so dark, and they couldn't use lamps or light fires. Although for some reason unknown to Adrian, one of the legionaries was charged with carrying a clay fire-pot. They travelled east for several miles, still sticking to cover as much as possible, until they eventually found evidence of log cutting. A considerable number of people had been involved, which pointed more to an army, than to peasant farmers clearing ground. Adrian ordered the men to move as quietly as possible.

They were inching their way along a wide ditch, when a large posse of men fell on them. Adrian's helmet was knocked off his head. He felt a searing pain in his scalp. He drew his sword, only to have it knocked instantly out of his hand. He was surrounded by enemy troops. He stood helplessly, blood running into his eyes and down his face, watching his legionaries run for their lives. The enemy were so pleased to have caught a tribune, they weren't that interested in pursuing the others, although several did make a half-hearted effort to run after them, and managed to grab a few.

Adrian was marched to the enemy camp, which was so near, and so obvious, surrounded by a deep ditch with vertical sides and a rampart in front of the wooden palisade. How could they have missed it? His hands were forced behind his back and tied too tightly. He protested, but the soldiers just laughed. They stripped off his armour. Then they tied his feet together, and lifted him up bodily onto a trestle table. Two remained with him while the rest went off to report their prize captive with great glee.

Nothing happened for an hour, during which time the pain in Adrian's tightly bound hands became worse and worse, until he could almost think of nothing else. He made his brain face the fact that he knew his own side's battle plans, and that someone would try and force information out of him. He determined to give nothing away, not even his name, but oh, God, if only his hands could be untied.

A figure approached, wearing a helmet and elaborate armour, surrounded by a group of impeccably turned out legionaries and a couple of nicely dressed servants. Dessy and Adrian had once met for an hour, many years ago at Dessy's wedding. Not since. Neither had any idea who the other was.

Decimus looked curiously at Adrian, and removed his own helmet, whereupon the servants swiftly unbuckled his armour. A camp prefect wouldn't normally be expected to interrogate a prisoner. Dessy had been delighted to leave that part of his military duties behind, but a tribune, however young and inexperienced, was quite a prize. Over the years Dessy had refined his techniques to such an extent that he usually had prisoners eating out of his hand in no time, metaphorically speaking, he smiled to himself. He didn't think this wounded youngster would cause him any problems. The boy looked familiar. But that was the trouble with civil war, friend and foe looked much the same.

Decimus came over with a warm friendly smile, and perched on the edge of the table, attempting to interpret Adrian's expression. He saw the dread, terror, and pain, but there was something else, determination?

"So who do we have here, all trussed up like a goose ready to roast?" asked Decimus.

"We found this tribune and a group of legionaries about a quarter of a mile from camp, Sir."

Decimus touched Adrian's arm lightly. "Do you have a name, Tribune?"

"I don't intend to give you any information," Adrian replied with an effort.

"Not even your name?" Decimus asked, still smiling.

"No." Adrian shook his head miserably.

Dessy laughed. "Then I'll have to name you myself, I suppose. You're new to all this, aren't you? You look very young to me. I think I'll call you, 'Baby Boy.'"

The legionaries laughed as well.

"I'm eighteen," Adrian said desperately. He was shifting around on the table now, in so much discomfort, he was unable to keep still.

"So old," smiled Decimus. "But I thought you weren't going to give me any information?"

The pain in Adrian's hands was overwhelming. He couldn't think straight anymore. "No, I...." he gasped out. "I........I'm sorry." He felt so confused, the agony of his hands too much for coherence.

Decimus continued to scrutinise Adrian's face. "You are in a lot of pain, aren't you, baby boy?" Clearly he would get nothing out of this lad until he was sorted out. "Are you going to tell me why? No?"

Dessy grasped the boy's chin and tilted his head down. He inspected the damage. "You've quite a nasty scalp wound, but it's not that, is it, baby?" He walked round behind Adrian, and spotted the white bloodless hands. "Ah, now I see."

Decimus carefully cut the too-tight knots with the point of his dagger. The cords loosened, and fell onto the table. "Untie his feet," he ordered one of the legionaries, "and find the idiot who tied the tribune up."

Adrian tried to move his stiff shoulders. He couldn't help but let out a sob, as the blood started to trickle back into his fingers. Tears ran down his face and dripped onto his tunic. Decimus picked up one of his hands and began to gently massage the fingers. In a quiet voice he told one of the servants to do the same to the other hand.

"Now, boy, let me see you try to close your hands," Dessy ordered. "Look! Try and make a fist, like this," he demonstrated.

He wasn't at all surprised to find that the boy obeyed him without thinking, but Adrian's swollen fingers were so painful and stiff, he couldn't move them much at all.

A terrified legionary appeared.

"In another hour the tribune's hands would have become permanently useless because he was tied too tightly. Go and tell your centurion you are to receive twenty lashes for idiocy," said Dessy, "and then come back here and apologise to the tribune."

The legionary saluted and walked away, shoulders drooping in dejection.

"You need a drink, baby boy," said Decimus. "And so do I."

One of the servants poured out a large mug of wine. Decimus drank deeply, then held out the mug to be refilled.

"You'll like this," he told his prisoner. "It will help your hands. Here, I'll hold it for you."

Adrian was hot and thirsty. He knew the wine might weaken his resistance, but on the other hand perhaps it would give him some courage. He felt so shaken and helpless, and his head ached dreadfully. He tried to work out why his interrogator was being kind to him, but couldn't come up with any satisfactory explanation.

Once Decimus was satisfied that the boy had drunk a sufficient quantity, he suggested a visit to the latrine trench, which was accepted with the usual eagerness. Dessy helped the boy off the table, holding him under his arms. Adrian could feel the strangely intimate warmth of his body, so close to him. Decimus made sure his prisoner could stand unaided, although Adrian was a little unsteady at first, and had him taken over. By the time the soldiers brought the boy back, Dessy had all the equipment he needed.

Adrian was stripped of his clothes, making him feel even more terrified. Then he was pulled round so his body could be examined for wounds, just as if he were a slave being assessed for market, he thought in despair.

"Could be a lot worse," said Dessy cheerfully. He pushed his victim down onto a stool. "Your Mama wouldn't like the state of you at present," Dessy smiled at the sick expression on the young man's face. "So I'm going to stitch you back together again. I want you to keep working away at your hands. I know it hurts, but the more you try to move your fingers, the quicker you will recover. Will you be able to keep still?"

Adrian thought he could.

"Close your eyes, then," Dessy ordered.

"Why?" asked Adrian, fearfully.

"I'm going to pour vinegar over this scalp wound, to disinfect it. You won't like it if it goes in your eyes," Decimus explained. "And I'm afraid your scalp will sting a bit. Sorry about that."

A little later he said, "You have blood all over your eyelids, baby boy, so keep them closed for the moment."

Decimus gently bathed his prisoner's face and then began the suturing. This wasn't going anything like Adrian's imaginings. It felt odd and painful having the skin of his scalp tugged and pulled and stitched together, but it was bearable. He wondered about Max. What had happened to him? And when was the torture going to start?

"That's my good boy," Dessy murmured absently as he was nearing the end of his repair work. He bathed the stitches in vinegar, warning again that it might sting. He looked down at Adrian and smiled at him. "How are you managing? Alright?"

Adrian agreed he was alright.

"But you're shaking," Dessy pointed out. "What are you afraid of? Me?"

Adrian shivered. "Yes, you." He thought for a moment. "And spiders," he added.

Decimus laughed aloud. "Spiders! So all we have to do to scare you is produce some large hairy spiders?"

"No." Adrian decided he must have drunk far too much wine. He'd never told anyone else of this weird fear of his. "Ones that take you by surprise. Those ones."

Decimus heard a muffled exclamation from one of his legionaries.

"For the Gods' sake," Dessy exclaimed. "Not you, too, Piso?"

"I don't like them, Sir, and that's a fact. Don't get me wrong. I can manage to kill them alright."

"I should fucking well hope so," said Dessy.

"It's the ghost wot I'm scared of," piped up another legionary. "Spiders is alright."

"What ghost?"

"I dunno 'oo it is, Sir, cos it ain't got no 'ed. I see'd it when I wos on guard duty one night. It followed me round, like."

"Pompey, then?" suggested Dessy.

"No, Sir, not Pompey."

"Why not, if it was headless?"

"Well, Sir, it wos wearin' a dress."

This caused a bout of hilarity. Even Adrian was smiling.

Dessy smiled down at him in turn. "See what you've started? Anything else? Rats? Scorpions? Snakes?"

"Finding out that I'm a coward," Adrian whispered.

Jupiter! This was altogether too much honesty. "No. you're not a coward. Of course not. You wouldn't be here if you were. Anything but," said Dessy. "Listen, my lamb, it's not cowardice to talk to me, but sweet reason. You are bound to tell me all you know. It is inevitable."

"I don't believe you," said Adrian. But he did.

"Let me see your hand," said Dessy.

Adrian held out his right hand.

"No, baby. Your other hand."

Decimus held Adrian's left hand in his own. Adrian tried to grip him, with some success, as he thought that was what was intended. He had been lulled into a strange feeling of safety. Decimus disabused him.

"Now, my son. To be serious. We really need to talk. I need information from you."

"I've told you already. I can't talk," Adrian protested. Terror returned instantly.

"Of course you can, my dear boy. Everyone talks to me. Better that you do it sooner rather than later. I have no desire to hurt you. But I will do everything necessary to obtain all the information you have in your head."

"I can't. I just can't. I'm sorry."

"No. It's me that is sorry," sighed Dessy. "We will have to get started then."

Adrian thought he sounded sad.

The legionaries automatically moved into action. There was no need for orders. They had done this many times before. One picked up Adrian's right wrist and arm, gripping him tightly. Adrian felt two hands come from behind him, pressing down on his shoulders. As he twisted round to see behind him, Dessy savagely pulled back the middle finger of his left hand. Adrian screamed in shock, and tried unsuccessfully to pull away.

"I have dislocated your finger," Dessy explained dispassionately. "It hurts, doesn't it? I can make it hurt much more, quite easily." He moved the finger backwards and forwards, making Adrian gasp with pain. "So you see you will talk to me, baby boy, as you have no alternative. Now, what is your name?"

Adrian gritted his teeth, summoned up his courage, and refused to answer.

"Do you know how many joints you have in your body?" Dessy asked patiently. There was still no answer. "More than a hundred. I'm afraid I will have to go on dislocating each one until you talk to me. I will stop as soon as you do so. So come on, my lamb, I don't want to have to hurt you any more. Tell me your name, just to start with."

To Dessy's great surprise, the youngster still shook his head, although pale with shock. Most unusual. By now he should have been pouring forth information.

"Fuck," Dessy swore. This stubborn youngster might have to be really damaged. He gestured to his legionaries to start the process.

Adrian groaned aloud as the intensity of pain increased, then lost consciousness altogether when it became too much for his brain to cope with. He passed out just as the bone from his upper arm detached from its socket with a clicking noise.

"We've lost him, Sir," said one of Dessy's men. They carried the boy over to a battered-looking couch, and laid him down tenderly. It took a while for consciousness to return. Decimus was ready, for this moment often proved fruitful.

The boy was coming round. "Lucius?" said Dessy, speaking quietly in his ear. "Are you Lucius?" he queried again.

"Not Lucius........Adrian. I'm Adrian," said the befuddled boy. "Oh, my arm, my arm."

Something stirred at the back of Dessy's brain. He remembered Cassius saying, 'Adrian is such a stubborn child.' He looked down at the youngster lying stretched out in front of him. Adrian opened his eyes and attempted to sit up, clutching his shoulder, and rocking backwards and forwards in an effort to cope with the searing pain. Decimus saw the close family resemblance. He reacted so violently, so unusually, that his men were shocked into silence.

Decimus struck Adrian hard across the face, yelling at him. "How dare you fight for Pompey, Adrian. Your father died for Caesar. You are a traitor, do you hear me? A traitor to Caesar, to your father, and to your family."

Decimus took hold of the boy's shoulders and shook him hard, making him scream in agony. "You are going to talk to me now. You are going to tell me everything you know."

Adrian was shaken to the core. He told Dessy everything.

Decimus sent for his commander and explained the battle plans as recounted to him by Adrian.

"What do you think, Dessy?" Caesar asked.

'Dessy.' Adrian knew that name from somewhere. Knew this man from somewhere, who clearly also knew him. But he couldn't think where. His brain wouldn't work, pain kept interrupting his thoughts. His arm throbbed and throbbed.

"He's a decoy."

"A decoy?" whispered Adrian in shock.

Decimus slapped him again and told him to shut his traitorous mouth. Adrian subsided into whimpers.

"He comes from an unimportant family. Labienus considered him expendable, making sure we would capture him. I think we are being enticed into thinking we know their plans. They have no intention of an ambush where they've suggested to this idiot. Probably much sooner on the march."

Caesar agreed. "And what do you want to do with Cassius's son, Dessy?"

"He's a traitor," Dessy reiterated, sending up a plea to the Gods that his strategy would work. It almost did.

Caesar looked at the naked young man stretched out before him, a pathetic creature, writhing and moaning in agony, his left arm sticking out at an odd angle from his shoulder.

"Are you trying to manipulate me by any chance, Dessy?" Caesar asked, smiling into his eyes.

Decimus felt his heart miss a beat. "Not at all, Sir," he replied, trying to keep all emotion out of his voice. There was a long pause.

"But he's so young. I think we can give him a second chance. I'm sure you will be able to convince him to fight for us," said Caesar, still smiling benignly. He left, amused at Dessy's attempt at subterfuge, but pleased to think of his clemency to the son of an old friend.

A tall, blond, beautiful, bearded young cavalry commander approached them.

"We've captured another one, Sir. I'm afraid he's a bit cut about."

Adrian looked up at the figure. He knew him at once. All became clear. He called out, his voice weak and strained. "Cierán?"

"Master Adrian!" said Cierán, sounding pleased.

"Cierán, oh Cierán," sobbed Adrian, holding out his uninjured arm.

Cierán looked at Decimus, who nodded. "Hang on to him, Cierán." he said. "I'll have to reduce the dislocation. He's not going to manage to keep still, poor lamb."

Adrian had some idea of what was coming. He tensed himself. Cierán had his arms tight round him. The pain was overwhelming; Adrian nearly passed out again. He sat up, feeling so sick, leaning helplessly against Cierán, but thinking that at last he had an ally.

Afterwards Dessy carefully strapped Adrian's injured arm to his chest with padding and bandages, then he said, "Go on, Cierán. Make him better. I've sent for Musa. I'll need to see to the other one. What is his name, Adrian?"

"Max. Maximus."

"A friend, is he?"

"Yes, Sir. Please.....please.....?"

"No need to worry, Adrian. He'll be fine."

Adrian collapsed into tears of relief. Cierán put his arms around the sobbing boy, and started talking, soothing, comforting. Decimus felt he could safely leave everything to his freedman.

Adrian woke several times in the night, despite the disgusting concoction Marcellus's uncle forced him to drink. He found himself in a palatial tent, being nursed by his own father's slaves. Max was lying in a cot next to him. Adrian was so relieved, for Max confirmed all he had told Dessy, without putting up much of a resistance. He had been so badly wounded while trying to avoid capture.

"My arm," moaned Adrian. "My arm."

Cierán hauled himself up from a deep sleep, got up and came over to him.

"My arm," Adrian repeated. "A wolf is eating my arm," he sobbed.

"Wolf gone away now, Master Adrian," Cierán said. He brought over the lamp to see, then lifted the boy to a sitting position, softly talking words of comfort and reassurance. The bandages were cutting into Adrian's swollen flesh, so they were loosened, refastened, and more pain killer administered, despite Adrian's protests.

"Wolf gone away now," Cierán repeated. "Go back to sleep, Master Adrian."

The realisation that the information obtained from the two young tribunes was in the nature of a ruse enabled Caesar's forces to thoroughly rout a part of Sextus Pompeius's cavalry. It was a while before the two boys recovered their health. During this period Decimus treated them with the greatest kindness, having them conveyed from camp to camp in a litter, as he thought the jolting of a carriage over the poor roads of the province would be far too uncomfortable for them. But once Decimus decided they were fit enough to be useful, his attitude towards them changed for the worse, as far as the boys were concerned.

Decimus was pleased to find them both so frightened of him, he had no trouble at all with either.

"You will do exactly as I say, when I say. Do you hear me?" he screamed in their faces.

They agreed at once.

Dessy had firm ideas of how to train officers, thinking that they should know something of the hardships endured by the men they commanded. Accordingly he made the two boys perform the most menial tasks to start with. They were busily engaged in sharpening and polishing swords and spears when Decimus called them to come and meet Quintus Martius, a military tribune who had deserted the enemy camp, and had come to join with Caesar.

"That's what you two should have done," said Dessy afterwards. "Much less painful."

When part of their own cavalry was torn to pieces, Caesar decided the time was ripe for Decimus to be sent back to Rome to raise badly needed reinforcements, and also to have another attempt at persuading Atia to allow Gaius Octavius to join them.

On the way back to Rome Decimus bullied the boys mercilessly. He made them choose the camp site, and then tore their decision to pieces. They had to drill the legionaries accompanying them, to his mocking comments, write out lists of equipment required, only to be told they were all wrong. They were forced to ride non-stop for hours, as far as the horses could take them. Adrian was made to wear a lead sheath on his left arm, to strengthen his muscles, Dessy said. They were questioned repeatedly over tactics and battle stratagems, the formation of armies, the use of cavalry, when to keep back reinforcements, and how to fortify a camp.

It was no better once they had boarded the ship to take them to Capua. They were made to care for the nervous horses and mules in the hold. This included mucking out the stalls and jettisoning the resulting filth over the side of the ship. If Decimus wasn't satisfied with their efforts, they received a humiliating beating in front of the jeering ship's company. At the end of each of these exhausting days, Cierán and his fellow freedmen fed them, bathed them, massaged them, told them it would get much much worse, laughed at them, drank with them, and put them to bed.

BOOK 2 : CHAPTER 3

Rome

"I think it's important that he comes with me," Decimus explained as he lay next to the naked body of Atia, stroking her breasts with his fingers.

"Why so?" Atia asked, although she knew the reason. She had been over it so many times in her head.

"He has no legitimate children."

"He's got that bastard son with Queen Cleopatra."

"He's got bastard sons all over the place. None legitimate. Gaius Octavius is the only close legal relative. Come on, Atia. I'll look after him. He'll be perfectly safe, I promise you."

"Publius Crassus wasn't safe. Nor was his father. How can you guarantee safety when you are fighting a war?"

"But my dear. We have so nearly won. Caesar wishes Gaius to be in at the death."

In at the death! How glibly men talked about death. She had been in at the death of her husband and it was a hideous experience. Perhaps men's protestations of love were all shallow. That they simply couldn't care deeply for another human being. Not like mothers. Mothers would do anything, anything to protect their young. Not launch them into the middle of a war.

"But there's still Labienus to contend with, and Pompey's sons."

"They're a spent force, my darling." Although Decimus had been surprised by the number of Gauls committed to fight with Labienus. Perhaps their hatred of Caesar outweighed all other considerations. He couldn't persuade his lady love this session. So he could look forward to more amorous days like this. Wonderful. Of course Atia knew that as soon as she agreed, he would be off again. So, a tricky task.

The two boys were seated in the wooden arena built on the Campus Martius for the Triumphal Games hosted by Caesar. They were watching a gory spectacle, a savage boxing match between two naked men using the heavy metal-spiked gloves. Gaius Octavius was leaning forwards eagerly, lips parted in excitement, as they watched the slim, very young gladiator being pounded by his huge opponent. The gladiator's eyes were swollen so much he could no longer see properly, his lips were cut, bloody bruises and gashes were appearing all over his torso.

Abruptly Marcellus got to his feet, stumbling over the legs of the rest of the audience, who were all still enthralled. He pushed his way out to the exit, and then sat down on the pavement, leaning against the outside wooden wall of the arena. He could hear the shouts of the crowd still, and felt sickened by the whole procedure. The shouts crescendoed to a roar of approval. Half an hour later Gaius Octavius found his friend still propped up by the wall. He sat down next to him, to the consternation of his slaves. Gaius put an arm round Marcellus.

"What?" Gaius asked.

"You know what. It's all wrong. They weren't properly matched. It was just a blood bath. I don't want to see any more." Marcellus pushed himself up from the wall. "I'm going home."

"I'll come with you, then," said Gaius Octavius.

"You don't have to."

"Of course I don't have to. I want to."

"Why? Why are you friends with me?"

"Come to the pub and I'll explain."

They crossed the road, and entered a taverna with Marcellus's servant clucking his disapproval at every step, until Marcellus turned on him and ordered him home.

"I couldn't leave you, Master," said Ambrosius. "I would be failing in my duty to your distinguished father, if I left you in a place such as this. With no one to guard you."

Gaius Octavius found it highly amusing that this plump and unarmed slave should think he could do anything to protect his master, but Marcellus flushed with embarrassment.

Gaius took charge. "You!" he shouted. "Either you obey your master, or I will have you flogged right now."

Marcellus protested immediately. "No, you can't do that, Gaius. He's been with me for years."

"Then he should know his place by now," said Gaius Octavius tartly.

They settled themselves in the shade of a date palm, with tankards of wine, and some pickled eggs, which Gaius loved, but Marcellus loathed.

"You are my conscience," Gaius explained. "I don't have one." He took out his penknife and opened up the fork. He speared an egg, and put it into his mouth whole. "That boy, now," he continued indistinctly. "As far as I'm concerned it's tough titty. That's life. Get on with it and stop whimpering."

"Death for him," Marcellus objected.

Agrippa arrived, flushed with triumph, as he had bet heavily on the eventual winning gladiator. He suggested they play at dice, aware that Lucanus gave his son little money to spend.

"Come on, Marcellus. Prove you're a man," he grinned. "Double or quits."

Marcellus heard the inward suck of breath from Ambrosius, who was standing just behind him, as he recklessly wagered five gold pieces on the throw of the dice. After losing these first five pieces, Marcellus was so cross that he promptly wagered another five gold pieces, all the money he had in the world, just to demonstrate to his servant that he was the master, and his actions were not to be criticised by an elderly slave, however long the man had been in his service.

Marcellus lost the next five gold pieces as well, and was then furious with himself and his slave. He went home, deciding to have it out with his father. Ambrosius was an embarrassment. He could perfectly well look after Marcellus's little brother. Meanwhile Marcellus would like a younger and more obedient slave. He explained how impossible it was to punish Ambrosius.

"I'm sixteen years old, Dad. I don't need a nursemaid any more."

His father promised to think it over, realising that his elder son did have a point.

BOOK 2 : CHAPTER 4

Slave market, Rome.

In the morning Marcellus walked with his fussing servant to the slave market. His father had deliberately given him only a small amount of money, the amount he suggested that Ambrosius was worth. It was unlikely that Marcellus would be able to purchase any proper body servants who would know what was required of them. He glanced round at the mass of naked men and boys. Some immediately straightened themselves and smiled ingratiatingly, desperate to be bought by a youth who looked as if he had a bit of money behind him. Marcellus's clothes were excellent, his fine wool tunic being heavily embroidered and interlaced with gold thread. His bracelets and necklace were also of gold, beautifully wrought into delicate patterns of leaves and flowers. He looked rich.

There was nothing immediately obvious. But then, tucked away behind a group of healthy, expensive-looking specimens, he found a little huddle of slaves, two small children, and two straggly-bearded men, all thin, dirty, and ill-looking. The older man had a soiled bandage tied around one leg. He appeared feverish, sweating and shivering. The younger fair-haired man had suffered a severe scourging, his back was a mess of contusions and cuts. They crouched looking up at him, tense, expectant, and fearful. Marcellus decided that none of them could be worth much.

He spoke to one of the overseers and demanded to take a closer look, starting with the youngest, a thin pale child. To begin with the overseer tried to steer him towards the expensive servants, but Marcellus shook his head, saying he hadn't a lot of money to spend.

The little boy looked up in terror as the overseer approached. He started to sob with a hopeless low keening sound as he was being dragged over to the examination block. Marcellus thought he could see urine dribbling down the child's legs. The boy must have wet himself with fright. The child was made to stand up on the block. The overseer pointed to the urine, and then slapped the boy across the face, which made blood drip from the child's nose to join the mucus and tears already coursing down his cheeks.

Marcellus was angry. "Leave him alone. Can't you see he's scared?" he said crossly. "Get a cloth so he can wipe himself, and get those other three as well for me to look at." Marcellus was used to being obeyed.

A lackey appeared with a damp cloth, and made an effort to clean up the still sobbing child.

Marcellus took hold of the child's arm. The boy was dirty, painfully thin, and his blond hair was dull, long and unkempt. It looked as though the slave dealer regarded the child as a lost cause. The overseer brought over the other three with some reluctance, the two men moving with obvious difficulty, the one with the bandage limping heavily.

Marcellus had never bought a slave before, and hadn't much idea of what to do. He wished his father had come along to assist, but Lucanus had deliberately said he was busy this morning. Marcellus handled the child with firm but gentle fingers, and talked to him all the time. He pushed back the ragged fringe from the boy's forehead, exposing a dark purple bruise underneath the hair.

"Listen, my little one, I'm not going to hurt you," Marcellus said. "Can you speak Latin; can you understand anything I say?"

The boy continued to sob. The overseer jabbed the boy in the chest, causing him to gasp with pain. "Answer, you ignoramus!" he yelled, his face thrust forwards and spattering the boy with saliva.

Marcellus had had quite enough of the overseer. "Go away," he said to him angrily. "And don't return until I summon you." He turned his attention back to the child, trying to reassure him by talking to him in a calm steady voice. "My father has told me to buy a slave to replace my old servant, but I don't have much money to spend. Open your mouth, now."

The boy clearly understood nothing, didn't speak Latin, so Marcellus opened his own mouth. "Like this, see?"

The boy screamed, "*No, oh no, no! Don't eat me! Please don't eat me*!"

He shrank back, terrified. The overseer stepped forward to administer another blow, but Marcellus stopped him at once. Marcellus felt a pleasurable glow as he recognised the boy's words. The boy was speaking Gallic. Gallic that Marcellus could readily understand. But why on earth would the poor child think he was going to be eaten? The shocking answer came almost immediately, as an interruption occurred. A thickset man pushed his way towards the group.

"Where's the dog meat, then?" the man asked impatiently.

Marcellus saw the sick slave look up at the words. Their eyes met. The sick man made the tiniest gesture of appeal, his palms upwards to the children, still staring straight at Marcellus. Marcellus was sure the man had understood the words and was begging for help for the children, although apparently not for himself.

The thickset man grabbed hold of the other child. "Is this all you've got for me today?" he asked the overseer, looking round at the little group.

"I'm in the market for these slaves," said Marcellus with a frown. Were they really to be butchered by this man? Or was it just a bad joke?

"What, all of them, or just the kid?"

"All of them," replied Marcellus. He saw the sick man mutter something to the bearded youngster next to him.

"No, Master, no!" Ambrosius cried in vexation. "Your distinguished father will be furious! They are barbarians! They are not suitable, Master. Not at all suitable. They are dangerous, dangerous."

Marcellus looked at the trembling child he was still holding by the wrist. "Oh, I think not," he said.

The slave dealer appeared, bowing to Marcellus and ignoring the thickset man.

"How can I help you, Your Honour?" he enquired.

"How much for these?" Marcellus asked, indicating the four slaves.

"Look here, I'll give you seven for them," said the thickset man quickly. "Two each for the kids, and three for the other one. That one's worthless," he ended, pointing to the sick man.

Again Marcellus was aware that the dark-haired slave understood the words. He caught the hint of the faintest of wry smiles, as the man looked directly into his eyes.

"I'll give you ten for them," Marcellus said firmly. He didn't know if they were dealing in denarii, sestercii, or gold pieces. If it was gold he was out of the bidding completely.

"Got a pet lion to feed, have you?" said the thickset man in amusement. "Well I'm not paying any more for them. They're all yours."

Marcellus looked directly back at the dark-haired slave. "No, I've no lions, bears, or wolves in my house."

"Master, no, no, no!" cried Ambrosius.

"Ten sestertii then. Agreed," said the dealer, and held out his hand.

Marcellus shook hands on the deal, and wondered how on earth he was going to explain to his father that he had just bought four sick slaves. At least he should be pleased with the price. He walked over to talk to his purchases. The dealer followed him, carrying a stool, which he then placed on the ground, bowing obsequiously.

Marcellus sat down gingerly. The stool looked grimy, like the slaves. "You speak Latin," he said to the dark-haired slave.

"A small," said the man, holding up his fingers to demonstrate how little he could understand.

"No, a little," smiled Marcellus. "You speak Latin a little."

"A little? No a small?"

"A little," Marcellus repeated.

"You buy us?" asked the dark-haired man.

"Yes, I've bought all four of you."

"Not for eat?"

Marcellus shook his head. "No, not to eat." He repeated it in Gallic, but he didn't think the children understood his words.

His father walked through the archway into the dealer's premises at that moment, to see his son sitting surrounded by four unkempt dirty skinny sick slaves, who were kneeling patiently on the ground. Marcellus's servant began to make his excuses at once.

"I tried to stop it, Sir, I did truly, but the young Master wouldn't listen, Sir," Ambrosius complained.

"And since when has it been your place to question my son's judgement?" Lucanus asked angrily.

All the time, thought Marcellus.

His father surveyed the human wrecks at his son's feet. "And just how do you propose to get them back to our house?" he enquired.

"I will ask my father for his advice in the matter," Marcellus replied with a straight face. "Dad, they were to be sold for dog meat. I won't have it!"

"They need to be clothed, fed and watered, and that one needs a doctor," said his father. "I suggest we take them to the taverna across the road. We are due to meet some friends of yours there shortly. Then we can organise a wagon to get these slaves home. They don't look as if they could walk any distance."

For a few denarii the slave dealer produced some pieces of sacking to be twisted round the adult slaves' hips. He made a hole in the centre of a couple more pieces, placed them over the children's heads, and tied a length of rope round their waists. The younger boy looked down at the sacking and started crying again.

Marcellus wondered who the friends were, whom they were to meet at the taverna. He didn't have to wait long. A group of familiar figures made their way into the tavern's gardens. Gaius Octavius and Marcus Agrippa ran up to Marcellus, each grabbed an arm, and pulled him round in an excited circle.

"We're going to Spain," yelled Agrippa.

"You're coming too," yelled Gaius.

Decimus approached the group more slowly, smiling broadly, accompanied by Adrian, Max, and his Gauls. There were kisses and hugs all round, and partial explanations. Agrippa gave Adrian a none-too-friendly punch in the ribs.

"Changed sides already, have you, Adrian?" he said, and laughed.

Marcellus found his friend Adrian to be subdued, not at all like his usual self.

"I've been deputed to take you lot to join Caesar in Spain. Just my rotten luck," Decimus said. "So you will all do exactly as I say, which will make a nice change."

The young men laughed. Gaius Octavius, who knew all about the slave purchase idea, looked at the group of four dishevelled slaves.

"What have you been up to, Marcellus?" he grinned. "More Cupids?"

"He's starting a hospital," Agrippa suggested.

Decimus was crouched down, talking to the exhausted slaves, and examining one of the children. "He's lousy," he declared. "They will need to be shaved. Feed them little and often to start with. I'll sort them out for you when we get home, if you like, Marcellus. Musa can have a look at them."

Marcellus was only too thankful to agree.

Once home they discovered the little boys had been told by a centurion that they were to be eaten when they reached Rome, but first they would have to be beaten all over their bodies to tenderise their flesh. The centurion had thought this a great joke, and walked away grinning, leaving behind two terrified children. The boys stopped eating, partly through fright, partly because there wasn't much familiar about the food they were offered, and partly in the hope that they might be considered too thin to eat. The fair man had been trying to defend one of children from an assault by a guard, and had killed the man. Hence the severe punishment. The dealer wanted to rid himself of the dark-haired man so as not to infect the rest of his property.

Dessy told his nephew that slaves as badly damaged as these, especially the children, may well have problems.

"What sort of problems, Sir?"

"Problems such as wetting the bed, or nightmares. The older ones may think of suicide, initially. So be careful. Don't expect too much to start with." It was only recently that Dessy had learnt about Ethela's terrible nightmares.

Dessy's orderly Musa was left to nurse them all back to health. None of them would be fit soon enough to take to Spain. But this turned out to be no problem at all, as Egnatius presented Marcellus with two expensive, intelligent, and smoothly-trained slaves.

The three excited youngsters rushed round to see Octavia and tell her the news. They were going to war. Marcellus had images in his mind of astonishing bravery, on his part, brilliant tactics, on his part, and mercy to the defeated, also on his part. Agrippa was thinking more practically, of how much he could take with him. Gaius Octavius decided to order a decorative breastplate, one engraved with heroes.

Octavia was so pleased to see them. Her husband noticed with some dismay how her face lit up when the boys arrived. His wife was becoming more and more prone to fits of depression. Claudius thought he knew why. Lack of sex was known to be bad for women, and here he was, depriving his wife of a basic human right. At present he couldn't think how to overcome the problem, though occasionally ideas flitted through his mind. Outrageous ideas. However the present political climate precluded any solution. He needed to tread warily. Caesar had ostensibly forgiven him for his actions against him which had precipitated the civil war, but he must watch his step.

How like Marcellus, thought Octavia when she heard about his recent purchases, always so kind and sweet-natured. She thought a poem might be difficult, especially one dealing with slavery, starvation, and death. She was horrified when she discovered the slave children's story.

"Our slaves are freed when they become too old to work," she explained.

"Then what?" asked Marcellus. "Do they beg in the street?"

"Not at all," said Octavia indignantly. "They are given a little sum of money, and they are always allowed to come back to this house to eat, and get shelter. They aren't slaughtered, I do know that."

Octavia resolved to enquire more deeply into her own household. Her old nurse was pensioned off, she knew, but she wasn't so sure about the menials. Marcellus thought he would investigate the fate of the old useless slaves in his own household. But Gaius and Agrippa said that slaves were slaves. If their master decided that they were to be put down, the two boys couldn't see any problem with that.

There was some delay as Gaius Octavius succumbed to one of his terrible chest infections. He was feverish, coughing and wheezing. Lady Atia refused to allow him to travel until he was fully fit again. Decimus sent off some of the cavalry reinforcements under the command of Lucius Asprenas. Meanwhile he was able to see Atia every day, ostensibly to enquire about Gaius Octavius.

Some days after the slave purchases, Decimus told Marcellus he needed him to accompany him to the wooden arena.

Marcellus knew it was to be dismantled shortly, and didn't understand why they were going there. "Because there is something I need you to see," was the only explanation he got from his uncle.

Quintus Cicero was sitting in the front row reserved for the Senators. As soon as he saw Decimus he beckoned him over, greeting him with enthusiasm, explaining that his brother Marcus would be joining them.

"Marcus was defending Publius Vetto, but he was found guilty. He is being executed this morning, and my brother feels he should be there to witness his demise."

They took the seats offered by Quintus Cicero. As soon as the organisers saw Marcus Cicero entering the the stands, the proceedings began.

Marcellus had an uninterrupted view of the arena floor. First came a group of pale-faced men, with their hands tied behind them, driven into the arena with blows from cudgels and whips. They were fastened in turn to wooden posts dotted at regular intervals around the arena's edge. Proceedings were paused so that the audience could lay bets as to who would be killed first. There was a strong whiff of animal scent, then the small audience caught the sounds they had been waiting for, the roar and bark of ravenous beasts, desperate to eat.

"See that lion with the black mane?" Marcus Cicero asked Marcellus. "He's disposed of fifty-five men already, to my certain knowledge."

The execution of criminals by wild animals was a spectacle that Marcellus usually took pains to avoid. He found the whole procedure nauseating. The shrieks of the victims, the groans and yells of the crowds, the smell of blood, guts, and faeces, both human and animal were an affront to his senses. He tried to close his eyes and cover his ears, but his uncle pulled his hands away, saying, "No, Marcellus. You are to watch it all."

Publius Vetto, being one of the equites class, was brought on separately. Cicero leant forward with interest. Vetto waved to him.

"Putting on a good show, anyway," remarked Cicero, raising his arm in acknowledgement.

When the old, sick, crippled, or blind slaves were dragged in to meet their deaths, male and female, with some children as well, Marcellus could stand it no longer. He started to cry, sobbing into his hands. This time Dessy made no effort to stop him.

Two hours later the arena was cleared of animals and human debris, the sand smoothed ready for the afternoon's gladiatorial contest.

"What did you think of our morning's entertainment?" Decimus asked his nephew.

Marcellus considered. He'd had a bit of time to recover. He had a good idea of why he had been made to witness the carnage. "I suppose it's a rough and ready form of justice for the criminals. After all they have committed horrendous crimes against the State."

"Not all of them were criminals, my boy," Marcus Cicero explained. "Vetto was innocent of any crime, and a couple of the others as well, I can assure you."

"Then why was he executed?" Marcellus asked in horror.

"Someone powerful, more powerful than me, for instance, wanted him out of the way. It was a put-up job, by all accounts. The magistrate was heavily bribed."

"But that's terrible," said Marcellus. "It's unjust! And to have those pathetic slaves disposed of in such a way. I had no idea."

"Their owners get a small fee, you see, for the entertainment value," Marcus Cicero explained. "There has to be some way to deal with the useless, the unwanted and unloved. Freeing them can be dangerous. Some turn into aggressive beggars, others just starve to death and litter the streets with their corpses. Then the authorities have the problem of disposal. Be reassured, though, young man. Most conscientious masters dispose of their slaves in a more humane fashion, or free them, even allowing them food and shelter, or a small pension."

"I must find out what happens to our slaves." Marcellus was feeling quite agitated. He could recall a couple of family slaves who had simply disappeared. He'd always naively assumed that they had been sold, though they were worthless, to all intents and purposes.

Decimus spoke quietly. "You managed well today, Marcellus. It's not a pretty sight. And now you know that sometimes the innocent are killed along with the guilty. The Roman Army is a bit like those ravenous animals. It's a vicious beast. When we fight the enemy, nothing is allowed to stand in our way, not men, nor women, nor children, nor animals, not even corn."

"Corn?" said Marcellus in bewilderment.

"We lay waste the crops to starve the enemy to death. Of course they try to do the same to us. So everyone is affected, everyone starves, women, children, babies. Those children of yours look well-fed compared to some walking skeletons I've seen. Not that they walk for long. Now we have virtually won the war against the Pompeian forces. This will be in the nature of a mopping-up exercise, a punishment campaign to make sure the province is completely subdued. It won't be a pretty sight, either. Caesar stops at nothing to get his way."

Marcus Cicero interrupted. "A just war waged on behalf of the Republic should limit the destruction of life and property of the enemy, by using only the necessary force needed to achieve the objective. But many generals feel that all actions in war are lawful. They will use lies, trickery, murder, poison, on the innocents as well as the combatants, sometimes cutting off the enemy's water supply as well as food. There is always collateral damage, my boy."

"Look at those poor devils at Alesia. The civilians expelled from the city," Quintus Cicero added. "We had starving women and children begging for food, but quite rightly in my opinion, Caesar forbade us to feed any of them. Otherwise we may not have had enough supplies to feed our own men. One has to be pragmatic when fighting a war."

Marcellus was worried. "Surely we should always try to do what is just and right and reasonable, as the Gods have told us."

"No!" Decimus was emphatic. "Our job is to obey orders. The orders of our superiors. There is no room for disagreement. Can you do that, Marcellus? Could you perform an unjust act if I ordered it?"

"I suppose I'd have to," Marcellus said, hesitantly.

"Think long and hard about it. If you change your mind about coming to Further Spain, I will understand. You are a kind man. Not particularly one of our Roman virtues, but I would hate you to lose that quality."

"Further Spain is well named," said Quintus Cicero. "Basically Caesar will be able to do anything he likes."

"Isn't he also managing to do that here?" his brother remarked dryly. "He's written to ask the Senate for his dictatorship to be extended for a further ten years."

Decimus and Marcellus were invited back to lunch with the two Ciceros, where Decimus enjoyed hearing of the awfulness of Mark Antony, whom Caesar had left in charge of Italy as Master of Horse. It appeared that Antony had spent his time indulging in every vice and every extravagance, having lavish banquets and many love affairs, while Caesar was roughing it in the field of battle. There was no love lost between Cicero and Antony.

BOOK 2 : CHAPTER 5

Mare Nostrum, The Mediterranean, 46 BC

The Uncle Dessy who took charge of them was nothing like the Uncle Dessy Marcellus had known and loved for the sixteen years of his life. This uncle made them write out a list of everything they would be allowed to take with them on the campaign. Then he tore the lists up in front of them.

"No, Gaius, you will take two slaves, not ten, and only slaves that can ride a horse, and fight if necessary. Marcus Agrippa, you will have one pack mule only. What the hell do you want all this paper for, Marcellus? To write poems? I will make sure you never have a free moment to do so."

Decimus had arranged for a fleet at Genoa to be readied to transport these important young men to Further Spain. In addition he was to pick up cavalry reinforcements on his way through Italy from the pro-Caesar garrison towns and cities.

Dessy carried out the youngsters' military training on the journey just as brutally as he had with Max and Adrian. The other boys were surprised at how much Max and Adrian seemed to know, much more than they knew. When Dessy asked them for the points to be looked at, when assessing a place for the army camp site, Marcellus struggled, trying to think. Agrippa was better, but could only come up with level ground and a water supply. Adrian reeled off a long list, which all made perfect sense.

One evening in their tent, while Decimus was cross-questioning them about the salient points it was essential to discover from captured enemy spies, he walked over to Adrian and reached up into the air above his head, clutching at an invisible object. Then he exited the tent, and stood outside, brushing the remains of the spider from his hands.

"Was it....?"

"Yes. It is no more."

"It's so stupid," Adrian confessed.

"You're not alone, Adrian. Nonius Vibius, a nasty piece of work if ever I saw one, has his tent searched from top to bottom every evening before he goes in it. We're all scared of something."

"What are you scared of, Sir?" Agrippa wanted to know.

"No one's ever asked me that." Dessy looked round at them all. "Disfigurement. More specifically, facial disfigurement. I don't care about the scars on my body from swords, or darts, or arrows. But a spear in the face? Somehow I know I would find that hard to cope with."

"What about you, Cierán? What are Gauls scared of?"

"My most terrifying moment was when I was first sold. The slave dealer grabbed hold of my balls, and asked my master if I was to be castrated."

"For the Gods' sake'!"

The young men looked at him in horror.

"Fortunately for me, Dessy said no."

"I'd forgotten that," said Dessy.

Cierán smiled. "I haven't."

He should have agreed, Decimus thought to himself. Then those frightening ideas about Ella, his beautiful blonde daughter, would never occur, and he could sleep at night.

Decimus barked out orders and expected to be instantly obeyed. The accompanying legionaries were kind and sympathetic. These boys were to be their future officers, after all, but they weren't allowed to help them, when they got things wrong, nor were the Gauls. When they made camp one night on the journey to their embarkation port, Marcellus forgot to light the cooking fire from the fire-pot. To his horror he was forced to bend over, his tunic lifted, his subucula pulled down, and he received three cuts with the cane on his bare buttocks. He felt a rage he couldn't disguise. No one had beaten him since Octavia's wedding. He stared resentfully at his uncle. Dessy told him that if he didn't take that look off his face he would take it off for him. Hastily Marcellus looked down at the ground. Afterwards Decimus ruffled his hair, and said, "It's not so easy to grow up and be a proper soldier, is it, Marcellus?" and laughed at his expression. But before reaching the port they had all had a taste of Dessy's vine-stick.

The embarkation of the group took a whole day. First they sacrificed to Neptune, at an ungodly hour according to Marcellus. He couldn't imagine Neptune being awake when it was only just daybreak. Marcellus, Gaius and Agrippa were ordered to coax their horses, mules and pack animals down the ramp into their stalls in the hold of the ship. They found this task more difficult than they'd expected. Most of the fleet set off the next morning. Their ship was rowed out of the harbour by three tow-boats. Once released, the ship swept out to sea, using the three large sails, and the one smaller one, as well as oars, making for Valentia.

The voyage took Marcus Agrippa by surprise. He found he loved the feel of the ship shifting restlessly under his feet. He watched the rowers in fascination as they kept perfectly in time with each other. The ship had two banks of oars. The oarsmen needed to be so skilled to avoid clashing with each other, but they managed it. Agrippa enjoyed spending long hours with the captain, learning how to reef or shake out the sails, according to the power of the wind; how the twin steering oars steadied the ship, setting her on her course. On one occasion he decided to see what happened when he caused chaos. Without warning he violently pushed down onto the handle of an oar. The unfortunate rower caught a crab, the oar handle jerking backwards and hitting him on the chest. The adjacent rowers were furious as their oars were jerked out of synchronisation. They knew they would all be punished.

Agrippa protested that it was all his fault, as the overseer came over to lash at the rowers. Decimus appeared, wanting to know what happened. After the overseer had explained, Decimus insisted that Agrippa change places with the rower, and handed the rower the whip, telling him to use it if Agrippa wasn't pulling his weight. An hour later Decimus came to see the result. Agrippa was pulling as hard as he could. The rower said that as he was trying so hard and was so young, he hadn't administered any punishment. After that Agrippa developed an affinity with the rowers, finding out the conditions they worked under, sometimes sharing his supper with them. Some were free, and working for money, some hoped for citizenship, some were convicted criminals. But all were subject to the same harsh discipline.

Before they arrived at their destination the weather took a severe turn for the worse, with a fierce cross wind increasing to gale force, causing the captain to reef in all sails, and rely on the rowers. But the rowers were having huge difficulty making any headway, as the waves increased in amplitude, with the ship plummeting to the depths, then being tossed up again. Waves crashed over the bows, covering the decks, and drenching the sailors. They had to hang onto the rails to move safely anywhere about the ship. It took four men to hold each steering oar steady, but they were fighting a losing battle against the elements. In the hold the horses were stamping and rearing in fright, battering their hooves against their stalls.

The ship pitched violently as one of the steering oars snapped under the strain. Sailors tumbled across the tilted deck. The ship slowly rotated, buffeted by the wind. It was being blown side-on towards the rocky shoreline. The other steering oar was retrieved from the water; the captain saw no point in going round in circles. He had a screamed conversation with Decimus over the tumult of crashing waves and howling wind. Ropes and creaking timbers behind them protested at unaccustomed strain.

"We're heading to the rocks, Sir," yelled the captain. "We'd better get ready to abandon ship. She'll be smashed up for sure."

The captain proved prophetic. The ship was inexorably heading towards the jagged rocks of the shore. Before reaching it a fearsome crashing tearing sound told them all that the hull had been breached by rocks below the water line. Giant waves tugged the hull off the rocks again, leaving a huge gaping hole in the ship's side.

Dessy took charge. "Is anyone trying to repair the hole?" The captain replied in the affirmative. A group of men were at present trying desperately to plug the torn flesh of the ship with a crushed-up leather sail. The water was still gushing past them, despite their efforts.

Decimus ordered his nervous men to dispense with their armour, but not their swords. "Unchain the galley slaves," Dessy yelled over the tumult. "I want ten oars to be lashed together, to make a raft."

This was a lot easier said than done on the slippery tilting deck. But they succeeded, even though the ship was now being tossed about like a God's plaything, listing heavily to port and sinking ever lower in the water. But the influx of seawater into the hold made the ship's movement slower. In the distance, out of the looming spray, they could see a ridge of rock forming an impenetrable barrier.

Decimus ordered the rowers to throw the oars into the water, together with anything else made of wood. "Now who can and who can't swim?" Decimus demanded. He had always ensured that his own men could swim. Most of the sailors couldn't swim, their superstitious nature thinking the ability to swim would be more likely to cause them to be shipwrecked.

"Once past the rocks the sea is a lot calmer," Decimus shouted. "It's not far to landfall. About a quarter of a mile. All those who can't swim, dive in now and grab an oar. Three can hang on to one oar. The rest of us will attempt to get you to land." He told the boys that they were to stay close to Cierán, and obey his orders.

"But Cierán's a fucking....." began Agrippa, and then hastily changed it to "Yes, Sir. Cierán's in charge," when he saw the look on Dessy's face.

Decimus grabbed the twin sacks of gold coins he kept in his tiny cabin by the masthead, and tied them to his improvised raft Then he collected Óengus and Darreth, ordering them to follow him, but to take care. He took a knife in his mouth, and climbed down into the hold with them. They desperately needed the horses, and any equipment he could salvage. They had a hard time, standing up to their waists in sea water, trying to avoid being kicked in the head by terrified animals. Once freed most of the horses and mules made their way towards the daylight of the gaping hold.

The sea was warm, but some men were badly stung by jelly fish, some were too exhausted to keep going, and some just gave up. Many never managed to reach the calmer waters past the menacing black rocks, being smashed to death by the powerful waves. Several of the men had fractures after these collisions, or limbs with deep gashes. All were bruised and battered by the sheer force of the storm. Cierán shouted encouragement, grabbed oars and tugged them in the right direction, giving rudimentary swimming lessons at the same time. "Kick your legs out. Push the oar in front of you. That's right, well done," he encouraged. But it was hard to get the oar going steadily towards the shore. Some managed it, many didn't. Gaius Octavius and Marcellus swam together, attempting to encourage anyone they came across. It took over an hour for them to reach land, and they were the best swimmers. The loaded raft floated shorewards, pushed by the wind and tide.

Finally the ship shuddered into the rocks, with a deafening crash of splintering splitting wooden beams.

"Jump, jump," screamed Decimus. "Jump now."

Sailors, soldiers and boys who had been too terrified to abandon the ship, leapt into the maelstrom, to grab hold of anything able to float.

Slowly, majestically, the broken prow of the ship rose up high out of the water, and then with a ghastly inevitability, the whole edifice keeled over onto its side, and half-submerged. A jumble of torn timbers, ripped sails, and broken masts leered intermittently out of the waves, silhouetted incongruously against the sky line.

The main group made land hours later, to find most of the horses and pack mules had already stumbled up the beach, and were busily cropping the few patches of grass. Decimus crawled out of the sea, supported by Darreth, and clutching his chest, a full hour after the others. Cierán wanted to know what the problem was. Dessy found it painful even to talk.

"I got kicked in the ribs by one of the horses. It's bloody sore. Cierán, you will have to take charge. We need to meet up with Asprenas and the cavalry. I wonder how many of the ships managed to find safe harbour?"

The surviving rowers, sailors, ship's officers, and captain were told to look after themselves. There weren't enough horses for them. Cierán ordered them to go inland with the injured, and remain under cover. This was hostile territory, after all, and if they stayed on the beach they would be spotted by any passing ship or boat.

The rest of them had to walk or ride without saddles. Dessy had managed to salvage most of the bridles, but he was sure the weight of saddles as well would have sunk his raft. Óengus had a cross and sore Decimus in front of him on his horse. Cierán insisted they travelled by night and slept by day. First they appropriated one of the local farms, telling the inhabitants they would not be harmed, but taking their food supplies, their two horses, and all their fodder. Marcellus protested that they should only take half the supplies. But Cierán explained that in that case they would just take longer to starve to death. Marcellus had to hope that their neighbours would rally round.

They followed the coast road, eventually reaching Valentia, where they were relieved to find some of the ships, and a lot of cavalry. It was now much safer to proceed by day and strike inland towards their own forces. Decimus, still grumbling, managed to ride by himself again.

Marcellus was shocked and horrified when they finally arrived at the camp outside Córduba. Both sides were occupied in hand to hand fighting over the stone-built bridge across the river, piling up corpses at either end in a macabre competition. The stench of decomposing bodies was appalling. Flies hovered in thick clouds over the carcasses, with the local vultures fighting off ravens and rats to feast on decaying flesh. All of which made for great difficulty in eating, Marcellus found, when seated at the banquet provided by Caesar to celebrate their safe arrival. Not that anyone else seemed that bothered. He supposed he would just have to get used to the stench, or starve.

Caesar was delighted with the story of the shipwreck, singling out Gaius Octavius, praising his cool head and courage. He had to start thinking about his heir, he realised. There was a slight chance he would be killed before this war ended. Although Queen Cleopatra had assured him that her year-old son Caesarion was his child, Caesar was still legally married to his Roman wife, Calpurnia. Rome wouldn't take kindly to an heir who was half Egyptian and a bastard, let alone an infant, whereas Gaius was wholly Roman, and wholly legitimate. However he wanted to see his great nephew in action before he made up his mind. But this was a good beginning.

It was quite late at night when Cierán took Marcellus over to the luxuriously furnished tent, which evidently they were to share. Inside were a little knot of nicely dressed slaves. Each one came forward in turn to kneel at Cierán's feet and kiss his hand, and be embraced by their master. Cierán explained to them that they were to serve Master Marcellus as well as they served him. Marcellus was so pleased to be stripped and given a lovely comfortable warm bed to sleep in. He felt exhausted, slightly drunk, and nonplussed by the formality with which the slaves were treating Cierán.

Marcellus didn't believe Uncle Dessy's description of them being on the verge of victory. He was set to work the next morning, supervising the transport of wood from the countryside in order to build the replacement siege towers. The Córdubans were successfully burning some of them to the ground.

To Marcellus's amazement he was told Cierán and his fellow Gauls were each given decurion rank at the start of the civil war, and each were put in charge of a cavalry section. But they had fought so successfully, they were now senior cavalry officers, each in charge of a thousand men and horses. Cierán had overall responsibility for the whole contingent. No wonder Decimus had put him in command. Marcellus could see that the Gauls were now seriously rich as well, apparently having taken enthusiastic part in looting the captured cities during the campaigns, as well as receiving considerable monetary reward from Caesar. They had their own slaves and horses. Astonishing that they had acted more like servants on their journey, looking after the boys so well and so kindly.

Cierán explained. "You needed somebody on your side. Someone you could rely on. Someone you trusted not to hurt you. So did Max and Adrian at first. Dessy can appear to be quite brutal when he is training men, frightening sometimes. He couldn't both train you and look after you all as well. So he asked us if we could help him. And we were pleased to do so. Has Adrian ever told you what happened to him?"

"No, Sir." There was a space up between them, and he hadn't known why.

"I would ask him about his capture. And try to understand. He finds it upsetting to talk about. Oh, and keep Agrippa away from him."

It was strange to be calling Cierán 'Sir' at first. But Cierán had such an aura of authority, so it wasn't difficult. The Gauls had no problem killing Roman citizens. Marcellus thought they rather enjoyed it. Except that apparently they would be made citizens themselves, once the war was finally over.

Uncle Dessy was proved to be quite correct. The end was near. Once Córduba surrendered, after its citizens were promised their lives, other towns fell more easily, one after the other.

Marcellus had what he thought at first was a hilarious conversation with his uncle.

"Just a word of advice, Marcellus," Dessy started.

"Yes, Sir?"

"Well, if you get to fancy any of the young girls in the towns......"

"You mean virgins?"

"Yes, virgins." Dessy paused, thinking how to frame the words. "Look, you might need a bit of lubrication."

"Oh." Marcellus found his mind filling with images of his uncle needing a bit of lubrication. He was trying hard not to laugh out loud.

"Yes. And it's best to avoid the rough stuff."

"The rough stuff?"

"Yes. Look, if it's their first time, don't be too vigorous, alright?"

"I'll bear it in mind, Sir."

Fortunately for his relationship with his uncle, Decimus rode on ahead, relieved to have performed his duty, as he saw it.

Marcellus was able to have hysterics in peace. He could hardly wait to relay this conversation to Marcus Agrippa. But then he remembered something he had almost forgotten. How as a small child he had heard someone crying as if their heart would break. He had gone to investigate. He'd found Uncle Dessy's slave girl sobbing her heart out in Cierán's arms. He could picture her still, a very young girl, a very unhappy girl, being comforted by a big boy with long golden hair. His first memory of Ethela. He stopped laughing.

Increasing numbers deserted to join Caesar, even though there was a trickle also in the opposite direction. Once the senior officers, as well as ordinary legionaries and slaves, began to desert Gnaeus Pompey it was obvious the war was at last coming to a bloody conclusion.

The final pitched battle took place at Munda, where Dessy's training had so endeared his young protégés to Caesar, they were each put in charge of a cohort. Decimus wondered if Atia would ever forgive him, if she knew what danger her only son was in. No, probably not. And he wouldn't blame her, as unlike Caesar's usual practise they were fighting in a severely disadvantageous position. Gnaeus Pompey's forces were on high ground in front of the fortified city, whereas they had to fight uphill over marshy territory. But Caesar's tactics won the day. Decimus and the tenth legion began driving back the enemy on the right wing, whereupon Caesar summoned the left cavalry wing forwards into a classic pincer movement. The Pompeian lines were broken, the enemy retreated full tilt back into the fortified town. Labienus was killed by an accurate spear shot from one of the Gallic princes leading the cavalry.

Sextus Pompey was back in Córduba when news came of the defeat. He took the remains of the Pompeian fleet out to sea.

Marcellus knew he was changing day by day. Increasingly the horrors of war left him unmoved. Munda was now under siege, surrounded by the bodies of the slain enemy on top of the earth rampart, with severed heads mounted on top of the corpses, their faces turned to the town. But although the smell was disgusting, it no longer bothered him, which was just as well. He thought he would now be able to go back to the wooden arena, without getting upset. Well, as long as he didn't know the victims personally. That might be a lot more difficult.

The mopping-up exercise became more sordid the longer it went on. One by one the Pompeian towns were taken, with increasing numbers of enemy casualties. Retribution untempered by mercy was the order of the day. Caesar invited Gaius Octavius to share his carriage, as they were travelling from one camp to another. As usual, when they arrived, Dessy's tent was erected first. Gaius erupted into the entrance while Dessy was giving the boys their orders for the evening.

"He wants to suck my dick!" he blurted out.

The others laughed aloud. Marcus Agrippa ruffled his hair affectionately.

"You shouldn't be so beautiful, darling," he said.

But Dessy could see it was no laughing matter for Gaius. He snapped at the others to get going, sat Gaius down at the table, poured beakers of wine for both of them, and then seated himself opposite the distraught boy, covering his hands with his own.

"It's alright. It will be alright. He doesn't pursue the unwilling, Gaius. When you see him tomorrow it will be just as if nothing has happened."

"How do you know, Sir?"

Dessy laughed. "He came on to me once, years ago, when I was young and handsome."

"You still look pretty good," Gaius admitted. "And obviously Mother thinks so."

Decimus choked on his wine. "Does she?" he managed to gasp out.

"Oh, come on, Sir. Everyone knows you've been fucking Mother for years."

Gaius was beginning to recover his composure. He studied the stunned speechless Decimus. It was true. There were some greying hairs at the temples, but Decimus remained extremely good-looking, distinguished even. "Anyway, thanks for your advice. It gave me a bit of a shock." He grinned. "I see I've given you a bit of a shock, too."

This was worrying. Gaius assured Dessy that although all the children in the annexe knew, the information was never passed on to anyone else, as Cierán threatened to wring their necks if it got out.

News came that Gnaeus Pompey was dead, betrayed. His head was brought to Hispalis and exhibited to the local populace. By September the province was fully pacified, although Sextus Pompey, having retired with his fleet to the Balearic Islands, would be a future problem, one to be set aside for the moment. They could all return to Rome for yet another of Caesar's Triumphs, leaving behind garrisons in all the major cities.

BOOK 2 : CHAPTER 6

Apollonia, in Illyria, Winter/Spring, 45/44 BC

The young men were sent to Apollonia to finish their education and military training under the harsh regime of the Camp Prefect. They preferred the more gentle tuition they received from Cierán and his colleagues, during which they learnt how to manage cavalry operations. They would be collected up when Caesar set out on the long-planned war against Parthia. But this was so frustrating. They knew that masses of exciting changes were being forced through the Senate by the Dictator; they wanted to be there in Rome, to take part, to see the results.

Decimus would not allow any slackness. He told them he intended to make them the best generals Rome had ever possessed.

"Generals, Sir?" Agrippa was astonished.

"Not now, you idiot. In the future. You should make decent military tribunes, though, by the time I've finished with you here."

They were talking about courage one night. How to instil bravery into their own soldiers. Decimus explained how the system worked, how having one cohesive body of men enabled the army as a whole to perform unimaginable feats of daring. How the constant drilling and fierce discipline made men obey orders, even orders that seemed suicidal. On rare occasions the army had been called on to kill one in ten of its own men after a mutiny, the sentence duly carried out, the men drawing straws to find out who would be the victims. Although more often decimation was used as a threat rather than the actuality, as it led to severely disaffected troops.

"Who is the bravest man you have ever met, Sir?" Agrippa wanted to know.

"I think it must be Adrian," said Dessy without hesitation.

"Adrian?" Agrippa laughed in disbelief. "Our Adrian? Adrian who is scared of spiders?"

Dessy was frowning, remembering unpleasant details that he usually tried to suppress. "Yes. Our Adrian. Though at the time he was Gnaeus Pompey's Adrian. He was only eighteen, and had been in the army for three weeks. But he wouldn't even give me his name until I hurt him so badly he passed out. Although there was a Gaul, one of the Nervii, who ran him close. But he was older, a married man with children. And of course there was Cassius, Adrian's father. But he was also reckless on that last day, as well as brave. Sometimes courage runs in families."

"You don't mean me," Adrian whispered.

"Yes, of course I mean you. I presume it was a serious question, deserving a serious answer. But if you have no wish to discuss it further, we will leave the subject alone for the time being."

"I find it difficult to talk about. But I did tell Marcellus."

Decimus lightly touched his left shoulder. "Good?" he asked.

"Fine," Adrian answered. "Normal."

Dessy smiled in relief. "Your choice of confidant does you credit. I do wonder sometimes why I have any friends left," he continued sadly.

"It's because you're the best, Sir," said Adrian. He felt for Dessy's hand and gripped it in his own. "We know you're the best."

They stared into each other's eyes. "Thank you, Adrian," said Dessy. He was forgiven. He had never been sure up till now.

Marcellus had hoped to be back in Rome, so he could see his mother and father and the family, but was allowed only a fleeting visit before being ordered to Illyria. Especially he wanted to see Octavia. He missed her so much. He wrote as often as he could, Uncle Dessy still not allowing much time for a flourishing poet to put his thoughts together in verse, even when Marcellus pointed out that Caesar himself wrote poetry. Decimus merely remarked that Caesar had finished his army training, whereas as far as he could see, Marcellus had only just started his.

All winter, legal reforms poured out of Rome, mainly to the benefit of the plebeians, and to the detriment of the aristocratic faction. The Senate was kept busy. Lucanus wrote to his brother, keeping him abreast of the news.

"I agree with many of the reforms, brother. In January we will at last have a proper calendar, no longer interfered with by the priests. But Caesar has asked to be made dictator in perpetuity. He rivals Sulla, no, he exceeds Sulla in ambition. There are plots swirling around the Senate, with men whispering in corners. I don't like it. We have heard that Queen Cleopatra has not only claimed her son Caesarion to have been fathered by Caesar, she has also made the boy co-ruler of Egypt with her. And Caesar hasn't issued any denial of paternity."

Lucanus met Marcus Cicero at the door of the Senate when the law was proposed which gave Caesar the perpetual dictatorship. "We are putting our heads in a noose," he declared.

But Cicero sneered back. "Come on, Luke. Everyone knows your brother sups at Lady Atia's table when in Rome. No doubt Caesar can count on your full support."

Ye Gods, thought Lucanus. Does everyone know of Dessy's affairs?

In the spring Caesar's intentions became more obvious. He issued coins with his crowned head on one side, something only done in the past by Roman kings. In the present Republic the patricians well knew that only the Gods or dead heroes were portrayed in this fashion. By now Caesar had greatly offended many and greatly rewarded many. The city was divided in its loyalties. The members of the aristocratic faction were still powerful holders of land and wealth, but, as always, the plebeians favoured Caesar. At the feast of Lupercalia, Mark Antony made several attempts to crown Caesar with a wreath, with roars of approval from the crowd, only for Caesar to repeatedly lay it aside. Even so, he ordered the wreath to be taken to the temple, not to be destroyed. Rumours were flying around that Caesar wanted kingship. The plots came thick and fast to stop him. And prophecies of doom.

When Decimus was informed that his brother was at the camp gate demanding admittance, he knew something momentous must have occurred.

Luke hugged and kissed him.

"Alright. Don't keep me in suspense. What's happened?"

"Caesar's been assassinated."

"What?" Decimus was shocked to the core of his being. "When did it happen?"

"On the Ides of March. Outside the Theatre of Pompey."

"How ironic."

"He's made Gaius Octavius his adopted son and heir."

"By all the fucking Gods! Not Caesarion?"

"No. Not Caesarion. I thought I'd better come myself."

Decimus sent for Gaius Octavius first, wanting to tell him privately. When Gaius arrived, Decimus held up his hand in salute. "Hail, Caesar," he said softly. He had always been Caesar's man. He owed almost everything to him. He wasn't going to change loyalties now.

"What, Sir? What do you mean?" Gaius looked in bewilderment from one brother to the other.

Decimus pushed him down into a chair, and handed him a beaker of wine. Then he told him.

Gaius sat quietly at first. "Who was responsible?" he asked, when he had recovered from the initial shock.

"There are thought to be about sixty conspirators," Luke explained. "The main instigators were Marcus Brutus and his cousin, Junius Brutus..."

"Sixty conspirators? Marcus Brutus? How can that be, Sir? Marcus Brutus was one of Caesar's greatest friends. I know he fought with Pompey, but Caesar forgave him for that, didn't he? I thought they got on well with each other."

"So were some of the others apparently friends, Servilius Casca and Cassius Longinus, for instance. The post mortem examination showed that Caesar had been stabbed twenty-three times, so at least twenty-three Senators are implicated."

Lucanus was able to relate all the details, as he had been present at the appalling event. This was rocking the entire Roman Republic to its foundations, he explained.

Gaius sat with his hands clenched tight in his lap. "With the help of Jupiter, Greatest and Best, I will make sure Caesar is avenged," he said. "This I swear to you both. I will kill every one of the traitors."

"That may not prove to be an easy task," Lucanus murmured.

Decimus summoned the senior officers and his protégés, to break the incredible, almost unbelievable news. They had a conference that night.

"Your revered mother and stepfather are convinced you should do nothing, Gaius."

"No!" Gaius shouted.

"They think any action on your part would be far too risky," Luke explained. "Mark Antony has already seized all Caesar's papers, and the treasury. He is now sole Consul. At present Caesar's wife Calpernia is lodged with him." Was that in case Calpernia proved to be pregnant? Luke wondered. So Antony could dispose of any future threat to his authority?

"What about the assassins?" Gaius Octavius asked presently, when he'd had time to absorb this information.

"The Senate has agreed an amnesty for them. They wish to avoid any further bloodshed. Many Senators feel yet another civil war might prove disastrous. And many Senators have sympathy for the assassins, thinking Caesar was overreaching himself and desiring kingship. But Antony's funeral speech whipped up so much ill-feeling among the citizens, most of the liberatores, as they call themselves, have fled from Rome at present. One of them, Junius Brutus, has retreated to Cisalpine Gaul. He's just outside Mutina, with four legions under his command. He insists that Caesar allowed him this province, and that the Senate ratified it. This despite the fact that he plunged his dagger into Caesar's breast. Antony is trying to pass a law proclaiming the province as his, which means more trouble."

"I agree with Lady Atia," said the legate. "Gaius, it's an unholy mess at present. You can take refuge with the troops in

Macedonia until we see how things work out. There would be no problem with that. You will come to no harm there."

"What do you think, Sir?" Gaius asked Decimus.

"I'm sorry, Gaius. I disagree with Atia and Philippus. And with my commander. There's no way you can do nothing. Do nothing and Antony will have you killed. In my opinion we should return to Rome. The sooner the better. We need your great uncle's legionaries."

"His father's legionaries, Dessy. I think it would be better from now on, for him to be known as Gaius Julius Caesar Octavius. If we are going to make a move we will need to emphasise the point repeatedly. He is Caesar's heir and Caesar's adopted son."

Decimus smiled. "A commitment from my brother. Now that is unusual. Gaius, my dear boy, it is up to you to decide, of course. You are still so young and untested. But in my opinion you have the makings of a great man. In fact I am mightily impressed with all of you youngsters." These were the first words of praise Decimus had ever uttered about them. The young men were astonished.

Gaius reached out and clasped the hands of Dessy and Luke. "Thank you, Sirs, for your advice. I think I'll sleep on it. But I agree I should take my adoptive father's full name." He already knew what his actions would be. He'd made the decision years ago.

Decimus organised ships to take as many troops as he could muster back to Rome with them. It took some time to arrange. They landed at Lupiae, where Gaius discovered the whole contents of Caesar's will, which made him heir to two thirds of Caesar's estate. So he would have a considerable fortune to consolidate his political position. First though he had to prise it out of the hands of Mark Antony. Not easy.

They were met at Brundisium by an enthusiastic crowd of Caesar's soldiers. It was fortunate that the army was already being assembled to fight the Parthians, Dessy thought. It made his job much easier. On Gaius's behalf he commandeered the funds set aside in Brundisium for the Parthian war, and ensured a guard was put over them, organising their safe removal to Rome.

Gaius was excited when he heard this news. "This is good. Money is vital. We need to pay the troops handsomely. We could do with a man possessed of a good business brain."

"I have just such a one in mind, Sir," said Dessy.

Gaius laughed aloud. This was the first time Decimus had addressed him as 'Sir.'

"Thank you, Dessy," he replied, grinning.

Once back in Rome Decimus sought an interview with Antony. He brought a couple of his Gallic slaves with him, to be on the safe side. He was ushered into a room full of supplicants for Consul Antony's favour. Antony and his wife Fulvia were seated on elaborately carved chairs on a raised dais, but as soon as Antony caught sight of him, he was whisked away to a small side room, where Antony promptly joined him.

"Fulvia can deal with that lot," Antony grinned. "It's good to see you, Dessy. You're a wonderful excuse. Have you brought your protégé with you? No? Shame. I want to meet him. I've never had a chance to congratulate him on his success in Africa."

A servant arrived with a tray of savouries, but Dessy waved them away.

"Hey, I don't keep poisoned food around, just in case you should come to visit," Antony laughed. He poured two glasses of wine from a flagon, handed one to Dessy, and drank deeply from his own. "What can I do for you, Dessy?"

"I'm not hungry, actually. I've just had lunch with my father-in-law, which means I am stuffed full," Dessy explained. "Gaius Julius Caesar Octavius has authorised me to act on his behalf. He wants his inheritance."

"No. Absolutely not. He's a kid, Dessy. If I give him the money he'll start to think he's important. He'll try and play at politics. Politics is a dangerous game to play at present. When I feel we are in a more stable situation I will release his money. Until then I'm going to save him from himself."

"You're wrong, Antony. He's not a child any longer. There was a good reason for Caesar choosing him as his heir. I admit it was a bit silly awarding him military honours for Africa, when he hadn't even been there, but he has been doing some hard fighting in Spain. He is well able to look after himself. He won't do anything foolish, I'll see to that."

"Nothing doing, Dessy. Tell him from me to be a good boy, and leave the governing to those who know how to do it."

Decimus got up to leave. As he turned to go Antony said, "I hear you got your girl back."

Dessy spun round, shocked.

"Ethela. She's back with you, isn't she?"

"Are you threatening me?" Decimus demanded.

"For the Gods' sakes, Dessy. No, I'm not fucking threatening you! I'm just glad you got her back. That's all."

"Sorry," Dessy muttered, feeling a little ashamed.

"I don't make war on women, Dessy. I have a much better use for them. You should know that of me."

Dessy was pleased to have Egnatius Juvenalis on his side, gaining his support with no difficulty. He made a further visit to Veronica's tomb with him. But this he did automatically, every time he was in Rome. He loved his father-in-law more and more as the years went by. Egnatius agreed to look after money matters for this new political party. A party backed by increasing numbers of veteran troops. He made the tentative suggestion that to counteract Antony's withholding of Caesar's fortune, Gaius should sequester the tribute paid by the Eastern provinces, held at the temple of Venus. To Dessy's surprise, Gaius agreed at once. A young man of rapid decision, obviously. Which was just as well. A lot needed doing, and needed doing quickly. Dessy marched on the temple and insisted the priests allow him access to the money stored in the strong boxes, deep inside the temple walls. He handed the hoard over to Egnatius, who was now appointed as official paymaster to Gaius's soldiers. Egnatius made sure that the rate of pay exceeded the norm.

"Loyalty can be bought and sold, Dessy my boy. Remember that," said Egnatius.

Decimus summoned all his old army friends and acquaintances, gathering a considerable force, making Arretium his military base, north of Rome. By the end of the summer he could count on three thousand of Caesar's former troops, who would be willing to fight for Gaius Julius Caesar Octavius.

BOOK 2 : CHAPTER 7

House of Lucius Philippus, May to December, 44 BC

To start with, Dessy had a vicious quarrel with Atia, she blaming her son's decision on Dessy's 'malign influence.' After she shouted these words at him, they parted on the worst of terms. But once she saw how determined Gaius was, she realised Dessy hadn't had much option. Philippus made her understand that Antony was a considerable threat to her boy. And Dessy, with his veterans, stood between Antony and the death of her son. She hastened to summon him again, but she didn't apologise.

"You always put me last," Atia complained. "I am the very last person on your list that you must see."

"You sent me away, my adorable and unreasonable love," said Dessy, pulling her into his arms.

She was so hungry for his body, she almost ripped the clothes of him, kissing him with a pent-up, all-consuming passion. Dessy was overwhelmed by her.

"Hey, hey! Slow down, my beautiful girl, or I'll be finished before we've even started," he laughed at her.

"Then you'll just have to start again," she said, in deadly earnest.

They came together with a violence that Dessy found slightly unnerving. Atia was kissing and biting, almost sobbing in her eagerness, covering his neck and body with little darts with her lips and teeth, pressing herself so close, almost suffocating him with her arms held tight around his neck. He caught her wrists, and disengaged himself momentarily, but she leaned herself forward, rubbing her breasts against his chest, and pressing her groin against his, so he gave in, taking her face in his hands.

"My turn," he said, smiling. He led her over to the bed, and unpinned her dress, letting it fall in soft folds onto the floor around her, then he gently pushed her down onto the couch. The Gods knew he didn't need any more arousing, but he forced himself to lie next to her, to kiss and caress her slowly, until he knew she was at the peak of anticipation. The sex was perfect, as always, ever-increasing pleasure ending in a long-lasting crescendo of blissful sensation. But he had to waste so much time afterwards soothing her fears. He discovered that his mistress thought he didn't love her any more. Apparently she was too old, she was too ugly, and he loved Ethela more. Dessy kissed her and petted her, attempting to give her instant reassurance after every miserable protestation.

"My darling girl, how can you say anything so stupid," Dessy whispered, gazing down at her body stretched out on the couch before him, "when you are the most beautiful woman in the world. I love you, Atia. I will always love you. You are the most wonderful thing that ever happened to me." He had to reiterate his undying love for her over and over again to satisfy her.

At last she became calmer. All the same Decimus was mightily relieved to disentangle himself from her, and return exhausted to his undemanding freedwoman.

There was never any sign from Philippus that he knew his wife was in love with Dessy, had been in love with Dessy for years now. For the last year Philippus had given up performing his marital obligations, preferring the intellectual thrill of conspiring with other members of the Senate. Now he was stepfather to the new Caesar, he relished the action, bringing together all the old Caesar's allies, of which there were still more than enemies in the Senate, and far more in the general population. Caesar was their hero. They were quite prepared to make young Gaius Caesar Octavius their new hero, especially as Caesar had left them money in his will. The Senate forced Antony to distribute the largess, but he still refused to give Gaius Octavius the money left him by his adoptive father.

Octavia was grateful for the political turmoil. It meant she had little time to think about Marcellus, or dwell on her desperate longing for babies of her own to love. She knew time was passing her by. There was so much to do to support her brother, endless dinner parties to be arranged. She was a little concerned that her brother Gaius was becoming distant from her. He no longer confided his dreams and ambitions to her, like he used to. Perhaps because he was distrustful of her, or thought she couldn't keep his secrets. Although she had never divulged anything about him to anyone. She also thought he was becoming a little too self-important. He was quite rude to Claudius at one dinner.

After she had visited her sister-in-law Popilia and admired her baby son, just two weeks old, and brother to little Cornelia, Claudius found her weeping in the summer house he had built for her in the garden.

"My dearest girl, what has happened to upset you?" he asked her.

But Octavia had no desire to reproach him in any way. Popilia sympathised with her, but couldn't think of a solution, other than the ones Octavia had already tried. Like having one of the slave babies close to her. But that didn't work. She wanted her own children. All her friends had children by now, some of them were proud mothers of a family. Atia continued to nag at her, but she had so little affinity with her mother at present. She could do nothing right for her. Atia told her she wasn't doing enough for Gaius, but she truly had no idea of what else could be done. There were political dinners almost every night.

When Octavia stopped rushing around attending to the needs of everyone else, as she curled up in her lonely bed, Marcellus would come into her thoughts and she couldn't banish him. He hardly came to the house any more, and then only when he had received a formal invitation. Clearly he no longer found her interesting. She was no longer his muse. Perhaps he had found love elsewhere. Not altogether surprising, he was such a lovely and attractive boy.

The young men formed a tight-knit inner group round Decimus and Lucanus; Gaius, Agrippa, Adrian, Max, and Marcellus, dining together more often than not. Though Dessy's father Marcus often went to dine at Cierán's house, where he felt he was treated with a proper deference. He loved the formal old-fashioned way Cierán ran his household. He was aware that his country was passing into the hands of inexperienced youth. Youth which had no regard for the lessons of history. And no manners. Marcus hated being sidelined in his own house. His views were either ignored or ridiculed by the youngsters. But when Gaius cut through one of his stories, saying they had heard it all before and didn't wish to hear it again, Gaius found himself hauled out into the courtyard by Decimus.

Dessy had him pinned up against the wall. "You will go back in there and grovel to my father. And if you don't, I will rip out your guts and tie them round your neck. Do you hear me, *Sir*?"

Gaius managed to confirm that he did with some difficulty, Dessy's hands round his throat making any speech an effort.

Decimus banged Gaius's head against the wall. "Furthermore, from now on, you will treat our elder citizens with proper respect. Or I and my brother will wash our hands of you. Do you understand, *Sir*?"

"Yes, Dessy," Gaius gasped out again.

"You need them on your side, you young fool. Father has a huge circle of friends, most of whom have sons and grandsons. They meet at the baths to talk about the dreadful manners of the young. You are *not* going to give them any ammunition. On the contrary, from henceforth your manners will be exemplary, won't they?"

"Yes, Dessy," Gaius agreed fervently. "Please! I can't breathe!"

Decimus ignored him. "My father's great friend Cicero is planning to return to Rome, and take his place again in the Senate, now that your adoptive father Caesar is dead."

"Oh, is he, Dessy?" Gaius was astonished. "Is Cicero a friend of your father?"

"Yes. They fought together, years ago. They write each other letters bemoaning the state of the world and deploring Mark Antony and the present situation. Now do you understand?"

"Yes, of course. Please will you let go of my neck?"

"Right. Now go and grovel." Decimus released the pressure on his victim's neck, and gave him a resounding box on the ears, making Gaius's head spin. "You can be arrogant when you have some solid achievement to be arrogant about."

Marcus was much gratified when Gaius knelt before him and humbly begged his pardon, excusing himself on the grounds of the excellent wine he had been served in Marcus's house being too much for his immature brain to cope with. At least some of today's youth knew how to apologise properly for their errors.

A valuable lesson had been instilled into Gaius's mind. He realised Dessy was correct, and altered his behaviour accordingly, making sure that he acted with great civility towards the Senators. He was also polite to the plebeians, earning him some much-needed popularity.

Cicero was intrigued to meet with the young Gaius Caesar Octavius, gladly accepting an invitation to dine at his old friend Marcus Taurus's house to meet him. There Gaius behaved with decorum, using his charm, good-looks, and politeness to great effect. Cicero was soon bowled over by him. Luke played his part as well, mobilising support in the Senate, getting both the Cicero brothers onside. Marcus Cicero declared Gaius to be 'a wonderful example of traditional piety to the youth of today,' causing Marcellus and Agrippa to hoot with laughter when they heard reports of the speech.

Many Senators made the mistake of thinking young Gaius could easily be manipulated. Luke failed to disabuse them. In no time at all Cicero and the aristocratic party in the Senate, the Optimates, decided that Gaius should be made a Senator. No one was quite sure where the suggestion came from, but all agreed on its immediate implementation. Which meant that Gaius was gradually becoming more and more aligned with his adoptive father's assassins, and against Antony. The Optimates wanted to cling to the Republic, and thus to their land and wealth, and naively hoped that young Gaius Caesar Octavius could be a popular leader of the plebeians, but controlled like a puppet by his seniors in the Senate.

One night Portia shouted that she had had enough of men conspiring in corners, and lost her temper with Lucanus, a rare event. Usually Portia behaved with propriety, however annoying her husband was. This annoyance was occurring with ever increasing frequency, especially when he told her she wouldn't understand, when a child of three could see clearly what was happening. Certainly her friend Atia knew all there was to know, and passed on masses of information with barely suppressed fury, which was supposed by the men to be strictly confidential. Portia knew why. In Atia's opinion, far too freely expressed to her friend Portia, Decimus was spending too much time dining with his freedwoman Ethela and his male friends, hatching plots to bring ever more important men over to her son's side. Atia despised herself for being jealous of a young barbarian girl, even though she saw more of Decimus that summer than she had for years. Atia was never fully satisfied.

Portia found she was beginning to forget what she was and was not supposed to know. A little shaken by his cross wife, Lucanus attempted to sum up the complex political situation.

"My dear, the assassination of Caesar has left a power vacuum at the centre of our lives. The dictator is gone, and with him the threat of restored monarchy, so the Senate thought, as did the assassins, the liberatores, as they style themselves. But here we have Mark Antony ruling as sole Consul, and refusing to hand over Gaius Octavius's inheritance."

"Gaius Julius Caesar Octavius's inheritance," put in Gaius mischievously.

"Gaius Julius Caesar Octavius's inheritance," corrected Luke with a smile.

"Oh, alright. You can just call me "Sire," said Gaius, grinning. Then he saw Decimus looking at him. "Only joking, Dessy," he said quickly.

Marcellus and Agrippa combined to quell him, but Decimus was staring at him, thinking in his mind that it wouldn't be just a joke for much longer, if Gaius had his way. A Senator at the age of nineteen was simply unheard of.

Lucanus waited for the young men to stop fooling around, then continued. "Mark Antony is too divisive, and is thought to be too ambitious. When Caesar left him in charge of Italy he did not govern wisely or well. It was a relief when Aemilius Lepidus was appointed instead."

"Marcus Cicero is distrustful of Antony, and constantly speaks against him in the Senate," added Decimus.

"I feel Cicero has a sneaking admiration for the liberatores. He helped broker the amnesty for them," Gaius complained.

"You are right that he is anxious to restore a proper Republic, but the Senate comprises many men of disparate views, many supporting Antony, many supporting the actions of the liberatores, and many supporting Cicero."

"Haven't you already decided on next year's Consuls, though?" Portia asked, knowing the answer. "Men of good sense and conservative views, so I've heard."

"You've been listening to Mother," said Gaius. "No one is supposed to know until after the election, darling Lady Portia."

"Antony is promoting a law to enable him to govern Cisalpine Gaul next year, rather than Macedonia, the province awarded to him by the Senate."

"And what's wrong with that?" Portia demanded.

"Everything. For one thing the province is held at present by Junius Brutus, one of the assassins. If Antony succeeds in dislodging Brutus he will have his legions just outside Italy. If anything goes against him he will invade, like Caesar did four years ago."

"As I see it, Sir, we have problems all over the Republic," said Gaius. "There are generals in every province, each commanding a number of legions. To me they all represent a threat to the Republic. And of my adoptive father's assassins, Marcus Brutus has three legions in Macedonia, and Cassius Longinus has four in Syria."

"Almost half the Senate think their intentions were pure, especially they think that of Marcus Brutus. He was your father's great friend, after all."

"The Gods preserve me from such friends," said Gaius.

"No. we will preserve you, Gaius," said Marcellus.

"I'll drink to that," added Marcus Agrippa.

The relative peace of this summer allowed Decimus to continue to muster veteran troops to young Caesar's cause. Egnatius supervised their pay. Dessy was able to visit Atia frequently, although Atia complained it was never frequent enough. He also felt an increasing sense of relief when he returned home to Ethela. Ethela demanded nothing of him. It didn't appear to bother her whether or not he bought her presents. Her only concern was for her son, Mochán. He was thirteen years old now, growing into a lovely looking child, tall and blond, with his father's smile, and eyes bright with intelligence. Veronica's son Lucas was more solidly built, more like a little bull, Dessy laughed as he cuddled him. His other son was slow, but determined not to be left behind by the others. Decimus had wisely decided that they should all be educated together. The child he adored, though, was his little girl, Ella, now eight years old. He would sit her on his knee and play with her, letting her pull his beard and necklace, and cover his face with her kisses. He made sure she was also properly educated. He didn't want another Veronica. The uncomfortable thoughts that surfaced about her paternity were pushed firmly back to the bottom of his mind.

Decimus used his young men as adjutants, sending them out to all his old friends and acquaintances, to whip up support for Gaius Caesar Octavius. He made sure they always had a party of his Gallic slaves acting as armed bodyguards. It took persistence to stop Gaius from continually threatening to assassinate Mark Antony. Gaius thought it was the only way he could get his inheritance. Dessy told him to be patient, which was not a virtue given to Gaius. The boy wanted immediate action. Fortunately two of Antony's legions stationed at Brundisium defected to join the Caesarian forces when they heard about the increased pay offered to the men, the famed Legio Martia and the Legio Macedonia, despite threats and entreaties from Mark Antony.

Looking back afterwards Marcellus decided he was too young and too close to Gaius Octavius to fully understand the heterogenous forces that were unleashed during that pivotal year, although his father did his best to explain matters to him. But the various political factions shifted continually, coming together and making strange alliances, splitting apart again, and then reforming. The Optimates party and the Populares party were becoming blurred round the edges.

Marcellus enjoyed that summer. It felt exciting to be among Gaius's close friends, in at the centre of action. Present at all the dinners when intrigues were launched to bring more and more adherents to the 'young Caesar.' Gaius constantly emphasised his new name. Risky as well, he knew. But with Uncle Dessy around he always felt safe. Had felt safe even on the battlefield, when the front of his brain knew he was anything but safe, and taking appalling risks.

When at home Marcellus had a pleasant time visiting his old friends, always with his four adult slaves armed for his protection. His slave children were sweet, well-fed, now looking more like normal children. They were also mischievous. He hadn't wanted to use physical punishment on them, remembering Ennius and his own childhood, but in the end he had to produce a cane and make them behave with proper respect for the house steward.

Marcellus spent most of the summer riding backwards and forwards from place to place at his uncle's behest. Which was just as well, he thought ruefully to himself. He needed an excuse to keep away from Octavia. Usually he would call round to see her whenever he was in Rome, and was always given a warm welcome by her husband, Claudius. Caesar hadn't pursued Claudius for his actions against him, when Claudius was Consul six years ago. Marcellus presumed this was to do with the family ties, though clearly these didn't count for much if you happened to be Pompey, Caesar's former son-in-law. But recently, the more he saw of Octavia, the worse it became.

He was in love with her. Now he knew what those words meant. He no longer just loved her, he was in love. Passionately in love. But there was nothing he could do about it. The more he wanted to kiss her, hold her, enfold her in his arms, the more difficult it became to visit, making empty conversation, reciting his inane poems, while all the time he was longing to cover her with kisses and crush her to his breast. Everything she said, every movement she made increased his longing to possess her properly. He was worried that he would give himself away all too soon. Marcellus assumed that Claudius, who usually sat with them, professing to admire the poems, and feigning interest in everything he was doing, was just being polite.

Here Marcellus was in error. Claudius was perfectly happy to encourage a handsome young man to his house. He thought Marcellus's poems were becoming more and more mature, some of them quite exceptional. Now the youngster had experienced warfare for himself, his poems rang with truth. Marcellus was a pleasure to look at and to listen to. Claudius was also intrigued to witness the young man's confusion whenever Octavia spoke to him. Both Octavia and Marcellus had discovered a surprising habit of blushing recently. Claudius was fairly sure that these two were in love. He would never relinquish Octavia, though, especially as her brother was gaining more political and military influence every day. He knew Decimus Taurus thought highly of young Gaius Caesar Octavius, and would back him to the hilt. A great man to have on your side.

Antony refused to vote for Caesar's deification. This lost him several allies in the Senate, and caused great offence amongst the citizens. They hadn't in any case agreed with the amnesty for the assassins. Most of the liberatores had already fled from Rome.

As winter approached, Cicero made ever more inflammatory speeches against Antony, causing them to be published. They were read eagerly by the populace. Cicero's obstructive actions against Antony worsened. January would see the installation of the two new Consuls, Aulus Hirtius and Vibius Pansa, neither of whom were friends of Antony. Nor was the general public, which remembered all too well how badly Antony had governed Italy, spending his time drinking and whoring, while Caesar, his commander, was supposedly roughing it in the field. Had they but known it, Caesar had spent a lot of his time doing much the same thing. Although unlike Antony, he could be abstemious when necessary.

At the end of November, with the Senate and the public against him, Antony ordered his remaining legions in Brundisium to join him. He left Rome, took command of his legions, and marched north to Mutina to claim Cisalpine Gaul as his province. The assassin Junius Brutus, with three legions of his own, refused to give it up. So Antony settled down to encircle and besiege him, to the despair of the Senate. Yet another civil war was about to break out, when the country desperately needed peace.

Cicero had already managed to have Gaius elected as a Senator, ridiculous given his youth. Senators weren't supposed to be appointed until they had reached thirty-five years of age. But now he promoted a bill to have Gaius made Propraetor, which would instantly legitimise his accumulation of troops. The law was duly passed. That night at the celebratory dinner Lucanus addressed Gaius as 'Sire,' more in jest than in earnest. But Gaius took it seriously.

"'Sir' will do, Luke," he said. "For now."

"We'd better watch our step," grinned Agrippa.

"I think we better had," whispered Adrian, in all seriousness. "He always wanted to be a great man. He's halfway there already."

"For fuck's sake!" Agrippa exclaimed in exasperation. "He's done sod all, so far."

Gaius overheard. He rose to his feet, tapped his glass with his knife for silence, and made a short speech. "I know you all think I'm much too young for this position, especially Dessy and my mother." He bowed to each of them in turn. "But I swear to you that I will do my utmost to live up to it. You won't have cause to be ashamed of me. I hope to make you all proud to be part of our endeavour to restore our beloved Republic to its former state."

Marcus Cicero proposed a toast. "To the people of Rome and the reinstatement of our Republic."

As one they stood up and raised their glasses, drained the wine, and then hurled the glasses to the floor, to the horror of Portia and Atia, who both knew how much such a gesture cost.

"My best glasses," hissed Portia to Atia, who squeezed her hand in sympathy.

Atia was feeling pleased with life at last. It was good to know that her wonderful son was surrounded by men of sense, men who could be trusted. She knew as well that she would have Dessy to herself all night, as her husband Philippus was away, exhorting the citizens of Arpinum to support his stepson.

BOOK 2: CHAPTER 8

House of Marcus Statilius Taurus, January 43 BC

Atia arrived at Portia's house in an agitated state.

"Whatever's the matter darling," said Portia, as Atia sat down on the couch and burst into tears.

"I'm pregnant," said Atia.

"Congratulations," said Portia, thinking she was missing something.

"Don't be daft," snapped Atia. She dried her tears with the back of her hand, and rubbed her face vigorously. "My husband hasn't touched me for over a year. It's Dessy's!"

"For the Gods' sake! Why didn't you take precautions?"

"Of course I took precautions. Do you take me for a fool? I've taken precautions for the last twelve years, but this time they failed. Here I am, a woman of forty-one and pregnant. But my twenty-six year old daughter is barren. One of the Gods' jokes I suppose," she added bitterly. Atia came to the point abruptly. "Portia, I need help. I need an abortionist. Servants talk. You know what they're like, so I'll have to stay here for a day or two afterwards."

Portia recoiled in horror. "I'm not going to help you to abort Dessy's child," she said. "I've lost two little sons. Life is sacred."

"So you won't help me then? You, my so-called friend, won't help me when I really need help? I'm too old, for this, Portia. Much too old."

"I'll help you. Of course I'll help you. But, good grief, darling. You may well die under the hands of an abortionist. Have you thought of that? Let's think what to do for the best, not the worst." Portia was silent for a moment, her mind turning over possibilities. "You've had two normal deliveries. I'll help you to conceal the pregnancy."

Atia laughed. "Philippus won't notice a pregnancy. He's far too wrapped up in his own importance to notice his wife. But I have a feeling he might notice a baby. And these normal deliveries were years ago. Gaius is twenty years old, for the Gods' sake."

"We must plan this. When is the baby due? Do you have any idea?"

"Oh yes. I've hardly seen Dessy. I know exactly when this little monster was conceived. Dessy never touches me when I'm menstruating, or even when he thinks I'm about to start. He's so squeamish. He has a horror of menstrual blood."

"Luke is the same. It must be the way they were brought up. There were no sisters to enlighten them that we don't actually turn into raving lunatics."

"I've heard nothing from Dessy since December, and the last time I had a period was in November."

"So you think it will be born in September, all being well?"

"All being well?" Atia laughed a mirthless mocking laugh. "Yes. Then what?"

"I think we must ask Dessy."

"No!"

"But Atia, if it's his baby, surely he is entitled to have some say in its future? After all Philippus could divorce you, and then you and Dessy could marry."

"Really, Portia? It may interest you to know that the last time Dessy and I were together I gave him an ultimatum. I told him to get rid of Ethela. He refused. We had a terrible row. I said terrible things. Oh Portia, why was I such a fool?" Atia began crying again. Portia moved to sit by her side and take her in her arms.

"He said I was being unreasonable," sobbed Atia. "He said he didn't want to see me again. He said I was a stupid jealous woman, and that he didn't want anything more to do with me." Atia collapsed into a soggy heap.

"He didn't mean it, darling."

"I think he did. I hardly saw him last autumn, even though he was in Rome. And of course when I did see him I was angry with him. So he's right. It is all my fault. I've driven him away."

"When he knows you are pregnant with his child he will come running back to you. But he won't get rid of Ethela. For one thing the children adore her. She is a second mother to little Lucas, and her own boy and girl wouldn't be able to cope without her. Yes, Dessy does dote on her. He always has and he always will. He is loyal to her. So you will have to grin and bear and share with Ethela."

"Portia, you are to tell him nothing of this. Do you hear me? Nothing. He is not to know."

BOOK 2 : CHAPTER 9

Spring 43 BC

Once the new Consuls, Aulus Hirtius and Vibius Pansa, had taken up their posts at the beginning of January, the Senate turned its attention to the north of Italy. It was decided to send an embassy to Antony, ordering him to desist from attempting to fight Junius Brutus. They returned empty handed. The Senate was furious. More war!

As a consequence Cicero persuaded the Senate to declare Antony an 'enemy of the State,' and issue an ultimatum. This was a thoroughly vindictive ruling, meaning that if Antony were to be apprehended, he would be flogged to death without trial. Lucius Philippus and Decimus Taurus were ordered to present the ultimatum to Antony, as they 'knew each other so well.' Some of the Senators found this ambiguous statement amusing. Dessy kept a careful guard on his conversations with Atia's husband.

They travelled north with Dessy's usual bodyguard, as well as Cierán and some of his Gallic cavalry, just to be on the safe side. Decimus was able to ascertain the positioning of Antony's vanguard around the Via Aemilia, and the fortifications of Antony's camp, which were in good order. Not surprising. Antony wasn't lacking in military skill. And he still had some of Caesar's veterans, especially the second legion, noted for their fighting spirit. Antony would be a hard nut to crack, Dessy thought.

When Philippus and Decimus appeared at the praesidium, Antony looked at them both and laughed aloud, but luckily said nothing outrageous. He read the ultimatum, and laughed again.

"So now I'm an enemy of the State, am I? How my fortunes do fluctuate. No way am I giving up my province. Why doesn't the Senate support me? They passed the law giving it to me in the first place. You'd better stay for dinner, Philippus, and you too, Dessy."

It was a superb dinner. Antony was a good host. The wine was of excellent quality. Decimus and Antony sat companionably chewing over past times. Good times, too, some of them. The evening was spent saying, "Do you remember when............." and they did remember, and laughed together. Although Antony plied Dessy with drink, Dessy was careful to give away no information about the Senate's available resources, or its future actions. Philippus was sidelined, only able to listen, but not contribute. He had never fought alongside Antony.

Afterwards Cierán and his men reported that they too had been well-fed. Clearly Antony and his soldiers weren't short of supplies. Cierán had noted a weaker point in the fortifications, information that was to prove immensely rewarding. Dessy knew that Publius Bassus was marching north from Picenum, with three more legions loyal to Antony. Altogether Antony was a formidable force. But then so was Junius Brutus. He too had fought with Caesar, commanding a brilliant Roman naval force when defeating the Venetii in a sea battle off the coast of Normandy, during the Gallic Wars. Caesar was able to sell the entire Venetii tribe into slavery as a result.

Dessy was thoughtful when they rode back to Rome to deliver Antony's answer. The new Consuls were attempting to raise as many recruits as possible through January and February. But these were raw untrained troops. Dessy didn't think they would be a lot of use. The three veteran legions he had accumulated for Gaius at Arretium, together with the two legions of Antony's that had defected, would be needed if the Senate decided to act.

The Senate did so decide, and ordered Gaius Caesar Octavius's forces to join with Consul Aulus Hirtius and the two legions of defectors at Ariminum on the east coast. Aulus Hirtius wasn't well, but nobly agreed to go anyway. The combined forces marched north to attack Antony at Mutina.

It was all too easy to dispose of Antony's vanguard, with their positions well known, but Decimus urged caution. He decided to set up camp at Bononia, making use of the tiny garrison quarters already in place. Decimus suggested they wait until the other Consul, Vibius Pansa, arrived with the new recruits before launching an all-out assault, even though their numbers were advantageous. He saw no point in taking unnecessary risks with young Gaius.

Mark Antony launched an attack on their camp, which they easily repulsed. Then Antony's scouts reported the arrival of Vibius Pansa with the four legions of newly recruited men along the Via Aemilia. Leaving his brother in charge of the siege, Antony set out on an ambush in the darkness, his soldiers splitting into two groups. He used his excellent cavalry forces along the road to engage with Pansa's forces, luring them into the trap.

Hirtius sent out his strongest legion, the Legio Martia, to join up with Pansa's recruits when told of his approach from the south. Decimus put Adrian and Maximus in charge of the two praetorian cohorts of six hundred men each. At least these troops were properly trained.

The legion was ordered to divide and take cover. Adrian and Max found themselves separated again. It was pitch black as they stumbled through the tall reeds on either side of the road. The ground underfoot was marshy and treacherous. Soon they could hear strangely subdued sounds of battle. There were screams and yelps of pain, clashes of weapons, and running feet, but none of the usual shouting. Some of Pansa's terrified recruits were fleeing from the fighting. The veterans decided that these youngsters were worse than useless, and would just get in everyone's way, so they were ushered back to Bononia. The battle was fought in almost total silence, raging all through the night, each side determined to succeed. Pansa suffered a severe wound in the chest from a javelin, and was removed to Bononia as well, accompanied by Max, who had a sword thrust penetrate his right shoulder. In the end, at daybreak, Antony's forces prevailed; their opponents fled back to their camp, pursued by the enemy, who inflicted heavy losses. The Legio Martia reformed and remained outside the camp to successfully repulse Antony's men. Adrian was thankful to remain in one piece.

Delighted with their success the Antonian legions marched back towards their camp at Mutina along the Via Aemilia, not knowing that Pansa had already summoned additional assistance from Hirtius and Gaius Caesar Octavius. Now Hirtius ordered the Macedonia legion into action. They came upon the two legions of Antony's troops, exhausted from the night-long battle, and defeated them easily. Antony beat a hasty retreat. After two days and nights of bloody fighting, the trampled ground was covered with the corpses of men and horses, severed limbs, abandoned weapons, helmets, and the shields of the dead soldiers.

Despite having done nothing except repulse some feeble attacks mounted by Antony's brother Lucius, Gaius Caesar Octavius was lifted high up on two shields, while his men shouted that he was 'Imperator,' to Decimus's amusement. But the indecisive end result was an appalling loss of life of many superb soldiers. Pansa and Antony both lost half of their forces. And Pansa's wound subsequently proved fatal.

Marcus Cicero was euphoric initially with the report of the battle from Hirtius, and called for fifty days' thanksgiving, praising Hirtius and Pansa to the skies, but hardly mentioning Gaius Caesar Octavius, to Gaius's disgust.

Six days later Decimus considered the legionaries were sufficiently rested to be deployed again. He suggested that as Antony couldn't be induced to fight a pitched battle, his camp should be attacked at the weakest point as noted by Cierán, where the ground was unfavourable for extensive defence works. And an attempt made to bring supplies up to the besieged Junius Brutus and his force in Mutina.

Antony sent two legions, twelve thousand veterans, to fight against Hirtius and Gaius. While the battle was raging Hirtius made the rash but brave decision to make for Antony's tent. At the same time Junius Brutus made a sally from Mutina. Gaius found himself in the thick of the fighting. He could no longer see the battle standard.

"Where are we?" he yelled to the centurion next to him, who was vigorously wielding his sword with great effect.

"The standard bearer's gone down, Caesar," the centurion screamed back.

Gaius shouldered his way through the swaying fighting throng until he reached the crouched figure of the standard-bearer.

"Get this man to safety," yelled Gaius. He picked up the standard, shoved it on his left shoulder, and thrust himself towards the front of the line, sword in hand. Up ahead he heard a shout of rage and despair from his men.

"What is it? What is it?" Gaius shouted.

"The Consul Hirtius, Sir. He's gone down. Looks like he might be dead," bawled someone in his ear.

"We must get to him. We must get his body at least," Gaius yelled back, and charged forward again, raising the standard high in the air. "Come on, you men."

Dessy appeared out of the melee. "What do you think you're doing?" he demanded.

"I must get the Consul," said Gaius, his voice hoarse from yelling.

"He's dead, Caesar."

"I know. I know. I will bring his body back for burial."

"No, my lamb," Dessy shouted. "We are not going to risk a live commander for a dead one. With Vibius Pansa out of action, you are now in sole charge. We must keep you safe." He twisted round for help, relieved to find Darreth right behind him. "Darreth, get Caesar back to safety."

As Darreth turned to usher Gaius back through the lines, a javelin hurtled out of the heavens, impaling him. It passed straight through his thorax. Dessy could see the point sticking out of the front of his chest. Darreth didn't make a sound: he was dead instantly. Decimus hardly moved. He yelled for Cierán to get Caesar to safety. Then he pulled the spear out of Darreth's back, and knelt on the ground, cradling the body in his arms.

"Sod Hirtius," Dessy shouted to his men. "Get this boy back to my tent. He means more to me than a dead Consul." Then he hurled himself into the fray once more.

Both armies retreated back to their camps to take stock of the day's events. Óengus was beside himself with grief. Decimus assured him that he would erect a memorial cenotaph to Darreth when they returned to Rome. It cast a terrible pall over their victory. Dessy had Darreth buried with full military honours, having discovered that the Belgians like the Helvetians had a horror of cremation, thinking their souls would be destroyed by fire. Cierán and Laeforis combined to sing the lament, a hauntingly sad song, that had everyone weeping at the end.

Mark Antony knew how close he had come to annihilation. He was unaware that Hirtius had died, and didn't know that four of the legions ranged against him comprised only raw recruits. Thinking retreat was the safest option, he pulled out his forces that night, and marched them westwards to await the arrival of his reinforcements from Picenum, leaving behind his dead and wounded on the battlefield.

This action shocked his opponents, but Decimus knew it could be put to good use. He advised Gaius to arrange for both their dead and Antony's dead to be buried in trenches, and for the wounded on both sides to be tended.

"Why on earth should we do that?" Gaius asked.

"Any that recover will fight for us, that's why. Now, Sir, go around all the tents, and explain that Antony has left his dead and wounded in the lurch. And that we will treat them honourably. Make sure you enquire about the health of our men. Sympathise with the bereaved and wounded. And praise them to the skies for their valour against a well-armed and well-disciplined foe."

As soon as Junius Brutus's forces found the siege lifted, they deserted wholesale to join with Gaius Julius Caesar Octavius, to his delight. He was now in command of eight legions. Alright, some of them weren't much use as a fighting force, but he knew Dessy would make sure they were properly trained, soon enough.

It took a week to list all the names on the discarded shields, and to bury the dead. Dessy ensured as well that the wounded had adequate treatment. He arranged for those unable to walk to be transported back to Rome. In the meantime they received instructions and information from the Senate. Decimus handed the letter from Lucanus to Gaius.

"Cicero claimed in the Senate that we suffered no loss of life."

"What an idiot."

"And you can see, Caesar, my brother thinks the Senate was much more against you, and much more for Junius Brutus. While we've been fighting Antony, the Senate has given the fleet to Sextus Pompeius, Macedonia to Marcus Brutus, and Syria to Cassius Longinus."

"Your brother is quite correct," said Gaius. "Look at this. The Senate has issued orders for me to hand my legions over to the command of Junius Brutus."

Decimus thought the instruction hilarious. "Well, you're not going to do that, are you, my lovely boy?"

"Certainly not," said Gaius. "We'll tell the Senate to fuck off. Marcellus, put that in more emollient terms for me, will you? You're good with words."

"Certainly, Caesar," said Marcellus.

"Why do the Senate think the legionaries will fight for Caesar's assassin?" Dessy asked.

"The Gods know, I don't," said Gaius. He was a little despondent, because again Cicero had praised the noble sacrifice of Hirtius and Pansa in the Senate, and still given little credence to Gaius Julius Caesar Octavius.

But the men knew. The men exalted. They had another Caesar. One who didn't flinch at the enemy. One who advanced fighting mad. One who charged forward holding the battle standard high, without thought for his own safety. One who was concerned for his men. A hero. Their hero.

Men continued to flood in from Junius Brutus's camp in Mutina. Brutus found his position increasingly untenable. He fled towards the east coast, hoping to get a ship and join his cousin Marcus Brutus in Macedonia. Dessy sent Cierán and his Gauls out to stop him. He thought it would be good for Óengus to get revenge on someone, even if it wasn't the correct culprit.

It was a hard desperate ride to catch up with the few fugitives. Cierán, Óengus, and their men travelled fast by day and some of the night, having to utilise the spare horses they had brought with them. Sometimes feed for the horses took precedence over their own requirements. They arrived at Arminius to find themselves unexpectedly surrounded by a large troop of Antony's Gallic cavalry, dressed in their usual trousers and tunics. Cierán ordered his men to sheath their weapons. He shouted a greeting in the South Gallic language. The leader came up to him, saluted, and greeted him in his own Northern tongue. Cierán responded, replying politely, and gave his name.

"Cierán the Helvetian, the Wise and Just?" asked the leader.

"That was my father," Cierán smiled.

"You are also Cierán, the Wise and Just, so we have heard, Sir."

"Are we after the same prey, by any chance? Junius Brutus?"

The leader smiled back. "Sir, we already have him. Come and see."

Brutus was a sorry sight, dirty, bloody, and dishevelled. He had been stripped of his armour, but still managed to hold up his head, and rain curses on his captors, predicting dire consequences for them all.

"We are the Venetii. It is our right to execute this criminal," said the leader. "Do you agree, Sir?"

Cierán gestured with his hand. "You have every right." He turned to face Junius Brutus. "Sir, we come from Caesar, and these men come from Mark Antony. The consequences to us will be entirely beneficial, I assure you."

Junius Brutus became the first of Caesar's assassins to be killed. Cierán was allowed to retrieve the letters from Brutus's co-conspirators, appropriately edged with blood, from the headless corpse.

BOOK 2 : CHAPTER 10

A month later, to its horror, the Senate discovered that Antony and his men had managed to reach Gallia Narbonensis and had joined forces with Aemilius Lepidus. He had also sent emissaries to Lucius Plancus in Celtic Gaul. Together they had a combined strength of seventeen legions and ten thousand cavalry. A formidable force. The Senate hastened to order Gaius Caesar Octavius to block the three legions marching to join Antony from Picenum.

At their council meeting Gaius and his senior officers chewed over the need to consolidate their power base.

Decimus summed up the situation. "We have eight legions, admittedly only four of them with good soldiers, the other four not much tried and tested as yet, although at least they've started their training. But still, it's sufficient to terrify the Senate. As far as I can see, Caesar, you can either ally yourself with Marcus Brutus and Cassius Longinus......"

"Never!" Gaius shouted.

"Then we had better make an accord with Antony. A staunch friend of your adoptive father, after all."

"But not to me," said Gaius.

"Let me see what I can do with Antony," said Dessy. "But first we must deal with the Senate."

"What do you suggest then, Dessy?"

"You have eight legions. The Senate have none. I think we should march to Rome, and set up camp just outside. That should give the Senate something to think about."

"That sounds good to me," said Gaius. "Does everyone agree?" There were no dissenting voices. The officers were feeling outraged at the Senate's equivocation. "Well then, Dessy, go to the Senate, and deliver the message. Tell them I refuse to give up my legions."

"I'll put preparations in train at once," said Dessy. "And while you're about it, there is a vacancy for a Consul, is there not?"

Gaius looked thoughtful.

"Aim high. Aim for their faces. That's what your father Caesar always used to say."

Gaius smiled. "Quite right, Dessy. Aim high. Say to the Senate that I respectfully request that they appoint me as Consul. But make sure they know I'll take it by force if necessary."

"And if I am to talk to Antony, perhaps you should also insist that the Senate's edict describing him as an 'Enemy of the State' be rescinded?"

Decimus decided to take his young men with him. Max needed time to heal. His shoulder was stiff and painful to move still. Adrian was sympathetic, remembering his own experience. Óengus needed consoling. Basically though, Dessy thought the rest of them were excellent company. They made him laugh, and after losing Darreth he needed someone to make him laugh. Sometimes they even managed to make Óengus laugh, but not often. Somehow Decimus had got to expect that they would all be fine, all survive to live many more days. He'd thought Cassius's death would be enough to satisfy the Gods. Well it doesn't do to be complacent. War always means death for some, why should those he love be spared? Why should he be spared, come to that?

Decimus failed to convince the Senate of the necessity to accede to the new Gaius Julius Caesar's requests. They were horrified. Aemilius Lepidus, now a close ally of Mark Antony, had reached Rome before him. He invited Decimus to dinner, which brought forth an interesting proposal. Dessy returned to give Gaius the message, leaving his young officers in Rome. He thought they deserved a reward of some sort. They had all fought hard and well, especially he singled out Adrian and Maximus. He was proud of them. And Óengus needed to be with Cierán, who was proving adept at finding the right words to help him overcome his anguish at the loss of his much-loved brother.

Decimus found it impossible to get to grips with the training of the four legions of raw recruits while they were on the march south to Rome. A rapid march at that, often more than the usual twenty miles a day. But the commanders knew the reason for speed. Gaius Caesar Octavius needed to consolidate his position. Once back in Rome Decimus thought he would institute a strict training regime for the untested recruits. He knew how effective his centurions were, choosing only the very best to lead the exhaustive programme. And a Caesar needed an army, a powerful army. Dessy would ensure that was exactly what he had.

By July Gaius was back in Rome, in command of an eight legion army camped just outside the city boundary. By August he was inducted as Consul by the Senate, together with his cousin, Quintus Pedius.

BOOK 2 : CHAPTER 11

House of Claudius Marcellus, July 43 BC

It was wonderful to be back in Rome, despite the summer heat. The city was always so full of life. Just strolling through the streets, greeting friends and acquaintances, looking at a miscellany of commodities to buy, was so much pleasure after the rigours and anxieties of war. Marcellus was always accompanied by his Gallic slaves, though, even at the baths. Decimus insisted. There was still so much unrest bubbling away just beneath the surface. These were dangerous times.

Marcellus received an invitation from Claudius, saying how much he and his wife Octavia had missed his visits while he was away on affairs of state. Would he consider coming round to their house and telling them about his experiences?

When he arrived Claudius looked at this confident, tanned, virile young man, and at last came to a decision. Possibly a dangerous decision, but Octavia's brother appeared to be fairly politically secure at present, with an army and Decimus Taurus to support him. And Claudius loved his wife. His exceptional wife, a beautiful girl, who had never reproached him, never even mentioned what she had discovered during that unannounced visit to his bedroom. She knew all about his affairs with the boys at the baths, and ignored all the gossip about him, refusing to discuss her husband's proclivities with her mother, or anyone else.

"I'll walk back with you, if I may," Claudius announced, as Marcellus was taking his leave after the briefest of visits.

Octavia looked up at this. She had an underlying fear that her husband might be interested in her Marcellus. She always thought of him as her Marcellus. She had no desire to share him with her husband, but she could see the attraction. Marcellus was turning into a young man as beautiful almost as her brother, although in a different darker way. She would have loved to kiss him on those smiling lips, be held in those strong arms, rub her cheek against his dear face. It was not fated to be, and she must bury those thoughts deep, deep inside.

As they walked through the streets Claudius decided it was time to act. He waited until there was no one in earshot, then slowed his pace, allowing the attendants to move further ahead of them.

"You may have noticed, Marcellus, that my dear wife is a little pulled down at present."

Marcellus had noticed. But it seemed to him Octavia had been ‘pulled down’ for years. And he thought he knew why. No babies. He said as much, as politely as he could.

"Sir, I think Lady Octavia has always wanted her own family. It is a sadness that so far it hasn’t pleased the Gods to give her what she wants."

"That’s because my wife is still a virgin."

Marcellus stopped dead in the street. "What? What do you mean?" he asked falteringly, his mind reeling in shock.

"It is difficult to put it more plainly. My wife is a virgin. With her I am unable to obtain an erection. I do not intend to provide you with any further information as to my physical problems. The question is only, ‘What can be done about it?’"

"Oh yes, yes of course. That’s the question." Marcellus wondered if his companion was having a fit of madness.

Claudius was smiling at the young man's bewilderment. "I have given this problem a great deal of thought over the years." He wasn't going to tell Marcellus all the various remedies he had subjected himself to, with no success. It was too humiliating. This present conversation was bad enough. And now even the most beautiful boys were unable to help him. "I have decided that you are the solution."

"Oh," said Marcellus faintly, "I'm the solution."

"I will explain to my wife that I have consulted with the Gods." Which was only too true. What a lot of effort and money he had spent in useless sacrifices to Venus. "They have chosen a representative who will come to her at night." Claudius nearly choked on the bitter words. "And have intercourse with her. She will be blindfolded."

"She'll never agree, Sir."

"Yes, she will. My wife is a dear, obedient, credulous girl. She will do as her husband orders."

"Why are you telling me this, Sir?" But he knew why. His mind was reeling in the shock of the idea, as Claudius's meaning hit home.

"Marcellus, you have loved Octavia for many years. And she loves you. I think, observing you both recently, that she is in love with you, and you with her. Am I right?"

Marcellus was feeling more and more uncomfortable with this conversation. He blushed to the roots of his hair. It was all too true. He found himself desperate to crush Octavia in his arms, to cover her dear face with kisses, to hold her close to his body and feel the warm perfume of her skin.

"You don't have to answer," Claudius smiled. "However, should you agree to my proposal, there is a downside."

"Which is?" Marcellus managed to gasp out.

"You will marry my niece Cornelia. A pleasant girl, but plain."

"Oh my God," said Marcellus. "Let me get this right. I'm to fuck your wife and marry your niece."

"Admirably succinct," Claudius replied dryly.

"But isn't it a crime? I mean allowing your wife to be seduced by another man? I thought that was a crime."

"No one will ever know. I will insist that you be masked at all times. Octavia will not know who you are. You will merely be an instrument of the Gods. Go away, my boy, and think it over. I will invite my niece to visit us tomorrow. If you put in an appearance, I will know you are interested. If not, my dear wife will have to content herself with the life she has. I would trust no one else with her. Only you. You are a dear boy, and will do nothing ever to hurt her."

Claudius was fond of his niece, an intelligent girl, who deserved better than a life as a Vestal Virgin. And there would need to be some kind of smoke screen to camouflage the truth.

Marcellus arrived back at his house in a state of shock. This needed thinking out. Was it some sort of plot? He knew that in theory a husband could kill either participant if his wife was found in an adulterous liaison with another man, although admittedly he had never heard such a thing actually happening. Anyway, surely he was far too unimportant to be worth killing? Claudius could be jealous, though, concocting the story of his infertility just to give him an excuse to kill his rival. It seemed so unlikely. Marcellus was pretty sure that Claudius liked him and enjoyed his company. And what a story to make up.

He decided to put in an appearance the next day and couldn't understand why Claudius thought his niece to be plain. Marcellus thought she would have been quite a pretty girl, if only she hadn't a wine-stain coloured blemish obscuring part of her complexion and extending downwards into her neck. He wondered how far it went. Unlike his lovely Octavia, her face was still young and unformed. She was conscious of her defect, sitting turning her face away from him, so he got up and deliberately sat on her affected side, seeking to engage her in conversation. To his amazement she smiled shyly back at him, and said how much she admired his poetry. Then she correctly quoted one of his love poems, a good one he thought. Apparently this Cornelia thought so too. He decided to consult his Uncle Dessy as soon as he was back in Rome, a man of affairs, well, one affair at least.

Decimus was a little surprised on his return, when almost immediately Marcellus asked to discuss something with him, something so secret that no servants were to be allowed anywhere near them. He wondered what trouble his nephew had got himself into.

"Can I get my horse stabled first?"

"Yes, of course, Sir."

Once this was achieved Marcellus started to explain his dilemma, and concluded, "You know all about these things, don't you, Uncle Dessy?"

"Meaning what exactly, Marcellus?"

"Well, everyone knows you've been fucking Lady Atia for years."

"Oh yes?" said Dessy. "And just how did you know that?"

"I thought everybody knew," said Marcellus. He thought it best not to explain that they had all peered through the shutters to see a naked Decimus and Atia sprawled out on the bed in the annexe.

"For the Gods' sake!" said Dessy.

"So what do you think, Uncle Dessy? Will you help me?"

"Of course, Marcellus, I will always help you."

Marcellus could see that even Uncle Dessy was taken aback at Claudius's bizarre suggestion.

"If he loves his wife so much he'll allow someone else to father her children, I don't see why he doesn't divorce her, so she can marry you."

"I think he's frightened that if he divorces Octavia her brother might punish him for precipitating the civil war when he was Consul. And I doubt if Gaius will allow her to marry me. I'm no one important."

Decimus frowned at that. "My dear boy, you become more and more important every day. However, if you wish it, I will help you to take this chance offered by Claudius, and risk no other at the moment, just in case you lose everything. Are you sure you will be able to cope with young Cornelia as well?"

Marcellus thought it would be no problem.

BOOK 2 : CHAPTER 12

House of Claudius Marcellus

They were to meet in the summer house at the bottom of the garden. A couch was already installed, as it was a place where Octavia went often to cry unseen. She had her pride. Her husband's explanation she found hard to believe. But she desperately wanted to believe in it. Claudius said he had consulted the Gods on many occasions, but at last he'd had an answer. Apparently the Gods knew her to be a good and virtuous girl, who always properly celebrated the holy days. The Goddess Juno had watched her as she kissed the feet of her statue, and anointed her with costly perfumes. They knew she knelt for hours with prayers and entreaties. They were aware of her enormous sacrifices. So they would reward her for her piety. She was to have children, the Gods had decided. An angel would come to her at night. But she would have to be blindfolded, lest the sight of the angel blinded her with his radiance. The angel would wear a mask.

It was just as well Marcellus didn't know he was to be radiant. He was standing outside the garden gate, waiting for Claudius to usher him to his assignation. It had been raining. A quiet drizzle, unlike his heartbeat, which was sounding loud and rapid in his ears. He was so nervous. He hadn't thought he would be so nervous. He wondered if all bridegrooms felt like this before the wedding. He would find that out soon enough. His parents had jumped at the chance of him being allied to Claudius, a Senator and former Consul. His marriage to Cornelia was to take place in a few weeks' time.

The gate creaked open. To his surprise Ganainm appeared before him, holding a lantern. Ganainm bowed to him, smiled, and took his hand. Of course, a speechless man who loved Marcellus would be unlikely to betray any of this to another person. Marcellus felt a certain relief. Ganainm led him through the garden, brushing past wet leaves and the scented roses, until they arrived at the little summer house. Ganainm pushed open the door, bowed again, gave Marcellus the lantern and walked away.

The aroma of sandalwood, Marcellus's favourite perfume, drifted into the room. Marcellus could hear his own harsh breathing. He waited in the doorway, transfixed by the sight of his love. Octavia stood before a cluster of oil lamps. She was wearing her wedding dress, but no veil. Her eyes were covered with a blindfold. Her hair shone luminous around her dear head like a halo of light. He thought he had never seen anything or anyone more beautiful, as she tilted her face up towards him.

Something snapped deep down inside Octavia. "Marcellus, take that stupid mask off," she ordered.

As he stood dumbfounded, she ripped off her blindfold and the cap she wore on her head, shaking out her long softly curling hair, lustrous in the lamplight. She looked at Marcellus and suddenly she laughed, her lovely gurgling laugh. Sheepishly he removed the mask.

"How did you know it was me?" he asked.

"Because you walk like Marcellus, and you smell like Marcellus, and you cough like Marcellus."

"I didn't know I was coughing. I was nervous."

Octavia laughed again. "For goodness sake, you've known me long enough."

"What shall we do now," asked Marcellus, thoroughly bewildered.

"You make love to me, and then I have a baby, and then I will be happy ever after, or that's what my poor husband hopes."

"Oh."

"Yes," Octavia sighed. "For an intelligent man, he's remarkably stupid. Never mind. Look, at least we can have supper."

"Oh good. I've eaten nothing all day."

"No. Nor me, either." They both laughed this time.

"Let's sit down then, and eat."

They sat together, side by side, the closest he had managed to get to her for years. Marcellus decided it was time to take charge. This opportunity was simply too good to miss. There she was, his beloved, looking even more beautiful than usual, with her face flushed in excitement. "Don't you want me to make love to you, Octavia?" Marcellus whispered. He leaned towards her and kissed her cheek.

"Do you want to?"

"You know I've loved you all my life."

"I hope you didn't want to make love to me when you were six!"

"No of course not. But recently, no, not even recently, things changed. I found I wanted to touch you, hold you, kiss you. And as I couldn't it became a torture for me, so I stayed away, and tried not to think about you. But it didn't work. I've thought about you night and day, when sometimes I should have really been thinking of something else, like how to stay alive."

"So that's why you wouldn't come. Oh Marcellus, Marcellus. You've made me so happy. I thought you didn't love me any more. And I know it's torture, but that was so awful, thinking you no longer cared. I'd prefer the torture."

Claudius left them strictly alone that night. In the morning Ganainm came to escort Marcellus back to his own house, going by such tiny alleyways Marcellus was soon lost.

The sound of singing echoed through the house. Octavia hadn't sung like that since they were first married, Claudius remembered in shock. He met his wife at breakfast. She looked at him with such an expression, brimming with so much joy in her face. It was a look he had never seen before.

"You seem happy this morning, my dear," he said, kissing her fingers. "I trust you weren't too bored last evening. Did you manage to sleep well?"

"No, I did manage to sleep, Sir. But I think I will continue to sleep in the summer house for now?"

"My dear, all I wish is for your happiness."

Octavia was overcome. "Thank you, Sir," was all she could managed to say.

No one seemed that surprised when Decimus announced that he would supervise the troops guarding the streets of Rome in the evenings, but Portia wasn't sure why Marcellus had to be involved.

"Don't you worry. I'll look after him. And so will his slaves."

BOOK 2 : CHAPTER 13

House of Marcus Statilius Taurus, September 43 BC

Everyone who was anyone was present at the splendid banquet laid on by Marcus Statilius Taurus in celebration of their victory and their safe return. He had to wait until his son Decimus had stopped galloping the length and breath of Italy, negotiating a meeting with Antony and Lepidus. This was to take place in October at Bononia.

Portia had spent a harassed month, getting the whole evening organised, arranging for the hire of musicians and dancers, and pouring over menus. Her former secretary spent hours writing out the elaborate invitations, to Cierán's disgust. He wanted his wife to himself.

Portia arranged for Atia to have a comfortable seat on her husband Philippus's couch, well padded with cushions, as Atia was now near her time, and found herself beset with unaccustomed aches and pains. Her feet and legs were swollen. Walking was difficult, so she travelled in a litter. She didn't want Dessy to see her, but Philippus insisted she attend the dinner to honour her son. He was baffled by his wife's unwillingness in the last few months to venture out of the house. Not even to the baths. He put it down to indigestion.

Dessy was shocked by Atia's appearance. She looked haggard and pale, and why on earth was she wearing that unflattering garment? So wrapped round with material that her usual slender figure was obscured. He tried to speak to her, but she turned away, allowing her dress to slip, giving him a deliberate cold shoulder. Dessy was too proud to be snubbed by a woman, so he made no further attempt to engage his former mistress in conversation, and summoned Ethela and the very new baby to join him on his couch, to Atia's chagrin.

Dessy loved watching Ethela suckling the infant, exposing her beautiful creamy breasts to his gaze.

Ethela was angry with him. "I am not a weapon," she hissed. "You are being a bad man, Dessy."

Octavia came over to inspect Ethela's new arrival. She dropped a kiss on the baby's tiny forehead. The baby opened her eyes and stared at her with unfocused gaze. Octavia was enchanted. "Oh, she's so beautiful, Sir. You must be so proud."

Dessy agreed, laughing. "All my children are beautiful. There have never been such beautiful children in the world before. May the Gods always protect them, and not be jealous." He thought he had never seen Octavia look so lovely herself. Her smile was dazzling.

Octavia almost danced over to her mother's side. "I think I'm pregnant, Mother," she whispered excitedly. If she was looking for praise she was in error. Atia gave her a scornful glance and said acidly, "Not before time."

"Mother, couldn't you be pleased for me just once?" Octavia pleaded. If only she knew in what way she had offended her mother, so as to make Atia hate her. Because that's what she felt. That her mother hated her. It was a horrible feeling.

Octavia returned to find Claudius, but he had gone in search of Marcellus. She could see them discussing her animatedly. Marcellus rushed over. He wanted dearly to take her in his arms and kiss her sweet mouth, but that would need to wait for a more opportune moment.

"You clever girl," Marcellus whispered.

As Ethela leaned back against her master, holding her tiny baby daughter in her arms, Atia gave a loud cry and rose staggering to her feet. All the guests turned to look at her. She was pale and gasping in pain, with a shimmering of sweat on her face, clutching at her side. Dessy ignored her, thinking she was indulging in histrionics because of Ethela, but Portia knew better. She grasped her friend under the arm and summoned assistance at once.

"Oh look, Lady Atia," said young Lucas. "Your dress is all red at the back. You must have sat on some cherries." Which was strange, Lucas thought, as there weren't any cherries. It was altogether the wrong time of year for cherries. He tried to puzzle it out.

Portia was alarmed, realising Atia could well be in labour. It would be unfortunate if her friend was to produce a baby in Dessy's house, as things stood between them at present. Atia was becoming whiter, the blood appearing in spots on the floor as she tried to walk out of the room. Portia looked round for help, summoning Cierán with a beckoning hand.

"Take Lady Atia to my room, please, dear Cierán," she whispered urgently. "She is unwell."

Cierán clasped Atia under her arms, and supported her for a few steps. Atia let out a sharp cry of anguish as her legs buckled beneath her. Cierán lifted her up in his arms, and discovered some of the truth of the situation.

"Lady, I'll carry you. Don't worry, don't worry," he said, adopting his usual calm tone of voice. Cierán was always good in any emergency. He knew the way to Portia's room, carrying his burden effortlessly in his strong arms.

Portia swiftly followed them into the room, and shut the door. "What is it, darling? Are you having labour pains, do you think? Have your waters broken?"

"I don't know, Portia," Atia gasped out. "This doesn't feel like labour to me. It's agony, constant agony. Pain all over my abdomen. Something's wrong, Portia." She paused to gather her remaining strength to speak. "Something's badly wrong. I feel so ....I feel so weak.......I feel so dizzy......oh God, this pain's terrible, terrible. Make it stop, Portia. Please darling." Atia moaned again in terrible discomfort, writhing on Portia's bed, sometimes clutching her hand, sometimes the coverlet. She tried to sit up, shifting backwards and forwards a little, all the while the blood draining from her cheeks. Her lips looked almost colourless. "Get me Musa. I need Musa. Please, Portia."

Portia sped back to the dining room, and stood over Dessy.

"Dessy, I need Musa," she whispered urgently. "Now. At once. Get him for me, please."

Decimus laughed. He'd had a lot to drink already. He spoke a little too loudly. "Why, Portia? Is Atia having hysterics again? Just slap her face. That's what I did."

Portia was furious with him. "How dare you!" she hissed at him. "You are despicable. How dare you talk like that about her! Get me Musa. Now, I said. At once!" Portia turned on her heel and walked out of the room, closely followed by Ethela and Octavia.

Decimus was astonished. But realising that his beloved sister-in-law was really upset and cross with him, he sent for his physician. Cierán appeared to inform him that the doctor was already with Lady Atia.

"I think she's having a baby, Dessy," whispered Cierán.

Decimus looked up at him in bewilderment. Then he too rose and walked out of the room, making straight for Portia's bedroom.

He found Atia lying stretched out on the couch, apologising to Portia over and over for the mess she was making, both physically and socially. She also apologised to Musa, as she was having such difficulty lying still.

Musa managed to make a thorough examination, despite his patient's constant movements. He soon realised that Atia was heavily pregnant and bleeding internally, as well as vaginally. This was something he could do nothing whatsoever about. Haemorrhage during childbirth was a major cause of death. There was no way of stopping the bleeding. Atia's pulse was so rapid; she was sucking in air in great gasps in an effort to breathe. He could see that she was losing the battle for life. As she became weaker, her struggles lessened. He took her hand.

"My dear lady, you must make your peace with the Gods. I fear there is nothing more I can do for you."

Dessy heard these words as he entered the bedroom. He saw Atia's body, the swollen abdomen taut with the massive blood loss between the wall of the womb and the placenta. He looked in bewilderment at his mistress, then walked over to the couch and pushed Musa out of the way.

"Darling Atia, you mustn't die. My dearest love, you mustn't die."

Atia opened her eyes. She attempted to raise herself. "Dessy," she gasped out."Save the child. It's yours, my darling. Our child. Save the baby." Her eyes closed. She flopped back onto the couch, as the blood slowed to a trickle. "Musa, I order you ....this is an order.......do whatever it takes.... Whatever it takes........"

"Child? What child?" Dessy yelled. "What is she talking about?"

"Your child," snapped Portia. "Musa, you must do as she asked. Be quick."

Musa dived into his case of instruments, produced a scalpel, and made the incision. A flood of blood poured out of the wound. His hands groped around inside and found the tiny infant. He delivered the baby out of the cavity with the greatest care. Then he held the baby up by the heels, and lightly tapped the creased buttocks. Nothing happened. The baby was laid next to its mother, where it lay blue and motionless.

Octavia was in shock. But she reacted instinctively, moving towards her mother. She plucked the baby from the couch, and handed it to Ethela. Ethela sat down on the edge of the couch, and began to massage the tiny limbs. The rest of them stood in a circle round her. The baby twitched its little legs, then gave out a thin cry. Ethela slipped down her dress from her shoulder and held the baby to her nipple, rubbing its little mouth backwards and forwards. The baby cried more strongly, and then made a feeble effort at sucking.

Gaius stood in the entrance. "What the hell is going on?" he demanded.

Portia rushed to cover up the body of her friend, as Ethela moved past Gaius and out of the room with the baby in her arms.

Musa bowed low. "I am so sorry to have to tell you, my Lord, that your mother has suffered a catastrophic haemorrhage from the womb, no doubt due to a cancerous growth."

"What do you mean? What catastrophic haemorrhage?"

Musa stood aside to reveal the ashen face of Atia, and the pools of blood over the sheets and on the floor.

"Mother, Oh Mother." Gaius dropped to his knees beside the couch. Decimus moved swiftly to block his view of the body.

"My dear boy. Your mother didn't want to be seen like this. Let us leave the women to restore order and dignity, before we take our farewells."

Gaius allowed himself to be shepherded out of the room, his toga stained with his mother's blood where he had knelt by her. Portia shooed Octavia out as well, then she and her maids set to work to clean and clear up.

Musa stitched the wound with neat subcuticular stitches, leaving only a thin red line to show the opening where the baby had entered the world. Portia decided it had to be given out that Atia's child was actually the twin of Ethela's new baby. The truth must be concealed from Philippus and Gaius.

Philippus was bewildered, standing in front of his dead wife, shaking his head. "I thought it was indigestion," he said plaintively. "She wouldn't go out anymore, not even to the baths. But I just thought it was indigestion."

"Why didn't she tell me about this cancer? Why did she keep it secret?" Gaius demanded in a rage.

"No doubt she didn't wish to give you her troubles when you have so much else to think about," said Philippus sadly. "Such a wonderful woman. Always putting her children first."

True enough. Politics paid no attention to medical catastrophes. Gaius had little time to mourn his mother. He had to set out almost immediately to meet with Antony and Lepidus.

BOOK 2 : CHAPTER 14

Bononia, October 43 BC

The three of them met in a room without slaves or others present, apart from a single young secretary, who sat with piles of closely written parchment in front of him, lists of names of all the Senators and knights. Dessy was turned away at the door by Antony, who said he wasn't wanted.

"Just hang on a moment," yelled Decimus. "Caesar, eat nothing and drink nothing in this room. Not unless it is brought by one of your own servants."

"How melodramatic," Lepidus laughed. "Do you think we're going to poison him?"

"I'd put nothing past you," snarled Decimus.

"What's the deal?" asked Antony, once Decimus was manhandled away.

"We would like to join forces with you both. Then if we combine, we can take on my father's assassins. I understand from Decimus Taurus that you have already agreed to this."

Antony nodded. "Very well, it's agreed."

The three men shook each other's hands.

"But first we need to clear out that nest of vipers in the Senate, the Optimates," said Antony. "I suggest we issue a proscription against their names. Unless they flee into exile they can be killed by anyone, who can then claim a reward. But we will confiscate all their land and possessions."

Aemilius Lepidus agreed with enthusiasm. "They are a dagger in our sides. We must steel ourselves to be utterly ruthless.

In any case, we need money and land for our legionaries. This is a right and proper way to get it. Two birds with one stone."

"Correct," said Antony. "We mustn't allow sentiment to interfere. We must be practical." He looked at twenty-year-old Gaius Julius Caesar Octavius, who was still wearing the dark tunic of mourning for the recent death of his mother. Antony thought the young man would be easy to handle.

Gaius signalled his agreement, thinking that it would be useful to get rid of so many aristocrats who had always been against Caesar, the popular party and reform. They were desperate to hang onto their power, money, land, and seats in the Senate. But Gaius hadn't known until the others started to produce actual names, just how appalling the blood-letting was going to be. He had enough sense to realise this would stain his reputation for years afterwards. But he was outmanoeuvred by the wiles of the two more senior politicians. They played him skilfully, reeling him in like a fish.

"You need to rid yourself of the Cicero brothers," Antony suggested. "They are past masters at plotting."

Gaius frowned in annoyance. "How can I possibly do that? It was Marcus Cicero who urged the Senate to make me a Senator, even though I was theoretically far too young. And he allowed me to vote with the Consuls."

"He was doing it all for his own benefit. He thought you could be easily manipulated, not realising that you are entirely your own man, with your own principles, and that you make your own decisions."

Gaius was feeling that at last someone was recognising his innate abilities and rightness to be considered one of the greatest Romans. "He also did his best to make me Consul. By then he must have discovered that I am not easy to control. So I don't wish him or his brother to be proscribed."

"How about this letter, then." Antony quoted the damning letter from Marcus Cicero to his friend Trebonius, one of the assassins. "'How I wish you had invited me to that superb banquet on the Ides of March.' That's what your precious Cicero wrote. Not exactly friendly towards you or your father, is it, young Caesar?"

"Are you serious about this, or not?" Lepidus butted in. "This is a golden opportunity to stabilise the Republic. It needs us three acting in concert. And we have to harden ourselves to perform unpleasant tasks. We are surgeons, cutting into the rotting corpse of the Optimates. I have volunteered my own brother."

Gaius gasped in surprise.

"And I have given my uncle, Lucius Antonius, to be listed," Antony declared. "If you're not up to it, Gaius, my lad, you'd better retreat to some island or other, until Lepidus and I have dealt with our mutual enemies."

"Of course I'm serious," said Gaius.

"I want Dessy proscribed, then," said Antony, watching in satisfaction the expression of horror on Gaius's face. "He's an arrogant bastard, far too cocky for a jumped-up centurion."

"Well you can't have him, either," Gaius reacted angrily.

"Not just him. I want his brother as well, and that nephew of his. What's he called? Titus? Marcellus? The one that writes dreadful poetry. He keeps changing his name. Trying to confuse us maybe." Antony laughed. "What do you think, Lepidus? Add Dessy and his crew?"

"Okay by me," said Lepidus. "I'd include their father as well. He's a friend of Cicero's. Get rid of the lot of them."

"Two to one, Gaius. Sorry."

Gaius panicked. "No, no. Alright. Leave Dessy alone. Leave his family alone. You can have the two Cicero brothers after all."

It took them two days to thrash out all the names. As each name was added, Gaius began to experience a feeling of exhilaration at the power he wielded, every suggestion of his being added to the list.

"Anyone ever heard of Titus Volusenus?" Lepidus asked.

"He's a friend of mine. A charming man. Unambitious. Likes to do the right thing. He's Gaius's father," Antony explained.

"Oh, him. We need to keep him, then. Don't ever upset Gaius Volusenus."

"There's another one afterwards on this list that I've never met," complained Gaius. "Antistus Petronius Antinous Allanus. He can't have been much in Rome."

"Good grief, you can't have him proscribed," said Antony hastily.

"And why not?"

"He was my medical officer. A brilliant physician and surgeon. One day we may have need of his services. He performed the post mortem on your father."

"I remember him. A hulking great bloke, with blond hair," said Lepidus.

"That's him."

"Fair enough," said Gaius, who had a great respect for physicians.

By the time they exited the meeting room, there were three hundred Senators to be proscribed, and nearly two thousand of the Equites rank. Antony gestured to the young secretary who had kept the copies of the names, three separate lists for the three 'Triumvirs,' as Antony termed them.

"Kill him," said Antony to the guards. Gaius spun round to face him. "We don't want any witnesses, do we?"

"I suppose not," Gaius agreed, with a sick feeling in his stomach. What would everyone say about this appalling blood-letting? Nothing good, he was quite sure. And no one would hear of his efforts to spare those holding important public offices, many of whom had performed their functions with great ability. And he would never be forgiven for allowing the Cicero brothers to be added to the list.

Decimus grabbed the list out of his hand. He skimmed through the names, nearly choking when he came to Marcus and Quintus Cicero. "Are you quite mad?" he demanded, white with fury that his idiotic commander had agreed to this horror.

"Are you questioning my decisions?" snapped Gaius, consumed with guilt.

"Yes, Caesar," said Dessy.

"They wanted you," shouted Gaius. "And not just you, your entire family."

"No, they didn't," Decimus said angrily. "They wanted Marcus Cicero, and now you've just handed him to them on a plate. Damn Antony!"

"Don't you dare criticise me," Gaius shouted even louder. "Just you remember your place. And it is not to tell me what and what not to do! I'm in charge, I'm the Consul, not you!"

Decimus looked at him as if seeing him for the first time. "As you please, Caesar," he said. He saluted, turned on his heel and began to walk away.

"Dessy, you mustn't desert me. Not now. Not when there's so much still to do. Dessy? Dessy!"

"No. I'm too old for this. I can't be doing with temper tantrums from kids who are so bloody clever. I'm leaving the army. I've done my time. I don't have to do any more. I quit!"

"Maybe I should add your name to the proscribed list after all, then."

"You do that. See if I give a fuck."

Gaius stopped yelling. "It's because of Mother, isn't it? That's why you're so........."

Decimus turned on him savagely. "Don't you dare say another word."

"But Dessy, I'm devastated as well. It's not just you. We both loved her so much. Listen, we can mourn her properly when we return to Rome. I will build a mausoleum of such magnificence. It will do her justice, I assure you."

"You're a fool," Dessy told him. "Don't you know already rumours are circulating that you killed Hirtius in the confusion of the battle, and that you poisoned Pansa? What sort of a reputation will you have, if this goes through? Even the plebeians will think you're a monster."

It took Gaius an hour to talk Decimus round. "In the Spring we are to go after Marcus Brutus and Cassius Longinus in Macedonia. I need you, Dessy. Your country needs you. For the Gods' sake don't leave me to cope with Antony by myself," he argued. At last he was successful. Decimus agreed to stay on until either the assassins were annihilated, or they were.

"But that's it," he declared. "After that I'm retiring to bring up my children in peace on my estate." And I'll be with Ethela, he thought, my beautiful, sweet, anything but jealous Ethela.

Gaius and Decimus took the list of names, and ambushed Antony in his tent. Antony was chatting to his wife Fulvia, with his son on his lap and his little daughter leaning against his chair. He looked the epitome of a peaceful family man. Which just shows how deceptive appearances can be, thought Dessy.

Gaius was introduced to Fulvia's eldest daughter Clodia, a pretty shy girl, fathered by Fulvia's first husband, and thus Antony's step daughter. When they got down to business Gaius explained that in retrospect he had concluded that the proscription of a third of the Senate would do none of them any good.

Antony laughed. "You mean Dessy is getting cold feet," he sneered. But Antony had been having similar doubts. Perhaps the three of them were being overzealous.

Lady Fulvia vehemently disagreed. She was all for the original list. The men managed to get the list whittled down to a sixth of the Senate, but no further. Antony and Lepidus and especially Fulvia, refused to yield any more. The Cicero brothers stayed on the list, Fulvia insisted.

One hundred and forty Senators were proscribed, and nearly a thousand knights. Some managed to flee into exile, with their wives, family and gold, mostly to Sextus Pompey, who was now holding Sicily and Sardinia. Their property was confiscated. Marcus Cicero tried unsuccessfully to escape. He was caught while trying to get to Macedonia. His severed head and hands were displayed in the Forum in Rome. The cowed Senate passed the Lex Titia, agreeing that Antony, Lepidus and the young Caesar become the Committee of Three for the Ordering of the State for five years, forming the second, but this time official Triumvirate. Gaius was betrothed to Antony's stepdaughter to consolidate the agreement. All his close friends were inducted as Senators, despite their youth, Marcellus, Agrippa, and Adrian.

BOOK 2 : CHAPTER 15

House of Claudius Marcellus, Spring 42 BC

On the first of January the tame Senate declared the original Gaius Julius Caesar to be divine, and authorised his worship in various temples, with Mark Antony designated as his high priest.

At the end of January Gaius, Agrippa, and Marcellus walked round to Claudius's house to congratulate Octavia on the birth of her son. They all brought presents for the baby. Marcellus also brought a poem, but this was strictly only for Octavia to see.

Octavia, looking a little pale, and still rather plump, proudly exhibited her tiny son. She was blissfully happy. The three young men gazed in awe.

"He's so small," whispered Gaius, as if a loud noise would blow the child away.

Octavia laughed. "He was quite big enough for me." She was still so sore, but the baby was worth it.

"What's his name?"

"His name is Marcellus," said a smiling Claudius.

"Looks like you," grinned Agrippa, tapping Marcellus lightly on the shoulder.

There was an instant's shocked silence, then Gaius punched Agrippa so hard that, taken completely unawares, he fell to the ground. Gaius was white with anger.

"If Caesar's wife must be above suspicion, then the same rule applies to Caesar's sister," shouted Gaius.

"It was a fucking joke, you bastard," yelled Agrippa from the floor.

"Boys, stop this. Stop it at once," Octavia pleaded.

"I'm not a boy. I'm the son of the Divine Julius, and I will not permit insults to my sister to go unavenged."

Marcellus picked up the baby and said lightly, "Poor baby. You've a lot to live up to." He kissed the baby's tiny cheek, and placed him carefully back in the crib.

"He'll manage fine. I'll see to that," said Gaius, beginning to simmer down.

Marcellus helped Agrippa up from the floor. "Don't say anything. Don't make things worse for Octavia," he said.

Agrippa looked daggers at Gaius, but held his tongue. The young men didn't stay too long, being told by an embarrassed Claudius that Octavia still needed plenty of rest.

Marcellus realised he would have to wait some time before he could see his love again, and that their liaison was becoming dangerous for all involved. But other considerations worried him much more than the danger. Now Octavia had a son, would she still want him? He wanted her, quite desperately.

He found Cornelia to be sweet and loving. There was no problem at all making love to her. She appeared to be so grateful that Marcellus had deigned to marry a girl with such a deformity. When Claudius announced their marriage to Gaius, Gaius had turned to Marcellus laughing, and said, "Oh I suppose all cats look alike in the dark." Which remark made Cornelia cry a little. When Octavia tried to call her brother to order for displaying such atrocious manners, he told her abruptly to shut up.

Now Cornelia was pregnant as well. She confessed that she was frightened her children would also be affected by the skin stain. Marcellus asked Musa's opinion, which was that this was unlikely, to the couple's great relief. When Cornelia's pregnancy was advanced Marcellus had to make do with the bath girls. He had one he liked very much, an adventurous girl, who taught him a lot. But she was expensive, and now he was starting a family he was beginning to take life a little more seriously. If he was killed in the forthcoming campaign, how would his wife and son fare? Of course, it might be a girl. Well, he didn't mind either way. As long as Cornelia survived. That was the main thing.

He remembered Aunt Veronica with crystal clarity. He thought about her a lot. He didn't want Cornelia to feel that she was second best, and that he didn't love her enough, like Uncle Dessy. Was that why Aunt Veronica had died, as Dessy had claimed one night in Spain, after a hard fight, and when he was too drunk to know what he was saying?

Marcellus loved his uncle with all his heart, still. But he could see that Uncle Dessy wasn't the perfect human being he had thought him when he was a child. There were flaws. Possibly involving Lady Atia, Marcellus thought, as well as Aunt Veronica. He wondered if Dessy ever considered marrying again. But he seemed perfectly happy with Ethela.

Marcellus was pleased to receive an invitation almost immediately, summoning him back to Claudius's house.

"I understand you will be departing for Macedonia, in the near future, my boy," said Claudius.

"Yes, Sir. We are hoping to ship twenty-eight legions over there, to take on Brutus and Cassius. They have also amassed a huge number of troops, mainly from the eastern provinces and kingdoms. It will be a long drawn out campaign, according to my uncle. A difficult logistical problem for him to solve."

"And we hear my niece Cornelia is expecting a baby. How is she?"

"She seems to be managing fine, so far. Her health is good."

The most unexpected event was when his wife came to his bedroom one morning and recited his new poem.

"We have unlocked the secrets of the Universe
"Together we have touched such joy, such wonder
"As we thought only the immortals could obtain.
"When our bodies lay together we made a new hope,
"Our love holds the key. We have created life itself.

"It's so beautiful, Sir. And that is just how I feel as well. How clever you are to make our feelings into a poem."

Of course, Octavia must have shown his wife the poem. Oh well. There were bound to be some minor complications.

"You don't mind, do you, Octavia? It's not as if she is anything like you. You're not to be jealous." Not like your mother, thought Marcellus.

"Of course not," Octavia laughed. "It was my idea."

"What do you mean?"

"That you should marry Cornelia. She's a lovely girl, but so lacking in confidence because of the stain on her skin. I knew you would be kind to her. I love her dearly. She is clever and brave. She goes to the baths despite the other women pointing and commenting."

"Does she know about us, then?"

"No. No one knows. No one will ever know. Claud is emphatic about that. So Baby Marcellus is his baby. You will never be able to claim him," Octavia finished sadly.

"Is he to be the only one, Octavia?"

"No. Don't you remember? We had four babies."

"Of course I remember. So I will see you again and again, until there are four, and then you will be rid of me."

"You are so stupid sometimes. You will be rid of me before I ever wish you to go. You must take care, my darling. It is so difficult for us women to stay behind, knowing nothing of the dangers you face, but imagining everything."

"Octavia, more of my relatives have died having babies than ever died fighting battles. You are the brave ones."

BOOK 2 : CHAPTER 16

Philippi, March to October, 42 BC

Lepidus was to remain in Italy. He gave up his seven legions to Antony, a huge tactical mistake on his part, in the light of future events. Rather to their surprise Marcellus, Adrian and Maximus found themselves each in charge of a legion. Unfortunately not the legions of veterans they'd hoped for, but of novices. Twenty-eight legions and thirteen thousand cavalry were gathered at Brundisium under the command of the other two Triumvirs, Mark Antony and twenty-two year old Gaius Julius Caesar. Lepidus travelled with them. As Pontifex Maximus, he performed the main role in the ritual purification of the army before hostilities commenced. Because of the numbers involved, this took days longer than usual, leaving the two other Triumvirs hopping with impatience. But Lepidus refused to be hurried.

The embarkation was fraught with difficulties, but eventually most of the men, horses, mules, wagons and baggage were successfully ferried across the Adriatic, landing at Dyrrhachium. Two legions were kept in reserve with the fleet. The vast army, one of the largest ever known, set out on the Via Egnatia, crossing Illyria and Macedonia. Decimus's organisational skills were in great demand. A scouting army of eight legions was sent forward to find the positions of Brutus and Cassius's camps. They succeeded in getting the required information, only to be routed, having to withdraw to take up a defensive position a few miles west of Philippi.

Gaius arrived at Dyrrhachium in a litter, feverish, coughing and wheezing terribly.

"You're not ill again, are you?" Agrippa demanded. "For heavens sake! Can't you stop being sick for once?"

"No," said Gaius. "Agrippa, you may have to be in charge of the army."

Agrippa swore at him. "Sweet fucking Jupiter! We need you. We need a Caesar at the head. I'm not the same."

"There are plenty of good officers," croaked Gaius. "And Dessy. Just do whatever he says."

Decimus sent Musa to him, as Musa was willing to try an unorthodox approach to alleviate Gaius's symptoms. Later, when Dessy walked into Gaius's tent, he was hardly able to see through the clouds of steam emanating from a myriad of vessels perched on charcoal braziers. A pungent aroma from the balsam permeated the tent. Gaius appeared from under a towel, looking dreadful, unshaven, sweaty and still feverish. Musa was busy cooling him down with cold compresses.

"I think there is a little improvement, Sir," Musa claimed.

"Why do we always have to campaign at this time of the year?" Gaius complained amid bouts of coughing. "I'm always worse in the Spring."

Once Gaius had fallen into an uneasy sleep, still disturbed by the intermittent coughing, Musa sought out his former master. "Sir, I know I owe you everything, but you are never ill. Would you permit me to serve Caesar instead of you? He says that when he's ill, he feels much safer if I attend him."

"On one condition," Dessy smiled.

"What's that, Sir?"

"That you treat me if ever I am ill or injured. I would feel much safer with you around as well."

"Of course, Sir. I am your freedman. I will always be there if needed."

The scouts reported back. The Liboratores' camps were just a short distance west of Philippi. Marcus Brutus's forces were north of the road, surrounded by impassible hills, Cassius Longinus's camp was south of the road, surrounded by impassible marshes. Both camps were heavily fortified. They appeared to have a large force of foot soldiers, and a massive cavalry contingent.

Antony camped opposite Cassius in the south, while Gaius, having temporarily recovered his health, camped opposite Brutus in the north. There was bad news. The Liboratores had succeeded in raising an enormous fleet of one hundred and thirty ships, which were now patrolling the Illyrian coast, attempting to prevent any supplies being landed for the Triumvirs. They had wiped out the two reserve legions. Decimus was forced to send a legion all the way south to Achaia to gather the vast quantities needed to feed the mass of soldiers, horses, and pack-animals.

Egnatius somehow managed to avoid his ships being intercepted. He arrived with many wagons laden with silver table-ware, luxurious mattresses, blankets, food, fodder, and expensive wines. He also brought more money. Antony was pleased to make the acquaintance of a fellow epicure, and the morale of the troops was boosted by the promise of an additional 5,000 denarii for each soldier and 25,000 for each centurion.

The tactics of the Liboratores became evident. They hoped to starve the opposing army and avoid a pitched battle. Antony tried to tempt them into a decisive engagement several times, drawing up his troops in formation in full view of the enemy. The months were rolling by and he felt they were getting nowhere. Brutus and Cassius refused to fight, but they were worried about the possibility of desertion. Many of their soldiers had previously fought for Caesar in the civil war against Pompey. Cassius made a speech, saying, "Don't be concerned if you have previously fought under Caesar. You weren't his soldiers, but our country's soldiers." He added a gift of 1,500 denarii for each legionary and 7,500 for each centurion. This served only to amplify the desertions, thus proving Egnatius's point. Somehow the soldiers always knew how much money the opposition was getting.

An exasperated Antony decided to bring matters to a head. In great secrecy and trying to make as little noise as possible, he started using his men and camp slaves to build a causeway through the marshes towards the part of Cassius's camp that couldn't be properly fortified due to the swampy ground. He was so successful that at last the Liboratores had to fight, or be surrounded, trapped on both east and west sides of the Via Egnatia, and unable to obtain any supplies from the south. On the third of October battle commenced.

Once lined up, Brutus's forces attacked Gaius's line, without waiting for the signal to start. The force of this unexpected early thrust took Gaius's troops by surprise, causing panic in their ranks. They crumbled. Decimus shouted in vain to the men to stand fast, keep their positions, and if they had to retreat, to do so in an orderly fashion back to camp, but many turned to run in all directions. Cierán saw Dessy go down in the melee. Instantly Dessy's tent-mates charged forward to surround him with a wall of steel. Cierán manoeuvred his horse close to the front of the fighting, his mounted troops clearing a protective space through the chaos. Laeforis scooped up the body of the Camp Prefect. Dessy was alive and groaning in agony. He was dumped unceremoniously on Cierán's horse.

"We need to get him to safety, but where?" Cierán shouted.

The fighting was breaking up into disorderly groups of retreating men, slipping and sliding on the dead and wounded bodies of their comrades. The battlefield was so huge it was hard to see exactly what was going on, but there were many hundreds of casualties from their side, both men and horses, piling up in jumbled bloody heaps.

Adrian appeared out of the dust. "Our camp's overrun, Cierán," he yelled. "Is that Dessy? Fucking hell! Right, you cross the road and make for Antony's camp. Their line has pushed forward, so it should be safe. Take your men with you. Max and I will gather up as many as we can, and join Marcellus and Agrippa to reform our line. We'll join you in the south, once things have stabilised."

"Where's Gaius Caesar, Sir?"

"No idea. We lost him in the confusion. It's Marcus Agrippa who is attempting to keep the legions together. Brutus's troops are so busy looting our camp, we have a breathing space."

Laeforis gathered up his force and charged towards the fleeing troops, to find Marcellus in the thick of the fighting, attempting to make his men stand fast, to no avail. Their legion had succumbed, losing the battle standard. The Gallic cavalry shouted encouragement, riding up and down the lines, persuading the foot soldiers to turn round and reform. They hurled their spears at the enemy, whenever they were sure of their identity, which was proving difficult among the chaos.

Gaius's men succeeded in regrouping in the end. It was a struggle fighting their way out of the battle, but eventually they joined up with Antony's reserves. Their casualties were enormous, sixteen thousand men killed or severely wounded, and three battle standards lost.

They discovered Antony's legions had had a much more successful day, having pushed right into Cassius's camp, destroying the palisade and filling up the ditch in the process.

It was dark by the time Gaius Caesar's exhausted officers and men were able to retreat to the relative safety of Antony's camp. A group of senior officers were escorted into the praesidium. One of them walked up to Antony and saluted.

"Sir, I have our camp prefect here, Decimus Taurus. He's wounded quite badly."

"And who are you?"

"I'm Titus Statilius Taurus, Sir. You wished to have me proscribed for writing execrable poetry, if you remember."

"Ah, the poet commonly known as Marcellus, nephew of my old army pal Dessy?"

"That's me, Sir."

"Bring Dessy in here." Antony turned to his slaves. "Summon the surgeon, and bring more lights."

Cierán carried Dessy into the tent. "He's quite cut about, and his elbow is dislocated. I can deal with that bit."

Adrian burst out laughing. "Can I watch while you do it, Cierán?"

"Stow it, Adrian," growled Dessy. He was in no mood for laughter. Antony had won and he had failed. It hurt more than his wounds.

"We've lost Caesar, Sir."

"You don't say," smiled Antony. "Don't worry about him. He'll be skulking somewhere in the marshes. We'll look for him in the morning. In the meantime we'd better find some accommodation for you guys. We'll be generous, and share our tents with you, and even our supper, if you promise to behave. I claim the poet." He laughed at the look of astonishment on

Marcellus's face. "You can recite some of your poems to me. That should help me get to sleep."

There was a minor disturbance in the night when Marcellus's slaves were brought to Antony's luxurious tent, the men having fought their way ferociously out of their camp, in order to protect the children. One of the children burst into tears of relief when he found his master.

"*I thought you had died,*" sobbed the child.

"*Not yet,*" whispered Marcellus, with his arms round the boy. "*Don't make a noise, baby boy. We mustn't wake the commander.*"

"He's already awake," snapped a voice. Antony appeared out of the gloom, holding one of the lanterns.

Marcellus found himself apologising, but to his surprise Antony swiftly arranged for his slaves' wounds to be tended, and the children tucked up snuggly on warm bedding.

Antony sat on Marcellus's improvised bed. "Nice kids," he said. He liked the affectionate way Marcellus had dealt with the scared youngsters. "They have such beautiful manners. Must be from Gaul."

"Yes, Sir. They tend to panic if I'm not around. Which is why I brought them with me." Marcellus thought he should explain.

"I like kids. I've some of my own. Lovely kids." Antony spent the next hour regaling Marcellus with tales of his children's escapades, when Marcellus wanted nothing more than to get some sleep. When Marcellus failed to stop himself yawning Antony laughed at him, and ordered him back to bed, to his relief.

In the morning came the astounding news that Cassius had killed himself, thinking erroneously that both wings of the Liberatores army had suffered a humiliating defeat. Gaius was found hiding in the marshes with Musa, but minus his cloak and horse. He never properly explained his absence, but he was coughing and wheezing badly again. Decimus was pleased that Cassius was out of the way, he being a good commander. Dessy claimed that Brutus was no great military mind. But as he didn't make much sense during the next few days, Antony took no notice.

It was an enjoyable experience sharing a tent with Antony, Marcellus found. A convivial teasing atmosphere prevailed, though Antony didn't mince his words about Gaius and his disappearance. And he also rubbed in the fact that his forces had overwhelmingly won the first engagement, whereas Marcellus's legion had melted away in the heat of the battle.

One evening Antony told Marcellus that he had an extra special wine on the table. He encouraged Marcellus to taste it, asking his opinion.

"Isn't it one of the best wines you have ever tasted?"

Marcellus thought it was more like vinegar, but felt he had to agree with his host. At which point Antony and the other senior officers roared with laughter. They were all in on the joke, as it was vinegar.

"The best vinegar though," said Marcellus with a smile.

The contrast with Gaius was brought into stark relief when Marcellus went to retrieve his horse from the stable block one morning. He caught the sound of someone sobbing. In the corner of the tack room he found Sarmentus, Gaius's page boy, crying his heart out.

"What's the matter, boy?" Marcellus asked. He touched the boy's shoulder, causing a yelp of pain. So the boy had been beaten for some misdemeanour or other.

"Sorry, sorry. I didn't mean to hurt you."

"He said I looked miserable, so he said he would give me a good reason to be miserable. And then.......then....." The boy choked with sobs again.

Marcellus could remember seeing him before at Octavia's house, where he had appeared to be an affectionate little boy with a sunny disposition. He was owned by Claudius's friend Favonius. Since Favonius had died, and Gaius had bought him, the boy had changed dramatically. It was true, he did look miserable most of the time, perhaps missing his former master. More likely to be Gaius's fault though. It must be hard to belong to a master with no conscience. Marcellus knew that Gaius could be cruel at times.

"Listen, I'm going to tell your master that I've found you distraught, because you think he doesn't love you any more."

"I *hate* him," whispered the boy.

"Don't *ever* say that. Not even to me. The Gods know what he would do to you, if he ever found out the truth."

Marcellus found Gaius doing nothing very much, while his uncle Decimus was bent over piles of papers. He related his find in the stables.

"It must be so hard for the boy, loving you so much, and with you being the son of the Divine. I expect your gaze alone is enough to terrify him."

"Do you really think so?" Gaius was delighted.

"I've heard that your eyes shine with radiance. Of course I'm used to it, so I don't even notice."

"Probably not," said Gaius wistfully.

"Stop it, Mark," Decimus intervened. "He is conceited enough already. Don't make him even worse."

"Oh, you were joking."

"Poor Sarmentus isn't a joke. He is heartbroken."

"Oh, alright. I'll go and make the kid better."

"Do you mind running your divine eyes over this lot first?" Decimus said.

"Why? What is it?"

"We've lost so many officers and men. I'm having to change things round a bit."

"What was all that about?" asked Dessy, when Gaius had left.

Marcellus explained.

"Our divine commander is a sadistic bastard. I am so glad you are nothing like your friend, Marcellus. Or his divine father."

Slowly Antony consolidated his position, moving his forces ever further to the east, forcing Brutus to extend his line. Antony stationed Gaius and his legions opposite the enemy camp. After almost three weeks Brutus's troops had had enough of playing a waiting game. Brutus had no idea that the Triumvirs' navy and two reinforcement legions had been defeated at sea. Men began to desert in ever greater numbers, going back to their homes in the east, or surreptitiously joining the Triumvirs, mostly during the night.

The second pitched battle took place on the twenty-third of October. Decimus was still an invalid and wasn't allowed to take part. He consoled himself by inspecting the camp fortifications, tent lines, and stabling from a litter, finding fault with everything and everyone, until Antony ordered him to stay in his tent until the battle was fought and won, or he would clap him in irons.

Gaius's foot soldiers broke through the eastern overstretched lines of the opposing army, and seized Brutus's camp, preventing his soldiers from regrouping in turn, a small consolation for the first battle. Gaius ordered that anyone found looting and not fighting to the end of the day would be put to death immediately. He wanted desperately to avenge his previous humiliation.

Antony's men fought at close combat with Brutus's troops, both sides pressing hard and not yielding to begin with. The slaughter was terrible. The enemy troops managed to push forward on the left side, but Marcellus and Adrian with their men, broke through the weaker central part of the Liberatores army, and then encircled the disordered enemy in a pincer movement, attacking the rear of the column. The three lines of Brutus's troops tried to pull back, but had no camp to retreat to, their base being occupied by Gaius and the rest of his forces. The lines became entangled. Brutus managed to escape with only four legions and a few of his officers. They fled to the nearby hills, where Brutus committed suicide a few days later, knowing that surrender was inevitable. Victory for Antony. And also a little victory for Gaius Caesar.

Both Triumvirs stood sombrely before the corpse of Brutus.

"A brilliant victory," declared Antony. "My Caesar is avenged." He saluted the corpse, and ordered it to be wrapped in his own purple cloak.

"Let's have his head cut off and exhibited in the Forum," Gaius suggested. "It might deter others from unlawful assassination."

Antony disagreed, so Gaius went off to jeer at a group of nobles who had surrendered to Antony, rather than to him.

The legionaries had still much clearing up to do. They buried the dead enemy as well as their own dead. There was a suitable ceremony celebrating their glorious sacrifice for the sake of the supposed new republic.

The victory banquet was a long drawn out affair, as it was hosted by Egnatius. Antony had managed to requisition some ‘working girls’ from the city, so his officers were happy. He startled Gaius by saying, "Now my dear Caesar, we must think what to do next. I have this feeling that our colleague Aemilius Lepidus, will have trouble controlling Spain. I suggest he has only Africa to govern. Do you agree?"

Again Gaius felt the thrill of power, so much power. He could do so much good with it, and repair some of the damage caused by these dreadful civil wars. The Republic was crying out for stability. He had some ideas of how to achieve it, in which Antony didn’t figure.

"And how will we divide the rest of our country?"

"I suggest you have Italy and Spain. I prefer the Eastern lands myself. I’ll take Macedonia, Greece, Egypt and the eastern provinces. But I’ll keep Gaul."

Italy and Spain. It would do for a start, thought Gaius.

"Egypt now. There’s a rich country. You should visit sometime."

"And Cleopatra?"

Antony grinned, "Oh yes, there’s always Cleopatra. Now don’t go running to Dessy to find out if he approves."

"I won’t. From now on I make my own decisions. That is what Dessy wanted when he trained us. Always he made us think for ourselves."

Decimus announced that henceforth he was retiring. He’d had enough of fighting. He wanted some peace. Although in his mind he was sure he’d be summoned back one day. He couldn’t see Antony and Gaius sharing power amicably for long. He thought Gaius was becoming a little too autocratic. Antony thought so, too, and spent the rest of the evening telling Gaius how useless he was, and that he had achieved nothing much.

"That's because Dessy was there, fucking things up," said Gaius smiling.

"I do not....." Dessy started in outrage.

"Rise to the bait," Gaius continued. Everyone laughed.

"If you weren't a Propraetor....."

"Yes I know. You'd thrash me. Thank the Gods for the Senate. At least they do some useful things."

BOOK 2 : CHAPTER 17

House of Marcus Statilius Taurus, Winter 42 / 41 BC

The news from the battle front was swiftly relayed to Rome and reported to the Senate. One evening, when the women were gathered at Portia's house to celebrate their menfolk's safe deliverance, Octavia declared with delight that she was sure she was pregnant again. Cornelia's face lit up with pleasure.

"Our children will be able to play together, and be good friends, won't they, Octavia. And just think, if one is a boy and one is a girl, maybe one day they will marry. Won't that be lovely?"

For the first time in her life Octavia felt a pang of jealousy, and some misgiving. But she mustn't be like her mother. She looked in horror at Claudius. Why hadn't they foreseen this?

"I think we had better wait and see what the Gods bring us, my dears," Claudius declared, wondering how to prevent such a calamity in the future. He would have to find a way.

"And if you do have a son, what will you call him, Marcellus or Titus?" Portia asked.

"I think we'll stick to Titus in future," said Cornelia earnestly. "It will avoid confusion."

Dessy stood smiling in the doorway of the courtyard. Ethela was playing with the children, just like she had all those years ago, with Cierán and Laeforis. The children were throwing a ball to each other, and Ethela was attempting to snatch it from them, with little success. Dessy ran into the yard, jumped in the air, and caught it for her. He handed it to her with a bow.

"For you, Ethela," he said.

She laughed, and flung her arms round his neck. "You're home, you're home. Oh I thank the Gods."

Decimus decided that jumping to catch balls was to be a thing of the past. His knees were sore.

Nobody batted an eyelid when Dessy announced that he was going to marry Ethela. Even Marcus couldn't be bothered to raise any objection. Besides how could there be any? Ethela had been successfully raising all Dessy's children for years, treating Atia's daughter Honoria just as lovingly as the way she treated her own girls. Not that Marcus or anyone else knew the truth about Honoria. Nor were they ever likely to know. All those intimately concerned knew how dangerous it would be if the truth were revealed.

"You wish to make sure Honoria is a Roman Citizen? This is why you marry me?" Ethela asked Decimus.

"No, my beautiful girl. I'm marrying you because I love you," Dessy answered. "I hope you love me. But I'm too scared to ask you."

Ethela laughed. "It took a long long time, Dessy. But now I do."

The wedding was necessarily a low key affair, Ethela being a barbarian and a freedwoman. Even so, everyone came to the banquet afterwards. Octavia was supported by her husband and Marcellus as she was heavily pregnant again. Gaius presented the happy couple with a magnificent silver dinner service.

Ethela was disgusted. "We already have one," she pointed out to her husband.

"Be grateful. You can always sell it when times are hard."

"Can they be hard again? For us?" Ethela turned to him, hoping for reassurance.

"My darling girl, even if I am killed, you and the children will be fine. There's nothing to worry about." He put his arm round his new wife. "Are you still having those nightmares, my love?"

"Not so bad. Better when you are home."

Decimus felt sure the nightmares were about him, but Ethela would never say. He looked back sometimes at the beginning of their relationship. Knowing what he knew now, it should all have been so different. Fourteen-year-old captive girls should not be subjugated by Roman centurions. It had long lasting effects. Dessy didn't ponder for long, though, thrusting unwelcome thoughts aside. He was doing his best to make up for his deficiencies in the past, he told himself. And he was sure he had now managed to convince himself that Ella was his own darling, and not .... Best not to name names.

After the happy throng had toasted the newly-weds there was a hiatus.

"What's the next toast?" asked Agrippa.

Gaius grinned. "Unfinished business." His eyes met Decimus's and they both laughed, knowing he meant Antony.

The young men rose to their feet in a body. and declared, "To unfinished business."

"Don't you dare smash the glasses," cried Portia.

One month later a solid gold dinner service arrived, courtesy of Antony. Dessy was all for sending it back, but Ethela said it was no problem. They could always give it to another couple for a wedding gift.

"For Gaius Caesar, when he divorces Antony's stepdaughter, and marries someone else," Ethela suggested, laughing.

Within a year Gaius had to send for Decimus again. And got the gold dinner service.

BOOK 2 : CHAPTER 18

Rome, 41 BC to 40 BC

It was all very well winning the war against his adoptive father's assassins, but Gaius was finding winning the peace more of a problem. There were thousands of legionaries now on both sides due to be discharged. And discharge meant he was to provide each of them with a grant of land and money. And if he didn't satisfy them, any disaffected soldiers might well side with his political opponents. He had no obvious opponents at present, but events changed so quickly. Any one of the remaining Senators might try to challenge his authority. In addition, all the auxiliary troops had to be awarded Roman citizenship and their share of the booty.

Unfortunately there wasn't any more land available. Antony had waltzed off to Egypt to ally himself with Queen Cleopatra and finally make the war on Parthia, that had been planned by Caesar before his assassination four years ago, leaving Gaius to solve an insoluble problem. Gaius had a conference with Decimus and Egnatius. Egnatius thought the only solution would be to confiscate more land, but Dessy advised against any more proscriptions, thinking Gaius was already beginning to look like a despot.

It seemed to be the only feasible solution. Safer to alienate citizens than soldiers. They hadn't reckoned with the result. Eighteen cities and their citizens had to be denuded of their land, which caused much anguish. At the same time Gaius handed his wife, Fulvia's daughter and Antony's stepdaughter, back to her mother, saying the marriage had never been consummated. Gaius then hastily married Scribonia, a close relative of Sextus Pompey, to keep Pompey as an ally. Not that it worked. Pompey was still ruling Sicilia, Sardinia and the seas with his fleet, intercepting the grain ships destined for Rome. Italy was starving.

Dessy was fast asleep. With great trepidation, his slave shook him awake.

"Go away," growled Dessy.

"Master, Marcus Agrippa is here to see you."

Decimus groaned, and rolled over in the bed to the warm patch where Ethela should have been. But she was already up and serving breakfast to her unexpected guests.

"Tell him I set off for Britain yesterday."

"Very well, Master," replied the slave, sounding dubious.

Fuck, fuck, fuck, Dessy thought to himself. Was he never to get any peace? He heaved himself out of bed, put on his dressing gown, and ambled into the dining room to find Agrippa consuming a hearty breakfast, surrounded by his officers and Dessy's sons, eager to hear the news. Dessy sat down to join them. The boys listened intently.

Ella appeared, carrying a tray of fruit. Irritably Dessy snapped at her, ordering her to cover her hair.

"But her hair is beautiful," said Agrippa. "Why should she cover it up?"

"It's immodest," said Dessy, cross at being challenged on this sensitive subject. "She's my daughter. I want her to keep her hair covered. Do you have a problem with that?"

"No," said Agrippa, surprised at Dessy's belligerent tone of voice. "Not at all, Sir."

"Good," said Dessy. "Now, what's up? Why are you here?"

"Lucius Antonius, the Consul is what's up. As Antony is in Egypt the citizens are looking to his brother to redress their grievances against Gaius and the land allocations."

"By doing what, exactly?"

"Raising legions. A great many Senators have sided with Lucius and the dispossessed citizens. Some of their own land holdings were seized illegally by Gaius's veteran soldiers, idiots that they are. And Antony's wife Fulvia wants her husband to come home, not be ensnared by that 'harlot of Egypt', as she terms Cleopatra."

"She's missed the boat there," said Dessy.

"Apparently Lady Fulvia has been trailing around the colonies of veteran troops, reminding them that everything they owned was due to Antony. Lucius and Fulvia want Antony to be installed as the sole ruler of Rome. Which is why they are raising troops."

"Hell!" said Dessy. "We'll have to put a stop to that."

"First Master Agrippa can stop the cavalry from ruining my garden," said a cross Ethela. "Some of the horses are trying to eat my vegetables."

Agrippa apologised and hurried outside. With a sigh Decimus ordered his armour to be readied and his charger saddled and bridled.

"Can we go with you, Sir?" Mochán begged.

"Certainly not," said Ethela, in horror at the thought.

"Maybe next time," said his father. It would take too long to persuade Ethela to let the boys fight. There were more pressing concerns.

Lucius Antonius had no difficulty raising eight legions. He thought he could gain some revenge for his defeat by Gaius's forces at Mutina. And Fulvia thought Antony would come back to her as soon as he heard what she was doing. And she was furious with Gaius for publicly demeaning her daughter. They marched on Rome to try and force the Senate to abolish the Triumvirate and install Antony as sole ruler, but had to retreat when confronted by Gaius's army, ending up at the city of Perusia.

Decimus sited his camp just outside the city walls, while Gaius and Agrippa set in motion siege preparations with redoubts and fortifications all round the city to prevent any foodstuffs reaching the citizens. It took two months to starve the inhabitants into surrender. Lucius and Fulvia had miscalculated badly, hoping for reinforcements from Italy and the East, which didn't arrive. The city was sacked and burnt, and many people killed.

Gaius sent Lucius off to govern Spain, not daring to kill Antony's brother. He forced Fulvia and her children to retire to Greece to meet with her irate husband in Athens. Antony was furious with her for meddling in his affairs, ordering her to go to Sicyon and to stay there.

However Gaius ordered the execution of the three hundred Senators and knights who had fought against him and with Lucius and Fulvia. The Senators hadn't imagined such an appalling outcome when they surrendered, but their pleas for mercy were ignored. "No, you must die," was all Gaius would reply, with gruesome satisfaction. The executions were carried out at the temple of the divine Julius Caesar on the Ides of March. Human sacrifice. The temple floor was awash with blood. This gave Gaius more land and considerably more money. But made him look like a bloody tyrant, Dessy told him to his face.

Gaius no longer accepted criticism from anyone. "The Senate has to learn to side with me," Gaius yelled at him. "Fight against me and you will not be spared. That lesson still needs to be rammed home. I am not my father. I don't do clemency."

"No, you certainly are not your father. Don't you see that every time you have someone executed you create more hatred? And telling those poor devils they must die when they have begged for mercy and repented? What's wrong with you?"

"They are traitors. And I need the money. It's as simple as that. Stop questioning my decisions, Dessy. You are here to obey orders, nothing else."

The victorious army returned to Rome, announcements of the horrendous execution of Senators and knights preceding them. When Gaius entered the Senate House he found the remaining Senators subdued, and eager to vote through any laws he suggested. Gaius asked that he be declared, 'Gaius Julius Caesar, Son of the Divine, Imperator.' The Senate hastily agreed. He toyed with the idea of adding 'the August' to his titles, but decided to keep that for a more propitious moment.

BOOK 2 : CHAPTER 19

Rome, Spring 40 BC

There seemed to be nothing but war, war, and more war, Octavia thought to herself. She was pretty sure she was now beginning her third pregnancy. She'd had no menses for three months and she was feeling so weary. Her brother and her darling Marcellus were off fighting Antony's wife Fulvia and Antony's brother Lucius in central Italy, while Antony was living it up with Queen Cleopatra in Alexandria. Did he even know what his wife was up to, Octavia wondered?

Claudius had developed a persistent cough recently, that was getting on her nerves. She ordered him to see a physician. They didn't have one of their own in the house, and Gaius had taken Musa with him as usual. Gaius wouldn't travel without him, he had so much faith in his abilities. Octavia thought Musa was a cure in himself. The awful wheezing Gaius was subject to every spring had virtually disappeared since Musa's appointment as personal physician.

Sympathy and sensible advice was forthcoming from Portia, who was a better mother to her than her own had been, soothing her many anxieties. Octavia loved her visits. She always felt better after seeing her. She would have liked to have confided her secret to Portia, but agreed with her husband that the fewer people who knew, the safer she and the children would be.

There were worries that even Portia could do nothing about. Octavia adored her two children. Little Marcellus could stand up unaided, and scamper about the courtyard. He was a fearless child, forever tripping up and falling over. But he had the same weak lungs as her brother, with bouts of fever, coughing and wheezing through the long dark frightening winter months. Now Octavia understood her mother's preoccupation with Gaius when he was a child. She could hardly bear to leave little Marcellus when he was ill.

Fortunately baby Claudia was a placid healthy child, who showed no signs of weakness, thanks be to the Gods.

The physicians Claudius consulted gave him many different foul-tasting remedies, but nothing worked. Weight started to fall off him. He became intermittently feverish, with dreadful sweats at night time particularly. His cough produced bloody sputum. By now Octavia was seriously worried. She sent to her brother for Musa, but Gaius refused to allow him any leave. Claudius took to his bed, as he no longer had the strength or willpower to get up. Octavia nursed him herself, doing everything she could think of to ease his suffering. She had a pillow made for him stuffed with goose-down and scented with herbs. She organised broths and savoury jellies to try and get him to eat. Both Claudius and Octavia knew he was fighting a loosing battle. Claudius wanted her to face up to reality. His voice was weak and constantly interrupted by dreadful bouts of coughing.

"My dearest wife, do not be sad for me when I am gone. I've had a full life and achieved much. If you would ensure that my military and civilian posts are correctly displayed on my grave stone I will die a happy man."

"No, no, no! You mustn't die. You mustn't leave me. Everyone leaves me, Father, Mother, and now my husband. I can't bear it, Claudius. You must stop dying and start living for me. Please, my dearest kindest husband, please try harder to live."

"We must all die, darling girl. We must accept our fate. Stop crying. You will make yourself ill. Ask Lady Portia if she will be good enough to stay with you. It will only be for a few days more."

Antony landed at Brundisium with his children and his legions to confront Gaius, angry that his wife and brother had been forced to surrender to a man he considered an upstart. And furious at yet another delay in starting the war on Parthia. Gaius marched his legions south and moved to meet him. But Dessy was still angry with him, because of the executions of the Senators and knights after the siege of Perusia. Dessy thought Gaius's actions quite unnecessarily cruel, a severe misjudgement. He sent Cierán with a letter to his opposite number in Antony's camp, a fellow Caesarian veteran. Dessy asked for a meeting between opposing centurions to discuss the imminent war.

Gaius was astonished one morning to witness a hundred or so centurions riding out of camp, with Decimus at their head.

"What's going on?" Gaius yelled at Marcellus.

"Sir, I think my uncle wishes to negotiate, rather than fight."

"How dare he dispute my authority," shouted an incensed Gaius. "I'll have him killed."

"Then I would be forced to kill you in turn, Sir. I think you had better calm down, Gaius, and find out the result of the meeting."

"Are you threatening me?"

"Yes. If not me, it will be one of his soldiers. Do you want to be assassinated? You are going about it the right way. Dessy is loved by his men."

As Gaius knew this to be true, he forced himself to speak more calmly. "Who's he meeting?"

"Antony's camp prefect."

The meeting of centurions took their lead from Decimus Taurus and overwhelmingly decided that they would all refuse to fight. There had been too much indiscriminate use of Caesar's veteran troops against each other. It was almost fratricide, said Dessy. Antony's centurions agreed and mutinied as well. There would be no war. Not this time.

Marcellus was ordered to arrange a meeting between Antony and Gaius, as he was beginning to know Antony well and liked what he knew. The two Triumvirs met and effected a reconciliation, brokered by Dessy and Marcellus. Antony was dressed in a dark tunic of mourning, because he had just heard news that his wife Fulvia had died in Sicyon. Gaius hastily proffered his condolences. These were received graciously enough.

Gaius hurried on to explain why he had ditched Antony's step-daughter and married Scribonia, in case it rankled. "We've also problems with Pompey's son, Sextus Pompey," he told Antony. "At present his fleet is barricading us, preventing the corn supplies reaching Italy. People are beginning to starve. Sextus wants to be the third Triumvir."

"He doesn't want much," Antony declared, astonished.

"He wants to be a member of the College of Augurs and a Consul as well."

They agreed Sextus would have to be placated at present, as Antony was too involved in the eastern provinces to spare time and effort to fight him. Although Sextus didn't supplant Lepidus in Africa, he was allowed Sicily, Corsica, the Peloponnese, and Sardinia to rule, and was designated to be Consul in five years' time. Both Gaius and Antony knew he would have to be dealt with at some stage, but not just now. In addition Sextus successfully negotiated the end of the proscriptions instituted by the Triumvirs. Many Senators had fled to him to avoid being executed. Now they were allowed to return to Rome in safety.

Twenty-five year old Marcus Agrippa was made Governor of Gaul, managing to cross the Rhine, defeating the threatening German tribes. On his return to Rome, he came into his own, joining up a small sea port with two inland lakes, not visible from the coast by the patrolling fleet of Sextus Pompey. Here he arranged for ships to be built and over twenty thousand men to be mustered and trained in naval warfare. Ready to challenge Sextus, should it become necessary.

Marcellus went to visit Octavia, as soon as he learnt the upsetting news of Claudius's death, a man he had grown to love over the years. A man who had made his own dreams come true. Inwardly Marcellus was pleased to see that Octavia was pregnant again with another child to add to his and her collection, but he had too much sensitivity to comment. He kissed her hand, and said how sorry he was to hear the sad news about Claudius. He thought his darling looked devastated. He hadn't realised that she loved Claudius so much, and said so. It gave him a shock.

Octavia tried to explain. "Whatever he was like with other people, he has always been such a kind and generous protector to me. He loved me. He would do anything to make me happy, as you know. I could do no wrong in his eyes. I miss him so much."

As she then burst into tears, Marcellus felt able to take her in his arms to comfort her, despite the presence of the servants.

Fleetingly he thought about divorcing Cornelia, and approaching Gaius for permission to marry his sister. But he knew he couldn't do such a thing. He loved his dear little Cornelia, and she adored him. It would break her heart. Only the other night she had said she thought him a God come to earth. How else could he produce such wonderful poetry? And she was also expecting another child. No. It was impossible.

But Octavia was such an important political figure. Who would Gaius marry her to next, if not to him, he wondered anxiously. Although any thought of marriage should wait for Octavia to recover from her husband's death. The Roman period of mourning was always at least ten months, from the purely practical desire to ensure the parentage of any posthumous offspring.

. Gaius asked Marcellus to accompany him on a visit to Antony and his children in his house in Rome. As they were walking along, Gaius casually asked Marcellus if he wished to marry his sister Octavia, now she was widowed. Marcellus found his head spinning. He never thought the suggestion would come from Gaius. Apologetically he explained that it had always been his dream. But that now he was married to the dearest girl in the world. And there was simply no way he could divorce her.

"Well it's entirely up to you," declared Gaius. "Don't forget I asked you first, though."

Marcellus wondered what he meant. He was soon to find out.

Antony had a lovely house, crammed with rich Egyptian artefacts. Marcellus would have liked the chance to examine them. But Gaius's opening words took his breath away.

"In order to cement our new understanding, Antony, I am offering you my sister Octavia in marriage."

"What?" Antony and Marcellus said in unison. Marcellus stared open-mouthed at Gaius. So Gaius had planned this all along, knowing that Marcellus wouldn't be able to divorce his wife. No doubt if Marcellus had said 'Yes' to the proposal, Gaius would have backed off immediately.

"You may have heard that her husband Claudius Marcellus, has just died," Gaius continued.

"Fortuitous," grinned Antony.

"She's upset. Very upset. She's strangely sentimental."

Antony laughed. "I think I would be the perfect man to help her overcome her grief."

The self-satisfied grin on his face made Marcellus want to hit him. Hard. Clearly Antony wasn't mourning Fulvia.

"But Octavia is expecting her husband's child," Marcellus protested, lying through his teeth. "Surely no marriage can take place at present?"

"It won't be a problem, my dear Marcellus. At the moment the Senate will agree to anything I suggest."

Gaius's smug look was almost more than Marcellus could bear. He hated them both. He was forced to lose the love of his life, because he was a man of principle, he told himself. His lovely girl was a pawn to cement an alliance between two of the most selfish bastards on the planet. It was so unfair. His poor darling Octavia to be married to a man whom everyone knew was the world's worst philanderer. Why, news had just come that Queen Cleopatra had given birth to twins, claiming they were Antony's. And Antony hadn't bothered to deny it.

"The nest of vipers has transformed into a cage of rabbits," Gaius observed to Agrippa as they walked round to Octavia's house on a visit of condolence. Although it was more of a procession than a walk. It was no longer safe to be strolling through the streets of Rome with only a couple of attendants in tow, not after the bloody executions of so many Romans. Now Gaius went nowhere without a cohort of the tenth legion acting as a bodyguard, while Agrippa felt safer with at least twenty of his slaves armed and ready to strike if necessary.

Little Marcellus managed a creditable bow. Gaius swept him up into his arms and kissed him. Octavia kissed Gaius. Then Agrippa kissed her hand, and said how sorry he was to hear the sad news about Claudius.

Without any preamble, Gaius told his sister to dry her tears, as she would shortly be marrying Mark Antony.

"I'm sure Antony doesn't want a weeping bride," Gaius added with impatience.

"But I don't want to marry Antony," Octavia cried in shock. "I want to marry Marcellus." Was the one hope she was clinging to about to be swept away?

Gaius snorted in disgust. "Well Marcellus doesn't want to marry you."

"Have you asked him?" Octavia cried in anguish.

"Certainly. He says he is married to the dearest girl in the world."

Octavia stared at him, stupefied. Of course Marcellus wouldn't divorce Cornelia. How could she have ever thought otherwise?

"It doesn't matter in the slightest what you want and don't want, my girl. My needs come first. The Republic's needs come first. You will marry Antony. And you will be a good and loyal wife to him."

Octavia was devastated. She found it hard to think rationally. "How can I?" she protested, stalling for time. "I am pregnant. I can't be married to anyone yet."

"The Senate will agree, my dear. They will do anything I ask. They have no choice. You have no choice. Swear it. Swear it to me now, Octavia."

Octavia knew she would have to give in. Her brother was now all-powerful. She couldn't withstand him. And rebellion might lead to her beloved Marcellus being harmed, let alone dear Cornelia. And that mustn't happen. She hesitated only for an instant. "Very well," she said slowly, with a heavy heart, "I swear I will be a good and loyal wife to Antony."

"That's my good obedient sister." Gaius was relieved. He thought he might have to issue threats. He was very fond of his sister. But if needs must.......

When they left, Octavia found herself numb, almost unable to think clearly. She'd had such a shock. First she experienced an unjustified rage against Claudius, for dying at such an inappropriate time. She banished the thought almost immediately. Poor dear Claudius. He hadn't wanted to die, but accepted his fate with such good grace.

What did she know about Antony? He was forty-three years old, only fourteen years older than she was. Marcellus had told her how much he loved his children and stepchildren. He was in the middle of an affair with Queen Cleopatra, who had just had twins by him, it was rumoured. Though it seemed he had also loved his wife Fulvia. If she was to be a loyal wife to Antony, Octavia decided it would be best to start with the children. They must be feeling bereft with their mother dying so suddenly.

The marriage was enthusiastically received by the Roman citizens and the legions. Peace at last. Antony was relieved as well. Now he could get on with his war in the east against Parthia. He wanted to recover the Eagles lost years ago. And maybe catch up with Cleopatra again soon, and see his twins for himself. First he visited Decimus with a warning.

"I don't want that nephew of yours sniffing round my wife," said Antony.

"What do you mean?"

"You know exactly what I mean. The poet. Titus Marcellus, or whatever his name is. I won't have him anywhere near my wife. Or I'll have him killed."

A tearful Octavia said the same thing. "No, Marcellus. You must stay away from me. He is dangerous. He will kill you and think nothing of it."

It was impossible for Marcellus to be absent from the wedding, though. His wife was Octavia's cousin. And Octavia insisted Cornelia and her husband be present. Agrippa had fun reminding Marcellus of Octavia's previous wedding, but couldn't raise even a smile. It seemed to him that Marcellus was acting as if he was at a funeral rather than a wedding. So those two did love each other. Interesting.

There were crowds in the streets, hopeful that this cementing of alliances might at last bring a peace that was permanent. Nearly every citizen had a family member or more than one, who had been killed or wounded in these endless civil wars.

Her own two children accompanied Octavia to Antony's house after the ceremony. Octavia warmly embraced Clodia, thinking how cruel Gaius had been to dump her so publicly. Octavia told Clodia she would be such a help to her in her new role as Antony's wife. She hugged Antony's two boys, Marcus and Iullus, and told her new husband that she was delighted to have Fulvia's children in her household.

"I will love them and care for them as if they are my own, Sir," she declared.

This pleased Antony, who was very much a family man. He loved all his children.

"Very well. You may have your tame poet after all, as a reward for your goodness and generosity of spirit." He picked up little Marcellus and kissed his cheek. "Now who do you remind me of? Not Claudius. Someone else." There was a tantalising memory at the back of his mind, that some time in the distant past he had seen a little boy very similar to this one.

Octavia was confused and a little anxious. "Do you mean Marcellus?"

"Of course I mean Marcellus. Titus Statilius Taurus Marcellus. He can come with us to Athens and bring that pretty little wife of his with him."

Octavia was pleased that others could see through the wine-stain and know just how pretty her young cousin was, but rather worried that Antony had noticed her. Women were not safe when Antony was around. Marcellus was delighted with the news. But Octavia emphasised that they must no longer be lovers. She was now in a marriage ordered by the State, confirmed by the Senate. She had no desire to precipitate another war between her new husband and her brother. Marcellus wondered if he would be able to cope with her proximity without being able to hold her, kiss her, and love her. More and more though he loved his wife. She was so in love with him it was impossible not to reciprocate. It was so strange to love two women simultaneously. But then Uncle Dessy had managed fine for years.

As Antony was five years younger than Claudius, and a raging heterosexual, there was no question about consummating the marriage. He was so different from her darling Marcellus. There was no kissing and caressing. It was a straight in and out performance. She could tell Antony was pleased with himself, lying back with a satisfied grin on his features. Presumably Queen Cleopatra enjoyed being bent over and treated like a prostitute. Octavia did not.

BOOK 3

Mea pulchra Octavia,
ego protector tuus sum venire.
Nos mos premo in unum
infantes ut geminae.
Dato et basiorum.

Fragment attributed to 'Marcellus'

My lovely Octavia, I will keep you safe
No harm will come to you. We will snuggle together
Like twin babies. And exchange our kisses ..."

BOOK 3: CHAPTER 1

Athens, 39 BC

Decimus turned down Antony's offer to accompany him to Greece, so as to begin the build up in the war against Parthia. He had bought a large estate adjoining his own, and was busy dividing it up amongst his former tent-mates. They had looked after him brilliantly for over twenty years. Now it was his turn to reward them. Laeforis was occupied as well, arranging to have part of his land drained, far more interested in farming than campaigning. But after they checked with their former master, that he would have no objection, Cierán and Óengus accepted the invitation, as long as their wives and families could go, and remain safely in Athens, when hostilities finally commenced. Cierán had heard so much about Athens from Penelope. He was curious to see what this ancient seat of civilisation was like. And he had always enjoyed Óengus's company. Óengus was a good conversationalist, and invariably came up with new and fascinating ideas about the world.

In some ways their departure was a relief for Decimus. He could still see no evidence of himself in eleven year old Ella. Cierán was a frequent visitor to his house, treating Ethela and Ella with affectionate respect, in his charming Gallic way. But when the three of them were together, Decimus found it increasingly hard to suppress his suspicions. He tried repeatedly to convince himself that it didn't matter, that a mistake made in the distant past had no longer any relevance, but he didn't have much success.

Antony found it difficult to think of waging a war without having Decimus Taurus around. Although they didn't see eye to eye on so many things, he knew he would miss Dessy's brilliant abilities in the training of troops. There was no-one better than Dessy in organising and establishing their camps on the most favourable sites, and maintaining adequate supplies of weapons, water, fuel, food and fodder. Still, he would have Marcellus, whom he had appointed as quaestor, and Cierán and Óengus Taurus, two superb cavalry commanders.

Marcellus stood pressed against the prow of the ship transporting them across the Ionian Sea, gazing down anxiously into the deep waters. The voyage would take three days. As soon as they set off, he started to worry. He worried about the children falling in and drowning, although he had insisted on safety rails being fastened all round the ship. Mostly he worried about being shipwrecked. He wished he could be as sanguine as Agrippa, who always relished any chance to be at sea. He felt his bladder contract with fear, when the ship unexpectedly pitched sideways a little.

Cierán knew what Marcellus was thinking, and made his way over with his eldest child, to offer reassurance. The sea was just a little too choppy for comfort.

"What a perfect day," Cierán started. "I'm glad the sea is comparatively calm, otherwise the horses tend to get nervous. Why don't you come and see the dolphins, Mark? The children have been watching them. They are putting on an acrobatic display just for us."

Marcellus allowed himself to be guided through the press of people covering the slippery canting deck. Every so often a wave would toss up and drench the shrieking passengers nearest the ship's side. Groups were sitting with arms around each other, their heads covered, mouthing prayers to Neptune and Poseidon, or standing and clutching nervously onto the rails.

Sure enough, when he came to the stern, Marcellus could see a pod of dolphins frolicking through the churning waters in the wake of the ship. He remembered Octavia telling him about the dolphins she had seen when she was a child, accompanying her father on a ship from Macedonia. Maybe these were the same ones. Cierán told his son to fetch the other children, so they could all see the spectacle. Even the wives were coaxed out of the tiny cabin, apart from poor Dora, Óengus's wife, who had been seized with sea-sickness as soon as they set out. Cierán took the baby from Penelope's arms, and kissed her tiny cheek.

"She mustn't be in the sun for long, or she'll get sunburnt," said Penelope. Cierán's little daughter was as fair as her father, but his boys were dark, like their mother.

Just then one of the dolphins leapt into the air, spun round, and crashed back into the waves.

"Can we have one of them as a pet?" asked one of the awed children. The adults laughed at the absurdity. Marcellus found his anxiety subsiding with this little domestic scene. There was nothing to worry about, he told himself repeatedly. All the same, he was only too pleased when the ship finally entered the port at Patrae after two more days at sea. He much preferred the road journey to Athens, with the women and children ensconced in comfortable carriages. So did Dora.

Octavia staggered around the Governor's palace in Athens, in the last stages of pregnancy. She wondered tiredly why it was only women who had babies. Why couldn't the men take a turn, instead of spending their time fighting and killing other men? This pregnancy was unlike her previous ones. She felt exhausted. Her feet were swollen. She had difficulty recognising the pallid face that stared back at her from the mirror. In the last few days the baby appeared to be sitting on top of her bladder. Sleep was constantly broken by a terrible urge to pee. She was breathless when climbing the many stairs. Maybe she shouldn't have had another baby so quickly after Claudia was born. But when she was in Rome with Marcellus, it had seemed important not to waste time.

To her horror she heard a commotion in the courtyard outside. She groaned inwardly.

Her steward appeared. "Madam, some guests have arrived."

No, not more guests. She was fed up with guests. There had been a constant stream of visitors, ever since they arrived in Athens.

"Please inform my husband," ordered Octavia. "Can you deal with them without me? I'm so tired today."

"Of course, Madam. But I think you'll want to see these visitors."

"Why?"

A laughing voice she knew so well, came through the open doorway.

"There's a lot of stairs," said Marcellus. "Very grand."

But when he entered the room and caught sight of her, he shouted in alarm. "Octavia! My dear girl, you don't look at all well."

Octavia caught the note of concern in his voice. Just then the baby appeared to give an almighty kick. She gasped and clutched her stomach. Marcellus was beside her in an instant.

Octavia was vaguely aware of the rest of the party. She tried to smile at Cornelia. Marcellus was holding her in his arms.

Her husband's voice echoed round the room. "Get your fucking hands off my wife."

"Go to hell," snapped Marcellus.

Fluid flooded over the floor. Marcellus and Cierán carried the half-fainting Octavia over to a couch. "No, no," Octavia protested weakly. "I'll stain the couch. My dress is all wet."

Penelope swung into action. "Lady Octavia's waters have broken. Please take her to her bedroom. And send for the midwife," she ordered the steward. "Don't worry about the couch," she whispered to Octavia. "I'll sort it out."

Antony made himself scarce. He was squeamish about childbirth. A job for women as far as he was concerned. Although he remembered to apologise to Marcellus later.

"It's a girl. A beautiful girl," Cornelia announced that night. "Claudia Minor. And Octavia is fine, but rather tired. Would you like to see the baby?"

"Yes," said Marcellus.

"No," said Antony.

"I thought you liked babies," said Marcellus in surprise.

"I like kids, my own kids," Antony explained. "Babies are boring. For the first two years all they do is yell blue murder, guzzle milk and shit all over the place. Take my advice. Leave babies to the womenfolk. However we'd better have a drink to celebrate."

Athens was a magical city, Marcellus found. A city filled with beautiful buildings and beautiful minds. He was fascinated by the multiple open-air schools of philosophers and teachers, with their adherents all gathered around in a circle, but anyone allowed to listen and join in. To start with he wandered the streets in a daze of wonder, looking, listening, and absorbing the precious details. He was pleased to discover that his efforts at poetry were greatly appreciated by the Athenians. Many more knew of his poetry than knew of his military exploits. Cierán and Óengus often accompanied him on his explorations, delighting in the change of scene. Cierán decided he preferred the clean cut lines and purity of the Greek temples to those of Rome. The Acropolis was breathtaking in its magnificence, the Parthenon temple to the Goddess Athena was perfection in stone, he declared.

They made some interesting discoveries about their host. Antony made much of the Greeks, ensuring he attended all the important religious festivals. He had been inducted into their most sacred mysteries. In turn he was highly regarded by many important Athenians. He had a true love of new ideas. His palace was always filled with the most interesting men and even women. He was happy to let anyone air their views without censorship. The Greeks felt secure under his authority. Antony was no tyrant. And when news came that his lieutenant Publius Bassus had achieved great military success in Parthia, he was happy to receive him with full military honours, and award him a Triumph in Rome.

But only Antony was allowed to indulge in practical jokes, Marcellus swiftly discovered. His host's mood could change at lightning speed from genial to aggressive, especially in the evenings after an alcohol-fuelled dinner.

At first Octavia found it difficult to be so near Marcellus, but they gradually became used to the changed circumstances. Marcellus began to enjoy Octavia more for her nimble mind than for anything else. Once she had recovered her strength she began teaching Antony's two sons by Fulvia, and caring for her own little children by Marcellus. (Only the wrong Marcellus. Still, nobody knew apart from Uncle Dessy, who would never tell anyone, and Ganainm, who couldn't tell anyone.)

As an occasional treat Cierán and Óengus took the boys out for some sword and javelin practise.

"Aren't they a bit young?" Octavia queried.

"Romans are never too young to learn how to kill," said Óengus, for which cynical remark Cierán told him off, as he could see the women were shocked.

"It is good to learn how to kill animals for food or protection," Cierán explained hastily.

The women thought that might explain the javelin practise, but not the sword play.

Octavia was pregnant again all too soon, this time by Antony, which curtailed her activities. Antony wished her to take the greatest care of herself. It was a relief to her to have Cornelia, Penelope, and Dora with her for company. Not that Dora ever said much. She was too overwhelmed by these erudite women. Penelope took over the teaching of the children when it proved too much for Octavia to manage. The women were a little disconcerted to discover that external expeditions by females were frowned on in Athens. A pity. They would have liked to visit the markets. And it was annoying when their husbands gave rapturous descriptions of what they had seen on their excursions.

Antony cut short Marcellus's explorations. He wanted Marcellus to use his intelligence, charm and good looks to help achieve alliances with the surrounding client kings, most of whom had supported the Liberatores in the recent war. And he needed Marcellus's help in restoring his legions to their full numbers, and get them in order. Óengus and Cierán were engaged in purchasing sufficient horses, and practising military manoeuvres with the cavalry. The overall schemes that Decimus had introduced into the training of officers and men were quickly put in place. Which was just as well, because the Parthians didn't wait to be invaded. They invaded instead.

Eighteen months after their arrival in Athens, Octavia was safely delivered of another daughter, Antonia, which led to problems. Although Antony had his pick of many attractive slave girls, he wished to restart conjugal relations as soon as possible. Octavia would have liked a respite.

"For fuck's sake, Octavia, I'm all wet!" Antony yelled at her one night.

"I'm sorry," she said. "It's milk. I thought I heard the baby. It just comes out."

"Get a wet nurse," snapped Antony. His love of his children did not extend to him being in any way inconvenienced.

"I'm sorry," Octavia said again. "I thought you would want me to feed the baby myself."

"If I'd wanted to spend my nights covered in milk, I'd have married a cow."

Despite her success in running the palace smoothly and entertaining many important kings and princes, she knew that Antony was becoming tired of her. Not that he was all that enamoured of her to start with. He was increasingly bad-tempered with her. Within two years she was pregnant again, but to her dismay she felt that her husband was perpetually comparing her in his mind with Queen Cleopatra.

"Why can't you be more alluring?" he asked her. "Can't you wear a sexy dress sometimes instead of those awful all-enveloping clothes? Something smooth and silky?"

"I'm five months pregnant," Octavia objected. "Just you try and be alluring and sexy with a belly that sticks out and a feeling of constant nausea."

"Some women mange it," Antony grumbled. Even when expecting twins.

He did appreciate her skills as a wife with superb political acumen, able to cope charmingly with his many putative allies, men who were liable to take offence at any perceived slight. Even seating some of them together in the dining hall required considerable diplomacy, an art Octavia had learnt from her mother. He rewarded her efforts by procuring some wonderful perfumes for her, and beautiful silk materials, for which she was grateful. It was lovely to be dressed in cool silk. So it wasn't all bad. She felt she was living on the edge of a precipice, though, no longer on a solid ground of affection, as she'd had with Claudius. And she didn't want to complain to Marcellus, as that would be disloyal, and Octavia was a woman who kept her promises.

Unfortunately Antony picked a quarrel with her brother. Octavia was sure Antony had misinterpreted one of Gaius's speeches, but she couldn't persuade her husband of Gaius's good intentions. Antony was suspicious, accusing Gaius of plotting against him.

Marcellus rode up through the bustling throng on the Via Piraica, towards the Governor's palace. He was so glad to be back in this wonderful city. He looked forward to seeing Octavia. And his darling wife. And the little ones. Marcellus loved all of them. He had been away for so long. He ushered the Syrian envoys into the palace and made his way through the guards to the main hall. Antony was there with one of his secretaries. Marcellus smiled, and walked up to him, expecting Antony's usual affectionate greeting.

Antony looked at him, then turned to his secretary. "And who have we here?"

"Titus Statilius Taurus, Sir."

"Ah yes. Titus."

Was Antony pretending not to know him? Another of his practical jokes, Marcellus wondered. "I've just returned from Syria, Sir. The treaty is signed and sealed. I've brought these envoys, so you may confirm the obligations on both sides."

"Treaty sealed?" said Antony. "Well, this calls for a celebration." He wandered over to a side table and poured out a generous quantity of wine into two glasses. He took some large gulps, and then stared at Marcellus. The world came back into focus.

"Marcellus!" He almost shouted with relief. "I look forward to hearing a poem on the difficulties of signing a treaty."

"It was really weird," Marcellus related to Octavia and Cornelia later in the evening. "He didn't seem to know who I was. Has he ever been like that before?"

"He's very bad at remembering people's names. He always has a secretary by him to prompt him."

"But the nomenclatura had already announced me."

Antony was his usual cheerful joking self at dinner, so Marcellus put the problem on one side. But Cierán told him that Antony was having increasing lapses of memory.

"Often he can't remember my name, so he calls me the javelin thrower. I think he drinks far too much. Then he gets irritable, and snaps at Octavia." Cierán found it was all he could do to refrain from leaping to her defence. He liked and admired Octavia. She had a wonderful way of speaking, with good use of language and clarity of thought. She was enjoying teaching the Gauls the rudiments of Greek philosophy, when they had a spare moment, which wasn't often.

The fragile peace between Sextus Pompey and the Triumvirs was breaking down, Sextus was betrayed, three of his legions deserting to join Gaius Caesar. So Sextus began to blockade the Mediterranean again, starving the Italian towns. This time he demanded control of Greece.

BOOK 3 : CHAPTER 2

Tarantum, 37 BC

The Triumvirs' term of office was coming to an end. With Antony's lieutenant Publius Bassus doing so well with his wars in Syria and Parthia, Antony was desperate to get some glory for himself in the east, but couldn't get the troops promised by Gaius because of the blockade. Gaius badly needed Antony's help and Antony's ships in order to confront Sextus. It didn't help that Antony had taken offence at more of Gaius's reported speeches. He reluctantly sailed for Italy once again, with his wife and children, and a fleet of three hundred ships, stuffed with marines, to find out what the hell was going on. He ordered Marcellus and his family to come as well, explaining that he had nominated Marcellus to be Consul with Agrippa. He wanted someone on his side in the Senate. And he had learned to love Marcellus, a true Athenian in spirit, secretly admiring his poetry even as he teased him unmercifully about it. Marcellus had been a little reluctant to leave Athens and Antony. And Antony was equally sorry to lose him. He was such a lovely interesting companion.

Before Antony's fleet arrived, Gaius, in a stupid act of aggression, ordered the port of Brundisium to be closed to him. Octavia was terrified when she discovered this, convinced that Gaius and Antony would start fighting each other again. This idiotic action of her brother's was the last thing she needed. She reassured Antony, telling him she would travel to Rome with Marcellus and his wife, to seek clarification and another reconciliation, despite being heavily pregnant. Antony's fleet sailed to Tarantum instead, a few miles further north.

Octavia found it hard to be clambering on and off boats in her condition. But Marcellus and Cornelia were always present, Marcellus with a supporting arm round her waist, and Cornelia gripping her hand. She was thankful to rest back in a well-padded litter for her journey. She knew Marcellus was secretly terrified that she might go into labour on the way.

Messengers were dispatched to Rome, telling of Octavia's imminent arrival. Gaius was shocked when he heard that she was coming to see him. He felt guilty, knowing her condition. He set out straight away with his bodyguard and with Marcus Agrippa to advise him, as Decimus Taurus was still insisting that he had retired from public life.

Octavia and her companions hadn't travelled any distance before they were met on the way. With tears in her eyes Octavia begged Gaius to see reason.

"Dearest Gaius, can't you see that if you fight Antony, I am bound to lose either a brother or a husband?"

Marcellus added his voice to hers. He thought Gaius's action incredibly stupid.

"Oh, very well. Have it your own way." Gaius was easily persuaded. He had been thinking on the journey. He did love Octavia, and maybe now wasn't the time to wage war against Antony. Better to wait until after Antony had conquered Parthia.

They all boarded Antony's flagship for an opulent banquet, which was rather wasted on Gaius and Octavia. They had been brought up on much simpler fare. Octavia's anxiety had destroyed her appetite. She didn't have much room left for food, the baby lying uncomfortably, right up to her stomach. She hadn't felt hungry for days. Gaius didn't drink much, either, but

Marcellus made up for him. Antony liked to have drinking companions, and by now Marcellus was used to raucous drunken nights with an inebriated Antony.

The peace terms were that Antony would leave Marcellus in command of one hundred of his warships for Gaius to use against Sextus Pompey, but he asked Gaius to supply legionaries for his Parthian war. Gaius promised him twenty thousand soldiers.

"I think we should inform the Senate that we Triumvirs will rule for a further five years," said Antony.

"And Lepidus?"

"Yes," said Antony. "We'll inform him as well."

Antony left Octavia behind in Rome with the children, where she arrived without mishap. To be honest he'd had enough of her. She was so bloody virtuous, never doing anything wrong, constantly nagging at him to perform his religious duties, reminding him of people's names, advising him of dates and meetings, criticising his judgements. She was more like a secretary than a wife. And pregnancy didn't suit her. She didn't blossom. She waddled round the palace, wearing dreadful clothes, always accompanied by hordes of kids. He liked kids, but for the Gods' sake, not all the time every single day. Anyway, she'd have her tame poet as well, he'd seen to that, so she should be happy. Occasionally Antony wondered if those two were up to anything, but he dismissed the idea. Altogether too adventurous for his irreproachable wife and his high-minded friend.

BOOK 3 : CHAPTER 3

Parthia, 37/36 BC

Antony and his forces sailed to Ephesus in Galatia, and then had a long march to Antioch, where he had arranged to meet up with Queen Cleopatra and her land army, already mobilised from Alexandria in Egypt. In addition Marcellus had arranged for several of the client kings to promise troops for the forthcoming battles against the invading Parthians.

All through the journey Antony was thinking of Cleopatra, his wonderful mistress, Queen of Egypt. A powerful woman, able to beguile him in so many different ways. Life was full of excitement, bed a place of infinite enchantments, making him feel like a god, Dionysus himself perhaps. He spent a couple of blissful months with Cleopatra. She was happy to assist him in his military endeavours, assigning the entire Egyptian army to be under his direction. Antony succeeded in combining his forces with hers, a total of nearly one hundred thousand men, before starting an ill-prepared war to repulse the Parthian invaders.

When Óengus and Cierán arrived with a large cavalry contingent, they set about finding out all they could about the Parthian army and Parthian territory. Wars between Rome and Parthia had been carried out for years, they discovered. There was a mine of information. In addition they questioned the auxiliaries from Armenia and Pontus. They would need to cross the Euphrates river. Then a high mountain barrier lay in the way of any invasion on their part. The south of the country was mostly hot desert and scrub. Arable land was farmed in basins between the mountains.

"Just like Helvetia, only hotter in the summer," said Cierán. They could see the snow-capped mountains in the far distance, very high mountains. "If we have to travel through those mountains in the winter months, it will be quite a problem." Cierán had a clear memory of such a journey undertaken many years ago. An unforgettable experience.

Óengus agreed with him. "We must be ready for any eventuality. That's what Dessy would say."

Their own cavalry forces were ordered to make every effort to provide themselves and their servants with warm waterproof clothing, ground sheets, sacking and straw, in addition to the usual baggage. Cierán ordered blankets for the horses. There would need to be a vast amount of food and fodder transported, as there would be little foraging available through the tree-clad foothills.

Canidius Crassus, one of Antony's senior officers, came to speak to them. "What's with all this heavy stuff?" he asked. "Why furs and suchlike? We're going to a desert country. It gets bloody hot."

Cierán was polite. "Sir, my former master, Decimus Taurus, always said that preparation is half the battle. We are going over mountains. High mountains. That may be easy enough in the summer, but we don't know how long this war will last. I feel it is better to take precautions."

The officer laughed, and went off to regale the rest of the officers' mess about the daft Gallic leaders and their hilarious 'precautions.' "Furs for the men and blankets for the horses. Would you believe?"

The mess found it most amusing. How could they possibly lose this war when they had such an enormous fighting force? It would be a swift Roman victory, no question.

When Cierán discovered that Antony was in so much of a hurry to bring about a decisive victory, he was proposing to leave behind the heavy baggage, the catapults and battering rams that were unobtainable in Parthia, he felt bold enough to confront him. He entered the praesidium to find Antony with a gaggle of untidy officers, bent over a map.

Cierán saluted. Antony looked up at Cierán, looked down at the map, then looked up at Cierán again. Then he belched, waved an arm in Cierán's direction, and said to the officers, "Ah, my javelin thrower." His speech was slurred. He belched again, and said, "Pardon." The officers sniggered.

Cierán was dismayed to find his commander and his officers already drunk halfway through the morning. Nevertheless he launched into his speech, adamant that taking on the Parthians without the usual Roman heavy weapons was tantamount to suicide. Cierán pointed out the problems Marcus Crassus had experienced, culminating in his death. Parthian cavalry were heavily armoured, equipped with long straight lances. It wasn't easy to fight them. The Romans would need ballistae and battering rams. But his mention of Decimus Taurus and preparation caused Antony's eyes to narrow. Cierán ended up shouting at his commander and getting nowhere. Coldly, Antony told him if he was too scared to fight, he had his permission to go.

"The baggage train will travel behind us, but they will move more slowly, as they may have to cut down trees in their way," said Antony. "We're not marching along proper Roman roads, but along tracks through forested areas. I've ordered two legions to act as a rearguard."

Cierán was sorely tempted to leave, sure that this expedition would end in another Roman disaster, but he decided to remain. He felt oddly responsible for Octavia's husband, not sure how distressed she would be if anything untoward happened to him. He could hear the officers' caustic comments about him, as he left headquarters and went over to join Óengus.

"Well?" Óengus asked.

"Nothing doing." Cierán spread his hands in a gesture of despair. "He got really angry when I mentioned Dessy. He says we can go."

"So are we going?"

"No. I'm staying. You go if you like."

"Now you are being daft."

Cierán heaved a sigh of relief.

Antony was missing Marcellus and his sage advice. He was even missing the poems, he discovered. For the last three years Marcellus had been a steadying influence on him. He was very like his Uncle Decimus in many ways. Left to his own devices, Antony knew he was apt to make the occasional catastrophic misjudgement. On the other hand Antony also knew that Marcellus would disapprove of his relationship with Queen Cleopatra. He was beginning to find it hard to be without her, which was partly the reason for his impatience over the Parthian war.

As foreseen by Cierán, the problems arose almost as soon as they started out. Despite Antony's ten thousand cavalry, it was impossible to protect the whole length of the supply chain. Mounted Parthians swooped down on the lightly guarded wagons, killed the guards, and carried the supplies away. By the time they reached the mountains the Romans had already lost the two legions acting as a rearguard.

It wasn't too difficult to negotiate the mountain passes during the warm spring and summer. Each valley seemed to support just one small town. The legionaries trampled through the carefully tended plots and vineyards, scattering the cattle and sheep. After firing the buildings and raping and slaughtering the inhabitants, the Romans didn't find a lot of provisions or booty left to take.

By mid-August the main army had arrived at Phraaspa, one of the principal cities of the Parthian empire, rising out of the flat plain like a miniature snow-covered volcano. Thick high white walls protected and encircled the city. Wisps of smoke from multiple cooking fires spiralled up into the thin air.

Antony settled down and made preparations for a long siege. He knew he had no means of destroying the city walls. And they were too high for a siege terrace to be practicable. He would have to force the issue by starving the inhabitants.

The first month was spent digging trenches and cutting down the stunted oaks and ash trees to be used to build redoubts and palisades. The cavalry were trying to protect the workers from the vicious attacks of the city dwellers, when Cierán caught sight of a glinting glistening mass in the far distance. He tried to make out what it was. The mass was moving towards them, semi-obscured by a haze of mist or dust. He called to Óengus, who had better eyesight.

"I think they're the cataphracts we've heard about," said Óengus, squinting and shading his eyes. "Can you see? Both the riders and the horses are covered with that scale armour. They look similar to the elephants we saw in the African campaign. Look at the size of those horses. They're the biggest I've ever seen."

Cierán could make out individual shapes as the cataphracts accelerated their pace. They could hear the sound of the huge lumbering horses being urged to a gallop, and the whoops and yells of their riders. He shouted for the men to abandon work and take up arms. They soon discovered that their arrows and bolts were insufficient to stop the enemy in its tracks. They resorted to hand to hand fighting, using swords and spears against the cataphracts' long heavy lances, without any great success.

At last the Parthian line broke and retreated, to the Romans' relief. They had been hard pressed, with many casualties. The legionaries pursued the enemy with the whoops and yells of their own battle cries. As soon as they saw that the Romans had abandoned their tight formation, the Parthians turned round, formed up and fired arrows and javelins at the scattered soldiers, causing horrendous losses. At the day's end the Romans had many men wounded and dead. A furious Antony accused one cohort of cowardice in the face of the enemy. He said they had run away, and would be punished by decimation. Angry and aggrieved soldiers drew lots to see which of them would be executed by their close comrades, the sentence swiftly carried out. This action of Antony's caused much bitterness and resentment amongst the remaining troops. The legionaries' confidence in a successful outcome to this war was severely shaken.

BOOK 3 : CHAPTER 4

Rome, 37 BC

Marcellus was relieved to hand over the rest of the fleet to Gaius. He still hated sailing across open sea with no land in sight. Memories of the shipwreck haunted his mind. He preferred to be in charge of a land army and feel solid ground under his feet. Gaius sensibly appointed Marcus Agrippa as his naval commander instead. Meanwhile Marcellus took his wife and little family, a boy and a girl so far, to his father's house in Rome. He decided he would need a lot of help from his father before being installed as Consul. The thought of it was a little overwhelming.

Lucanus worked hard on his son's behalf, ensuring that as Consul he would be enthusiastically welcomed by the Senate. Consuls were getting younger and younger.

Marcellus would have to stay in Rome for a year. His mother was delighted. Father and Grandfather would be so pleased as well, Marcellus thought. He would enjoy being a Consul with Agrippa. Even better, Octavia was back in Rome with the children but without Antony. He felt she was almost a part of him. But although Octavia was happy to see him, pleased to witness his love for his own children and also his love for Antony's children as well, she refused him her bed. She had sworn an oath to be loyal to Antony and that was that. Marcellus couldn't persuade her otherwise, and secretly he admired her for her stance. It would have been a risky procedure in any case. As he had his adorable Cornelia with him, it didn't worry him overmuch.

Marcellus was put in charge of Gaius's legions, preparing them to be battle ready, a job he was now well able to do. All the same, he wished Uncle Dessy hadn't retired from the army; he would have loved his uncle's assistance. But Marcellus had no difficulty controlling his officers and troops, instituting many of Dessy's training methods, most of which had by now become standard practise.

The peace didn't last long. As soon as they heard that Antony was back in Galatia, aiming to forge an alliance with Queen Cleopatra again, Gaius commenced hostilities. He was unsuccessful in his first attempts to defeat Sextus Pompey. His ships were hit by a violent storm and had to scuttle back to shore. Even so, quite a few were lost for good. Now Agrippa and Marcellus had finished their year as Consuls, Gaius handed control of the fleet to Agrippa, then he sent for Marcellus.

"Is the army readied for action, Marcellus?"

"Yes, there are no problems, Sir. The troops are well-trained and competent. What would you like me to do with the army?" Marcellus asked.

Gaius smiled. "You're to invade Sicily."

BOOK 3: CHAPTER 5

Villa of Decimus Statilius Taurus, 36 BC

A distant group of horsemen making a thunderous noise, careered down the road towards the villa, kicking up clouds of golden dust. Decimus saw them from the near field. He joined Laeforis, who was acting as his bailiff at present, and together they walked towards the visitors. Dessy shaded his eyes in an effort to identify them.

"It's Marcellus," said Laeforis, smiling.

The riders, all obviously experts, reined in their mounts to a walk. The horses' sides heaved with the recent exertion; their glossy coats were dulled with sweat, their breath condensing into clouds of tiny droplets in the chill spring air.

A delighted Decimus looked up to see his nephew Marcellus, and a whole squad of cavalry. He laughed with pleasure and turned to Laeforis. "We're being invaded."

Laeforis grinned and caught hold of Marcellus's bridle. "Come inside to the courtyard, Sir. There's a horse trough there."

The party dismounted and led their horses through the gate, towards the stables and the drinking trough. Dessy summoned his grooms to attend to them, watching with expert eye as the horses drank thirstily. Decimus patted the nearest animal on the neck, and then turned his attention to his visitor.

"Beautiful horses," said Dessy appreciatively.

Marcellus didn't prevaricate. It was not his way. "Uncle Dessy, you said you would always help me."

"A temporary madness," said Dessy, smiling. "What exactly do you want me to do this time?"

"I'm in charge of the army."

Dessy laughed again. "So I heard, Consul."

"I'm to invade Sicily. I need a camp prefect. One who knows what he's doing."

"Come and see Ethela. We will discuss your request over dinner."

So they were to take on Sextus Pompey and finish the job started by Caesar all those years ago. Unfortunately everyone knew that Sextus had governed his islands with considerable expertise, learnt from his father, no doubt. The proscribed Senators returning to Rome often voiced their opinion that Sicily was ruled better than most provinces. Not that anyone said this too loudly. Gaius was apt to take offence at any criticism. Marcellus was to command the Caesarian legions, with Max and Adrian acting as his deputies, while Aemilius Lepidus would have fourteen legions of his own.

"I'm flattered that you are asking me, an old man," Dessy said smiling, waiting for the protest. It didn't come. Ye Gods, he thought, my nephew really does think I'm old.

Marcellus thought the idea so stupid, it wasn't worth wasting his breath. "Lucas will have a position as military tribune, if you agree."

An excellent idea. He would be able to induct his son into the intricacies of army life, and protect him if necessary. Not that Lucas needed protection, he was a tough young man.

"And my other sons? What about Mochán and Manius?"

"Cavalry commanders, with your permission, Sir."

Ethela thought it was a dreadful idea and said so. "Your Uncle has much work to do here, Master Marcellus. And so have my boys. I do not wish them to be fighting."

All the boys protested immediately. They were so excited to be going to war, just like their father. Inwardly each wondered if he would ever match up to his father's reputation.

"If we go, my darling Ethela, and I haven't yet decided to do so, I promise to bring them all safely home." He had made just such a promise to Atia, he remembered. He had kept his word to her. It was the women who died, not the men. That made him think of Darreth, the exception. No military or medical skill could have saved him. It was just bad luck. Somehow his death, when he was on the point of refuge, was more poignant. Dessy had to push the thoughts away. He couldn't be sad when all around him were bursting with eagerness, wanting to ply Marcellus with questions. Ethela could see that her words would carry no weight at all.

The first success was down to Marcus Agrippa, whose brilliant naval tactics defeated some of Pompey's fleet, enabling Marcellus and Lepidus to land on Sicily without opposition. There they raced through the settlements, seizing towns with no great difficulty. Marcellus found it impossible to control his legionaries once they had burst through city gates. The soldiers fanned out, raping and looting as much as possible, intoxicated with the euphoria of easy victory. Fortunately they returned quickly, once the trumpets sounded the signal to retreat back to camp.

Agrippa polished off the remains of Pompey's fleet a month after the first naval encounter. Sextus Pompey fled with only a handful of supporters. He was caught at Miletus. It was thought that he would be executed without trial, whenever Antony returned from Parthia, as Gaius had already pronounced him an outlaw, without the rights of a Roman citizen.

Aemilius Lepidus wanted Sicily added to his African province, which would only be right and proper, as Lepidus was the third Triumvir. But the steady trickle of men deserting him in order to join with Marcellus, became a flood. The attraction proved to be mainly due to the camp prefect, and a large increase in salary negotiated by Egnatius, Marcellus found when questioning the deserters. They would much prefer to be with Dessy than with anyone else, they said. Dessy's men came home. And they all knew exactly how much Marcellus's legionaries were paid. More than twice the amount Lepidus awarded.

Gaius was able to strip the defenceless Lepidus of all his territory, allowing him only to continue in the post of Pontifex Maximus, the chief priest of the Roman Republic. Lepidus was forced to retire to a luxurious villa in Circeii, but was allowed to return to Rome frequently to carry out his official duties.

Marcellus was ordered to take his legions and make secure the African provinces that Lepidus had previously governed. He managed this with the continued assistance of his uncle, his cousins, and his friends. His officers were by now well used to the way he ran operations with meticulous preparation. He allowed no excuses for poor performance, and did not tolerate drunkenness or laziness. He was firm but fair in his dealings with the troops.

Marcellus met little in the way of resistance, making allies of many local leaders. He was careful to avoid any unnecessary massacres, rightly thinking that his spare use of force would be considered reasonable by the indigenous population. He endeavoured to exercise proper control over his men, telling them that they were to avoid upsetting the natives. When he returned to Rome, the Senate lost no time in awarding him a Triumph, having been heavily prompted by Gaius. There were enough opposition slain and prisoners captured to justify the award.

"So you have become a Great Man," Gaius declared gleefully, when he announced the news. "Just like I prophesied when we were children."

Marcellus laughed aloud. Gaius so loved being proved right. "Alright, I promise I won't fight you this time."

"I want you to come with me to Illyricum. There's trouble brewing in Dalmatia. I need a few heroic military exploits of my own, instead of always relying on you lot."

"What a cynic you are. Very well. But I'm busy right now."

"Yes, so I heard. Is it true that you are intending to build an amphitheatre of stone, a permanent structure?"

"Why not? I'm not as rich as you, but I've earned plenty of money with all these wars. I want to do something for the citizens. You and Agrippa have already done much to beautify the city. It's my turn."

Gaius agreed. He wondered if Marcellus was making a bid for popularity, but he couldn't bring himself to regard his childhood friend as in any way a rival. Besides, he didn't think Marcellus had a political bone in his body. He was wrong, but it took him some time to find out.

Decimus was awarded military honours, riding beside his nephew's triumphal chariot, with all his sons accompanying him. It was a truly amazing day for the Taurus family, who were now to be forever immortalised in stone by the amphitheatre of Titus Marcellus Statilius Taurus.

BOOK 3 : CHAPTER 6

Parthia to Galatia, Winter, 36/35 BC

After three months Antony gave up the siege of Praaspa. They were getting nowhere, constantly hammered by superior forces. It was time to beat a hasty retreat. He was haemorrhaging troops and horses from the frequent raids instigated by the closely-armoured enemy cavalry. He had sent for the heavy baggage, but none had arrived. The Romans' heavy weaponry was in all probability in the hands of the marauding Parthians. His officers were almost mutinous.

It was now November. Chill drying winds were blowing across the Parthian plains, kicking up one sandstorm after another, obscuring the sky with ominous ochre-tinted clouds. It seemed impossible to move outside the army tents, let alone fight. The abrasive sand particles whipped up into their faces, blocking noses, causing their skin to become painful, sore and excoriated. Their red-rimmed eyes stung, unable to peer through the fog of whirling spinning grains of sand. Everyone was coughing and choking, spitting out grit-laden saliva.

Unfortunately the storms failed to stop the Parthians, who descended from the city and erupted out of the plains in droves. They wrapped their silk scarves round their faces and helmets; so only their darting dark eyes could be seen. With blood-curdling yells and screeches they attacked the Roman redoubts, rounding up terrified prisoners and forcing them back behind the city walls, or herding them east, deep into their territory. There was never any sign that the city lacked provisions.

By the time the retreating Roman army reached the mountain passes, the temperature had plunged. Flurries of snow overlaid the roads, obscuring the way. The columns of weary and hungry marching men were continually harassed in the rear by the enemy looming out of the mists. Icy winds funnelled up the valleys, causing faces, fingers, and feet to freeze. The Egyptian troops suffered terribly. Although they were more reliable during the sandstorms, they were hopelessly unprepared for winter travel in mountains. At least the army was able to utilise the rough and ready camp sites they had built on their forward march, several months ago.

Despite Óengus and Cierán's Herculean efforts with their cavalry forces to patrol the marching men, fending off enemy attacks, they were continually harried by warmly-clad Parthians. The enemy had sure-footed ponies and deadly weapons, arrows, sling-shots, and javelins. There were frequent successful ambushes at the rear of the column.

Cierán's and Óengus's servants were made to give up their cloaks to Antony and his senior officers, to be distributed to some of the tribunes, and the shivering Egyptian captains. So the Gauls gave their slaves the horse blankets instead.

"It's best if we all sleep together," Cierán told his slaves. "That way we should stay warm." Each night he ordered that a layer of straw, kept for the purpose, be spread over the ground sheet, under the men's cloaks and blankets, in an attempt to insulate them from the freezing earth under their bodies.

Despite the difficulties, the Gallic commanders felt almost at home. They were used to travelling with an army through cold mountains. They organised and carried out hunting expeditions, and managed to catch some of the mountain animals, the wild boar, red deer, and mountain goats. But it was hard to find enough for the whole army, and they were still under sporadic attacks from the Parthians. Precious corn supplies were dwindling rapidly.

"This reminds me of those early nights in Gaul, when Laeforis and I were newly captured and sold to Dessy. We were always so cold. We had to huddle together for warmth," Cierán told Óengus as they rode side by side.

Óengus frowned. "I don't remember being that cold."

"No. By the time he bought you two, he'd learnt a bit about looking after us all. But to start with, we thought we always had to sleep outside the tent, until one night when it was pouring with rain, and Dessy came and yelled at us to stop behaving like idiots. Though we didn't know quite what he was saying, just that he was angry with us again. He had to drag us inside the tent. We couldn't understand him, and he didn't make much effort to understand us."

The army arrived at yet another burnt-out village. How the troops wished that they had refrained from stampeding the cattle and burning all the buildings on their original march. Still, there was some wood left that could be fired, so they could cook their tiny portions of meat and beans. And sometimes they found a few beasts that had managed to survive, despite lacking the care of a herdsman. An occasional chicken or two helped to eke out meagre supplies.

As his servants were preparing what little food there was, Cierán noticed his youngest slave coughing continually. The boy's face was flushed. He was feverish.

Cierán caught his hand. "Hey, boy. You didn't tell me you were unwell."

"I'm fine, Master," said the boy. He then had another paroxysm of coughing.

"You're anything but fine, my lad. Put that down and get to bed."

"Please, Master. I'm fine, really I am." The boy started to cry.

"He thinks he will be left behind to freeze," explained one of the other servants.

"Idiot. Of course I won't leave you behind. Have you had any supper?"

"Yes, Sir."

"He's had a little, Master."

"Good. I'll see if I can get something to help."

Cierán trudged off, his nailed boots crunching through the frozen ground as he made his way to the camp apothecary. He passed the massed black tents, silhouetted in sharp relief against the snow, illuminated by the brilliant starlight, even though there was no moon as yet. He gazed up at the sky in awe. It was good to sometimes stop fighting, and just relish the beauty of this roof-top world.

Someone tapped him lightly on the shoulder. He spun round, but no one was there, just the black tents standing to attention in serried rows. Cierán looked up at the stars again. His father's voice said, "The Greeks call it the plough." Were the words spoken aloud, or just in his head? He wasn't sure. His mind scrolled back through the years. He remembered the night he had stood gazing at the stars with his father, up in the clear air of the high mountains, when they were out on a hunting expedition. He could remember his father naming the constellations for him, and his feeling of wonder that his father knew so much more than other men.

Cierán returned to his own tent a little later, with a bitter brew of willow bark. He had difficulty persuading the boy to swallow any, the taste was so awful. He became exasperated. "This medicine has cost me more than you did," he said sternly. "So you are going to drink it. Just gulp it down quickly."

As the boy was worse the next morning, hardly able to stand, Cierán found him a place in one of the baggage wagons. Despite his fever, the boy was shivering. Cierán took off his own cloak and wrapped it round him, telling one of his other slaves to watch out for the boy.

An hour later Cierán found his slave cloak-less, blue-lipped with cold, his teeth jittering as he tried to explain that a centurion had wrested the cloak from him. Cierán rode along the line until he found the centurion in question. The officer was confronted by six feet of Gallic fury. Meekly he handed the cloak back, and swore to look after Cierán's sick slave in future.

"No," said Cierán. "Keep away from him. And keep away from me, or I'll kill you."

Word swiftly circulated that upsetting the cavalry commanders was a seriously bad idea.

At the end of each day, once his tent was erected and the bedding in place Cierán half-carried the boy to his tent. At first the boy was crying still, apologising over and over again for being a nuisance, till Cierán shut him up. Each morning he helped him back to the wagon. It was fully a week before the boy showed any signs of improvement, and another week before his master allowed him to march again for any distance.

The weather worsened. There were heavy snowfalls, followed by bitter frosts. The valley basins were sometimes so snow-filled, that trying to make camp in them was no longer feasible. The mountain air glittered with particles of ice. The paths were treacherous, causing men and horses to slip and slide. Wagons stuck fast. Cierán produced sacking to go under the wheels, in an attempt to get a grip on the ice. Sledges would have been much more practical, he thought to himself. There wasn't enough to eat for legionaries or animals, but at least they could eat in peace. Even the Parthians had decided the weather was so dreadful, they had given up their pursuit.

Cierán provided his sentries with fur-lined cloaks to keep them warm and dry while they guarded the overnight camps. He told them they had to try and keep moving backwards and forwards a little during the freezing nights. Even so, one morning he found one of his men frozen to death. The man was standing rigid in the snow, making no attempt to salute. His waxen face was fixed in a grimace, blue lips pulled back over stumps of yellow teeth. Cierán knew he was dead. He gave the body a gentle push. It toppled over like a log of wood.

Increasingly men fell by the wayside, sometimes due to wounds, more often due to privation. At first an effort was made to pick them up and transport them in the wagons, but eventually even this was abandoned, there were simply too many casualties. The mules couldn't pull the loaded wagons up the steep slopes. Antony ordered the sick and wounded to be turfed out into the snow, to die by the roadside, their cloaks and boots removed for the still-moving and living legionaries to use.

Some of the horses had to be slaughtered in an attempt to feed the officers and men. But fuel was almost impossible to find. The men got used to chewing frozen meat. By the time the army reached Ancyra in Galatia, Antony had lost upwards of thirty-two thousand men dead or captured, a third of his forces, ruining his reputation for military competence.

The two Gauls decided that they no longer wished to be allied to Antony. They sought his permission to return to Athens, collect up their wives and offspring, and head back to Rome. During their last evening a drunken Antony tried in vain to persuade them to stay. He apologised for his past mistakes, agreeing that they had been right and he had been wrong. But to no avail. Cierán was fed up with the disorganisation of the army, and he didn't much like Antony's officers, especially Canidius, who still tended to treat both Gauls with disdain. Especially when drunk. It was so different from campaigning with Dessy, when everything was so well ordered.

Cierán was surprised to feel a sense of elation, a lightness of spirit, when he returned to Rome. He discovered that Óengus felt the same way.

"It feels like my home city," Óengus confessed. "I've almost forgotten what my real home looked like. But we didn't have fountains and marble palaces, warmth in the winter, and heat in the summer. And food and drink fit for the Gods."

Cierán found himself agreeing. "We've turned into Romans," he said. But the realisation made him feel a terrible sense of loss for his own culture, his own religion, his own dead family. He would never be completely Roman, although his children would be. He must make a real effort to give them as much of his Helvetian heritage as possible, especially after that strange unexplained encounter in the high mountains, when his father had spoken to him.

It would not be possible to accommodate all their servants and baggage at the Taurus house, so they left most of their men and equipment at the army garrison. They realised something was badly wrong as soon as they turned in at the familiar street. A slave came running towards them.

"Please, Masters, could you try and make as little noise as possible? Lady Caecilia is gravely ill."

This was a bitter blow to Cierán. He had always held Lady Caecilia in the greatest affection and respect, ever since the time many years ago, when he had first sat by her side, and she had shown him sympathy and understanding.

"Is Master Decimus Taurus here?" Cierán asked.

"No, Master. But we expect him soon."

The Gauls handed their horses over to the grooms, and entered the silent house. Some of the servants had red-rimmed eyes. Caecilia was a much loved mistress.

Marcus and Lucanus made a great fuss of them both, but clearly had their minds on other matters. Marcus spent a great deal of his time in his wife's bedroom, where expensive aromatic pastilles burned day and night to ward off any evil spirits lurking about that might harm his dearest Caecilia. Portia and her maids were tireless in their efforts to ease her suffering, but everyone knew that her life was ending. Marcus was desperate to catch her last breath.

Dessy rushed up from the country to see his mother for the last time. He also wanted to see the Gauls and learn all about their experiences with Antony. It was a distraction from contemplating a future without his gentle mother. Decimus enjoyed hearing about Antony's incompetence, but hated the thought of a Roman defeat. At least none of the eagles were lost, unlike the disastrous campaign of Marcus Crassus.

"Mark Antony went through a marriage ceremony with Queen Cleopatra, before we set off to repel the Parthians," Cierán told them. "Should Lady Octavia be informed, do you think?"

"I'm sure Octavia has a pretty good idea of how things stand. She's no fool. Don't interfere between a man and his wife, or a man and his slaves. Better to await events," advised Dessy.

BOOK 3 : CHAPTER 7

Villa of Cierán Statilius Taurus, Winter, 35/34 BC

After the elaborate funeral rites, Decimus and the Gauls travelled back together to the country. It was a sombre journey, with Cierán and Óengus giving a blow by harrowing blow account of Antony's wasteful campaign.

"Laeforis has been keeping an eye on things for you," Dessy explained, "but it's always as well to have a look yourselves, though you've both got good bailiffs in my opinion. We've not had any major problems. The harvest was excellent. And you'll like the wine."

Their community was gradually taking shape. Dessy's tent-mates and their wives and children were an added bonus, as the Gauls knew them all well. They had fought so many campaigns together, they were old friends.

Cierán invited the entire Taurus family to join his household for the winter festivals at his villa. He knew that the recent death of Lady Caecilia had affected the family hugely. It had affected him too, but he felt that it was better for him to do all the organising, so the family didn't have to think or plan festivities while they were consumed with grief. Also he wanted his wife and children to know something of the way in which Helvetians celebrated the passing of the shortest days. He supervised the preparation of the rough cider which would be served to his field hands. The house slaves cut branches of butcher's broom, holly, and mistletoe. The women had fun decorating the villa with the shiny green leaves and bright red berries. They hung the mistletoe in strategic places.

Once all the guests had arrived and had been settled in their accommodation, the festivities started. The house slaves and field hands were summoned in addition, to witness while Cierán, Óengus, and Laeforis performed the sacrifice of the ox, pig, and goat.

After the ceremony Cierán's butchers got to work, skinning the animals and preparing them for roasting, the bullock for a full day and night. The bakers had been working overtime, producing many loaves of coarse bread. The next evening the farm hands with their women and children were marshalled into the near field, adjacent to the villa.

It was a chilly night. The adults stamped their feet, and blew on their fingers, their breath condensing in the night air. Penelope and her maids supervised the gifts of warm woollen cloaks and tunics to the men, and materials for the women and little ones, enough to make dresses, and clothes for all the children. They were told that their old clothes were to be handed in a few days later to be used as patches.

The smell of roasting meats was so enticing. Men and women became cheerful in anticipation of the feast ahead. Excited children raced round the field. Cierán made sure the overseers kept an eye on the crowd in case anyone caused trouble, especially as they weren't that used to drinking the rough cider. He didn't want any fights to break out.

Everyone in the house was advised to wrap up warm. As he held the adjacent estate Decimus arrived last with his family, all too aware that as soon as he saw Cierán and Ella together, the age-old problem would rear its head. He had taken a good drink beforehand in an effort to numb the feelings he knew were just under the surface of his mind.

Cierán welcomed them warmly, then he took Ethela by the hand and led her out into the garden. There every branch of every tree was hung with glowing lanterns. Bonfires flared and crackled from all the corners of the field. Smoke rose up, tinged with tiny glowing-red sparks. Pitch torches around the circumference of the garden illuminated their faces, and their breath.

"*This is for you, Ethela,*" said Cierán, speaking in German.

Ethela burst into tears. "*You've made me so happy,*" she said, hugging him. "*It's perfect. Just like it was at home.*"

"It's so beautiful," Portia declared.

"We should have snow though," Cierán sighed. "Or at least a good hard frost."

"No, we don't want that."

"This is how we celebrate in our home country, with lights, torches, and bonfires. Everyone is summoned to the feast, slaves as well," Cierán explained. "Sometimes a favourite horse, too."

One of the boys tweaked off the cap that Ella wore. Her beautiful blonde hair tumbled down to her shoulders. She turned swiftly to berate the boys.

Portia laughed. "You are so like your father, Ella."

Dessy looked at the three of them, Ethela, Ella and Cierán. So Portia knew the truth! She was in on the conspiracy. He felt a rage surging through him. He walked over to Cierán in one swift movement. Cierán turned to him with a smile, and started to say something. Decimus hit him as hard as he could. Cierán stepped backwards, then lost his footing and stumbled against Ethela. As she tried to hold him, Dessy struck him again. Cierán fell to the ground. There was a deathly silence.

Dessy stood over him. Cierán tried to sit up and was struck again. He lay back on the ground, feeling sick and dizzy.

"Traitor," snarled Decimus.

Ella was crying in her mother's arms. Óengus and Laeforis stepped into action, grabbing Dessy's wrists. He struggled to free himself. "Damn you, let me go!" Dessy shouted, trying to twist out of their hold on him.

"No, Master. You are frightening the children."

Only Ethela realised exactly what was going on. She spoke in rapid German. *"Dessy thinks Ella is Cierán's child. I've seen him looking at them both. I knew what he was thinking. He was wondering if she is his own Ella."*

Cierán succeeded in getting to his feet. He looked at Ethela, and then back at Dessy. Blood trickled down from one nostril. The youngest slave rushed over with basin and cloth.

"I'll kill him for you, Master," said the boy, quite distraught.

"You'll do no such thing, boy," said Cierán sternly. He took the cloth and wiped his face. "Let him go," he said.

They released Dessy's arms. The two of them stood looking at one another, Dessy breathing hard, still seething with a rage he was now unable to express.

"Have you finished, or do you want to hit me some more?" Cierán asked.

Decimus looked at him and then looked at Ethela. "You traitor," he spat at her. "I should have killed you both."

"Enough, Master," Laeforis shouted at him.

Decimus looked around. Everyone was still shocked. It had happened so quickly. But now people were moving. "I'm going," he said. "Enjoy your feast."

Cierán spoke with authority. "No, you're not. Bring him inside the house. Penelope, please take over, while I settle this problem with my Master."

"I'm going," Dessy repeated.

"I am sorry to overrule you, Master, but you are going nowhere. On the contrary you are coming inside my house." Cierán beckoned to his servants. "You too, please, Ethela, my dear." He used the endearment quite deliberately.

Decimus knew he was outnumbered. He was shocked at what he had just done, but was still furious with everyone.

Cierán made him sit in a chair, with Óengus and Laeforis standing by. Then he knelt at his master's feet, and said, "Give me your hands, Master."

"Go fuck yourself," snapped Decimus.

Cierán started speaking with slow deliberation. "When you first bought us, what, twenty-five years ago, it must be now?" He looked round at the others, who nodded in agreement. "Ethela and I were little more than children. We were fourteen years old. Remember, Master?"

Decimus couldn't bring himself to speak. He just slightly moved his head.

"You raped Ethela on her first night with you. A fourteen-year-old virgin who couldn't speak a word of Latin. Much less defend herself."

Decimus lifted his hand as if to ward off a blow. He stared at Cierán, taking in every word spoken.

"We were terrified of you," Cierán continued, "all three of us. So much so that Ethela was unable to eat. Which made Cassius Domitius's servants worried out of their minds, thinking that they would be blamed if Ethela got sick. So they indicated to me that I must try and do something about it, or everyone would be punished. And the Gods knew what horrors that would involve. We had just been branded. Remember, Master?"

There was no response, but Cierán knew his words were having a profound effect.

"So I promised Ethela that henceforth I would be her brother, and I would do my best to help her and look after her. We went to the camp altar. We thought Roman gods must be more powerful than Helvetian or German gods. I took a knife and I made a cut just above my wrist. Look, you can still see the scar." He held out his arm. "And I made a similar cut on Ethela's wrist." His voice dropped to a whisper. "Look, you can still see the scar."

Silently Ethela held out her hand. Decimus could see the tiny white mark on her skin. He'd never noticed it before.

"Laeforis bound our wrists together, so our blood intermingled. I swore to be a faithful brother to Ethela. She promised to be my sister. She has been my beloved sister for the last twenty-five years, and she has never been anything else."

Decimus had his hands over his face. Tears were trickling through his fingers.

"We got used to you. We were fed, after a fashion, and clothed. We began to have a glimmer of understanding of what we were expected to do. After Laeforis and I nearly died, you changed. You changed a lot. We felt safe, no longer scared of everything. We had Óengus as well, to explain things to us." Cierán paused. "But Ella is my baby."

Decimus was staring at him in shock.

"Ella is my baby," Cierán repeated, his voice cracked with emotion. "Because while you were away killing my fellow countrymen, I was delivering your little daughter at the side of the road. I was the first person to hold her. I kept her safe from harm all through our long journey. I have loved her ever since. She is special to me, as is my sister Ethela." His voice shook, so he stopped again, fighting to get himself under control. "Where were you, Master?"

There was no reply.

"Lady Portia told Ella that she was like her father, because she sounded just like you when she was telling off the boys."

There was still no response.

"Dessy, we have learned to love you, even though you were once our enemy." Cierán got to his feet. "So now you have totally fucked up our party, you'd better come and make amends."

Dessy took his hands away from his face, and looked straight at Cierán. "I'm so stupid."

"Too true," murmured Laeforis.

Decimus stood up. He felt a little unsteady. "Cierán, do you ever make mistakes?"

Cierán was laughing with relief now, with his arms around Ethela. "Occasionally we had our revenge."

Laeforis grinned. "We all spat in the pancake mixture."

Decimus swivelled round to face him. "What?"

"We all spat in the pancake mixture. You said it was delicious."

"What else?" Decimus was a bit shocked.

"That's enough truth for now," said Cierán. "We will leave you to speculate upon what form our revenge took. That should give you something real to worry about, bearing in mind we were little more than children." He stood smiling at his former master. "Let's wrap ourselves in our cloaks and go out and enjoy ourselves."

"I'm so sorry." Decimus held out his hands.

Cierán gripped them tightly. "I thought you would be. How long has this been festering in your brain?"

"That first night. When I'd come home, and there you all were. Ella seemed too good to be true, somehow. I kept trying to convince myself that it was so long ago, it no longer mattered. But it did."

"If you think back, you'll remember the time she was conceived."

"I'm so ashamed."

"Good. Remember that for the future. Things are not always what they seem. Come on. It's high time we started the party."

Cierán walked out of the house, straight over to Ella, and removed her cap. "Your hair is glorious. Don't be ashamed of what you are, a beautiful, intelligent, kind girl."

"Daddy says it's immodest."

Cierán kissed her. "Not any more." He walked over to the roasted ox, and cut the first slice of meat, to start the proceedings, to tumultuous applause. By now everyone was very hungry.

Marcus and Lucanus tried to offer apologies for their relative's dreadful behaviour, but Cierán laughingly dismissed their protests. "He's done much worse to me in the past," he said. It took a little time for Decimus to get into the spirit of the proceedings. Cierán knew he would get drunk, like his father, so kept a careful watch on him, ready with a guiding hand when necessary.

Marcus and Luke refrained from asking questions, as the problems appeared to be solved. As for Dessy, he felt a lightness of spirit in spite of his mother's death. How wonderful to know that Ella was his own sweet child, and that Cierán would forgive him almost anything.

There was a miscellaneous collection of musicians, and one or two of the field slaves had whistles and flutes. After everyone had eaten their fill, the music started and the scene was set for dancing.

The following night Cierán's youngest slave, still somewhat weak from the residue of his chest infection, was appointed to be king of Saturnalia. He had told the other household slaves so proudly, how his master had given him medicine that cost more than he did. He made lots of mistakes. For the Romans, the festivities became a lot more familiar.

BOOK 3 : CHAPTER 8

Rome to Athens, 34 BC

It was good to be back in harness again, Decimus declared, but it was better to be back at home. Everyone had returned in one piece, apart from a few minor cuts and scratches, thanks be to the Gods. He settled down to the enjoyment of family life and the running of his estates.

He didn't have peace for long. Octavia came to see him, begging him for help. She wanted to go to Greece with some of the troops Gaius had promised Antony, now Antony had lost so many men. Marcellus and Gaius were away fighting in Dalmatia, and she didn't know who else to ask. She thought Dessy's Gauls might help as well.

"But my dear girl, Antony is reported to have aligned himself with Queen Cleopatra." And in more ways than one, Dessy thought. The Queen had just had another baby. Probably Antony's.

"Dessy, I swore to my brother that I would be a loyal and faithful wife to Antony. I intend to keep my vow. Please, please help me."

He discovered that she was really worried about Antony.

"Look, Dessy. Read these letters. Antony doesn't write often. But these letters don't always make a lot of sense. He is full of conspiracy theories, but I don't think my brother has time to plot against him at present, now he is away fighting with Marcellus."

The letters were a confusing mishmash. There were paeans of praise for his lieutenant Publius Bassus, but also rambling descriptions of Cleopatra, sometimes far too graphic for comfort. Dessy wondered if Octavia had any idea of what exactly Antony was saying about his regal mistress. Antony's love for his Egyptian twins shone through the jumble of words, though, with funny little anecdotes about them that made Dessy smile. Antony was clearly anxious about his children in Rome, but hardly bothered even to enquire after Octavia's health.

Decimus did his best, but Gaius and Marcellus had taken the bulk of the legions to Dalmatia. The Gauls were reluctant to go back to Greece, but agreed to help Octavia, though they thought it would be a waste of time. Dessy found it hard to witness Octavia attempting to be a loyal wife to Antony, when Antony was anything but a loyal husband to her. Octavia raised a large sum of money and troops in her own name. She was popular among the plebeians, having the reputation of being a good virtuous wife, and a loving mother and stepmother. They arrived in Patrae with the two thousand legionaries Decimus had managed to recruit, plus cattle, horses, weapons, expensive gifts and expensive clothes for Antony and his client kings. Then they travelled the hundred and thirty miles to Athens.

It was no use. When Antony heard of her arrival, he refused to meet her. He sent a letter to her, ordering her to return to Rome. Because as soon as his darling Cleopatra heard of Octavia's arrival, she had stopped eating. She was fading away before his eyes. He couldn't stand to see her crying. Cleopatra was convinced he would desert her, despite his violent protestations of undying love.

For Decimus it had been a complete waste of time and effort. Octavia was in floods of tears, weeping on Dessy's shoulder. She found it was much more hurt pride than anything else. After all she didn't love Antony. He could be kind as long as it didn't interfere with any of his pleasures. But love? No. He loved only Queen Cleopatra, but that love was a kind of sickness, Octavia thought, when she reread his letters.

"You did your best, my dear. What more could you have done? Antony isn't made to be faithful. We men aren't made to be faithful, I'm afraid." Although Dessy was now perfectly satisfied with Ethela. He didn't bother to look anywhere else. Like his nephew he thought Octavia a beautiful woman, even more so now her features were more formed. Cleopatra was the same age as Octavia. Having seduced Caesar without too much difficulty, she had no problems with Antony. Perhaps she was skilled in areas that Octavia probably knew nothing about. Decimus had seen the Egyptian Queen at Caesar's house when she lived in Rome for two years. He didn't particularly like her olive skin and he thought her nose was too large for her face. It was Antony that mattered to these two women though, not him.

Lucanus returned from the Senate, bursting with news. He summoned his brother back to Rome.

"What's all the big excitement?" Decimus smiled, looking at his brother and father.

"Antony has successfully invaded Armenia again."

"It's about time he did something good."

"Yes, but he's celebrated this minor victory with a procession in Alexandria that has all the trappings of a Triumph. And listen to this. He's announced that he has broken with Gaius

Caesar. He's written to the Senate withdrawing from the Triumvirate."

"Good grief. He must be mad!"

Marcus broke in. "Possibly he was thinking Gaius would have to do the same."

"Gaius will never voluntarily relinquish any power. He still feels unsafe," Dessy said.

"You'd better send for your Gauls, Dessy. They may be needed."

Decimus agreed. But he wasn't sure in his own mind how Cierán and Óengus would react to the news.

Just one month later they heard that Antony had gone a reckless step further.

"He's declared Caesarion to be Caesar's legitimate and true heir," Luke informed them all. "He's given kingdoms to all his children, even some that aren't his to give. He has called it the 'Donations of Alexandria.' And he's proclaimed Cleopatra to be Queen of Kings and Queen of Egypt, and Caesarion to be King of Kings and rule as King of Egypt with his mother."

"Queen Cleopatra has put him up to this," said Cierán, frowning in annoyance. He quite liked Antony. And despite their differences, Antony had never tried to punish him while they were campaigning together. Even though Cierán had expressed his views more forcefully than perhaps a senior cavalry officer should. "I think his mind is no longer strong," he finished.

Decimus was appalled. "It's tantamount to a declaration of war."

"I'm very much afraid so," Luke said sadly. "This is dangerous for Gaius. His own claim to be Caesar's successor rests entirely on his adoption through Caesar's will. A legitimate heir born to the richest and most influential woman in the world is a direct threat, isn't it?"

It became difficult to keep abreast of the latest developments. Lucanus was able to report on the propaganda war which developed between Gaius and Antony. Messengers rushed backwards and forwards between the Senate and the Egyptian court. It appeared Antony accused Gaius of keeping the ships he had lent to him for the war on Sextus Pompey, and not dividing Sicily with him. And that he had taken the legions and revenue of Lepidus without sharing it with Antony. Finally he accused Gaius of being a low-born adventurer, who had forged Caesar's will.

"That last bit is not going to go down well," said Decimus gloomily.

"It didn't," said Luke. "So Gaius has retorted that Antony failed to share the spoils of Armenia with him, amongst other things. He's accused Antony of going native, preferring Greeks and Egyptians to his fellow Romans, making war without the authority of the Senate, and executing Sextus Pompey without a trial."

"No, just hang on there. I thought the Senate ruled that Sextus Pompey was an outlaw, an enemy of the state."

"I don't think niceties such as the law bother Gaius any more. He's also suggested that Antony intends to make Alexandria the capital city of the Republic, and rule as a king, with Caesarion to follow him. They're like a couple of squabbling children," Lucanus complained, "hurling insults at each other. And if one of them doesn't stop soon, it will come to blows. And we will all be dragged in again."

"Luke, it's been inevitable really, ever since Philippi, once they'd got rid of Lepidus and Sextus Pompey. I wonder who will win in the end?"

"You'll fight for Gaius, I suppose?"

"Against Antony? No," Dessy replied shortly. "I had enough of that at Mutina. He's never been my favourite person, but he's a comrade in arms. He was brilliant at Alesia when we fought Vercingetorix. Bloody brilliant. I suppose you will fight for Antony, Cierán, if it comes to it?"

"I shall do whatever you tell me to do, Sir."

"But you don't have to any more."

Cierán laughed at him. "Laeforis and Óengus obey me, because I am their chief. That will never change. I will obey you for the same reason. When I was sold all those years ago I had no country, no family, no freedom, no soul, and no chief. When you bought me, you became my chief. And you always will be. That will never change either."

"Oh," said Dessy. His eyes filled with tears. "I don't think I was a very good chief at first, was I?"

"No, you were fucking terrible," said Laeforis. Everyone laughed at that. Dessy dashed the tears from his eyes and hugged each of his Gauls in turn.

When Decimus discovered that Antony had written to Octavia, telling her he had divorced her, he called round to console her. But he found that even if Antony was sick in his mind, Octavia no longer cared.

"Any affection I felt for him vanished after our fruitless journey to Athens. He is an ungrateful disloyal man," Octavia declared.

"He's a selfish ignorant fool," said Dessy, shocked at Antony's callousness. "He doesn't appreciate the worth of what he was rejecting."

"He says he's married Cleopatra." Unexpectedly, Octavia started to cry, tears of humiliation. The children were at a loss to know what to do for their adored mother. Decimus put his arms round her and held her close against his chest, stroking her back and speaking soothing inanities. He didn't know what else to do. Octavia's tears turned to sobs, all the awfulness of the last few years taking her unawares. After a while she pulled away, and tried to compose herself.

"I'm sorry, Dessy. I've turned into one of those awful weepy females recently. I despise myself."

"I expect you'd rather I was Marcellus," Dessy smiled, as he wiped her face with his handkerchief.

"You're a comforting substitute. But I miss him so much."

The older children looked at each other in bewilderment. After all, Claudius had died years ago. It seemed odd that their mother was still so affected by his loss. No one enlightened them.

"Portia would like you to come and stay for a while. You will need to find a suitable house."

"I would like that very much. She has always been so kind, and such a help to me, especially after Mother died," said Octavia, still sniffing a little. She tried to smile at the anxious children.

"That's settled, then," said Decimus.

Gaius ordered swingeing taxes on the hapless Roman citizens to fill his depleted war chests. This made them very unhappy. Free men were to pay a fourth, and freed slaves an eighth, of their wealth and property. Cierán, Laeforis and Óengus were disgusted. Decimus wasn't that impressed, either.

Disorder ruled again. Gaius broke into the house of the Vestal Virgins and produced what he said was Antony's will. It appeared to give Antony's children Roman-conquered territories for his sons to rule, and on his death his tomb was to be in Alexandria.

At the end of the year the agreement between the three Triumvirs expired. It was not renewed. Both Consuls and a third of the Senate decamped to join Antony. The rest of the Senate deposed Antony from the Consulship for the next year, to which he had been designated, and declared war on Queen Cleopatra. The plebeians were in despair again. Yet more civil war!

BOOK 3: CHAPTER 9

West Coast of Greece, Rome, 32 to 31 BC

As soon as Antony read the declaration of war on his Royal mistress, he knew he had precipitated the final act between himself and that cowardly upstart, Gaius Julius Caesar. He was fed up with constantly looking over his shoulder to see what the poisonous little arriviste would do next. Initially he felt buoyed by his recent victory in Armenia, and the arrival of the Consuls, and so many senior Senators to his side. It was time to muster his army and navy, and ready them for the hard battles ahead.

Antony and Cleopatra moved their court to Ephesus, where an enormous fleet was gathering, a large part of which was supplied by Cleopatra. They had a party lasting several days. Antony wandered around in a drunken haze. Each morning he awoke with a horrible feeling of doom, hard to shake off. He had to have a drink or two before his mind returned to an even keel. He couldn't think of any reason. All the omens were favourable. An eagle had been seen circling over his house. A dead tree in the forum had sprung back to life. One of the city's seers had hailed him as the future emperor of the world. Perhaps he had offended the Gods in some way? He arranged several expensive sacrificial services to the Goddess Diana, asking for her assistance in the ensuing struggle, just to ensure his success. Not that there could be any question about it. He knew his victory was assured when he heard the news that Decimus Taurus had no intention of taking up arms against him.

A dreadful outbreak of malaria amongst Antony's rowers more than decimated their numbers, which was a little worrying. As a result, one of his generals suggested conceding the sea to the young Caesar and fighting only a land battle. He claimed that Antony was a superb army commander, conveniently overlooking the appalling mess Antony had made in Parthia. Cleopatra wouldn't hear of the idea. She wanted an easy means of escape, if things went wrong.

Antony summoned his land forces back from Armenia. The main fleet was transferred first to Athens, and then finally stationed in the huge safe harbour at Actium.

But Marcus Agrippa hadn't been idle all this while. He had already captured the Greek town of Methone. His nimble ships dominated the sea and all the ports along the coast. When Antony tried to take Corfu to maintain his supply route, he found his fleet barred. He had to retreat. And now Agrippa's ships were stationed across the mouth of the Ambracian gulf. So Antony's fleet was trapped.

Marcellus was still in Illyricum, establishing garrisons in all the principal towns, not aware of all that had been going on between Rome and Alexandria. When he was ordered by the Senate to bring the army to Actium, he wrote to his father, to try and discover the reason why. His father's letter of explanation was quite a shock.

Straight away Marcellus sent for his Uncle Decimus. Decimus replied that there was no way he was going to help fight Antony. He'd done so once; he wasn't prepared to do so again. This took Marcellus aback. He sat down in the evening to talk things over with his deputies and his officers. They were split, some agreeing with the war, but others disagreeing. Max thought they should be fighting with Antony and the Consuls rather than with Gaius Caesar, but he didn't know Gaius quite so well as the others. Marcellus came to a decision. He sent away any officers who had fought under Antony in the past, and felt a certain loyalty to him. Adrian persuaded Max to stay, but Max said he would have felt a lot happier if Decimus approved of this war.

Antony wrote to Octavia again, rudely ordering her to leave his house in Rome, but at the same time asking her to care for his children. Octavia knew things were coming to a head. She travelled fast, with a large escort. Thank goodness she had learnt to ride all those years ago, because there was a great need for speed. She was greeted warmly by Decimus and Ethela, although they were a little shocked to see her on horseback, and wearing a short tunic and trousers. Decimus snapped out orders to his grooms, and lifted her down off the horse. He could tell how agitated she was, with her flushed cheeks and chest heaving with emotion. He ushered her swiftly into the house.

"Dessy, have you heard the news?" Octavia burst out.

"What is the news, my dear?"

"Marcellus has been ordered to march to Actium. My brother means to make war on Antony and Cleopatra. Dessy, you must get the children for me."

Decimus guided her to a couch, while Ethela hastily produced a tray of refreshment. Gratefully Octavia gulped down some water, and attempted to compose herself. She smiled tremulously at them both.

"What children are we talking about?" Ethela asked.

"Cleopatra's children, and Antony's eldest son, Mark Antony Antyllus. My stepson. Antony sent for him a year ago. Now he has made him his heir." She broke off, looking beseechingly at her friends. "I know Antyllus well. He was with me in Athens. He is such a lovely boy. Please, Dessy, help me again."

"Of course he may be fighting at his father's side, in which case........." Dessy's voice trailed away, as Octavia stared at him, upset by the implication. Her eyes were moist with sudden tears. She sat looking distractedly at the mosaic on the dining room floor, then made an effort to continue.

"But Cleopatra's children are so young. The twins are just nine years old, and Ptolemy Philadelphus is only four. You must get them for me."

"And Caesarion?"

Octavia moved her hands in a gesture of despair. "That might be too much to hope for. You could try. He's just a seventeen-year-old boy."

Decimus rose to his feet. How could he refuse? He walked over to Octavia and grasped her hands. "Very well, lady. It will be as you command."

"Thank you, thank you. I knew I could rely on you."

Ethela suggested that she might like to freshen herself up and change, before they discussed anything further. Octavia agreed, laughing a little now she had achieved her purpose.

"I hope I haven't shocked you too much," she said.

Decimus wasn't shocked so much as struck by the beauty of Atia's daughter. She rivalled her mother for looks. No wonder his nephew was so besotted with her.

Later at dinner the conversation continued.

"I think there's definitely something wrong with Antony. Look at the last letter he sent me." Octavia handed over the papyrus.

Decimus was astonished when he read the letter. It was worse than the others, a long rambling epistle, varying in tone between threats and pleas, and not making much sense at all.

Marcellus marched his army south to Actium. Antony promptly had trenches dug, to deprive him of an adequate water supply. Marcellus desperately needed Uncle Dessy, who knew how to solve such problems. He sent again to his uncle, imploring him to come and help him. He felt just like Max, he realised. He didn't want to fight Antony either. No sooner had the letter been dispatched than Decimus himself appeared at the camp gates with Óengus, Laeforis, and Cierán. Marcellus was so delighted to see them all. They were escorted over to the praesidium where Decimus explained.

"Your Octavia is worried about the children."

"What children?"

"Her stepson Antyllus and Cleopatra's children. They are very young. Octavia thinks we might win. It looks as if Antony thinks so, too. I wonder why? He's asked her to look out for the children, though he didn't specify which children. Octavia thinks he means Antyllus and his children with Cleopatra."

"That girl is such a worrier! We haven't even started yet. Anyway I'm sure Cleopatra's children are safely tucked up in Alexandria."

Dessy showed Marcellus the strange letter from Antony to Octavia.

"Something's wrong," said Dessy. "Cierán said that Antony set off to wage war on the Parthians, but left all the heavy equipment to follow on behind. Why would he do such a thing when Cierán and Óengus were both yelling at him, and saying it was essential?"

"Yes, and look at his subsequent reckless behaviour. He used to be so reliable, so capable, such an expert politician. He's been a partner with Gaius for years. Why this drastic change?"

They could only speculate. Perhaps it was due to Cleopatra's baleful influence, Dessy thought. Perhaps Antony was losing his mind. Marcellus was more inclined to believe the latter.

Some of Antony's client kings heard that Titus Marcellus Statilius Taurus, whom they liked and trusted, was camped with an army at Actium. So many of them defected to join him, and ditched Antony.

The enormous popularity of Gaius with the legions secured the defection of the provinces of Cyrenaica and Greece to his side. At this point of strength, Gaius tried to arrange for a conference with Antony, but it was too late. His proposal was rejected out of hand. Yet another indication that something was wrong with Antony, Decimus surmised. What harm would a conference do?

Marcellus and his army occupied the northern spit of the gulf, where Antony had stationed some troops. But Cierán and his brother officers with their cavalry forces soon put paid to that. Cierán said he had given up trying to understand Roman politics. It was altogether too confusing.

"First Gaius fights against Antony at Mutina. Then he fights with Antony at Philippi. Now he fights against Antony again. Why can't they just make peace?"

Another large chunk of Antony's army deserted to join Marcellus and Dessy. Antony withdrew from the north to occupy only the southern peninsula. All was ready for the final showdown.

BOOK 3 : CHAPTER 10

West Coast of Greece, Alexandria, Egypt, 31 BC

It was Agrippa and his naval brilliance who won the Battle of Actium at sea. The two fleets engaged on the second of September. Antony had amassed more ships, but half of them were provided by Cleopatra. Many of his ships were the standard Roman warships, their towers filled with armed men, and fitted out with catapults. Good platforms for hurling weapons down onto Agrippa's smaller ships. Unfortunately for Antony, his depleted crews were too few and spread too thinly to act as a proper fighting force.

Cleopatra urged Antony to retreat to Alexandria and safety before the battle began. Antony agreed. He would attempt to sail with his warships out of the protection of the gulf, to face down Agrippa's blockade.

The sea was rough, which enabled Agrippa's ships to manoeuvre more efficiently. Two or three of them had to surround the larger unwieldy vessels of Antony, and rain arrows and stones down onto the towers of marines, as if they were attacking a fort rather than a ship. The ballistae were able to punch holes in the sides of Antony's ships, but they were so well-armoured, it was impossible to ram them. The big ships had no problem in ramming Agrippa's smaller vessels, crashing into their sides, and sending many of them to the bottom of the sea. Agrippa ordered pitch darts to be hurled in an effort to burn some of Antony's fleet. But the deciding factor was Agrippa's vast numbers of well-fed, well-trained, and well-armed men. One by one, a significant portion of Antony's ships were captured or engulfed in flames.

Cleopatra thought all was lost. She ordered her squadron to sail through the fleets of fighting, burning, battling ships. She headed out to sea and safety. Extraordinarily Antony, who should have known better, followed her in his flagship, having misinterpreted the signals, thinking he was losing everything. Marcellus and his men were watching closely on shore. It was unbelievable. Why in heaven's name had Cleopatra sailed away, and why on earth had Antony followed when, as far as Marcellus could see, there was no decisive victory apparent from either side at the present moment? Both had lost many ships. But Antony's retreat altered everything.

"He's like a dog following a bitch on heat," Marcellus remarked to Adrian.

"I suppose it's much the same. He can't keep away from her, can he?"

"I wish I didn't like him so much. It's easier to fight someone if they've harmed you, but he's always been so kind to me."

"You made your choice. Now stick by it." Adrian had run out of sympathy, having spent hours convincing Max to fight alongside them.

The rest of Antony's fleet watched in horror as their commander's flagship disappeared over the horizon. The captains and crews became disheartened and many surrendered. Why fight to the death if both your generals have turned tail and sailed away? With the heavy swell in late afternoon favouring his own ships, rather than Antony's larger Roman warships with their lofty superstructure, Agrippa's marines seized three hundred of Antony's ships and killed almost five thousand men. Agrippa and

Gaius spent the rest of the night organising rescue for the crews of the burning ships.

Once well clear of the battle, Cleopatra ordered her ship to pull alongside Antony's flagship. She invited Antony to come on board. She was horrified by the expression on his face when he clambered up the ladder onto the deck. He looked like a bewildered child. She ran to him, flinging her arms round his neck.

"We will be safe, my darling. Once we reach Egypt, we will be safe."

Antony pushed her away impatiently. What did safety matter? Winning was the only prize worth having. He had lost. All was lost. Instinct told him that this had been his final battle. He sat in the prow nearly all the way to Alexandria, covering his face with his hands. Only sixty of Antony's ships managed to escape Agrippa's blockade and reach Egypt with him.

Once they arrived in port Antony sent messages to all his friends. He still had many good friends. He gave them large quantities of money, gold and silver plate and begged them to get to Corinth and hide there until they could make their peace with Caesar.

In the meantime Antony sent instructions to Canidius, now the commander of his land forces, to march his army away to Galatia. Instead Canidius abandoned his troops and made his escape to Crete, with only his bodyguard and handful of servants to attend him, eventually arriving in Pelusium on the north coast of Egypt. A fatal mistake on his part, although it would be another year before he was caught.

When the news broke that Antony and Cleopatra had taken ship to Alexandria, and their general Canidius Crassus had fled as well, their land army became disheartened, though it was a full week before they could be persuaded that their leaders had deserted them entirely. It was so hard to believe. They surrendered to Marcellus in a body. Nineteen legions and a huge mass of Antony's cavalry defected to join Marcellus and Decimus.

Dessy advised postponing the invasion of Egypt until the following spring, by which time he hoped to have formed all the combined legions into one cohesive group. Gaius distributed the supplies he had captured from Antony, to the Greek cities that had been denuded of men, horses and food to feed Antony's army. Then the victors returned to Italy, as some of the remaining legions stationed at Brundisium as a back-up were fed up and threatening mutiny. An ultimatum from Gaius to decimate the lot of them and feed the rest on barley bread for the winter if they didn't obey their officers, brought the renegades to heel.

And Dessy. Dessy standing in front of ten thousand angry men, with his hands on his hips, treating them like naughty children, telling them he was ashamed of them. If they didn't behave themselves he wasn't going to take them to Egypt. They would have no extra pay, no loot, and no exotic women! Didn't they want to meet these alien Egyptian women with luscious mouths, desperate for love? Dark-skinned women with smooth limbs encased in softest silk? Olive-skinned women with firm breasts like pomegranates, raven-haired women dancing the forbidden dance of the seven veils? At the end of his speech the men were begging him to be allowed to fight, even promising to forego their pay, as long as he would take them with him. Dessy had no idea where these alien women came from. They just popped into his mind. He didn't usually have much imagination.

However as it had the desired effect, Gaius was now ready and able to invade Egypt.

BOOK 3 : CHAPTER 11

Egypt, 30 BC

There was almost no opposition when Gaius sailed into Alexandria with his army. Egypt was naked and defenceless. Antony had spent the last few months of his life in a state of indecision and hopelessness. Cleopatra was no help to him. There was no refuge he could think of. There was no way out. When Antony finally realised he was facing certain defeat at the end of an exciting life, he knew he had to kill himself. In some ways it would be a relief. He was worried about his children, though. Fulvia's son Iullus and Octavia's girls were safe in Rome, thanks be to the Gods, but his children by Cleopatra? He couldn't think of any way to help them, but he would try.

Antony sent his eldest son, Mark Antony Antyllus to Gaius, with an enormous sum of money, enough for a prince's ransom, he hoped. Gaius kept the money and sent Antyllus back to his father. Antony was in despair. He would just have to hope that Gaius Caesar wasn't as vicious as he thought him. And Dessy was there. Dessy, who loved children. He would leave him a letter, begging him to care for them all.

It could never be said that Antony lacked courage. He ordered his freedman to help him commit suicide, telling the man to hold his sword up, and fix it firmly so he could run onto it. A proper death, suitable for a defeated Roman general. He would join his ancestors. His servants were weeping, begging him to try to escape.

Antony shook his head. "There is no place left for me in this world. I must travel to the next one. Now, let me compose myself, and summon up my willpower."

He held his arms above his head. "Almighty Jupiter, receive me into your realm. Let me pass safely into the Elysian Fields, a warrior's reward for faithful service." He looked at the sharp point of his sword sticking up in the air. There is no way out, said his brain. There is no way out. He took some deep breaths, then he ran lightly over to the sword point, and at the last moment, jumped onto it with his full body weight.

It didn't work. He wasn't dead. He couldn't even commit suicide successfully, fatally injuring himself, but not being killed outright. Damn the Gods! Would none help him to die a decent death?

The pain was excruciating. He hadn't thought how bad it would be. He couldn't keep silent, grasping his abdominal wall with both his hands as his guts attempted to spill out, and writhing and groaning in agony. This didn't seem like a proper death. Couldn't he win any battle now, not even one with death?

His few remaining soldiers carried him to Cleopatra, who was hiding with her children and her maidservants in her own mausoleum. Antony died unpleasantly in her arms, a long drawn-out agony for both of them. The children watched their father in horror. How could this be happening?

The frightened children were found with their mother, clutching at her skirts. Antyllus and Caesarion were missing. Cleopatra was beyond grief, acting like an automaton after Antony's death. All she wanted to do was to join him. She cared nothing for the children, wandering around with a glazed defeated look on her face. The children could get no response at all from her. She ignored their questions. Her maids tried their best to comfort them, but they weren't much help. The children only wanted reassurance from their mother.

Gaius was desperate to have Cleopatra paraded in his Triumph. But even he could see how fragile was her mental state. He was sure she would try to cheat him by suicide. He told her she could perform the burial rites for Antony, thinking it might reconcile her to her own fate. But the complicated ritual had no effect on her. Nothing roused her from her apparent stupor. Afterwards she was kept prisoner in the mausoleum with her little children, where she sat picking at her food and gazing at the walls, saying almost nothing to the point. Her beautiful face was frozen in an unresponsive mask.

The letter from Antony was given to Decimus, imploring him as a fellow soldier and former comrade to look after the children. Unfortunately their fate rested with Gaius, who didn't do clemency.

The tutor of seventeen-year-old Mark Antony Antyllus, came to Gaius Caesar's army headquarters in Alexandria, to find Gaius fuming with rage. His soldiers had just discovered that Cleopatra had successfully managed to kill herself, despite all his precautions. What's more, she was joined in death by her two maids. Not only had an asp been smuggled in under a basket of figs, according to the terrified children, but someone had clearly brought in poison as well. The culprits would be severely punished. The guards were executed straight away. To get some revenge, Gaius ordered the execution of both Antyllus and Caesarion, saying in justification: "Two Caesars are one too many." He wanted the sentences carried out quickly, before Decimus got to hear of it and tried to stop him.

The tutor claimed to know where Antyllus was hiding. Gaius said that as the boy had fought with his father, he was to be considered a traitor. He looked round at his senior officers. Who could he trust to perform the deed? His gaze alighted on Cierán. Ah, a barbarian would have no qualms executing a seventeen-year-old Roman boy. He ordered Cierán to go with the tutor, and if they found the boy, he was to be beheaded.

Cierán protested immediately. "No, Sir. I can't do that. I knew him as a child. He's a nice kid. He doesn't deserve to die."

Gaius did not take kindly to dissent, and especially not dissent in front of his other officers. "Cierán, you are an officer. I am your commander. You obey my orders, or I will have you killed as well."

Cierán had one more attempt. "Yes, Sir. You are my commander. But your sister Octavia ordered us to bring back Antyllus."

Unfortunately this enraged Gaius even more. "My sister Octavia is not in command of the Republic. I am," he yelled. "Obey me, Cierán, or your life is forfeit."

Antyllus was found clinging to a statue of the divine Julius Caesar, but it afforded him no sanctuary. He was crying, on his knees to Cierán, begging for his life to be spared. Cierán crouched beside him, and put a hand on his shoulder. He could feel the boy trembling.

"No. This is not how great Romans die," Cierán told him. "I am going to kill you. I have been ordered to do so by Gaius Caesar himself. And I obey orders. But it will be swift. So you must be brave for me. You are to join your father in death, one of the greatest generals the world has ever known. You mustn't disgrace him. So stand up now, and face your fate."

Cierán pulled the boy upright and pushed him back against the stone plinth.

"Good," he said softly. "Be brave, Mark Antony Antyllus, and go with the Gods."

He saw dawning recognition in the boy's eyes.

"Cierán?" the boy said. "Cierán! No, no don't, don't!"

With a hand on the boy's shoulder again, Cierán drew his sword from its sheath, and plunged it straight under the ribs, directly into his victim's heart. There was a grunting sound and little blood, as the body buckled and slid down to the ground. Cierán ordered his men to behead the corpse, as that was the mode of execution ordered by Gaius. But Cierán couldn't bring himself to do it that way. He removed a large jewel hanging from around the boy's neck, and handed it to the tutor.

"Your reward," said Cierán.

The tutor was delighted, hastily stuffing the jewel into a pouch at his waist. Cierán's men were told to carry the corpse to join his step-mother in her mausoleum.

"But make sure her children are out of the way," he ordered.

Once they had returned to headquarters, Cierán approached Gaius and told him Antyllus was dead. But that the jewel he was wearing round his neck, had been taken surreptitiously by the tutor.

It wasn't a good day to be annoying Gaius Caesar. He had the tutor searched. The jewel was found in his belt. The tutor was dragged away to be crucified, screaming his protests.

"He gave it to me! That man, the blond one, he gave it to me. He said it was my reward!"

"Don't try and implicate me, you thief," said Cierán, with a look of disgust.

Later that day Cierán stood at the foot of the cross, gazing up at the twisted face of the tutor. "So die all betrayers," he said. It made him feel a bit better.

Adrian and his men were hunting for another seventeen-year-old boy, Caesarion, Caesar's son by Cleopatra, tragically named as Caesar's true heir by Antony. The trouble being that he was proving altogether too easy to find. A large procession had left Alexandria with the boy in question, heading for the port of Berenice.

Adrian and his soldiers caught up with the fugitives thirty miles south east of Alexandria. There was a mild and easily-won skirmish. Almost immediately the Egyptians laid down their arms.

Adrian ordered his men to kill the heavily-adorned terrified youngster, who was unbelievably still wearing the raised crown of Upper Egypt. The boy was also wearing a heavy gold chain round his neck. Two soldiers held his arms while another pulled the chain tight. The boy made odd guttural sounds of protest. Then he was dead. Why no screams or pleas for mercy? Adrian prised open the corpse's mouth to find the boy had had his tongue cut out.

"Cleopatra was a clever woman. So you were a decoy," he told the dead body. "I was a decoy once. Caesar spared me, so it is right that you also are spared, although this poor innocent boy had to die. I wonder where you are, Caesarion? Safe, somewhere far away, I hope."

The troop returned to Alexandria. Gaius was happy to accept the corpse as the real Caesarion. Adrian wondered what Cleopatra would think when she woke in the afterlife to find this unknown person in her tomb. But she must have planned it this way, he thought, so he stopped worrying about it.

When Decimus returned from rounding up the rest of Antony's soldiers and heard the shocking news, he found he had to deal with a distraught Cierán.

"I will never forgive Gaius," Cierán told him. "He said he would kill me if I didn't obey his orders."

"I'm afraid Gaius would truly have had you killed if you'd disobeyed him. He has no conscience."

"Antyllus knew me. He remembered me, just as I killed the poor child."

Decimus was frowning. "But when did you meet him?"

"When we were staying with Antony in Athens. We used to take the boys out for some exercise and weapon training."

"They can't have been very old?"

"No. They were small children. But he remembered me. He said my name. I killed a poor innocent boy. Lady Octavia will never forgive me. She loved Antony's boys, almost as much as she loved her own children."

Decimus sighed. "Cierán, we all have to obey orders. Obey our superiors. Look at the dreadful things I was ordered to do. Break a prisoner into pieces."

"But you put them back together again."

"No. There is always some part of them that is broken irrevocably. Just ask Adrian."

BOOK 3 : CHAPTER 12

House of Octavia

At last Cleopatra's traumatised children were given to Decimus Statilius Taurus to be cared for and brought back safely to Rome. He did his best to calm them and reassure them during the long journey, telling them that they would be going to their father's home city. At first they hardly ate anything, and had great difficulty in sleeping. Sleep was disturbed by terrifying nightmares.

Little Cleopatra took a great fancy to Cierán. She liked to sit on his lap and play with his hair. All the children liked him singing to them. It helped a great deal, especially at night when Laeforis would softly join in the lullabies, pulling Ptolemy Philadelphus onto his knees and rocking him to sleep.

By the time they arrived in Rome Dessy had become fond of them. They were nice, well-mannered, bright kids. He hoped Gaius Caesar wasn't going to be so evil as to harm them, but one never knew with Gaius. Once in Rome he installed them in his town house for Ethela to mother.

The Egyptian Triumph took a long time in the planning. This would be a Triumph to outdo even the Triumphs of the great Caesar and great Pompey. Decimus was horrified to find that the children would be involved. He had to hand them over on the morning of the Triumph. The children were paraded in front of Gaius Caesar's chariot, wearing heavy gold chains, behind a huge effigy of their mother, with an asp clinging to her arm. Gaius wanted to spite Cleopatra's ghost.

Dessy told Gaius that the chains were far too heavy for the children to carry. He thought the effigy of Cleopatra was disgusting. It would give the children worse nightmares for years to come, just as they had shown signs of improving. He'd ended up shouting again, but got nowhere. One day, he thought, Gaius would really carry out his threat and have him proscribed.

It was hot in the dusty streets. There was no shade. The noisy crowd were frightening the children, shouting and pressing forward, trying to squeeze through the guard of legionaries protecting the processors. The weight of the gold chains was dragging four-year-old Ptolemy Philadelphus's hands down to the ground. And his little arms ached. He couldn't manage it any longer. He sat down on the ground and howled. His big sister and brother gave up the unequal struggle and joined him. The crowd hissed its disapproval at Gaius, shouting, 'Shame, you big bully,' and 'They're just little kids,' and even worse, 'This isn't the Roman way,' and 'You fucking cruel bastard. What the hell do you think you're doing to those poor dears?' The crowd started booing, registering its displeasure in no uncertain terms. A stone whipped out of the baying mob, striking the triumphal chariot, causing the two horses to rear in alarm. The chariot skewed sideways. Two soldiers rushed to the horses' heads, as Gaius tried to get them back under control.

Decimus was purposefully riding in a group close by, so he could watch out for the children. He reined in his horse and twisted round in the saddle.

"Dessy!" screamed Gaius. "Do something, Dessy."

Decimus dismounted and looked around at the group of horsemen, trying to think who would be best. He picked up nine-year-old Cleopatra Selene. "You are going to ride on a horse with a good friend of yours. He will look after you until we are home again. Alright my precious one?"

The tearful little girl nodded. Dessy lifted her up carefully into Cierán's arms. He gave her twin brother Alexander Helios to his nephew Marcellus. Then he kissed little Ptolemy and lifted him onto his own horse. He hoped to the Gods that someone knew where the keys to the chains were. He ordered them to be produced straight away. If they didn't find them quickly, he thought he might kill Gaius himself with his bare hands. Dessy was in a rage.

Decimus was still angry when he went with Marcellus to accost Gaius that night. A crowd of hangers-on was milling around outside the house, hoping for favours from the victor. Dessy and Marcellus pushed their way through with little regard for niceties. They found Gaius closeted with Marcus Agrippa.

"Today it was a stone. Tomorrow it could be an arrow, or a javelin," Decimus began. "Caesar, you are going to have to change, if you wish to survive."

"Are you threatening me?" Gaius demanded angrily.

"No, it's the truth," said Agrippa. "That's what I've been trying to tell you. Stop acting like a cruel bastard. The plebeians won't stand for it any longer. They've had enough of your executions. They want a bit of stability and peace."

"As for forcing little children to march in chains, weren't you there when Caesar was booed in his Egyptian Triumph, for parading Cleopatra's young sister in chains?"

Marcellus agreed. "Gaius, you are a consummate politician. You always have been. Can't you mange the Senate and the plebeians without all these constant wars? We've had enough bloodshed."

"And raised taxes," added Agrippa. "That didn't go down at all well." He had nearly broken with Gaius, when he was forced to give up a quarter of his wealth.

Fortunately Gaius saw sense, rather shocked to find Agrippa against him for once. He resolved to ensure that the present peace was permanent. There were no internal threats to be dealt with anymore. He could already see various ways in which the Senate could be controlled. But he must be cautious. One step at a time. The plebeians did not take kindly to tyrants, Decimus had reminded him. And the Senate wouldn't put up with any attempt at kingship. If he wanted to avoid his adopted father's fate, he would have to find another way.

Gaius agreed to hand the children over to be raised by his sister. She had been equally furious with him when she heard about the executions of Antyllus and Caesarion.

"How could you?" she shouted at him. "How could you kill my stepson? Antyllus is just a child, a lovely boy. You made poor Cierán do the killing! That was wicked. And Caesarion, you've had him killed as well? Don't you realise how weak you look, making war on children? You are a monster, Gaius. I am ashamed of you, do you hear? Ashamed that I have a monster for a brother."

In vain Gaius tried to explain the political reasons for his seemingly harsh actions. Octavia could not be placated. He ended up promising not only that he would do no harm to the little ones, he also promised to give Octavia's daughters by Antony their father's estates in Italy. He also swore he would seek advantageous marriages for the girls, but Octavia insisted she be consulted on their futures, and demanded the right to veto any arrangements that she didn't agree with. Gaius caved in. He hated quarrelling with his sister.

Marcellus was holding the twin's hands, while Decimus was carrying Ptolemy Philadelphus.

"I'm sorry, 'Tavia. There are only three of them, but they all speak Greek," said Marcellus.

Octavia laughed the lovely gurgling laugh, that he knew so well. She looked at the anxious tearful children, little Ptolemy clinging desperately to Dessy's neck, half strangling him. "Oh you darlings," she exclaimed. "Come now. Come. You will stay with me always. There is nothing to worry about. I will take the greatest care of you all."

Octavia shooed the little group into the salon, where six children stood arrayed in their best clothes, and looking a little anxious in turn. What would these strange siblings be like? They didn't want to share their mother with anyone else.

"Now you must meet your half-brother, and half-sisters, and my three children who are no relation to you, you may be pleased to hear, because we are all going to stay together."

"For always?"

"Yes, my dear. For always, or until you are quite grown up and want to leave."

Octavia beckoned fifteen-year-old Iullus Antonius forward, who bowed to the children and smiled, saying: "You might not remember me, but we have met before."

"And this girl is big Antonia," Octavia continued. She could see Cleopatra's children were becoming confused by the number of new relatives. 'She is just a year younger than you two twins, and this is little Antonia, She is only six."

"What does it mean? Half-sister?" Cleopatra asked fearfully. The word conjured up in her mind was of children cut in two.

Octavia explained. "You all have the same father, my dears, Mark Antony, a most famous Roman. You can be proud of him. Can't they?" She appealed to the men.

Decimus and Marcellus hastened to agree with her.

"And these are my children," said Octavia. "This is my eldest, my son Marcellus."

Alexander turned to face Marcellus. "Your son, Sir?" he asked.

He hated lying to the boy. "No, not my son. But I love him as if he were," he said.

Octavia rushed on to avoid any dangerous comments. "And these are my girls, big Claudia and little Claudia. I think that is quite enough to be going on with. Let's all have something nice to eat, and then you can go and explore the house."

The three children bowed, rather overawed to meet so many relations at one go.

Marcellus looked at them all. "Nine children for you to play with, 'Tavia. That should be enough, even for you."

Octavia walked over and hugged him. She knew just how he felt about his own unacknowledged children. He loved them so much. He was so proud of Marcellus, his son and namesake.

All went relatively well until it was time for the men to leave, when the three newcomers became panicky. They had formed a firm attachment to Marcellus and Decimus, desperate for some adults to cling to after the dramatic loss of their parents. They had witnessed the death of their father in their mother's arms, his bloody clothes reddening her own. They had watched in horror as their darling mother lost her life, and their favourite attendants as well. Too much disaster for small children to manage successfully.

"We will come every day to see you, until you are happy and settled in," promised Marcellus.

"Every single day?"

"Every single day. I swear," said Marcellus. A wonderful excuse to see Octavia.

"And the others?"

Marcellus was puzzled. "What others, sweetheart?"

"The big big men," said Ptolemy. "The big men that sing."

Octavia was looking bewildered.

"You want them to come, too?" asked Marcellus.

The children nodded.

"My Gauls," Decimus explained with a smile. "They will deem it a great honour, I'm sure."

Marcellus lay on his back by Octavia's side. His arm was round her waist, and she rested her head on his shoulder, with her soft hair tickling his nose. But he didn't care. It was so wonderful to be with his beloved again. But that was a problem, because there was no doubt in his mind. Cornelia was his beloved as well. How could that be? He thought again about his Uncle Decimus. Perhaps it was just one of those things that run in families. Some men, especially Taurus men, could manage two love affairs of the same intensity at the same time.

"I've told my brother that I don't wish to marry again," said Octavia. "After all, I'm thirty-nine years old. Hardly the right age to start yet another family. To my surprise he agreed."

"You know, my darling, that I couldn't ever divorce Cornelia."

"I know. I'm glad. I love Cornelia. But I love you as well. I always will. I can't help it."

"That's good."

"But I must have no more babies." Octavia had thought a lot about her mother and her own situation. She used to think Dessy was so cruel to make Atia depend on him for all her happiness, and then leave her to go off fighting. But as soon as Marcellus returned from Egypt she knew she had to have him with her again. Even though it had been ten years since their last physical encounter. Cupid's darts were impossible to remove without severe damage, that she now understood. "So this will have to be the last time," she said, not even believing it herself.

Marcellus laughed and slid his hand down her so-familiar body to her groin. He stroked her pubic hair with his fingers. "You're not very convincing. We'll see how we cope with that. Don't women stop having babies after a time?"

Octavia had a fit of the giggles. "I can have you as my lover when I'm fifty, then. Well it's better than nothing. Something to look forward to." She wrapped her arms around Marcellus, breathing in his scent, a delicious mixture of fresh sweat and sandalwood, exulting in his hard muscular frame. "Abstinence till then."

"Abstinence till then," Marcellus agreed, as they came together in perfect harmony with each other.

After a month Decimus decided that the children could be safely left in Rome with Octavia. They had begun to settle in, making friends with the other children. Decimus travelled to his country home with his sons and his slaves, turning a great many things over in his mind. He didn't think his nephew would waste much time before reconnecting with Octavia in more ways than one. Mostly he thought about the big questions. Had he been right to fight for Gaius Julius Caesar against Pompey? Had he been right to fight with the young Gaius Julius Caesar against Antony? That was a really difficult question to answer. So he asked Cierán.

"You know what Caesar said before he crossed the Rubicon? The die is cast. It's too late now. You could order us to go back to Rome and assassinate Gaius. It would be so easy for us to do, and it would make me feel a lot better. But what would be the consequence? Chaos. More chaos. Look, give him a few years, and see how it goes."

"After all, you gave him a pretty drastic warning," Laeforis chimed in. "He'll understand what you meant. We would have to kill Agrippa as well."

"History would just repeat itself," Cierán added. "My father did not think our leaders were wise when they persuaded our people to destroy our homeland and cross the mountains to join with the Aeduans. But he said our duty was to obey our superiors."

"My life changed so much, when I bought you all."

"Ours changed a bit as well," said Cierán gravely. "Why weren't we killed along with our fathers and brothers?"

"Centurion Pullo wanted money. A good driving force."

Cierán was curious. "Did you ever ask your father whether you should fight for Caesar or Pompey?"

"He always maintains he knows nothing about politics."

"I think he knows a great deal."

There was no chance of conversation while they manoeuvred the horses past a large caravan of wagons. Then Decimus started again. "I did so many things wrong, not just with you Gauls."

"Like what?"

Dessy's mind sorted back through the years. "I should never have married Veronica."

"But then you wouldn't have Lucas," Cierán pointed out. "And you would not have been able to marry Lady Atia, in any case."

Dessy sighed. "I don't know what I was thinking of. Quarrelling with Atia, wasting all those months while she was pregnant with Honoria."

"My father said that once you have made a decision, it becomes the right decision. In life you will come to a fork in the road, choose the left or right path, you will still reach the same destination in the end."

Dessy was silent.

"I think he meant we will all die."

Dessy laughed aloud. "I did manage to work that one out, Cierán."

"If you had fought for Antony, he would have won," started Óengus. "But he drank too much, and we heard he didn't rule the country wisely, when Caesar left him in charge. He would go too far, and then someone would assassinate him, and then another Gaius would appear."

"He was fine in Athens, though. The Athenians loved him. We all did the best we could at the time," finished Cierán. "Enough of this soul searching. Let's stop at that taverna and have a drink. What do you think, Dessy?"

"Brilliant idea," Dessy agreed. Still, he was glad he'd thrashed things out with his Gauls. They always managed to make him feel so much better about himself.

The cavalcade walked their horses into the taverna's stable yard. They had been riding for quite a distance. Decimus looked down at the ground, and wondered how he was going to get off his horse safely. Cierán came over to help him.

"I'm getting old and stiff."

Cierán remembered his father saying that men and women started to age as soon as they were born. But this time he shoved thoughts of his father firmly away, as unnecessary. Carefully he helped his former master from his horse. "You do talk such rubbish, sometimes, Master," he laughed.

Decimus held him tightly for a moment. "I can't manage without you."

Cierán hugged him back. "You don't have to, Dessy."

Epilogue

Amphitheatre of Taurus, 29 BC

Any one who was of any importance, and many who weren't at all important, came to the opening of the new amphitheatre, built by Titus Marcellus Statilius Taurus, his gift to the people of Rome. Although in the future the first fourteen rows would be reserved for Senators, on this occasion, the dedication of the arena, the front rows were taken by many of Marcellus's friends, some of whom were not particularly distinguished citizens.

Billboards had been up for weeks around the city, advertising the programme of events. There was to be the usual procession, starting from the Temple of Victoria, where Statilius Taurus would sacrifice. Sacred chariots containing images of the Gods would precede the chariot of Taurus himself, so they could witness the forthcoming spectacle. A multiplicity of decorated carts, filled with dancers and acrobats, would be followed by the orchestra of drums, flutes, and trumpets, and lastly the splendidly-clad gladiators and their array of lethal weapons.

In the arena itself there would be clowns, exotic animals performing tricks, fights by armed men against fearsome beasts, and then a warm-up display by the assortment of gladiators before the actual bloody contests started. There were to be one hundred matched pairs of gladiators in total.

Light streamed through the window when his slave opened the shutters with a clatter, and woke Marcellus up. It was a beautiful morning. He kissed a sleepy Cornelia till she woke up properly, then he jumped out of bed and went to breathe in the cool early morning air. This was to be a momentous day for him and his family. He could already feel a surge of excitement rising in his breast as he caught the sound of the crowd gathered in the street outside, waiting expectantly for him to appear. They could carry on waiting. Marcellus wanted his breakfast.

"Nervous?" queried his father.

"I feel as if I'm about to go into battle," Marcellus admitted, ruefully.

"Good grief," said his mother, "do you always eat as much as that beforehand?"

"Of course, Mum. You need sustenance to fight all day. Sometimes all night as well."

He could clearly remember the feeling of exhaustion at the end of a hard day's fighting, and of terrible thirst and hunger as well.

"I think you've fought enough, darling," said Portia. "Surely it's time to stop." She spent a lot of time on her knees, praying to the Gods to spare her darlings when they were away, fighting. Marcellus decided to postpone telling his mother and his wife that he would shortly be off to Spain, with his brother as one of his legates, to take on the Cantabrians. His father had been more stoical. "If you die, then make sure you die in the right cause," he had told each son before the start of their military adventures.

After eating heartily, because he wasn't sure when he would have another opportunity, Marcellus donned the purple toga, with his slaves fussing around him, wanting their master to appear perfect. He had to parade round the house, showing himself off to the family and servants. Nobody wanted to miss out on this privilege of being so close to the main action. His children were full of awe for once. They had never seen their father look so impressive before. He seemed too important to hug, but Marcellus just laughed at them, and picked each child up in his arms for a 'special kiss,' he told them.

"Why, Daddy?" asked little Titus, his curiosity aroused.

"Because it's a 'special day,' a day our family will make history," answered his smiling father. History for all the right reasons, for a change. Something peaceful and constructive.

Marcellus strolled into the courtyard. He could hear the sounds of the procession assembling, so he went out into the street to inspect his chariot, which was to be drawn by two bullocks, led by slaves dressed only in golden cloaks. He greeted his cousin Lucas and his half-brothers, who were to accompany him on horseback. The crowd showed their appreciation by clapping and cheering, so he waved to them, which considerably increased the noise level.

His mother came out into the street to more cheers. She was pleased to see the phalanx of guards around her son's chariot, and the lictors drawn up in formation. Her boy would be quite safe. And dear Cierán and his fellow Gauls would all be there, thanks be to the Gods. Portia found herself worrying more rather than less about her children as they took their now prominent roles in society. Her daughters had made excellent alliances, partly due to her husband's, but mostly to Marcellus's fame. Though Portia had ensured that Lucanus didn't get too carried away with the girls. She didn't want her darlings to be married to important but ancient old men, after seeing what happened to Atia. The two girls were both wedded to up-and-coming handsome young men. And judging by the aura of happiness on their faces these days, Lucanus had chosen successfully for them.

At mid-morning Marcellus performed the sacrifice, assisted by his father, his young brother, and his uncle, to start proceedings. All went according to plan. When he left the temple he knelt on the front steps while Lucanus placed the golden chaplet on his head, to massive cheers from an excited throng of people, most of whom hadn't managed to obtain tickets for the actual event. They would only see the procession.

A fanfare of trumpets sounded, which startled one of the bullocks. The bestiarius had to hang on to the nose-rope with his whole weight, to get the beast back under control. Seeing this, Cierán ordered one of his men to get some additional rope, and tie it around both the bullocks' necks. He didn't want to witness Marcellus being toppled off his chariot.

Inside the arena excitement was mounting as the sounds of the procession were heard in the distance. When they turned the corner into the wide avenue of the Via Flaminia leading to his arena, Marcellus found the sight took his breath away, even though he had been able to closely supervise its construction. The three solid stone tiers rose majestically from the ground out of a seething mass of people, up to the sky almost, it seemed. The sun glinted off the myriad of bronze statues placed in the regular alcoves around the external walls. The gladiators were kept to the side, waiting to join the end of the parade. They were clad in their varied elaborate armour, and wrapped in purple cloaks adorned with gold thread. Marcellus has been lavish with the decorations of both the gladiators and their weapons. He wanted a truly memorable spectacle today.

The noise was almost overwhelming as they entered through the Gate of Life at the east end, causing the bullocks to try and play havoc again, making for much excitement among the spectators. Catastrophes happening to others were always a source of entertainment.

Fortunately the chariot remained in one piece. The procession carried on round the circumference of the arena, the clowns, jugglers, and acrobats performing their acts for the enthralled audience. Marcellus felt an inward relief as he descended, quite glad to leave the bullocks behind. He couldn't remember whose daft idea it was to have the beasts, so it was probably his own. He walked over to inspect the neatly laid out gleaming rows of swords, tridents, nets, and shields, and signalled his approval. Then, along with his many companions, he mounted the steps to take his place on the rostrum to thunderous applause. There were also some colourful comments and witticisms from the crowd, making him laugh, but he managed to answer back satisfactorily. He surveyed the throng of happy chattering people clustered around him.

Marcellus could see his dearest Octavia surrounded by her smiling children, and her wards. He beamed at them all. It would take a little time to greet all his relations and friends properly, but the crowd would just have to be patient. So he started with Octavia, kissing her hand, then he kissed his son Marcellus, then his daughters, the children he could never acknowledge. He shook hands with Iullus Antonius, lifted up each of the other children in his arms and kissed them one by one. Next came an embrace from Gaius Julius Caesar with his new wife Livia, and Livia's children from her first marriage.

"It looks terrific, Marcellus. Congratulations. It was a brilliant idea." Gaius wished he'd thought of it himself. A great way to keep the plebeians onside. Perhaps he would build something as grand. A theatre maybe, using some of the new building materials.

A minor disturbance occurred as Marcus arrived in his litter. Walking in the heat was becoming a little too much for him at his advanced age. His chest was puffed out with pride, he told his grandson. His cronies were becoming depleted, one by one exiting to be placed in their family vaults. But Marcellus knew that this elevation of the Taurus family was almost an adequate expiation for death as far as his grandfather was concerned. The Taurus family would be famous for evermore!

"If only your dear grandmother were here to see this," Marcus declared, with a tear in his eye.

"Yes I know, Grandfer. I wish she was here, as well. I'm afraid we can't have everything we wish for."

He greeted his own thrilled parents, Lucanus and Portia, and his sisters and their husbands, Here was Uncle Dessy again, this time with Aunt Ethela and all *their* children. It always seemed awkward to Marcellus to call her aunt and kiss her cheek on greeting. Because she still addressed him as Master Marcellus, even though he had tried to persuade her otherwise. Next came his comrades in arms, Marcus Agrippa the first among them, with Adrian and Maximus. Then his wonderful Gauls, those foreign men who were embedded in his soul, he loved them so much, Cierán, Laeforis, and Óengus, with their wives and numerous offspring.

And lastly Cornelia, his lovely Cornelia, and his own children, the ones he could claim publicly for himself. Sometimes he cursed Claudius for leaving him with this insupportable heart ache, unable to acknowledge his own flesh and blood. But he had a firm hand in their upbringing, Octavia saw to that. He was a substitute father to these supposed orphans. And he tried to treat them all the same, his own children by Octavia, Antony's children by Octavia, Antony's children by Cleopatra. He wanted them all to feel they could rely on him for love and affectionate guidance. And they did.

Almost time to begin. Marcellus was feeling distinctly nervous, which was ridiculous. No one was going to get killed, he'd told the referees. He had issued strict instructions on the subject. When he gave these instructions to the gladiator school he had hired for the occasion, the fighters cheered him. Nice to think they would all be expected to survive the combats, even if some were badly wounded.

Decimus and Gaius combined to accost him before taking their seats.

"So, Marcellus," said Dessy, "are you going to allow criminals to suffer damnation by wild beasts here?"

"Yes, of course."

"Even though some of them may be innocent victims?"

"If the courts have decided otherwise, who am I to disagree," claimed Marcellus.

"And slaves who have done no wrong, but who are old or crippled in some way?"

"Absolutely not," said Marcellus firmly. "They will have to go elsewhere. They are not polluting my arena by murdering slaves."

Gaius laughed. "No Cupids then?"

"No Cupids. I wonder what happened to him?"

"He died that night, poor little thing," said Dessy.

"Probably just as well," said Marcellus. "Can you imagine what that child went through to become a Cupid, having those wires thrust through his skin? And how old was he? Two? Three? It was barbaric."

Dessy said, "I'm glad I haven't changed you too much, Marcellus. How are you going to prevent it happening in the future?"

"Easily, Sir. The Senate have informed me that because of this amphitheatre, I have the right to choose a Praetor each year. So while I am alive, I will make sure any Praetor follows my instructions. And I will leave these instructions in my will."

"I was thinking of starting a hospital for slaves who were ill and turned out of their homes," Cierán added. "What do you think, Sir? If they recover they could be sold to get the costs back, and if they don't I would arrange have them properly buried."

"Even more important would be a medical school for surgeons," Gaius interrupted, not to be outdone in these charitable efforts. "I think it would be a good idea if I started one myself."

"With Musa in charge?" Dessy asked, laughing.

"Certainly not. He is exclusive to me."

"Don't forget he's mine when I fall sick."

"What about that medical officer of Antony's? The one that performed the post mortem on my father. Can anyone remember his name? He's a Senator."

The trumpets sounded.

"Come on Gaius," said Marcellus, "never mind post mortems. Let's start the games together, like we did all those years ago."

So they did.

Brief Bibliography

1.Commentarii de Bello Gallico
Julius Caesar
2.The Conquest of Gaul
Julius Caesar, translated by S. A. Hanford
3.The Civil War (including the Alexandrian War, the African War, and the Spanish War written by unknown authors)
Julius Caesar, translated by Jane F. Gardner
4. Lives of the noble Grecians and Romans
Plutarch
5. A Traveller in Rome
H. V. Morton
6. Everyday Life in Roman Times
Marjorie and C. H. B. Quennell
7. Doctors and Diseases in the Roman Empire
Ralph Jackson
8. Lives of the Caesars
Suetonius, translated by Catherine Edwards
9. **Daily Life in Ancient Rome**
Jérôme Carcopino
10. Selected Letters
Marcus Cicero, translated by D. R. Shackleton Bailey
11. The Reign of Augustus
Cassius Dio, translated by Ian Scott-Kilbert
12. **Res Gestae Divi Augusti**
Gaius Julius Caesar Octavianus Augustus, translated by Alison E Cooley
13. **The Early History of Rome**
Livy, translated by Aubrey De Sélincourt

14. De Medicina
Aulus Cornelius Celsus, translated by W. G. Spencer
15. Military defeats, Casualties of war, and the success of Rome
dissertation byBrian David Turner
16. Hostages in Republican Rome
by Cheryl Walker

Especial thanks to Wikipedia and many other Internet sites too numerous to mention.

21567798R00282

Printed in Great Britain
by Amazon